What's A Woman To Do?

Maritza P. Brown

iUniverse, Inc.
New York Bloomington

What's A Woman To Do?

Copyright © 2009 by Maritza P. Brown

All rights reserved. No part of this book may be used or reproduced by any means, graphic, electronic, or mechanical, including photocopying, recording, taping or by any information storage retrieval system without the written permission of the publisher except in the case of brief quotations embodied in critical articles and reviews.

This is a work of fiction. All of the characters, names, incidents, organizations, and dialogue in this novel are either the products of the author's imagination or are used fictitiously.

iUniverse books may be ordered through booksellers or by contacting:

iUniverse
1663 Liberty Drive
Bloomington, IN 47403
www.iuniverse.com
1-800-Authors (1-800-288-4677)

Because of the dynamic nature of the Internet, any Web addresses or links contained in this book may have changed since publication and may no longer be valid. The views expressed in this work are solely those of the author and do not necessarily reflect the views of the publisher, and the publisher hereby disclaims any responsibility for them.

ISBN: 978-1-4401-8824-4 (sc)
ISBN: 978-1-4401-8823-7 (ebk)

Printed in the United States of America

iUniverse rev. date: 01/07/2010

This book is dedicated to my daddy who I miss dearly.
I will always love you forever, and ever . . .

Henry Toliver Poindexter, III
June 5, 1938 - September 29, 2007

Acknowledgements and Thank Yous

First, and foremost, and as always, I would like to give thanks to God, who continues to sustain me through the hard times, so that I can continue to create and nourish the gift he has given me. I also would like to thank my mother, Roberta Johnson, who happens to be the best mother in the entire world … sorry y'all, God gave her to my siblings and me, and we are truly blessed. Thank you mommy for always being the rock I needed. I could not have come this far without your love, support and guidance. I also want to personally thank my literary muse and inspiration, Gloria A. Williams, who has always stood by me from the beginning and encourages me to follow through with my dream. I could not have completed yet another book without you Glo. Also, I want to say a special thank you to my two editors, Kimberly Clark-James and Stephanie Dellolio. Between the both of you, we managed to get through my typos, and missing commas (Steph), and with your suggestions and graphic designing skills (bookmarks) Kimmie, we completed another work of art. I want to say a special thank you to my sister Crystal Tashay Johnson who found Mr. Richard Gilliam in the last hour to design my book cover. Richard you did a wonderful job; I can't thank you enough. I also want to thank my best friends for life, Beverley Tinsley, Anissa Davis, Margaret Lark, Lashon Joyner, Geraldine Corley, Trina Dukes and Astrid "Aisha" Jean-Paul. You all continue to stand by me through thick and thin, and I am blessed to have you all in my life. I have to say thank you to my growing boys, Eric Donyae Marshall, II and Wesley Jabari Brown for always allowing me to have the peace and quiet I need to create. I love you! I would also like to thank my new writing partner in crime, Sydney Lyttle, for always being that ear when I need to brainstorm with someone at any given moment – much appreciated girl! To Jasmine

"Jazz" Williams – thank you girl for reading the manuscript for content and flow, as well as being there to coordinate my book signings. Thank you to my cousin-in-law Raeanne Adams for always supporting me, and my brother-in-law Robert Brown, Jr. for pushing me to complete this sequel. To my cousin, Joy Cobbs, thank you for taking the time to give this book one final read before sending it out into the world, it means more to me than you know – love ya! Thank you to my sister Renee McCord, my Auntie Raeanne Johnson-Vaughn and my husband, Travis Brown, for continuing to bear the brunt of my constant brainstorming, and for allowing me to bounce my ideas off of you throughout the course of finalizing this book. Finally, thank you to my true inspiration and the "real" writer of the family, my sister Shari Lynn Poindexter; it's because of you that I am writing today! To those whom I have not mentioned in this acknowledgement, thank you for your continued support.

The Prologue

June 8, 1996

Greenwich, CT

The Wedding Day

Here and Now

The euphoric soft blue sky combined with the cool pre-summer breeze provided the ideal day for a wedding. And, on this day, the Averys' massive Colonial home sitting stoically on three acres of land was a picture perfect setting for such an extravagant event. The secluded, delicately manicured backyard had been transformed into a scene that resembled a captured ceremony in any upscale wedding magazine: adorned with fresh magnolias and lilacs and laced with crisp linen covered tables and chairs beneath an oversized tent, the wedding planner had impeccably created a day that would be remembered forever.

The natural light illuminated Alex's bedroom, and the warmth from the sun touched her skin softly as she sat still on the edge of her bed. She tried not to wrinkle the nicely fitted chiffon dress that conveniently masked the extra weight she was still trying to lose after giving birth over six months ago. Her nerves were bundled, and she needed a few minutes alone to gain some composure before walking down the aisle. Alex looked over at her reflection in the oversized mirror attached to the antique dresser and silently complimented her mother for doing such a fine job with her make-up. She looked absolutely radiant. Alex breathed in deeply as she wiped her sweaty palms across the pastel floral bedspread. She tried to smile, but mixed emotions prevented the corners of her mouth to curve upwards. She felt both anxious and excited due to the numerous times she dreamt of this day as a child. Yet, the feeling of sadness and a tinge of envy filtered through Alex's being because this was Journey's day, and not her own. *Always the maid of honor, never the bride*, she thought remembering her other best friend Charlene's wedding some years ago down at the City Hall. She and Malcolm acted as the maid of honor and best man in the thirty-minute ceremony and made promises to one another that one day they too would share that special occasion. Alex leaned over and tugged at the tiny drawer of her nightstand. She pulled out a neatly folded piece of paper and, with a bit of hesitation, proceeded to unfold it. She stared at the scripted words as they spoke to her once again.

November 2, 1995

Alex, my love,

Writing this letter is certainly the hardest thing I have ever had to do. First, allow me to say that you have matured into an incredible woman, and I will always love you. From the moment I laid eyes on you on your first day of high school ten years ago, I knew that you were the keeper of my soul. You were and will always be the only woman for me. Yet, because of my childish actions, here I sit, trying to find the right words to leave with you, so that you will always know that my heart belongs to you. Back then, had I thought with my head and not with other parts of my body, our lives would be different now, and, more importantly, we'd be spending it together. And, although I love my son dearly, every time I see his mother, I am reminded of the price I continue to pay for my wrongdoing. When we finally reconnected, despite the fact you were carrying another man's baby, somehow I still believed that we could recreate what we once had. But, now, with the birth of your lovely daughter, I realize that I must continue to internally suffer as I allow your daughter's father the right to assist you in forming the loving family you so deserve. I would be less of a man not to. And, although setting you free causes me great pain, please know that if an opportunity ever presents itself for us to be together again, I will never allow anyone or anything to come between us. Please remember that my love for you is never ending and forever waiting.

Love Always,
Malcolm

Alex didn't feel the stream of tears flowing gently down her face. Instead, she reread the letter and cursed Malcolm for still owning her heart. This letter was the only remnant of their rekindling during her pregnancy. It was not the gift she expected from Malcolm when she finally came home from the hospital on that cool crisp November morning with her newborn in tow. Alex vividly remembered the very moment she found the single sheet of paper placed neatly on her pillowcase. She read it over, and over again before calling his cell phone and, once, she even called his home. The weeks passed by as Alex made several attempts to reach Malcolm to let him know that she resented him for making the decision to walk away without first consulting with her. He never answered. And, during the interim, Sway had in fact, proven himself to be the doting, loving father, just as Malcolm predicted he would be. Sway even attempted to become a monogamous man in an effort to show Alex he could change, but Alex often downplayed his sincerity toward her, and, instead, focused on how she and Sway would raise their daughter.

Today she wished she could have ignored her heart when it reminded her of the breakage men like Sway eventually caused. *If I could have only settled this would be my perfect wedding day,* Alex thought as she reached for a Kleenex from its box that sat on her nightstand. She gently blotted her face with the soft tissue in an effort to salvage the great make-up job that would now have to be retouched. The knock on her bedroom door caused her to quickly fold up the letter and throw it back into the drawer.

"Come in," Alex said, pushing the drawer in and trying to sit up straight.

"Hey Baby Girl," her father chimed as he stepped into her room.

"Hi Daddy; is Journey ready?" Alex responded with a weak smile.

"Almost, and she looks lovely. Your sisters are looking for you," Joseph replied, looking into his daughter's watery eyes. "But they can wait, tell Daddy what's wrong."

Alex knew that her father read her as soon as his shoes touched the plush carpet. She repositioned her body on the bed as her father sat down next to her, waiting to hear his daughter's woes.

"I guess I am just a little sad that this is Journey's day and not mine," Alex said candidly.

"But your day will come," Joseph assured her. "If I didn't think so, I would have never agreed to have anyone else's wedding here."

"Thank you Daddy, but I am not so sure," Alex said, smiling lovingly at her father.

"How can you not be so sure?" Joseph rhetorically asked. "You just had a baby six months ago, so you have not even given yourself a chance to get back out into the world. Not to mention that there is a handsome gentleman caller right outside who I bet would marry you today if you'd just say the word."

"I know Sway would marry me Daddy, but not for the right reasons. He only asks me because I have his baby," Alex quipped.

"Well, Baby Girl, back in my day, that was reason enough," Joseph confirmed.

Alex let out a loud sigh and patted her dad on his knee; "it's not enough for me, Daddy."

"Oh, I realize that, otherwise there would not be a whole lot of you single mothers running around. I know that you women today can take care of yourselves, so you feel you don't need a man," Joseph stated, half jokingly.

"That's right, Daddy, we are way more independent nowadays, but I still want a family of my own. I guess I just always dreamt that it would be with Malcolm. Especially after we reconnected," Alex sighed.

"Malcolm?" Joseph repeated. "Look Alex, I know that Malcolm was the love of your life just like I believe you are the love of his life, but you have to understand his position in all of this."

Alex looked over at her father as if he knew something she didn't. He did.

"What are you saying, Daddy?" Alex asked with squinted eyes.

"Just let me say that it broke that man's heart to have to walk away from you a second time, but the day after you had the baby, Malcolm told me that he called up to your hospital room to check on you, and Sway answered the phone," Joseph paused to give Alex a chance to recollect that memory.

She did remember, but she thought Sway was joking with her when she came out of the bathroom and he told her it was her "boyfriend" who called.

"Do you remember that Baby Girl?" Joseph asked before continuing. Alex shook her head yes.

"Well, that morning Malcolm came over to pick little Malachi up, and he and I talked. Not long, but long enough for him to tell me that his heart sank when he heard Sway's voice on the other end of that line because at that moment he knew the joy Sway must have felt in his heart. Malcolm told me that he would not be able to give you all that you deserve knowing that he did not allow Sway the opportunity to give you the life he was supposed to. Malcolm recognized that he had his chance and blew it," Joseph concluded.

Alex looked at her father in awe. She was amazed that he was just now divulging this information to her.

"Why are you just now telling me this, Daddy?" she asked, needing to know the answer.

"Malcolm asked me to keep it to myself. He needed a man to confide in, and I was happy to oblige. But, I tell you all of this now because I want you to let go of what you and Malcolm once had, and try to focus on what you have now. And, if you and Malcolm are ever rejoined, then you will know that it was truly meant to be," Joseph stated sternly in his fatherly tone of voice.

"You are right, Daddy, but I just thought that him coming back after the first time I let him go, proved that maybe it was real for us," Alex sulked.

"No Baby Girl, what you and Malcolm just went through was closure. You both needed to complete the chapter that was left abruptly and unfinished when you found him in bed with that girl. And, since you have forgiven him for his past infidelity, you are now setting him free without harboring any ill will or negative feelings, you understand?"

Joseph asked in a way that told Alex to nod her head yes despite whether she truly understood what he had just said or not.

"I think so," Alex forced a meek smile on her face to show her father that his words had helped uplift her spirits once again.

"Well good," he said, happy to see his baby girl smiling. "Now let's get down stairs before Journey and that big fella' Tiny get married without us!"

January – 1999

2½ years later…

Chapter 1

Pelham, New York
Alex
No Ordinary Love

The snow fell at a steady rapid pace as the wet flakes attached themselves to the blanket of snow already covering the roof of Alex's colonial home. The house was warm and cozy inside, and was overflowing with the aroma of gingerbread cookies that Marie and Stevie were baking in the kitchen. Alex was downstairs in her office having a teleconference with her newest clients, Makio Ono and Jin Sung from Japan. Learning Japanese had become her newest obstacle, and she was grateful that both Makio and Jin spoke fluent English.

"Yes, I understand Mr. Sung. I believe, based on the latest *Wall Street Report*, that venture should prove to be prosperous," Alex said with confidence.

She was thankful that she stayed up late the night before to watch the international stock market on *Bloomberg TV*. She was wrapping up the conference call when she heard the pitter-patter of her daughter's feet running down the long hallway, toward her office. Soon there was silence followed by a drumming harmony of little knocks at her office door.

"Mommy, Mommy!" Stevie sang while pounding her little fists on the door.

"Yes sir, I will be sure to e-mail you that information before noon tomorrow. I just have a little more research to do," Alex said into the receiver as she stood up to open the door to let Stevie in. "Before making my report final. OK then, tomorrow it is. Speak to you both soon," Alex said quickly into the phone before placing it on the receiver.

Stevie smiled brightly at her mother as soon as the door opened, and then she jumped into Alex's arms. Alex kissed Stevie's cheek over and over in the same spot creating an infectious laughter flowing from her daughter's tiny mouth. Stevie just turned three years old in October, and Alex wondered every day how time passes by so quickly. It seemed like it was just the other day when she was cradling Stevie in her arms.

"Heyyyy Baby!" Alex exclaimed, giving Stevie a bear hug. "How's my big girl today?"

She had not seen Stevie all morning. Her workday started at four o'clock in the morning (the downside of working with people who live on the other side of the world), and Stevie was still sound asleep when Alex checked in on her before locking herself in her office. Alex worked feverishly all morning and was ready to spend the rest of the day with her mother and daughter. The weatherman had predicted snow all day, so no one was dressed, and all three generations of the Avery women were draped in flannel from head to toe. Stevie's messy thick locks of brownish-red hair bounced off her shoulders as she wrapped her little arms around her mother's neck.

"Mommy, I was cookin'."

"You were? Well, let's go see what you made," Alex said, tightly holding Stevie and carrying her upstairs to the kitchen.

Alex found her mother sitting in her favorite seat at the table neatly tucked into the corner of the kitchen, reading the paper.

"The paperboy made it here in all this snow?" Alex rhetorically asked in amazement as she looked out of the kitchen window at the flurry of snow blustering in the wind.

"I know, I said the same thing. Remind me to give him a few extra dollars next week. He is a dedicated young fellow," Marie replied not looking up as she sipped on the brim of her coffee cup.

Alex sat Stevie in her booster seat that was strapped securely to one of the chairs that were placed around the kitchen table. Stevie immediately began to focus on the scattered Cheerios in front of her. Alex grabbed a coffee cup and poured her java to the rim. She learned to enjoy her coffee black through her numerous international business travels. It was easy to order in any language, and the absence of sugar and dairy was her way of saying she ate "healthy". She took a sip, sat down next to her mother, and reached for the business section of the newspaper when the doorbell rang.

"Who in the world could that be in all this snow?" Marie asked looking up over her reading glasses with a puzzled look on her face.

"I don't know, Ma, but whoever it is rode in on a snow mobile."

They both laughed as Alex stood up to answer the door. She wrapped the belt around her thick, white terry cloth robe and shuffled to the front door.

"Who is it?" Alex called out, wondering who was crazy enough to weather this storm.

"It's me! Open the door!"

Alex hurried to the door and unlocked it while turning the knob.

"Have you lost your mind, coming out here in this mess?" she asked rhetorically.

"I said to myself that if I am going to be snowed in, I should be snowed in with the women I love," Sway replied coolly as he walked over the threshold of the front door and shook the snow off his brown leather shearling coat.

He was as handsome as ever with his dark brown skin complexion reflecting off the bright white shearling fur. He reminded Alex of a young Richard Roundtree in his prime. She was happy he fought Mother Nature to be with his daughter during the storm.

"You never cease to amaze me, Steven McCoy. Come in; we are in the kitchen. You hungry?" she asked turning around and walking back into the kitchen.

Sway hung his coat on the self standing brass coat rack, slid his feet out of his unlaced Timberlands, which effortlessly color coordinated with his coat, and followed Alex into the kitchen.

"Where's my girl!" Sway sang out excitedly when he heard Stevie's mumbling.

"Daddyyyyy!" Stevie yelled holding her arms up for Sway to sweep her up into the sky. And, without any hesitation, Sway lifted Stevie out of the booster seat and into his arms while simultaneously bending down to kiss Marie's cheek in one fowl swoop saying, "hey Mama Avery."

"Steven, you drove here?" Marie asked not believing he was that crazy.

"Yes Ma'am. It's not that bad out there on the main roads, and I took my time. I just wanted to be here with my girls," he said showing off his sparkling white teeth and capturing Marie's heart.

Sway walked Stevie into the family room, plopped in a "Teletubbies" DVD, and sat on the plush carpet beside her. Marie finished scanning the paper and stood up to make Sway something to eat. She loved it when Sway came over because it gave her a chance to cook for a man. She missed doing that for Joseph. Besides, Sway was the only man who was ever there early enough to have breakfast.

One of the rules of Sway and Alex's unique relationship was not to bring their dates around their daughter, regardless of how serious the relationship seemed to be. They both knew that rule really applied to Sway since Alex seldom dated. As a matter of fact, at the present time the only sex partner Alex had was Sway. Nevertheless, he did not know that. Alex felt that would give him too much power, so she allowed him to think that she had other "interests" beside him. Although Alex hated playing games, she could not allow her feelings to evolve into something more for Sway. The simple fact was that she would do anything to protect her heart.

Nonetheless, Marie admired Sway. Since Stevie's birth, Marie often tried to encourage Alex to reconsider his numerous marriage proposals, which he still occasionally would ask. Yet, Alex stood firm on her decision to keep Sway as a friend, confidant, co-parent, and, sometimes, her lover. Sway was her forbidden fruit, and they both knew it. They both also knew that the most important aspect to any healthy relationship was trust, and Alex held no expectation in that realm when it came to Sway.

When she met him over four years ago, he made it clear to her that he was unable and unwilling to commit. She never forgot that. After Stevie was born, Sway asked Alex to marry him, and, for six consecutive months, he tried to convince Alex he had changed and was ready to give her his all. It wasn't until they were vacationing in the Bahamas for Stevie's first birthday that Alex had to be honest with Sway. She told him she would not marry him because if she had never gotten pregnant, he would not be proposing. Despite the love they had for one another, they both knew this was true. Alex also had to remind him that during her entire pregnancy, he did not believe Stevie was his. It wasn't until the night his baby girl arrived into the world that Sway chose to stop denying he was a father again. And since then, Sway continuously tried to compensate his selfish act by spending as much time with his daughter as possible. He was sorry for missing Alex's pregnancy and the delivery of his only daughter. He vowed that he would not miss other significant events that involved Stevie.

When it came to Alex, however, he eventually eased up from trying to persuade her to be his wife and, instead, concentrated on maintaining the special bond they created for the sake of their daughter. He respected Alex for being the independent woman she was, unlike the way his son's mother, Carmen, turned out to be. Carmen was an opportunist. The stereotypical, money grappling, trifling ass "baby mama" Sway tried to stay away from during his "hustling years". Yet, back then, there was something about Carmen. She was feisty and fearless when it came to getting her hands a little dirty, and she was always ready to make money. Not to mention she maintained an extremely high sex drive. She sucked Sway in with her intense temptation, and, before he knew it, Carmen had become Sway's "hood chick". She provided a place for him to chill, a safe haven for his drugs, and she stashed most of his money. On some level he trusted Carmen, but never opened himself up enough to love her, even after she told him she was pregnant with his son. Sway knew Carmen loved money more than she could ever love a man, and they both knew that she had hit the jackpot. And, although, Sway loved his son Cain dearly and took care of him like a father should, Sway never considered making Carmen his wife. Alex, on the other hand, was the only woman he ever thought worthy enough to be his wife, and she was impressively withstanding a strong resistance against him, deepening his love for her. He also found it to be rather sexy.

It was no fallacy that the tri-state area was teeming with an oversized population of women who would not hesitate to claim the position of Mrs. McCoy. Yet, Alex had the ability to dismiss Sway's proposals without a second thought. This showed Sway that Alex was a whole woman who did not need a man to complete her. The truth of this reality resulted in Sway feeling a two-fold emotion. Although it saddened him at times, it also satisfied him. He cherished this certainty because this woman who found him resistible was the same strong woman who was the mother of his daughter. Therefore, he knew Stevie was destined to become a strong woman of substance and integrity. Alex and Sway had a mutual agreement to co-parent and share custody of Stevie. As a good faith gesture, Alex agreed to live in Sway's house in Pelham, New York with the stipulation that he would allow her to take over the mortgage note. Sway admired her tenacity and determination to be independent. However, on the day that Alex moved in, she noticed a sealed envelope, addressed to her on the granite countertop of the island in the kitchen. With a quizzical look and a raised brow that caused her forehead to crinkle, Alex began to rip the envelope open with the nail of her pinky finger. As she examined the contents, her puzzled look transformed into a surprised snicker. Alex held in her hand the title deed to the house, which was in her name. Sway vowed to take care of her forever, and he meant it. Sway was also adamant about not having anyone take care of his daughter, except Alex. So, instead of Alex returning to work as the manager of his upscale male spa and barbershop, aptly named *The Candy Shop*, Sway convinced Alex to establish her own business-consulting firm. And, he made the start up easy by commingling her with his upscale clientele.

Sway hired the best contractors to convert his old workout room on the lower level of the home into an extraordinary office and small conference room. He wanted to make Alex as comfortable as possible at home while raising their child. Alex's initial thought was that Sway just wanted her out of the shop, so he could pursue the new flock of young, sexy female employees. Yet, it turned out to be a divine plan in everything that was transpiring because Alex's life began to unravel soon after she settled into her new workspace.

Upon completing the renovations of her new office in the winter of 1997, Alex's father died unexpectedly in the hospital while being treated for walking pneumonia. Joseph was considered to be the woven fabric that kept the Avery clan together. As soon as the doctor told Marie the bad news, the Avery women began to come undone. Alex's older sisters, Shawn and Reggie, were a lot stronger than she and their mother, Marie, but the shock of Joseph no longer being in their mist brought on a tortured feeling of hopelessness to them all. Although Sway was there to comfort Alex during her time of a terrible loss, the unexpected and sudden death of her daddy nearly destroyed Alex emotionally. In an effort to regain a balance in her life and tackle the overwhelming feeling of grief, Alex sought bereavement therapy as she came to terms with the unexpected death of her father.

After months of therapy, and with the guidance of her therapist, Dr. Monica Clark, she was able to accept her father passing and turn her focus in the direction of her new career. Within a year, her clientele had grown from a feeble four clients to a whopping twenty-three throughout the world. She traveled out of the country at least twice a month. Conveniently, the absence of Alex during these business trips allowed precious time for Sway to bond with their daughter.

****

The day had passed uneventfully as the snow slowly tapered off, and the evening sky began to hover over Alex's home. Sway tried to open his eyes from some much-needed rest. He neglected to mention to Alex when he arrived earlier in the day that he had come to her house directly from *The Champagne Room's* grand re-opening under new management. Sway and his partner, Romeo, sold the upscale gentlemen's strip club to a business investor who frequents the club and wanted in on the action.

Adam Rothstein was his name, and Sway liked his business etiquette. However, Sway was a little concerned with a white guy owning a strip club in the center of Harlem, but Adam always seemed to hold his own, and all of the ladies loved him. With the rapid success of their upscale barbershop and male spa, *The Candy Shop,* both Sway and Romeo's priorities had shifted during the past few years. They no longer held the same interest or passion for the strip club as they once did. The first *Candy Shop* opened in 1995 in a prime location in lower Manhattan, and, since then, three more shops had cropped up along the East Coast in Atlantic City, Washington D.C., and Philadelphia. Sway managed the Manhattan location, Romeo handled all of the activities in Atlantic City, and they hired highly experienced managers for their D.C. and Philly locations.

Sway made it a point to visit those locations at least once a month to ensure that those shops ran precisely like the others. That was the secret to their success with the shops. All of them practically looked the same, followed the same procedures, provided the same services to the upscale man, and, most importantly, all of the female employees looked like models and had bodies to die for. As always, the female employees were hand-picked by Sway and Romeo. Another great feature was that once the hefty annual membership fee was paid, a member could go to any one of the shops for service at any time. *The Candy Shop* was a one-stop shop for businessmen, athletes, and entertainers when they needed barbershop services as well as royal spa treatments. After the fourth shop opened in Philadelphia, Sway and Romeo started contemplating selling the strip club, and Adam was the best prospect to take it over and keep it running. Sway felt that it was not a coincidence when Adam approached them at the Thanksgiving Party and showed interest in a possible partnership. Adam informed Sway that he admired the way he and Romeo managed the strip club. He told Sway that their club was unlike the ordinary "ass and tit joint". He thought it had finesse and style. Sway did not waste anytime convincing Romeo that Adam was the man who could take over the club and keep it running as though management had never changed hands. Romeo had his initial reservations, but reluctantly agreed, and, in the end, had only one caveat: that he and Sway would be silent partners and continue to receive a percentage of the club's revenue. Sway initially felt that they should just sell the club and focus on the successful progression of the spas. Yet, on the other hand, he understood why Romeo did not want to relinquish all of their rights to the club. It held sentimental value for them both. *The Champagne Room* was the outlet that relieved Sway and Romeo from the streets and the drug game. It saved their lives. Sway acknowledged that and agreed with Romeo that Adam would hold the majority interest in the club, and they would only act as silent partners, advising only when asked. Adam guaranteed the guys that the club would not change its high standards and would still remain catering to upscale clientele. Sway knew that he could trust Adam because Adam was not only a savvy *Wall Street* businessman, but he loved all kinds of women, he was single, and he enjoyed making money. On some levels, Adam reminded Sway of himself with their only differences being the color of their skin, and Adam was college educated while Sway obtained his knowledge from the streets.

Sway and Romeo were equally impressed and both knew they had made the right decision by the turnout of Adam's grand opening. It was apparent that Adam had his own upscale following because the club was filled with upper-class white businessmen who were dressed as if they could depart the club's atmosphere smothered with flesh and lust and go directly to the boardroom to close a big deal. Sway and Romeo partied with Adam and his friends into the wee hours of the morning. Feeling completely exhausted, Sway exited the club that morning and was greeted by massive snow flurries. Sway remembered looking up into the bright-clouded sky and realizing that he had made the right choice to sell the club. He was getting too old for that kind of life.

Sway slowly rolled over onto his back in Alex's California king-size bed, layered with down-filled pillows and a matching comforter. He inhaled deeply to get a full whiff of Alex's scent that saturated her crisp linens. He always loved the way she smelled. As he laid there slumbering in the all too familiar sleeping quarters, Sway heard the doorknob turn. Lying still, Sway opened one eye to see who was entering.

"Get up sleepy head. Ma is making dinner, and Stevie was looking for you," Alex said plopping down on the bed sending a jolt through Sway's body.

"Mmmm … , what time is it?" he asked groggily.

"Six-thirty. Why do you have someplace to be?"

"No, I was just asking. I needed that sleep," he said stretching his arms and positioning his body to a sit up against the massive mahogany wood headboard.

"I was at Adam's grand opening last night, and, I have to say, I think he is going to be OK."

"That's nice," Alex said nonchalantly.

She was happy that Sway and Romeo decided to move forward. She felt that both men had outgrown the strip club scene.

"So did you see any of your *women* out last night?" Alex inquired, trying not to sound jealous.

"I always see them out. The question you really want to ask is whether or not I was with any of them. The answer to that question, would be no," he responded, looking Alex directly in the eyes to prove his truthfulness. "Besides, why do you care about them anyway?"

"I don't," she spat back. "I just don't want you laying up in my bed today if you were with someone else last night."

"Stop trippin', you know me better than that. If I was with someone last night, I would not be here right now," he said as a matter of fact, and pulled Alex close to him.

He kissed her lips softly to reassure her that she still held the torch to his heart. She pulled back from his touch and licked her lips. It had been awhile since their last sexual encounter, and that kiss made her insides tingle. The familiar feeling from deep below sent a signal telling her mind that it was time to re-connect once again with the man her body had grown to so deeply desire.

"You staying here tonight?" she asked, already knowing the answer.

"Yeah," Sway responded and slid back under the warmth of the soft plush comforter. "Wake me up when Mama Marie is done cooking."

Looking forward to the night ahead, Alex stood up from the bed and walked out of the room, leaving the door open.

Chapter 2

Harlem, U.S.A
Journey
You've Changed

Journey sat silently at the kitchen table, sipping on her piping hot coffee. She blankly stared out of the window at the remaining snowflakes from the storm, landing sporadically on the concrete sidewalk. She spent all day in bed healing from the day before. She was thankful that Tiny never came home from the gym they owned. Initially, she assumed he was snowed in and would not be home until the city cleared the streets, but the day was almost gone, the streets were free of snow and ice, and she still had not heard from her husband.

The once vibrant, petite, outgoing, pretty firecracker had turned into a shell of a woman who internalized her pain, and barely spoke to her family and friends. She was lonely and heartbroken. When she married Tiny almost three years ago, she thought she had met the man of her dreams. Despite the fact that they came from totally different backgrounds and their appearance was somewhat comical, Journey believed that they were a-match-made-in-heaven. Tiny stood at least 6'4" tall and was a 350 pound mass of muscle compared to her petite frame, barely weighing 100 pounds, and a height striving to reach five feet. He was from the projects in Flatbush, Brooklyn, and Journey was the embodiment of sunny California, where she was born and raised in Brentwood. Her parents had more money than Tiny's family would collectively ever make in their lifetimes. However, Journey never acted like a rich, snobby, money-encrusted valley girl. Tiny admired her for her modesty, which was one of the qualities that attracted him to her. Not to mention their sex life was explosive, and he protected her as if she was his lion cub. What Journey did not expect was that his need to protect her would eventually morph into a mountain of insecurities and down right out-of-control jealousy. When they both worked at *The Candy Shop,* he never appeared to be insecure and often played the part of the calm, cool, and collected head of security who adored one of the prettiest women working in the shop. Within a year of dating, they were married. It was not long after Tiny carried Journey over the threshold of the honeymoon suite that their relationship began to change drastically. Journey's inability to conceive and give birth to a child to carry on his name began to infuriate Tiny. Journey also suspected that his casual use of steroids to maintain his massive muscular frame was becoming more habitual and contributed to his recent violent mood swings. Over a year ago, when they decided to open a unisex gym named "*The Gem: Everyone's Best Friend,*" Journey saw signs of excessive steroid use. However, she overlooked the bad habit as his way of relieving the added stress of owning a business. It was not until a few months ago that the yelling and screaming became physical, and she found herself often times being choked breaths away from death. Whenever Tiny came home and found anything out of place, he would become angry, spark frivolous arguments and use them as an excuse to abuse her. His behavior had drastically changed. He was no longer the loving teddy bear she had fallen in love with. Instead, he had morphed into a beast that found solace in bullying her whenever the opportunity presented itself.

A single tear escaped Journey's eye as she mentally dissected the day before when Tiny forced himself upon her and verbally abused her while having his way with her. The degrading words rang and ruminated in her head.

"Shut up!" she remembered him screaming into her ear.

He had just come out of the bathroom, and he was wide-eyed like a crazed maniac. His mannerisms had changed from a tired man awakening from a good night's sleep to a man who had just been jolted with a burst of energy. Journey was still in bed. Since she worked from home, she did not have to get up to start her day until after eight o'clock.

"What the fuck are you still doing in bed?" he asked, stammering out of the bathroom.

"Huh," Journey said half asleep, still laying flat on her stomach.

Tiny grew increasingly angry when she did not immediately jump up to answer him, and he pounced on her, forcing his weight onto her back.

"Tinyyyyy!" she screamed before letting out a deep breath.

He was suffocating her. "Shut up!" he bellowed in her ear, with anger in his voice. "You want to lie in bed all morning when you should be up fixing my breakfast. But no, you want to lay here like a whore waiting to get fucked!" he said aggressively, pulling the cover off her small frame and firmly grasping at her panties.

"No Tiny, don't!" she cried. "I will make your breakfast, just get off me. I'll get up right now," she pleaded.

"Fuck it now, I want some pussy for breakfast," he said, tearing her panties from around her thighs, causing huge welt marks to form on her honey hued skin.

He pressed his massive body against Journey's back causing her to gasp for air. With one hand, he parted her legs and tried to slide his partially erect penis inside of her body. His forcefulness caused Journey to squirm, but she refused to scream. She knew the shrieking sound of fear would make him feel more powerful. Journey refused to fuel his madness, and she was not giving in to him that easily. Tiny rammed himself into her vagina as if he did not know and love Journey. She could feel her insides rip with each thrust, and her eyes began to water.

"Tiny stop, please!" she pleaded in a whisper.

"Shut up! It's not like this pussy is worth anything. It can't push out no babies, so what good is it," he managed to say while putting all of his energy into his painful penetration. "Besides, a woman who can't bear children ain't a real woman," he said belittling her while gasping for air as if he was running a marathon.

He pounded Journey's small frame for what seemed like an eternity, switching back and forth, harshly penetrating her vagina and anus. When he finally ejaculated inside of her and rolled over, she silently thanked God and wiped the tears from her eyes before he could see that he made her cry. Journey slid out of the bed that was drenched with his sweat and her blood and slowly walked into the bathroom. As she stood in front of the mirror examining her welted and bruised legs, she could hear Tiny moving about in the bedroom. *I hope to hell you are leaving,* she thought as she turned on the shower.

"Yo Journey!" she heard his baritone voice ring out from the bedroom. "I'm out. I will probably be home late tonight because of the storm that's coming. I love you," Tiny yelled with a smile on his face as if the brutal raping of his wife did not just occur.

Journey did not respond; instead, she crept into the shower and allowed the shower rain to wash over her bruised and swollen body.

****

Now, a day later, her body was still aching from his abuse, yet she was at ease because for the first time in a long time, she had gotten a full, peaceful night's rest. She thanked Mother Nature for creating a storm that was so great, it prevented Tiny from coming home. Journey stood up from the table and slowly walked over to the telephone that was mounted to the kitchen wall. She did not want to call Tiny, but knew if she did not, he would use her inattentiveness as a reason to cause another fight. She picked up the receiver with great hesitation and slowly dialed the gym's number. The phone rang several times before someone picked up.

"Thank you for calling The Gem: Everyone's Best Friend. Tanya speaking, how can I help you," a small, cheery voice sung through the phone line.

"Hi Tanya, is Tiny around?" Journey asked trying to sound as normal as possible. The last thing she needed was her staff speculating on her and Tiny's personal relationship, especially Tanya.

"Yup," Tanya's answer was prompt and succinct. "Hold on; let me go get him," she said in a snotty huff and slammed the phone down on the counter, sending a loud noise into Journey's ear.

Journey wanted to reach through the phone and choke her, but instead she smiled to herself, satisfied that she had once again pissed Tanya off. They hated each other. Tanya resented and envied Journey for being Tiny's wife, and Journey hated Tanya because she knew that Tiny was attracted to the fresh out of high school teen siren that resembled actress Nia Long. Journey once suspected that Tiny and Tanya were having an affair, and when she had finally found enough courage to approach him with her suspicions, Tiny with an open hand, shoved Journey in the face, pushing her to the ground. He knelt down next to her, wrapped his large hand around her throat, and told her to never question his loyalty to her again. Soon after that incident, he told Journey that she would have to work from home because he was turning her office into an additional spin cycle room. Journey immediately sensed that he was creating space between her and his little, young fantasy. Yet, no matter how true, she would not dare confront Tiny again. Instead, she justified the move with the sheer satisfaction of not having to see that young harlot everyday. So, without conflict, Journey accepted Tiny's proposal to work from home.

Journey held the phone to her ear, and listened to the bevy of conversations going on at the gym and wondered what was taking Tiny so long. After a few moments, she could hear Tiny's infectious baritone laugh as he neared the phone, and she braced herself for an earful. She did not know what to expect from her husband anymore.

"Yeah, hello," Tiny's deep voice traveled through the phone line and slapped Journey in the face.

"Hey, what's up?" Journey asked as nicely as possible, trying not to ruffle his feathers.

"Hey what's up? Did you miss me last night?" he asked half jokingly, as if he had not raped her the morning before.

She wanted to be honest and tell him 'hell no', but she also did not want a replay of the abuse she had already encountered, so she remained sweet as sugar with her response.

"You know I did. Why didn't you call me to say you were not coming home at all?" Journey asked as nicely as possible.

"It was late, and I got snowed in, so I knew you'd understand."

"When are you coming home? The roads must be clear where you are because the gym sounds packed."

"You know the gym is *always* packed. Rain, sleet or snow, nothing can keep these fitness freaks away," he said with a slight chuckle in his voice. "I will be home around eight, so be ready because we gonna catch a movie or something."

Journey warmed to his pleasantness and embraced it, even though she knew it would be short-lived. This all too familiar tone coming from Tiny's voice was the characteristic that she fell in love with.

"A movie sounds good. Maybe I'll call Alex and see if she and Sway would like to join us. We have not seen them since Christmas, and you know we missed her birthday dinner a few weeks ago," Journey said, thinking of the black eye Tiny had given her on Alex's birthday. Journey thought by going on a double date she would be protected because Tiny would behave around Sway. There was a silent pause, and finally he responded.

"Um, I guess that would be cool. Call them and see what's up, but we are going no matter what, so be ready and we can grab a bite to eat while we are out." He did not wait for a reply from Journey. Instead, he just hung up the phone.

She hated his extreme behavior, one minute he would act as if she were his precious cargo and the next he acted as if she was disposable trash. She hoped that Alex was free tonight because she needed a friend. As she poured another cup of coffee, Journey dialed Alex's number.

"Hello," a pleasant voice sang on the other end of the line.

"Hey, Mrs. Avery, its Journey, is Alex around?" Journey chimed in.

"Hey, Baby, yeah she's right here. Hold on a minute."

Marie handed Alex the phone and returned to the kitchen to finish preparing her meal.

Alex wondered whom her mother was calling "baby", but rationalized that it had to be someone close to the family. Cautiously, Alex pulled the phone to her ear, "hello."

"Hey girl, what's up?" Journey said, trying to sound cheerful and upbeat.

"I was wondering who Ma was talking to; what's up with you?"

"Nothing really, Tiny and I are going to check out a movie tonight and wanted to know if you and Sway wanted to join us. We can meet in the Bronx."

"Um, I am not sure. Sway is here, but he is sleeping. Let me call you back in a few, OK?" Alex said hesitantly, not really sure if she wanted to brave the winter night air.

"Oh, OK, but if you can, I really want you to come," Journey said somberly, sending Alex the hint that her friendship was needed.

Chapter 3

Alex

Count on me

Alex hung the phone up and debated on whether she really wanted to get dressed and deal with the wet, slushy residue that the snowstorm left behind. Yet, she could hear it in Journey's voice that they needed to see each other. Their friendship was solid however, since Journey and Tiny opened the gym, she and Alex barely spent any time together. The last time she seen Journey was around the holidays. Not to mention, Alex was still harboring some angry feelings towards Journey and Tiny for not showing up to her recent birthday dinner. Nevertheless, she could hear the longing in Journey's voice. Alex sensed that something was not right and felt the need for the two of them to reconnect.

She walked over to the oversized bay window in the living room and peered out into the black night. The bright snow illuminated the ground, and the branches of the leafless trees surrounded her home, creating a pleasant seclusion while at the same time making the night seem somewhat inviting. It was beautiful. She fixated her eyes on a large icicle dangling from the gutter that hung outside above the window. She watched the droplets of water that formed at the tip of the icicle descend to the ground. Alex was so deep in thought that she did not hear Sway creep up behind her.

"Hey, what are you thinking about?" he whispered into her ear as he hugged Alex around her waist.

Slightly startled, she grabbed his hand with force but quickly relaxed her grasp once she realized it was him. "Mmm ... nothing, just standing here debating on whether or not I want to go out tonight."

"Out! In this?" Sway questioned as if Alex had lost her mind.

"I know, I know," she said turning around to face him, "but Journey called and asked if we wanted to double with her and Tiny. They are going to catch a movie at Bay Plaza. I think she needs to talk to me."

"How are you two going to talk in the movie?" Sway asked with a puzzled look on his face. He often wondered how women were able to find time to run their mouths in any situation.

Annoyed, Alex answered, "in the bathroom." She looked at him as if he should have already known how she and Journey could communicate during the movie.

Sway laughed and shook his head. "You women, I swear," he said sitting down on the sofa. "Well, if you want to go, we can go, but that means you are staying at my place tonight." Sway looked over at Alex and waited for her reaction.

They both knew that he was not trudging through the snowy back roads of Pelham, twice in one night, despite the fact that he had driven his Range Rover instead of the BMW. Alex looked at Sway to see if he was really serious. She was the only woman who could just look into his eyes and know what mood he was in. She knew he was serious.

She wanted to hang out with Journey; it had been awhile. However, she also had a report due in the morning. She weighed her options and looked at Sway to make sure he had not softened within those few seconds. She walked over to him and sat on his lap.

"OK, cool, but that means we have to catch a late movie because I have to finish a report that's due in the morning."

Sway rubbed her thigh with a slight grip and simply said, "Cool."

Alex jumped up, told him that his dinner was ready in the kitchen, and that she'd be in her office for a couple of hours. She called Journey as soon as she settled into her plush, mahogany leather desk chair, and the two of them finalized their plans for the night.

****

Alex was able to wrap up her report earlier than she anticipated, and, by the time she shut down her computer, Sway had given Stevie a bath, read her a quick bedtime story, and tucked her in for the night. He and Alex were able to take their time getting dressed for the cold night ahead. Once layered in clothing that could bear the frigid weather waiting to embrace them, they both kissed Marie goodnight and headed for the door.

"I'll be home in the morning, Ma," Alex sang as she slipped into her warm shearling jacket. She wrapped her soft, angora scarf around her neck and went out of the front door, without waiting for her mother's response.

Sway was in the SUV, which was nice and warm. *I have to get one of those automatic car starters,* Alex thought as she climbed in. The sweet sound of Marvin Gaye delighted her ears as she got comfortable in the heated leather passenger seat. Sway looked at her for confirmation that she was ready and he pulled off smoothly as the tires made slushy tracks down the driveway. The main roads and highway were not as bad as the streets in Alex's secluded neighborhood. They were still slick and wet, but Sway's SUV hugged the curves of Interstate 95 as if the wet weather didn't exist. They arrived right on schedule with a few minutes to spare. Sway pulled into the Bay Plaza parking lot and looked around for Tiny's truck.

"It looks like we beat them here," he said looking out of his tinted window.

Alex sat comfortably in the cozy leather seat and stared at Sway's side view. He was an extraordinarily handsome man, ever more so now that he had an abundance of gray hair speckled throughout his low cropped 'fro'. His creamy chocolate skin only enhanced his pearly white teeth when he smiled, and sex appeal oozed from his pores. Tonight he looked good enough to eat.

After taking a second glance around the lot for Tiny and Journey, Sway looked over at Alex, who was gazing at him with hunger in her eyes. "What?" he asked with a nervous smile on his face. He quickly positioned the rearview mirror towards his face so he could check himself out.

"Nothing; I was just sitting here admiring how good you look," Alex said with a seductive grin.

Sway could tell by Alex's behavior that they were going to have an explosive night, and, for a split moment, he contemplated nixing the movie and taking Alex back to his place. Instead, he leaned over and kissed her lips softly. As he pulled back and started to open the door, Tiny pulled up in his new, shiny black Expedition and parked it along side Sway's Rover.

"What up, what up!" Tiny exclaimed as he jumped out of the truck, happy to see his homeboy.

He and Sway showed one another some brotherly love with a firm handshake and partial hug. Since opening the gym, Tiny rarely had the chance to see Sway.

As they talked, Journey and Alex hugged each other tightly and Journey whispered into Alex's ear. "Thanks, girl, for coming out tonight." Journey held back her emotions. A part of her wanted to be rescued from Tiny right there on the spot.

"Anytime, honey," Alex said pulling back and caressing Journey's face with her leather gloved hands. "I could hear it in your voice that you needed me so here I am. Let's go inside, so we can sneak off to the ladies room," Alex said, smiling and turning to see if the guys were ready to move forward. "You ready?" she asked Sway.

No words were spoken; both Sway and Tiny straightened up like soldiers, and followed the women into the theater complex. The two men simultaneously dug deep into their pockets and pulled out wads of money. Neither roll was bigger than the other, which clearly indicated that neither, Sway nor Tiny, was hurting for money. They quickly peeled back the crisp bills as if they were in a heated competition and handed Alex and Journey the money. While the ladies reviewed the streaming digital movie list that was displayed above the ticket counter, the guys went in the direction of the men's room. By the time they returned, Alex and Journey had purchased the tickets for the new Wesley Snipes movie, *Down in the Delta*. They motioned the guys over to where they waited in line to enter the theater.

Tiny walked up behind Journey and hugged her body tightly. From the onset, one would think that Tiny was the most loving man in the world. He rested his head on her shoulder and whispered in her ear. "You better behave tonight and watch what you say." His grip around her waist tightened. She smiled nervously to mask the fear that had just jolted the insides of her body.

"OK," she whispered back at him with a phony smile on her face.

As the couples waited in anticipation to enter the movie, Alex looked around the semi-packed theater lobby. Despite the weather, quite a few people needed to get out of the house. *We're not the only ones who decided to brave the cold*, she thought as she stood in front of Sway, leaned her head back against his chest and closed her eyes.

"You, OK?" Sway asked Alex with concern while softly touching her hair.

"Yeah, I'm OK," she responded as she opened her eyes and grabbed his hand and they began to follow the couple in front of them.

They moved with the crowd as if they were in a walk-a-thon until they branched off into the fourth row from the back of the theater and proceeded to sit down.

"Why are we sitting way back here?" Journey asked innocently at no one in particular.

No one answered; instead, Tiny shot Journey a glare that Alex caught out of the corner of her eye. It scared her. For a split second, she did not recognize Tiny. His facial expression was distorted, and he had an evil glare in his eyes. Journey quickly tensed up, and shifted in her seat to make herself as comfortable as she could. Her face became flush, and Alex could feel her fear.

"Hey girl, run with me to the ladies room before the movie starts," Alex said to Journey, interrupting the awkward moment the three of them shared.

Sway was oblivious to the whole scene. He was too busy reading the advertisements on the movie screen and making a mental note to talk to Romeo about placing an ad to promote *The Candy Shop*.

Journey stood up without saying a word and waited for Alex to follow suit. Alex quickly hopped up from her seat, and the two women swiftly walked up the aisle towards the exit.

"Hurry up!" Journey could hear Tiny bellowing as the large theater door closed behind her.

Alex barely pushed open the bathroom door before the questions began to roll from her tongue without pausing for Journey to answer.

"What's going on?" she finally asked, ending the thirty-second interrogation, staring at Journey with a tense, concerned look on her face.

Journey leaned against the cold, white porcelain sink and lowered her head. She was so embarrassed. She did not know where to start. Alex continued to stare at her, waiting patiently for an answer.

"Journey," Alex said softly, "tell me what's wrong."

Journey hesitated for a moment and contemplated whether or not this was the right time to tell Alex that Tiny had become an abusive terror. She quickly settled with keeping it a secret because Journey knew if she told Alex, Alex would not end the night without confronting Tiny, and making it known to Sway that his best friend was a punk. *Tiny would kill me tonight for sure*, Journey thought as she looked into Alex's waiting eyes.

Journey decided to divulge her infertility first and to use that misfortune as the excuse for Tiny's abusive behavior when she finally found enough courage to tell Alex about him. After all she had been through, Journey knew that Tiny would beat her bloody if Sway and Alex ever thought of him as a woman-beating coward. So, she thought carefully before speaking to not tarnish his character.

"We can't have children!" Journey shrilled.

"Oh, Honey!" Alex cried and embraced Journey.

They stood there for a moment to let the tears flow. Alex sympathized for Journey. She could not imagine not being able to bear children. Although her pregnancy was unplanned, Alex could not fathom the thought of living without her daughter.

"Journey, I am so sorry. Are you sure?" Alex asked in a whisper.

"Well, we go back to the doctor in a few weeks for the test results. I had my final fertility test done, so this will tell us for sure. I just know they are going to have bad news Alex," Journey cried, suppressing what she really wanted share with her best friend.

"Listen, you can't be negative. You guys have to think positive and stop trying so hard," Alex said, stepping back and grabbing Journey by the arms. "That doctor is going to have nothing but good news," Alex concluded, sounding as encouraging as she could. "Is that why Tiny is acting that way?" Alex asked, attempting to get to the bottom of Tiny's odd behavior she just witnessed.

"What way?" Journey asked, acting like she did not know what Alex was talking about.

"Journey, we've been friends too long. I saw how he looked at you in there and it scared me."

As the two best friends gazed at each other, both women hesitated to say the next word.

"Is he hitting you Journey?" Alex blurted out with a tinge of anger in her voice.

"Well, not really hitting me," Journey lied, "he just gets rough sometimes, and, lately, he has been overly possessive." She looked at Alex with a straight face trying to prove her honesty. Journey peered into her friend's concerned eyes and tried to gain some composure.

"Seriously, that's all it is Alex. We are just stressed about the results. You know Tiny would love nothing more than to have a baby boy," Journey said trying to smile.

She wanted to tell Alex the whole story, the real story. She wanted Alex to know about her concerns of Tiny abusing steroids and the brutal abuse. She wanted to share that her husband had raped her just the other morning, and how her body still ached from his unnecessary punishment.

Alex looked at Journey and tilted her head to the side. She stood there for a minute, trying to make sure Journey had nothing else to share. She finally hugged Journey again.

"Are you sure that's all Journey?" Alex asked as she pulled back and wiped Journey's face with her hands. Journey smiled with a phony reassurance and nodded her head.

"OK," Alex said, "let's get back in there before we both have to hear it!" They both giggled like high school girls and quickly walked back into the theater.

****

The movie dragged towards the end, but Alex did not mind. She could watch Wesley Snipes run bathwater all day because she enjoyed watching him do anything on the big screen. Both she and Journey began shaking Sway and Tiny awake as soon as the credits started to roll up the screen. The foursome shuffled out of the theater, and the coldness caused them to quicken their pace through the parking lot. As they reached their vehicles, there was little conversation between them. The time had finally caught up to them, and their bodies were feeling the effects of it being after one o'clock in the morning. Sway and Tiny tiredly turned to face each other and said their good-byes, while Alex walked Journey to the passenger side of Tiny's SUV.

"You are going to be OK," Alex reassured her friend as she hugged Journey tightly.

Journey nodded her head up and down with affirmation and climbed into the truck. Alex ran to get in the Range Rover as Sway revved the engine as if to say 'hurry up'. Each vehicle exited the plaza, going in opposite directions.

Chapter 4

Alex
Backstabbers

Sway drove in silence back to his place because Alex had fallen asleep as soon as she settled into her heated seat. He glanced over at her every time he stopped at a red light to admire her natural beauty. He loved her and often wished that they met under different circumstances. It had been almost five years since their first encounter on *125th Street* on that hot summer day. Romeo wanted her, and Alex wanted Sway. He could tell by the way she stared at him from the back seat of his *Legend* when he gave her a ride to work. *I miss that car,* he thought to himself as he turned onto Park Avenue. He knew from the moment he saw Alex that she was special. However, what he did not know was that she would become the only woman he would ever fall in love with. He never expected that she'd be the one; otherwise, he would have never started off their relationship on such a strict "no commitment" basis.

Over the years, he found that Alex was able to maintain the 'non-exclusive' bond he created, and, although he knew that she loved him, he also knew that she could not trust him. She was the dream he could never make come true, so he focused on business and money instead. Sway was all man. He prided himself for being a self-made millionaire before turning forty years old. His legacy was already established for his two children to inherit. He was thankful for many reasons that Alex had entered his world. He deeply believed that Alex played a dramatic part in his success.

He pulled into the underground parking lot of his apartment building on the Upper West Side of Manhattan and gracefully backed into his reserved parking space. He sat quietly looking at a peacefully sleeping Alex one last time before calling her name. He smiled to himself and started to get excited thinking about how he was going to make love to her. He felt slightly rejuvenated and called Alex's name softly. She responded by turning her head towards him and opening one eye. For a moment, she forgot where she was.

"Mmm," she moaned sleepily. "We're here?"

"Yeap," Sway said as he opened his door. He quickly ran to the passenger side of the car to aide Alex in stepping down from the truck.

The twosome slowly walked arm in arm through the brightly lit underground parking lot over to the stainless steel set of elevator doors. The heavy doors parted just as Sway pressed the button, as if it was waiting for his arrival. They eased in, and the doors closed behind them. Sway swiped his elevator card key to gain entry to the penthouse suites. The elevator traveled nonstop to the top and came to an abrupt halt. Alex followed Sway out of the elevator holding onto his coat tail. When they reached the door to his three bedroom apartment, he turned to Alex and asked, "Are you going to go to sleep on me?"

"That wasn't my intention," she seductively answered looking into his dark brown eyes.

Holding onto her words, he slid the card key into the slot and opened the door. He reached for the dimmer switch on the wall and rotated the dial until the room became illuminated with a candlelight like glow. His suite was spacious and immaculate. And, like the house Alex now lived in, this place was elaborately decorated with displays of artifacts and possessions collected during his worldwide excursions. His living room floor was covered with a smoke grey carpet he purchased from Persia, and it was an unspoken rule that all footwear was to be left at the door upon entering. To accommodate his infrequent visitors, he had several pairs of slippers neatly stacked in the coat closet. Alex kicked off her shoes as soon as she walked over the threshold. She immediately relished in the comfort that her feet felt from the soft Persian carpeting. She walked barefoot over to the burgundy Italian leather sofa and plopped down onto the soft cushion.

Sway darted off to the kitchen, and he was opening a bottle of wine when the phone rang. He rolled his eyes in annoyance of whoever was calling him at this hour. They were not adhering to his house rules. He knew it was not business, nor any of his friends because those calls came in on his cell phone. Only his lady-friends called his landline. For some reason, a woman feels special and in a class all by herself when she has a man's home number. Sway did not care one way or the other because he always made it a point to let all of his women friends know that he was a single man. Yet, he always treated his lady-friends like they were the "only one" when he spent time with each of them, so they all thought otherwise. Sway's lady-friends loved being treated like a queen. They each happily played his game, hoping to one day be chosen as the *one*. Unfortunately, for them, Alex held that position, and the irony of it all was that it was a position she did not care to have. She and Sway started out the same way he always started out with his women, as friends who ultimately had sexual benefits, and, because of the non-exclusiveness of their friendship, Alex could never trust him the way she wished she could. Instead, they enjoyed each other at times like the present evening.

The phone rang a total of three times before Sway's answering machine picked it up. Alex showed no reaction to the phone ringing at that time of night; instead, she looked at it, chuckled under her breath, and grabbed the remote to Sway's fifty-two inch plasma screen television that was neatly tucked inside the wall surrounded by a built-in bookshelf. Sway had an eclectic array of literature ranging from books about African American history to books on entrepreneurship and money management. Alex channel surfed and waited for Sway to return from the kitchen with her wine.

"You could have answered that!" she yelled at Sway from the living room.

"Please, Alex. You know me better than that. No one should be calling my house this late unless it's you or Carmen calling about my kids."

Alex chuckled and shook her head back and forth. She wondered why women put up with Sway's inability to commit. In her eyes, Sway was the type of man who could never have too much of anything, and that included women. Alex learned from the onset of their love affair that Sway would never be husband material. Yet, she accepted Sway for who he was because beneath his womanizing persona, he was a good man. She hoped that one day she would meet a man who wanted to share the same kind of monogamous relationship she craved, but, for now, she adapts like a chameleon to her current situation, and changes to the nature of Sway's environment when necessary.

Her mind drifted off as she snuggled up with one of the throw pillows on the sofa. For a split second, she thought of her high school sweetheart Malcolm, and how she once believed he was that special someone. He was her first and only real love. They were soul mates. As she continued to drift in her private moment, she accepted that time was the past. Both she and Malcolm were young and inexperienced. She sometimes wished that she and Malcolm could have rekindled their high school romance when they briefly reconnected during her pregnancy, but she had finally come to terms with never living out that dream. Alex still possessed the heartfelt letter Malcolm left for her the day after she gave birth to her daughter. And, although the last time she actually read it was almost three years ago on Journey's wedding day, she could recite it word for word if someone asked her to. Tears formed in her eyes at the thought of Malcolm walking out of her life, but she also understood his position. She had not seen nor heard from Malcolm except for a brief moment at her father's funeral. However, Malcolm made sure that he stayed ever-present in her mind by sending her flowers every mother's day. And, although she knew that she would always carry a torch for him in her heart, presently, raising her daughter and getting her business established were her only priorities, making the current set up she had with Sway work out just fine.

Sway returned to the living room pulling Alex back into reality and handed her a half-filled glass of red wine. She wiped her eye to erase the tear that had escaped as a result from her jog down memory lane, and nodded her head partly to thank him and partly to shake the memory of Malcolm back into her subconscious.

"Mmm … ," she moaned.

"I like the way that sounds," Sway said sitting down beside her, and taking a sip of his Hennessy. He knew that a lady preferred wine, so he kept a full stock. He, himself, was a cognac man. They looked at each other lustfully and drank their un-inhibitors in silence. Alex smiled as she finished off her wine and placed the empty glass on the coffee table in front of her. She stood up and stretched her arms.

"I'm going to take a shower, you comin'?" she asked as she turned and walked towards Sway's master bathroom quarters.

Sway, without hesitation, placed his empty glass on the coffee table, turned off the television, and followed Alex like a lost puppy dog. By the time they reached the bathroom, their bodies were bare, and his muscles flexed in the oversized mirror above the double sinks. The glass encased shower held no privacy as he watched the shower rain over Alex's lovely body before joining her. He was mesmerized by the way the soap clung to her honey soaked skin. He watched the soap suds wrap around the curves of her body followed by the water beads washing the foam away. He slowly opened the shower door and slid in behind her. He grabbed the soapy loofa sponge from her hand and proceeded to wash her back with it.

Alex stood still and enjoyed the soap enhanced body massage Sway was giving her. She turned around so he could massage the front of her body, and he proceeded with pleasure. As the water made the soap disappear from their bodies they embraced each other, and Sway told Alex that he loved her. He had gotten used to saying those words over the years, and they both knew he meant it. Alex leaned into his body and kissed him slowly. As their soft tongues passionately wrestled with one another causing their body temperatures to rise, Alex's nipples hardened against Sway's chiseled chest. The glass shower doors began to steam. Sway lifted Alex with ease, so she could wrap her petite legs around his firm chiseled waist, and she held on tightly to the back of his neck. Their lips never parted as he entered her moist flesh causing her eyes to open. He was already looking at her and smiled at the lovely expression her face made while he glided in and out of her body. With one hand, he reached for the shower knob and turned off the water. Holding her body with ease, he pushed the shower door open and carried her to the double sinks where her warm wet nakedness adhered itself to the cold porcelain sink. Sway looked at himself through the mirror as he pumped steadily. He took pride in knowing that he could still make a woman feel this way. Alex floated into her personal heaven as he put every effort into making her feel like this experience was all about her. She made short, breathy sounds as she came all over his being.

Sway looked at her as she smiled with her eyes closed, and he reveled at his accomplishment.

He lifted Alex from the sink and carried her to his king-size bed in the adjoining master bedroom. While still inside of her, he placed her body down gently on the bed and continued to make love to her. He stroked her as if they would never see each other again. After an hour of lovemaking, using different parts of his body to penetrate her inviting body, Sway finally climaxed inside of her. Completely exhausted, Sway rolled over beside her and smiled. Drenched with the moisture from their extensive love making session, Alex threw her arm across Sway's solid chest and thanked him once again for a job well done. He laughed and told her "anytime".

"Sway," Alex said, hoping he was not dozing off. "Are you ever going to tell me about this?" she asked as her index finger traced the bullet wound that scarred his stomach.

Sway opened his eyes and could feel her soft touch drawing circles in his stomach. That wound was his reminder to stay on the straight and narrow, and to never fall victim to the streets again.

"That's the exit wound from the bullet that almost paralyzed me," he said flatly.

He tried not to show any emotion, but the thought of that night was seared into his brain, and the incident remained etched in his memory as clear as the present moment. He knew that one day he would have to tell Alex what happened. She was the mother of his child, and she should know everything about him, but he still couldn't talk about it without becoming angry.

Instead, Sway closed his eyes again, and his mind flashed back to that cold night at the drug spot on *Amsterdam Avenue*. It was Sway's thirtieth birthday, and his boy, D-Money told him that he needed to "re-up" on their supply, and he promised that it would only take a minute. After that, they could stop by the strip joint before going to the club. Sway's best friend assured him that it was all good, and after they knocked off this pack they would be tenfold richer. Back then, everyone knew that money was Sway's only motivator. It was his only one true love next to his son. D-Money knew that Sway would be down for anything that generated dollars. What Sway did not know was that D-Money had a hidden agenda. D-Money's true intent was that only he'd be ten times richer, and snatching up Carmen was the added bonus. D-Money disapproved of the way Sway dismissed her. It did not help that D-Money cared deeply for Carmen, and he needed to finally be rid of his competition, to see if she was the one.

D-Money masterminded an elaborate scheme with Sway's street competition. The plan was to remove Sway from the drug game completely. The end result would be that D-Money would split Sway's massive territory among his rivals, making everyone richer, and making D-Money the new "man".

Sway silently recalled how D-Money pushed and pushed that night until finally Sway reluctantly agreed to go, but his gut kept telling him that something did not feel right. This feeling was heightened by the fact that he did not have his gun on him. Sway never carried his piece when partying, and D-Money knew that. There was nothing more dangerous than a heavily intoxicated man with a gun, so Sway always left his home. Sway remembered getting off the tight, urine stained elevator of the dingy apartment building and telling D-Money that something wasn't right.

"Chill!" he could still hear D-Money's voice echo in his head.

He followed D-Money down the dark hallway to the last door on the right. D-Money knocked three times, paused and then knocked twice more.

"What's up with the corny 'code' knock?" Sway remembered saying and laughing in D-Money's ear.

A light skinned, frail looking woman answered the door with her hair standing straight up on her head. Recognizing her, Sway thought to himself, *she used to dance at Sue's Rendezvous.* She was considered one of the finest red bones in the club, and her stripper routine always drew in the crowd. As they entered her musty, dirty, poorly lit apartment, D-Money asked for Paco. Sway caught a glimpse of her drawn in face and realized crack had gotten the best of her. She did not respond and, instead, looked at them both up and down, turned around and started walking down the dark hall. The two men followed her through the living room where three young thugs, who looked more scared than hard, sat stiffly on the dirt stained sofa. Sway looked at the three boys, shook his head, and continued to follow D-Money into the dimly lit kitchen. They were met by two big, black burly guys with guns drawn standing behind a small Columbian who was seated in one of the mix-matched kitchen chairs. He looked, at most, twenty years old and was playing a game of solitaire on the food stained kitchen table.

Sway wanted to laugh at the kid, but could see from his gun power that he had to be somebody in this game and refrained from giving him any signs of disrespect. Sway was surprised that he had never run into this kid before now. *Something's not right,* Sway's intuition kept reminding him. He stood silently behind D-Money with a stern look on his face to let it be known that he and D-Money were not to be reckoned with and that he was not new to the game.

"Speed this up," he said in low voice into D-Money's ear. D-Money shook his head and was greeted by the pint sized drug lord. The two immediately made eye contact, and D-Money turned around to look at Sway.

"Yo, my man, I gotta run to the bathroom real quick; I'll be right back," he nervously looked Sway in the eye.

D-Money looked back at the miniature man and while quickly walking away said, "hurry up and wrap that shit up for me, so we can get this money."

D-Money vanished through the back of the apartment as Sway stood there wondering what the fuck was going on. Before he could speak another word, the three young thugs walked up behind him and cocked their guns. Sway braced for the worst and decided to fight or die trying. He turned around quickly and punched one of the boys in the face. Before he could run past the other two boys, the two large black men began to fire their weapons and bullets began to fly haphazardly throughout the small dingy apartment. Sway tried to run but was stopped in his tracks by a sharp pain that ripped through his back. His legs began to lose their stability and his knees buckled beneath him as he fell to the floor. He could hear bullets ripping through the walls, and the woman's screams made the pain in his back more severe. Sway thought he was going to die on his birthday. He lay on the filthy beige carpet as his blood oozed out of the bullet wounds in his back. He could faintly hear D-Money's voice.

"Yo man, is he dead, let's get out of here!" D-Money nervously shouted.

Sway closed his eyes and purposely slowed his breathing, so he would appear to be dead. The men barely looked down at him as they ran out of the apartment, and the drug addicted woman called 911.

Thanks to the swift actions of that woman, the paramedics arrived at the crack spot in record time. The doctors were able to operate and remove the bullet that missed Sway's spine by a half an inch. The doctor told Sway that he was a lucky man. Sway knew that there had to be some divine intervention that saved his life that night, and, while recuperating in the hospital, he promised God that he would never sell drugs again.

That night his best friend tried to kill him. The one person he thought would always have his back. Sway felt betrayed, and he vowed that if he survived, he would find D-Money and make him pay.

Sway's body stiffened to Alex's touch, causing her to look at his face. His eyes were shut, but she could tell that he was deep in thought.

"Sway!" Alex said, shaking him.

Sway opened his eyes immediately and looked over at Alex. "Sorry, I was just thinking about that night. Man, I really thought I was going to die," he said in disbelief.

"I am sorry, Sway. I did not mean to make you upset by asking you about this. We don't have to talk about it right now," she said, regretting that she mentioned his wound again.

"Naw, it's OK. You should know what happened, and, one day, I promise that I will tell you the whole story, but, for now, let's just say that I use to have a best friend who turned out to be my worst enemy. We were partners in the drug game, and he made the decision one day that he wanted it all for himself. He tried to have me killed to take over my business and my life. But I didn't die that night," he said, feeling a wave of resentment toward his once best friend.

He grabbed Alex and pulled her close to his body. She reciprocated with a hug and kissed his bare chest.

"I'm glad you're still here," she said softly.

They lovingly kissed each other, and then Alex rested her head on his chest. Sway inhaled deeply and closed his eyes.

Chapter 5

Journey
There's a Stranger in My House

The tingling sensation penetrating through Journey's red flushed cheek reminded her that she was home. Tiny smacked her face as soon as they entered the foyer of their brownstone. She quickly turned on the light and shuffled through the living room. Her eyes welled up with tears, but she refused to let him see her cry. She was getting tired of his abuse, and suppressing her emotions was her only way of having some control in their volatile relationship.

"What was that for?" Journey asked as she walked into the kitchen.

She was tempted to grab the butcher knife that sat invitingly on the granite countertop and slit his throat, but he was not worth her freedom. Instead, she wiped her eyes quickly, and rubbed her bruised cheek.

"What in the hell were you two in the bathroom talking about?" he asked as he approached her.

She backed herself into her usual corner and waited for his fist to land somewhere on her body.

"We weren't talking about anything," Journey meekly answered.

Tiny's hand found solace around Journey's neck and he squeezed it tightly. Her entire face became flush as the pressure of his grasp restricted her blood circulation. Her eyes bulged slightly out of their sockets and began to tear up. She shook her head back and forth, but knew not to fight back. Part of her felt as if this was the last night of her life.

"You better not be telling Alex all of our fuckin' business! You hear me? You tellin' her that I hit on you?" he demanded to know as the glare in his eye dared her to say yes.

"No," she managed to say while grasping for air.

She grabbed Tiny's hand and tried to pry it from her neck. He loosened his grip slightly to allow air to flow down her windpipe.

"No Baby, I swear," she said with pleading eyes.

"You better not. I don't want Sway knowing my fuckin' business and how I handle my wife."

Tiny released his grip and walked out of the kitchen toward their bedroom.

Journey touched her neck with both hands and slowly slid down the wall to the floor, and began to sob quietly. She knew the real reason why Tiny did not want Sway and Alex to know he was beating her. He admired Sway, and he did not want to appear to be less of a man in Sway's eyes.

"Coward," she whispered under her breath.

She breathed deeply and held onto her knees tightly against her chest as she listened to him take a shower in their bathroom. Her good sense told her to get up, grab some of her clothes, and leave before he finished, but the fear that Tiny had filled her with through the years told her to stay put. She sobbed quietly and tried to remember where the relationship started to disintegrate.

Instead, her thoughts immediately took her back to a happier time. Tiny was in charge of security at the *Candy Shop*, and she was the head bartender. Sway and Alex were on vacation in the Bahamas, and the fling that Journey once had with Romeo had become no more than an occasional ride home after work. A slight grin developed on Journey's tear stained face as she remembered walking up to Tiny that night after the shop had closed. She could see the smile he had on his face as she approached him.

"Hey, you are Tiny, right?" she asked the large man sitting on the stool by the coat check counter.

Tiny's eyes wandered from Journey's pretty pedicured toes, past her toned fit body, and up to her gorgeous face. At first, he could not believe she was talking to him. She had been working there for more than six months and barely looked at him. However, he always noticed her. He was severely attracted to her fit, petite body and preferred her athletic look opposed to any of those thick, voluptuous *candy girls* who catered to the shop's clientele.

"Huh," he responded, looking into her light brown eyes. His dunce reply made Journey giggle, and she was kind of flattered because she never caught a guy that off guard before.

"Tiny. That is your name, right?" she repeated, showing her pearly whites.

"Yeah, that's me," Tiny replied and stood up from the stool. "What can I do for you?"

"Well, I hate to ask, but I need a ride home, and Romeo looks too fucked up to drive me anywhere. Do you mind?"

Tiny nervously grinned at the petite beauty and immediately took the opportunity to see what Journey was all about. He heard through shoptalk that she and Romeo had something going on, but when he confronted Romeo, he blew her off. He told Tiny she was just one of many and to "get in where he could fit in".

"No problem," he said in a low baritone voice, mesmerized by Journey's bright eyes.

She thanked him quickly and told him she had to grab her bag and would be right back. He stared at her firm backside that filled her form fitting jeans. Instantly, he started to get excited. College women like Journey normally intimidated Tiny, but, at the same time, those were the women he was attracted most to, and he was excited that he would finally have a chance with Journey. Before he could finish his daydream about her, Journey was back in his eyesight and ready to go.

They walked out of the shop together side by side over to Tiny's Ford Explorer, and he helped her into the passenger seat. He wasted very little time jumping into the driver's seat and speeding into the direction of Journey's place. He did not have to ask for directions because he had been to her house several times with Sway, but always stayed in the car.

"You know where I live?" Journey asked suspiciously.

"Yeah, I had to bring Sway there a few times," Tiny replied, nonchalantly.

They talked non-stop as Tiny drove swiftly through the Manhattan streets into Harlem. They discovered that they had more in common than they ever imagined. They loved to work out, took pleasure in watching old gangster movies, and enjoyed Thai food. Journey quickly eased into a comfort zone with Tiny and felt a connection that night. She never, in her wildest dreams, imagined herself dating a man of his size. His massiveness seemed like too much man for Journey's one hundred pound frame, but he seemed to be genuinely gentle. He walked her to the door that night and did not ask for a kiss; he took it. The intense moment reminded her when Alex's lesbian sister Reggie kissed Journey by surprise during the holidays one year. Just like then, she was caught totally off-guard. Yet, this time she willingly reciprocated and wrapped her arms around Tiny's thick neck as he bent down to enjoy the full embodiment of her embrace. Their tongues wrestled passionately with one another as their lips melted together. They kissed like lovers on their first date. As Journey pulled away, she found herself asking if he wanted to come in for a night cap.

"Journey!" Tiny's boisterous voice interrupted Journey's trip down memory lane and quickly reminded her that the Tiny she was now with is not that man who drove her home that night.

"Yes," she answered weakly.

"Get your ass in here. What are you doing?" he rhetorically asked in an irritated manner. He was upset that she was not in bed waiting for him when he got out of the shower.

"I'm comin'," she answered softly as she pried herself off of the floor and walked toward the bedroom.

When she reached the room, she was met with Tiny's large naked body sprawled across the oversized bed. Her body tensed up at the thought of him touching her after nearly strangling her just fifteen minutes earlier. Journey breathed in deeply and tried to relax.

"Go hop in the shower, and come back in here to make love to me," Tiny demanded.

Journey responded by turning around and walking into the bathroom, shutting the door behind her. She looked into the mirror above the sink and tried to encourage the miserable reflection gazing back at her.

"Just get it over with," she said to herself, trying to muster up some motivation. "Think about someone else tonight," she said, grinning at her reflection devilishly.

"Yo, hurry the fuck up in there. I don't hear no water runnin' or nothin'!" Tiny yelled from the bedroom. "My dick is getting hard!"

Journey scowled at the thought of him penetrating the inside of her precious body. He had come to not appreciate her goodness, and she was tired of him and his rough sexual nature. She was falling out of love with Tiny, and she could tell by the way he treated her that his feelings were mutual.

She shed her clothes quickly and jumped into the shower. She washed her body as quickly as she could, partly fearing that if she did not hurry, Tiny would come in and grab her by her hair and drag her to bed as he did in the past. Within moments, she was standing in front of him, draped in an oversized towel, and barely dry. Tiny looked at her as if she was helpless prey and he grew more excited at the fear he could plainly see in her eyes.

"Well, it's about time," he said with a satanic grin, "now get your little ass over here, and let me see if that no good snatch of yours can make me a baby tonight."

Those berating words pierced her heart, and a tear started to form in Journey's eye. She took a deep breath to stop it from flowing down her cheek. Instead, she created a fake smile, and shuffled slowly toward her husband.

February - 1999

Chapter 6

Journey

No More Tears

The quiet ride from Harlem to Rye, New York allowed Journey to mentally prepare for the outcome she and Tiny were anxiously waiting for. As Tiny pulled his SUV into the doctor's office parking lot, Journey's palms began to sweat, and she looked over at Tiny.

"I hope the doctor has good news today," she said, trying to believe that he would.

"He better have good news, or you will be sorry," Tiny responded without looking at her and jumped out of the SUV.

Journey looked at him as he walked towards the entrance of the doctor's office, leaving her behind sitting in the truck. She paused for a moment and shook her head. *God give me strength,* she thought as she jumped out of the SUV, and jogged to catch up to him. When she finally reached the door that he was holding open for her, the disgusted look on his face told her that she should have been right behind him.

"Sorry," she immediately apologized as she passed by him to enter the waiting room.

Journey approached the reception area and told the woman behind the counter her name and the name of the physician she was seeing. The receptionist quickly checked off Journey's name in the appointment book and handed her a clipboard.

"Complete these forms and return them with your insurance card," the woman said without looking up at Journey.

Journey grabbed the clipboard and a pen from the penholder on the counter, and sat down next to Tiny. She quickly completed the forms and grabbed her *Coach* bag to find her wallet. As she opened the large pocketbook, she immediately began to rummage through the mass of papers, date book, and makeup bag, in an effort to find the matching wallet. It was not until her fingers started rattling the loose change on the bottom of her bag when she looked up and noticed how much noise she was making. Tiny heaved a loud sigh and looked over at Journey.

"What ARE you looking for?" he asked annoyed that she was causing a small disturbance.

"I have to give them my insurance card," she answered and pulled her wallet out of the bag.

"You have to give them that damn insurance card every fuckin' time we come here?" he whispered in a huff.

"I guess so," Journey almost snapped as she looked at the lady sitting next to Tiny being entertained by the scene he was creating.

Journey stood up quickly, walked past Tiny and the amused woman beside him, and returned the forms to the receptionist. The receptionist sifted through the documents to ensure they were signed, and she made a copy of the insurance card.

"Here you go," the receptionist said, handing Journey the card. "The doctor will be with you shortly, Mrs. Moore."

Journey quickly sat back down in her seat and grabbed a *Parenting* magazine from the end table. The waiting room was child friendly and made Journey sad every time she came there for testing. The walls were painted with bright colors, and the office supplied a playroom for the children. The chairs in the adult waiting area were plush and comfortable. Tiny often moaned and groaned whenever they had to make an appointment to visit Dr. Kowalski, but Journey was adamant about being seen by this particular fertility specialist. She had her share of visits with the local specialists, and, with each one, she never felt a connection or had a sense of comfort when they consulted her on the matter of fertility. However, when she and Tiny had their first consultation with Dr. Kowalski, he immediately sensed Journey's pain and showed them compassion. The doctor's assurance that he would exhaust all of his resources in an effort to discover a way for Journey to conceive gave her much hope. This anticipation created the comfort she so desired. He came highly recommended by Alex's sister, Reggie and her life partner, Mia. They had been trying to have a child for a couple of years and hired several "sperm donors" to supply them with what Reggie was not biologically equipped to provide. After enduring her fourth miscarriage, Mia was overwhelmed with depression and decided to seek a fertility specialist to assist them in bearing children. A few of her friends recommended Dr. Kowalski. He turned out to be Reggie and Mia's Godsend. Their last attempt at conception not only worked, but it blessed the couple with twins, a boy and a girl.

Now Journey was praying that Dr. Kowalski would help perform a similar miracle with her body, and make it possible for her to give her husband the child he longed for. Journey's ultimate hope was that a child would turn her marriage into the one that Tiny promised her. Journey flipped through the pages of the magazine without retaining any information it provided. Her heart was too busy racing, and her mind kept spinning the same thought in her head, ***he's going to tell me I can't have children.***

"Mr. and Mrs. Timothy Moore!" the nurse called out as she opened the door leading to the doctors' offices and examination rooms.

Tiny and Journey stood up together like soldiers and followed the nurse to Dr. Kowalski's office.

"Please have a seat. The doctor will be right in," the nurse sang before quickly leaving the office and closing the door behind her.

Journey and Tiny sat silently in their seats and neither moved a muscle. Dr. Kowalski's corner office was designed like the average doctor's office, filled with rich, cherry mahogany wood furniture and deep burgundy leather chairs. His many credentials, encased in fine frames, hung proudly behind his large desk. A light knock on the door interrupted Journey's visual tour of his office. Dr. Kowalski entered the office and greeted his patients.

"Good afternoon Mr. and Mrs. Moore," he said cheerfully. His joyful mood had an infectious effect on Journey.

She instantly smiled brightly and stood up to shake his hand. Tiny followed suit, and they all sat down.

Dr. Kowalski pulled Journey's file from the neatly stacked pile on the left hand side of his desk and opened it carefully. "Hmm, let's see here," he said, flipping through his encrypted notes, "I have great news and not so great news; which do you want to hear first?"

"The great news," Tiny and Journey answered in unison.

"Well, OK. Mrs. Moore ...," Dr. Kowalski spoke clearly.

"Please, call me Journey," she interrupted him with a noticeable anxiousness in her voice.

"OK, Journey," the doctor continued, "the great news is that nothing is wrong with your reproductive organs. You had some blockage in your fallopian tubes due to the cysts that we found a few months ago, but, those have shrunk, and I believe that if I put you on the pill for a few months the cysts will dissolve completely."

Journey's face began to beam as she sighed in relief and smiled from ear to ear. She looked over at Tiny and grabbed his hand. "I'm fine Baby. See? I can have your babies after all," she said loudly and grew more excited, forgetting that she was in an office. She was blissfully happy. She could feel the tension that had solidified in her frontal lobe over the past few months immediately start to dissolve. The doctor was able to prove that her womb was truly healthy. Finally, Tiny could no longer taunt her by saying she was not enough of a woman.

Tiny held her hand tightly and looked into Dr. Kowalski eyes. He needed an answer as to why his wife was not conceiving his child.

"Well then, Doc, what's the not so great news?" Tiny asked calmly.

"Well, Mr. Moore, I am glad you asked because that part actually concerns you," Dr. Kowalski replied with a serious tone.

Tiny loosened his grip from Journey's hand and clasped his hands together. Tiny leaned towards Dr. Kowalski's desk to show the doctor had his full attention.

"How does this concern me?" Tiny questioned.

"You see, Mr. Moore, we have totally eliminated your wife as having any reproductive problems or setbacks, which now means we have to ensure that you do not have inabilities to perform either. Therefore, I am going to have to ask that you have some testing done."

Tiny stiffened in his chair and immediately felt that this man was questioning his manhood. His defensiveness filled the room. His behavior was typical and expected, and did not intimidate Dr. Kowalski at all. Instead, he assured Tiny that the tests were practically painless and would not be as tedious as Journey's tests were. Yet and still, Tiny was not comfortable. Dr. Kowalski then proceeded to ask Tiny a flurry of personal health questions that caused Tiny to grow agitated.

"I know some of these questions are personal Mr. Moore, but only a few more and then I will be able to determine which tests are needed. Now, in the past year have you had any problems becoming aroused or ejaculating?"

Tiny looked over at Journey for confirmation before stating that he had no problems in that department.

"Naw, Doc," Tiny chuckled in confidence. "I am straight when it comes to pleasing my wife."

Dr. Kowalski blushed and cleared his throat partly because he could not envision the two of them having sex without finding it incredibly awkward. As the doctor suppressed the inner amusement of his vision, he proceeded to ask his final question. It was essential that he worded it carefully, in an effort not to offend his burly, oversized client.

"Finally, within the past year, have you used any *performance* enhancing medicines or narcotics?"

An awkward silence suddenly filled the room as if the doctor had just called Tiny a nigger. At that moment, the tension could only be cut with a chainsaw. In unison, the three of them grew noticeably uncomfortable. Without thinking of the consequences of what Tiny might do when they returned home, Journey finally looked at Tiny and in a submissive, yet dutiful tone softly said, "Tell him everything babe. He has to know."

Tiny shot a glare over at Journey that if it had been a loaded gun, a bullet would have landed straight between her eyes. *Who are you to tell me what to say,* he thought as he pondered whether or not he should divulge his secret. Dr. Kowalski could see that Tiny was becoming more agitated.

"I have to ask this question sir because the use of particular steroids can result in a low sperm count in men, thus making it difficult to conceive," the doctor tried to explain.

"My sperm count ain't low," Tiny spat back at the doctor.

His uneasy tone and inability to stay still in his seat substantiated Dr. Kowalski's suspicions. Promptly the doctor accepted the unauthenticated answer and jotted down a "yes" next to the question on his pad. He then slapped the thin manila file folder closed, signifying the end of the couple's office visit. "OK then that is it for now. If you would be so kind to make an appointment sir on your way out, and we will get started with testing as soon as possible," Dr. Kowalski said calmly as he stood up and shook Tiny's hand. He walked them to the appointment desk, and using medical terminology, instructed the receptionist to set Tiny up for various types of testing. Tiny reluctantly agreed to the date the woman offered and walked out of the office leaving Journey trailing behind.

They jumped into the SUV and Tiny sped off as if they just robbed a bank. Journey did not want to open her mouth in fear that she would say the wrong thing again. Instead, she sat silently and looked out of the window in the opposite direction of Tiny's stare. Out of the corner of her eye, she tried to inconspicuously keep an eye on him. She could see that his gaze was fixated on the vehicle in front of them.

They were barely on the Interstate before Journey felt her face being smashed against the passenger side window. She immediately tasted the salt from the blood that oozed from the cut on the inside of her lip, and, as the initial shock wore off, she could hear Tiny's voice.

"How many fuckin' times I got to tell you to keep that fuckin' mouth shut!" he screamed over the music blaring out of the speakers. "What did you mean *tell him everything Baby?*" he rhetorically asked, mocking her at the same time.

"Everything like what! You don't fuckin' know shit!" he said, pushing his index finger into her head as hard as he could, causing her head to continuously bang against the window while he sped down the Interstate.

"I'm sorry!" Journey cried.

"You are sorry, a sorry piece of shit," he said, trying to make her feel less than the dirt on the bottom of his shoe. "That damn doctor don't know what the fuck he is talking about! I know my damn sperm ain't low," Tiny said, securing his manhood.

"I think he was trying to get … ," Journey tried to defend Dr. Kowalski's questionnaire, but Tiny's back hand came crashing against the left side of her eye and stopped her in mid-sentence.

"Shut the fuck up! You taking up for him now!" he shouted. His anger turned to rage. He sped pass the car beside him, cut it off, and got off Exit 13 on *Conner Street* in the Bronx. He sped down the ramp, and made a quick right into the gas station and stopped suddenly.

Journey's head jerked forward and she was thankful that she had her seat belt on or her head would have gone through the windshield. She had no idea why Tiny had darted off the highway. Familiar to being enthralled in his wrath, and now with a busted lip and black eye, she knew not to ask.

"Get out!" he yelled loudly while reaching over her to open the passenger door. He flung the door open and unhooked her seat belt.

"What?" Journey was stunned as she looked around at the unfamiliar surroundings. She did not know anyone in the Bronx, nor the area. As the side of her head pounded, it began to swell with disbelief that Tiny would leave her here stranded.

"I said get out!" Tiny looked in her eyes with such revulsion, it was apparent at that moment, that his wife meant nothing to him. It became clear to her that he was about to abandon her at that gas station.

"Call that fuckin' doctor you want to defend, and tell him to bring yo' ass home. I know for a fact that I can make babies," he said while pushing her out of the passenger seat. "Shit ..., I've pumped two babies in Tanya in this past year alone!"

Journey was unable to comprehend the words that came dashing out of his mouth. Before she could ask him to repeat the latter of his comment, her shoes began to slide on icy, oil slick ground beneath her. She tried to reach for the handle but Tiny had closed the passenger door before she could grab it and sped off. Journey quickly regained a steady gait. Stunned and shocked beyond belief she watched her husband dart out into the steady flow of traffic.

"Wait!" Journey screamed toward the taillights of the SUV. "My pocketbook!"

Journey looked helpless as the car disappeared before her tear-filled eyes, and she slowly turned around to face the onlookers who were able to see a great show at her expense. She touched her lip and then her eye, walked into the mini mart, and asked the store clerk to point her to the ladies bathroom. She entered the ladies bathroom, and the smell of aged urine engulfed her senses. She walked over to the mirror to examine her bruises. She cried for a full five minutes before splashing her face with cold water and walking back out into the store with as much dignity as she could muster.

"Can I please use your phone?" she asked helplessly.

The speechless store clerk quickly responded to her request and handed her the cordless phone without asking any questions. The few people standing in line stood motionless. It was clear to the onlookers that she needed help, but no one moved in her direction to come to her aide. Journey walked over to the far corner of the store and leaned against the glass with her back turned to her audience. She dialed Alex's phone number and silently prayed that her friend would answer.

Chapter 7

Alex

That's What Friends Are For

Alex was sitting up in bed with her laptop neatly resting on a pillow cushioned between it and her thighs. The television was on, but acted only as a temporary distraction when Alex's eyes started to strain. She had spent the past couple of weeks working feverishly on her Japanese contract and had to travel overseas one last time. She was making online reservations to Japan when her phone rang. She was hoping it was Sway. They had not spent any alone time together since their double date with Journey and Tiny. They saw each other briefly when he picked up and dropped Stevie off on the weekends, and he offered to spend the night on one or two occasions, but Alex's busy schedule made her decline up until now. She needed to feel his strong hands all over her body before flying to the other side of the world. She looked at the caller ID and did not recognize the number. The phone rang a total of four times before she picked up the receiver.

"Hello," Alex said into the handset, curious to find out who was calling from the unknown number.

"Alex." A weak, frail voice responded.

At first Alex did not recognize the voice; nonetheless, her stomach succumbed to a pang that made her instantly nervous.

"Journey! Baby what's wrong, where are you; what happened?" Alex could not stop questioning Journey long enough to get answers.

"I'm in the Bronx," Journey barely whimpered.

"The Bronx!" Alex screamed into Journey's ear. "Just tell me where you are and I am on my way." Alex talked fast into the phone as she sprung from the bed. Holding the phone between her ear and shoulder, she grabbed some sweats and furry boots from her closet and swiftly got dressed while carefully listening.

"I'm at … ," Journey paused and began looking around confused. "Excuse me, can you tell me where I am?" she asked no one in particular.

Two onlookers began to tell her the cross streets of the gas station, and Journey repeated their directions to Alex as if she was a parrot. "Please hurry" were the last words she spoke into the handset.

Alex pressed the "end" button on her handset and threw it onto the bed. She slid her feet into the boots and grabbed her keys and pocketbook from the chaise lounge in the corner of her bedroom. She trotted down the hallway and steps and out of the door so fast that she neglected to ask her mother to keep an eye on Stevie for her.

She sped her *Lexus RX330* down the narrow Pelham roads and grabbed her cell phone from her pocketbook sitting on the passenger seat. She quickly pressed two buttons on the small illuminated device and lifted it to her ear, while making a bend around the corner.

"Hello," Marie's voice sang into the phone.

"Hey Ma, it's me. Journey called and needs a ride. I will explain later," she said, keeping her sentences short. "I am not sure how long I am going to be. Can you put Stevie to bed for me?" she asked already knowing the answer.

"Of course; is Journey alright?" Marie pried, trying to get the gist of what was going on.

"Everything is OK. I will be home as soon as I can. Thanks Ma," Alex spoke quickly into the tiny phone and ended the call before her mother could ask any more questions. And, without interruption, she continued to steer the four-wheel drive suspension while the Bridgestone tires gripped the winding roads. She decided to take the back roads through Mount Vernon to avoid any unexpected traffic on Interstate 95. Alex's main objection was to reach her best friend in a fast and timely fashion.

****

Barely avoiding an oncoming car by a few inches, Alex whipped her SUV into the gas station parking lot.

"Oh! Sorry lady!" Alex yelled and waved at the woman in the other car. Alex knew the poor woman could not hear her, but Alex hoped that she read her lips. She pulled up to the curb of the mini-mart and blew her horn.

Feeling embarrassed and humiliated, Journey stepped out of the mart holding an ice pack on her left eye. She walked slowly over to Alex's truck and got in.

"Journey, what in the world happened to you?" Alex asked, with a horrified expression on her face. Her friend looked like she'd just been mugged.

Journey looked at Alex and could not say a word. Instead, she allowed the tears that she had been holding back, flow down her bruised face. "We had a fight." She finally managed to say.

"So, how did you end up here?" Alex said, looking around trying to make some sense of the whole situation.

"Just drive," Journey said buckling her seat belt. She wanted to be relieved of the stares and whispers surrounding her.

Alex caught on immediately and proceeded to drive off. She sped onto the highway and headed toward Harlem. They drove in silence. Alex decided to keep her mouth shut and allow Journey some time to gather her thoughts because they both knew Journey was not getting out of Alex's truck without telling her the entire story.

Journey pulled down the sun visor and looked at the little mirror embedded on the inner side of it. She touched her eye and could tell based on previous experiences that the puffiness and redness would be black and blue in the morning. She was thankful that she worked from home. At that moment, Journey fully understood the real reason Tiny persuaded her to work from home. In his rage, he allowed a few bones to fall out of his closet. Journey always knew something was going on between her husband and Tanya, but now her suspicions were confirmed. A wave of clarity came over her. Everything was starting to make sense.

Alex tried to pay attention to the road in front of her but could not help peeking at her friend's swollen face. It was apparent that Tiny had slapped her around pretty hard.

"Journey, you know we gotta talk right?" Alex said it as if she was reminding Journey.

"Mmm ... Hmm," Journey responded and was now looking at the cut on the inside of her lip.

This is the last time, Journey silently tried to convince herself. She knew that she had to leave Tiny or he would eventually kill her. Journey had watched enough episodes of *Oprah* to know when to get out of an abusive relationship. Her bruised reflection indicated that her time had come.

"I need a plan," Journey said, not realizing she was saying it out loud.

"What was that?" Alex asked, hoping she was ready to start at the beginning.

Journey looked at her friend with pleading eyes and said, "I am going to need you."

Alex gazed back at her frail friend and grabbed her hand tightly. "Whatever you need," Alex reassured her as she pulled up to the curb down the street from Journey and Tiny's place. Alex put the gear in park and unsnapped her seat belt to get comfortable. "OK. What's going on?"

"We went to the doctor today, and Tiny was not happy with what the doctor had to say," Journey said bluntly.

"Well, what did he say?" Alex asked, feeling like she was pulling teeth.

"Basically, he said that I am perfectly fine, and it's Tiny who may have the problem. Tiny could not take it and flipped out on me in the car and threw me out at the gas station."

"I knew he was putting his damn hands on you!" Alex said angrily.

"That doesn't matter anymore," Journey said coldly. "He said some things to me today Alex that I could never forgive him for. These bruises are just reminders that I have to leave sooner rather than later."

"How long has this been going on, Journey?"

"It's been almost a year now," Journey replied feeling somewhat numb. "It started with the verbal put downs and then a mush in the face here or there, but recently he has been using me as a punching bag," she said somberly looking down into her lap.

"WHAT?" Alex screamed.

Journey sat silently while Alex went on a thirty second rant calling Tiny every name in the book. In an instant, the moment became surreal. Journey could not believe she was finally sharing her hellish nightmare with Alex.

Trying to be as sensitive as possible, Alex tried calming down and concentrating on helping her friend. "Was he upset about the possibility of not being able to have children?" she asked, taking a deep breath.

"Well, yes and no," Journey said, trying to figure out in her mind if she should tell Alex the whole story, including Tiny's possible affair with Tanya.

"Tell it to me straight Journey, and stop beating around the bush," Alex said shifting in her seat and becoming slightly impatient.

"OK, OK. I did not want to say anything until after I see the asshole again, but at first I thought the abusive behavior was because we thought I could not conceive. But when Tiny kicked me out of the car, I could swear that he mentioned that Tanya was pregnant by him."

Alex's jaw visibly dropped causing Journey to chuckle.

"I know. Crazy, right?" Journey asked rhetorically while shaking her head up and down.

Alex closed her mouth in a slow motion and looked at Journey in disbelief. Tiny loved Journey. Alex would have never thought that he, of all men, would be so stereotypical and step out on his wife. She held higher expectations for Tiny, but she also knew something was not quite right since their last encounter at the movies.

"Tanya from the gym?" Alex finally asked, still half shocked. "Your counter girl? Isn't she, like, fifteen?" Alex asked half jokingly and covering her mouth to avoid laughing out loud.

"*Nineteen* and this is not funny," Journey said half laughing herself, while alternating the ice pack between her eye and lip.

Alex always had the ability to turn a hurtful situation into a lighthearted obstacle that they could face together.

"I know," Alex said, straightening up and gripping the steering wheel. "I am sorry, but Tiny should know better. He and Sway need to realize that they are a lot closer to forty than they are to twenty. So, is she pregnant now?" Alex asked confused.

"I don't know, that's why I really did not want to say anything, but I think they have been messing around for at least a year now. Remember when Tiny convinced me to work at home? I thought something was going on then, and that was the first time he actually mushed me in the face."

"Journey!" Alex responded not believing that in the last year her friend was being so violently abused.

"I know." Journey nodded, grabbing on to Alex's hand. "It's alright, Alex. After what happened today, Tiny will never have the opportunity to hurt me again," Journey said, trying to build confidence.

Journey reminded herself that the doctor gave her a clean bill of health. She indeed was fertile, which meant that she could have children, and, therefore, Tiny was wrong; she was in fact, all woman. Suddenly she could feel her self-esteem being restored. Her feelings of self-worth lifted several levels from the pit of nothingness, where Tiny had managed to place it in over time. At that moment, Journey made the decision to be the strong woman her parents raised her to be. The first step would be to leave the horrible situation that she was in. "Can I stay with you for a few days?" Journey asked, already knowing the answer.

"You know, you don't have to ask," Alex said, opening her car door. "Let's get some of your things now before your punk ass husband comes home."

Journey followed suit and slid out of the truck. Together they jogged up the steps toward the front door. The house was dark, which confirmed that Tiny was not at home. Journey was glad because she did not want to face him with Alex around. The women moved quickly through the house and gathered as many of Journey's things that their petite arms could hold and threw the bags in the back of the SUV. As Alex shut the lift-gate of the truck, Journey stared at her townhouse and contemplated running back to leave Tiny a note, but decided not to.

"*Fuck him*," she said as she turned around and hopped in the passenger side of the truck.

Chapter 8

Alex
If Only For One Night

Alex backed into her large cobblestone-brick paved driveway and into the two-car garage with precision. She and Journey leaped out of the SUV together as if it were choreographed, and rushed to open the lift gate. They unloaded the truck as quietly as possible. Neither of them realized that time had passed so quickly, and both Marie and Stevie were inside sound asleep.

Luckily, the guest bedroom Journey was going to use was near the entryway from the garage leading into the home. It made it easy for the women to unload Journey's belongings without creating a major stir. The added incentive was that the bedroom was on the basement level next to Alex's office, so Journey felt at ease knowing that she would have her privacy. She needed the alone time to decide on her next steps. Journey left the heaviest piece of luggage in the back of Alex's truck and decided that she would grab it in the morning because now it was time for a nightcap. They crept upstairs like two snickering teenagers sneaking in after curfew. They slid into the kitchen, and Alex turned the dimmer switch to illuminate the recessed lighting to a soft glow. She pulled out two martini glasses from the cabinet and excused herself briefly to grab the shaker and ingredients from the bar in the living room so she could whip up two strong apple martinis. Journey sat at the granite-tiled island in the middle of the kitchen floor and waited for Alex to return to demonstrate her bartending skills.

Journey's face was still hurting, and she suffered from a constant sting from the cut inside her lower lip. She needed a relaxant, and, at the moment, a martini was the remedy. Alex glided back into the kitchen and wasted very little time mixing and pouring her concoction into the martini glasses. Journey was impressed. Alex placed the glass filled with a lime green substance in front of Journey and sat down on the stool next to her. Alex lifted her glass and smiled.

"Here's to finding a new start," Alex said as a tear welled up in her eye.

Journey could not respond. She knew if she did, the tears would flow freely from her being, and she was tired of crying. A part of her realized that she needed to start over, but a small part of her still loved her husband and wanted to stay with him and force their marriage to work. She lifted her glass and nodded in agreement with her friend, and took a long sip from her glass. The combination of the ice-cold glass and alcohol cooled and numbed her swollen lip. Before she could pull the glass from her lips, the phone rang. A tinge of fear surged up her spine. She and Alex froze in their seats and looked at each other. Journey sat her martini glass down on the counter and continued to stare at Alex with frightful eyes.

"If it's him, I am not ready to talk to him," Journey whispered in a low voice.

"Girl, it better not be him," Alex said, easing off the stool and grabbing the phone without looking at the caller ID, and pressing the talk button before it could ring again to awake her mother and child. "Hello," she quickly said into the receiver, trying to hold back her attitude.

"What's up?" Sway's masculine voice rang in her ear.

"Oh, hey, what's up? You know what time it is right? Your child is sleeping," Alex said girlishly into the phone while looking at Journey with a grin on her face.

"I know she's sleep. I'm callin' for you," he said seductively.

"Oh, are you now? Well, you are going to have to call me tomorrow because Journey's staying over tonight. We have some women issues to discuss, so tonight's not a good night, if you know what I mean," Alex said sexily into the phone.

"Then come outside for a minute," he said calmly.

"What?" Alex responded, not believing that he was outside of her house.

She shuffled from the kitchen to the living room and peered out of the bay window into the black night. At first she did not notice his black BMW, but its shininess glimmered against the moonlight and lit up her eyes.

"Journey, I will be right back!" Alex yelled from the foyer and rushed outside. Alex wrapped her arms around her body and walked as fast as she could to the passenger side of Sway's car. She slid into the car seat and instantly, her backside was comforted by the warmth of the heated seat. The orange glow from the illuminated dashboard provided just enough light to allow the two of them to immediately lean into one another to kiss.

"How have you been?" Sway asked in a whisper as he pulled back from her soft lips.

They both knew what he meant. It had been a few weeks since their last intimate encounter.

"I've been good. I mean ..., I could be better but I have company, and you can't come in. I don't think it would be a good time," Alex responded with a little disappointment in her voice.

She was not upset that Journey was there, but she wished Sway would have come by earlier. And, more importantly, she did not want Sway to see the damage that Tiny had placed upon Journey's face.

"What's going on?" Sway asked with some concern. "Everything is OK with Journey, right?" he asked, looking at Alex in the eyes to ensure an honest response.

"Yeah, she will be OK," Alex responded down playing the situation. "You know how you men are, and she just needed some girl time. That's all. Now, I have a question," Alex said turning on her serious face.

"Why are you calling me so late? Couldn't find one of your *friends*?" Alex asked, hoping that he would have the right answer.

"You know that is never a problem. I just wanted to be with my lover tonight, not some friend," he said smiling confidently, knowing that those kinds of words often softened Alex, but thankfully never made her mushy.

Her ability to keep her guard up around him made her more attractive. It showed him she had strength. Alex smiled at his response and leaned in for another kiss. Their lips slightly touched as Sway's tongue slowly entered Alex's inviting mouth. She grabbed the back of his head as their kiss grew more passionate. Sway's hand traveled across her body with no planned destination but landed firmly on her right breast. He gently massaged it, causing her nipple to emerge and stand erect. Alex reciprocated by gently grasping his groin area and rubbed his partially erect penis through his slacks. She wanted him.

Sway could taste her sexual energy and pulled back from their kiss. "Let's go inside," he almost demanded.

"We can't," Alex replied disappointed and sexually frustrated.

"Why not, y'all don't have men in there with my baby right?" Sway asked with a raised brow. He could not believe he was asking Alex this question.

"No, silly. Journey and Tiny had an argument, and she is really upset, and I don't think I would be a good friend if I went back inside with you and left her hanging. I'm sorry," Alex said expressing her little girl pout that always made Sway melt.

Although Sway loved Journey like a sister, he was fully erect now and making love to Alex was his only pressing concern. He looked over at Alex and admired her beauty. Sway adjusted his car seat so that it leaned back horizontally into the back seat.

"Come'ere," he said, reaching his hand out to her.

Alex smiled a devilish grin. She quickly slid out of her sweats and panties before placing her hand inside of his and lifting her body over the gear shaft console.

"Sway, you are a bad boy. This is not what good girls like me do," Alex said getting more and more excited as she straddled his body as best she could with the limited space she had to work with.

Sway was hard and ready to feel Alex's warmth race through his body. Since his last encounter with Alex, he had one or two escapades with a couple of his *friends*, but sex with anyone other than Alex is just that – sex. The sheer act of satisfying his need for instant gratification was his only motivation when sexing those women. Yet, with Alex, it was love. He savored his time when making love to her, and his only mission with Alex was to please her. He slid his hardness into Alex's warmth as gently as he could, but the tightness of her flesh caused him to use some force creating a pleasurable pain in both their bodies. Alex stiffened as she sat upright on top of Sway's chiseled body, and he filled her petite frame with his thickness. She began to move in a steady slow motion, back and forth, up and down. Sway took hold of her hips and guided her body so that she could feel every inch of him. She was still the only woman he would have sex without using any protection, and it was at times like these he appreciated that incentive. The more Sway pounced Alex's body up and down on his waist, the more excited she became. The heat from their bodies caused the car windows to perspire, and Sway's BMW had the fresh scent of sex seeping through the leather seats.

"Damn, Girl," Sway managed to gasp in between each thrust.

Alex looked down at Sway with both love, and lust in her eyes and leaned in to lick his earlobe. Sway moaned in delight and wished he had more room to do more things to make Alex feel the way she was making him feel. He had never had sex in one of his cars before, and the lack of legroom reminded him why. They continued their lovemaking until the flicker of Alex's front porch light interrupted them. Alex sat up, and looked through the tinted glass window and was grateful no one could see inside of the car. She and Sway looked at each other and began to laugh. Neither of them had the opportunity to climax, which meant that they would have to see each other again real soon.

"I think I better get back inside," Alex said adjusting her shirt and un-straddling Sway to sit back in the passenger seat to slip back into her bottoms.

Sway sat up, zipped up his pants, and adjusted his seat back into the driving position. He looked over at Alex and wanted to kidnap her for the remainder of the night.

"Listen, I am going to call you in the morning so we can make an arrangement to finish what we started," Sway said looking at her up and down with hunger in his eyes.

"Please do," Alex said with the same hunger in her eyes. "But, don't forget, I am leaving for Japan in a few days."

They leaned into one another one final time, and Sway planted a soft kiss on Alex's smooth lips as she opened the passenger car door.

"Maybe I'll see you tomorrow," she said softly and slid out of the car.

"You can count on it," he responded.

Sway watched Alex briskly walk back into the house and close the door behind her. He shifted the gear into drive and sped out of the driveway wondering what he would do next since his night with Alex was not going to happen.

****

"I am so sorry!" Alex gasped coming in from the cold and closing the door behind her.

"Yeah, right! Y'all are so nasty!" Journey laughed. She was actually happy for the momentary distraction her best friend was providing. Journey's whole life had been turned inside out in the matter of hours, and Alex's schoolgirl behavior amused Journey, giving her something else to think about.

Alex knew she was busted, and she belted out a loud laugh that caused Journey to cover Alex's mouth.

"Shhh. You are going to wake up your mother!" Journey managed to say between her uncontrollable giggling.

"OK, OK!" Alex quipped while removing Journey's hand from her face.

"You know me too well," Alex said standing straight up and walking back into the kitchen. "But I really am sorry. I had no intention on staying out there that long." Alex lifted her glass from the same spot on the island where she had left it thirty minutes earlier. She took a long sip, savoring the vodka, apple flavor combination and licked her lips as she swallowed. For a split second, she wished Journey would have waited five more minutes before flicking that annoying porch light. She looked over at Journey's glass and could clearly see that it was filled to the brim.

"You were in here getting your drink on without me. How many does that one make?" Alex asked jokingly.

"You know I am a bartender! This makes three and counting," Journey said and took a quick sip.

Alex took another sip to join her and sat on the stool. Journey walked back over to her stool and sat down next to Alex.

"You did not say anything to Sway, did you?" Journey asked in a serious tone, immediately changing the mood.

"Hell no!" Alex nearly shouted. "You know I can't tell Sway that Tiny put his hands on you. He would flip out. I just told him you guys had a little argument and you needed some girl time," Alex said lowering her voice. She polished off her room temperature martini and stood up to shake up another one. The sound of the ringing phone startled both women and they found themselves frozen once again.

"Who in the hell?" Alex questioned while looking at the caller ID. "It's Tiny," she said looking over at Journey not knowing whether to answer it or not. "Do you want to talk to him?" Alex asked while simultaneously placing her finger on the talk button.

She was ready to give Tiny a piece of her mind, but knew enough not to interfere in their marital brawl. She would have to follow her best friend's lead. After all, this was not her battle or her man. Alex wanted Journey to say "no", which was all Alex needed to tell Tiny what a spineless punk he was. Instead, Alex watched Journey shake her head "yes". Alex let out a sigh of slight disappointment as Journey reached for the phone.

"Yeah, let me talk to that motherfucker," Journey said with much bravado and took the phone from the palm of Alex's hand. The confidence Journey gained from the intoxicating alcohol flowing through her veins showed Alex that she would be able to handle herself.

"What Tiny?" Journey asked without saying 'hello' first.

"I'm sorry Baby," Tiny said in a dull, sad voice, throwing Journey off.

She wanted to argue. She wanted to fight. "Whatever, Tiny! What do you want?" she asked.

"I want you to come home. I lost it earlier today; I am sorry," he pleaded.

Journey could hear it in his voice that he was feeling bad. She began to soften and looked over at Alex. Right then, Alex could see her friend melting right in front of her eyes. Journey turned away quickly from her friend's glare and walked into the living room to gain some privacy. She was confused. Her heart was telling her to listen to her husband, accept his apology, and to remember their vows. Yet, her head was telling her that love did not hurt and that her heart was being deceived.

"I'm not coming back home," she said as a matter fact, remembering the embarrassment she faced at that gas station in the Bronx. "What you did today, Tiny, was wrong. Not to mention that you have been fucking that little skank behind my back. How could you?" Journey asked holding back the same tears she had been suppressing all night.

"I said some stuff today, Baby, to make you mad," Tiny said softly into the phone, trying to down play his adulterous confession. "That's all that was. I was just mad at that fuckin' doctor trying to tell me that I am not a man!" his voice grew louder. He did not call Journey to get upset again. He wanted his wife to come home where she belonged and not at Alex's house, airing all of their dirty laundry. More importantly, he did not want Alex nor Sway looking at him in a different light. In Sway's eyes, Tiny was "the man", and real men did not hit women, under any circumstance – period.

"I'm coming to get you Baby, OK," he said, trying to stay calm.

"I already told you, I'm not coming back. I'm done. I am sick of how we have been lately, and I can't do it anymore Tiny," Journey cried into the phone.

Tiny could feel his control over Journey dwindling with every word she spoke. He could hear it in her voice that she had been drinking, but he knew that the new air of confidence in his wife was coming from the bond she shared with Alex. He needed her to come home. Alex sat in the kitchen trying to eavesdrop as best she could, and she was proud that Journey was not giving in so easily.

"I know, I know, Baby I have been wrong," Tiny agreed with Journey. "I was just frustrated with the baby thing, but now it's all good. Come home to your teddy bear."

Journey wanted to concede to her husband's request. Tiny's deep, seductive voice always had the ability to do that to her. "You cheated on me, Tiny?" Journey bluntly asked.

Tiny could not answer. He sat quietly, holding the phone to his ear, trying to decide whether to tell his wife the truth or what he thought she wanted to hear. He chose the latter. "No Baby, I told you. I said that shit about Tanya to make you mad," he lied.

"I never did anything with that girl. Just forget that I ever said that, OK," he pleaded.

"I can't forget what you said Tiny, not just like that," she replied and snapped her fingers. "There are too many things that make sense now, like you wanting me to work from home. And, you coming home at crazy times during the night sometimes," Journey began running down her mental list of neglect and betrayal.

Earlier that day as the words came barging out of his mouth; Tiny knew that he would have to work double time to get Journey to not believe the truth of his affair with Tanya. After he dumped Journey in the Bronx, he drove straight to Tanya's house and told her that the cat was out of the bag. Tanya's reaction to the news was sheer bliss. Excitably she began to tell Tiny how wonderful it would be to not have to hide how they felt for each other. She quickly disrobed, revealing her chocolate naked body. She wanted Tiny to have his way with her.

"Now the gym can be all ours!" He remembered Tanya saying. Her jovial behavior and blatant disregard to an important part of his life that was falling apart caused Tiny to step back and look at her.

He tried to resist and a part of him thought it best to end the ongoing affair with Tanya right then and there, but the desire he felt for her overwhelmed his better judgment and he took advantage of the situation. He left Tanya's apartment some hours later, feeling sorry for what he had done to Journey. He realized that he was where he was financially because of the hard work and financial resources of his wife, not some nineteen year old, nymphomaniac, barely holding a high school diploma. Yet, at the same time, he could not deny that Tanya provided him with a sexual explosion whenever they encountered. She was a freak in bed and performed the best fellacio he had ever had. He also could not deny his lack luster lovemaking skills with his wife since he started his elicit affair with Tanya. He vowed to make it right somehow with Journey, despite the fact that he was not letting Tanya go, just yet.

"Baby, you are putting too much thought into this. You know I work late trying to keep up with the competition, and I thought you would want to work from home especially since we were trying to have a baby," he said desperately, conning his way out of the mess he created.

Journey wiped her face, not knowing what to think or believe. The genuine sound of regret in Tiny's voice was driving her crazy. One minute he was bashing her head in and the next he was acting as if he could not breathe without her. One thing Journey knew for sure was that she would never go back home to Tiny if he was cheating on her.

She could not fathom the thought of sharing her husband with someone else, or him loving someone else the way he should be loving her.

"Tiny, tell me the truth, did you cheat on me with that whore!" she almost yelled into the phone.

"No Baby, I did not," he said clearly into the phone.

It was so much easier to lie to her over the phone than it would have been face to face; Tiny was grateful for that. He could hear Journey let out a sigh of relief. She wanted to believe that her husband was faithful. More than that, she needed to believe that their life together as she knew it had not been contaminated by an affair with their teenage employee.

"I am coming to get you Baby," Tiny said as if everything had been resolved.

"No, you are not. Tiny I can't live in a place where I am afraid," her voice was almost in a whisper.

"I promise I will never put my hands on you like that again, I swear," he said holding up his right hand as if she could see him taking an official oath.

Part of Journey knew he was lying but she wanted it to be true, so she forced herself to believe it. "You promise?" she asked again, sealing the deal.

"I promise, Baby, I will never do those things to you again or treat you like that. You deserve better," he said convincing her that her teddy bear was back.

"If you ever put your hands on me again Tiny, or if I find out you slept with that bitch, I swear, I will leave. Just walk out, no questions," she said with renewed confidence. It felt good to finally give Tiny some demands for a change. She liked it.

"I'm still not going to come home tonight," Journey concluded. "I will come home in a few days when Alex leaves for Japan."

Tiny wanted Journey to believe that he would do anything to make it right, so he complied with her makeshift plan.

"OK, Baby, but remember that I love you, and I am so sorry," Tiny said as lovingly as possible.

"I will see you in a few days when I get home," Journey softly replied, full of mixed emotions and suddenly unsure of her next move.

March - 1999

Chapter 9

Alex
Home

Alex clearly remembered arriving late to JFK Airport on a rainy, soggy Monday two weeks ago, due to a three-car pile up on the Long Island Expressway, and quickly checking her bags at the curbside check-in area. Although during the past few years, her career demanded that she jet set back and forth overseas, her fear of flying never faded.

Her heart palpitated as she boarded the huge Boeing jet airplane. She truly hated to fly. She was immediately greeted and seated by a pleasant stewardess. As far as Alex was concerned, the stewardess was too cheerful; however, she appreciated the woman's sincerity and her sense of calmness. As soon as Alex was comfortable in her business class window seat, her heart started to beat at a steady pace. The captain informed the passengers that they would be experiencing some turbulence throughout the flight due to the inclement weather. Alex closed her eyes and silently recited the *Lord's Prayer* and braced herself for a bumpy ride to the other side of the world.

However, the return flight from Japan was turning out to be far less painful. And, although the fear of flying still lingered, Alex was actually enjoying the view of the clear evening sky. The plane ride was smooth, turbulence free, and not to mention, it arrived in New York on time. As the plane touched down upon her return from a very productive, two-week business trip in a country she was growing to love, Alex breathed in deeply and thanked God for returning her home safely. Now she was eager to see her little girl.

As the stewardess announced that the passengers could remove their seat belts and move about the plane, Alex sprung up from her seat. Moving at a rapid pace, Alex gathered her paperwork she was working on and threw the pile in her briefcase. She quickly pulled her carry-on bag down from the compartment above her seat and joined the line of departing passengers. She was glad that the plane was not filled to its capacity because that allowed her to get off of it swiftly. Sway and Stevie were to pick her up and she hoped they were waiting. Not only did she miss Stevie, but she found herself feeling the same way toward Sway. She and Sway had some unfinished business to attend to since their impromptu rendezvous in front of her house on the heated leather seat in Sway's car was cut short. The combination of their conflicting schedules and Journey not going home until the day Alex left for her trip prevented them from seeing one another, until now. Alex had every intention on completing what they had started. That was one thing she prided herself on; she was a finisher, despite the task at hand.

Alex walked as fast as she could to the baggage claim area. She hovered over the conveyor belt, and waited for her luggage to come through the heavy, black plastic flaps dangling from the open space in the wall. After a few minutes, her *Louis Vuitton* luggage made an entrance through the black flaps and into Alex's eyesight. She moved closer to the conveyor belt and swiped her luggage from it before the luggage could pass her by. As she walked towards the passenger pick up area of the airport, she could see Stevie's wild, curly hair flailing on top of her head, while Sway held her high in his arms. Alex grew excited as her steps became shorter and quicker. The closer she got, the more visible the hand made sign that Stevie was holding became. Alex smiled and immediately knew that Sway and Stevie spent plenty of time doing what Stevie loved to do most: arts and crafts. The bright white construction paper had Alex Avery scribbled on it with Stevie's signature purple hearts border. Alex approached her family, dropped her luggage, and opened her arms wide for a much needed hug.

"Hi Mommy!" Stevie nearly screamed, handing Alex the sign.

"Hey Baby, I love my sign, thank you. How's my girl?" Alex asked as she relieved Sway's arms and took Stevie into hers.

She stood on her toes and planted a soft, seductive full closed mouth kiss on Sway's lips. They both savored the split second kiss and Sway bent down to pick up Alex's luggage.

"How was your trip?" he asked as they walked towards the parking lot.

"It was good. I am almost done with this project. I just have a few more loose ends to tie up, but thankfully I can do that from my home office. How was the Bahamas?" Alex asked.

"It was nice to spend some time with my kids, just me and them. Cain has really grown up. You had to see all of the local girls coming to the house all times of the night looking for him," Sway said, laughing at the memory. *Like father, like son.*

Once Alex firmed up her business trip a few weeks ago, Sway arranged for his son, Cain, to fly down from San Diego to the Bahamas to meet him and Stevie. Sway wanted to spend some time with his children. Although Cain was almost twenty-two years old, and there was such a great age difference between him and Stevie, it was important to Sway that his children knew one another.

Sway always regretted not being there for Cain, and now that he was considered to be a grown man, Sway felt a special need to bond with his son on a man-to-man level. Sway was cognizant of the necessary life skills that he wanted to impart on his son. He wanted his son to experience the joys of success in the absence of navigating illegal channels to attain it. Sway was building an empire, and he wanted Cain to inherit it. Sway's most recent investment was a cozy little beach house in Freeport, the main island of the Bahamas. This was Sway's fourth residential investment property. In addition, he owned the commercial properties in Atlantic City and Washington, D.C.

"I would love to see Cain. Did he go back home?" Alex asked.

"No, he's at your place with Mama Marie. He wanted to see you too, and I convinced him to stick around for another week to see what running my business is like," Sway said proudly.

Cain was graduating from the San Diego State University in May, and since his major was in business management, Sway was hoping Cain was ready to come back to New York and work in the family business. Alex looked over at Sway and could plainly see how pleased he was with Cain.

"He will learn a lot then. His father is very savvy when it comes to business," Alex said as they reached Sway's Range Rover in the short term parking lot.

He unlocked the doors, and while Alex placed Stevie in her booster seat and buckled her in, Sway threw her luggage in the back and hopped in the driver seat. He looked over and smiled at Alex.

"Thanks for the compliment," he said and leaned over to kiss her soft lips.

"Mmm … are you and Cain spending the night?" Alex asked, wanting more of what Sway had just given her.

"We can," he replied with a sexy look in his deep brown eyes.

No more had to be said. Sway eased out of the parking space and sped off toward the airport exit sign. Surprisingly, traffic was light and moved at a quick, steady pace. Just the way Sway liked traffic to flow. Stevie sat comfortably in her booster seat in the back of the SUV and asked Alex an array of questions about her trip to "hapan". She still could not pronounce the letter "j". She was an inquisitive child and very smart for a three and a half year old. Alex answered her questions as quickly as Stevie could ask them. Finally, after firing so many inquiries at her mother, Stevie dosed off. Alex then turned her attention over to Sway.

"So, did Cain and Stevie spend some brother-sister time together in the Bahamas?"

"Did they? She would not let Cain out of her sight," Sway replied with a light chuckle. "He had to take her to the beach every morning. And, every afternoon Stevie had a new arts and crafts project for them to create."

They both laughed and looked back at their little bundle of joy.

"Ahh, that's good. You know she hardly ever sees Cain, so I am glad that you took them on vacation together," Alex said.

"I really hope Cain decides to move back to the East Coast after graduation. I sometimes feel like I owe him so much since he moved away to California at an age when he needed me most," Sway concluded.

He could not help feeling a little guilty and was still slightly angry at himself for the way he used to live. The high price of that illegal lifestyle caused him to be separated from his son. Alex knew not to delve into why Carmen left New York because she already had an idea that it had something to do with Sway getting shot. Sway was still sensitive about that incident, so she left that part of his life alone.

"That would be nice," Alex chimed in, thinking how nice it would be to have Stevie's older brother living closer to them.

"Not to change the subject but I have to discuss a business proposition with you," Sway said, looking at Alex out of the corner of his eye.

"Oh yeah," Alex replied. Curious to know what Sway had in mind, Alex asked, "is this a real business proposition or the kind of proposition that I can possibly fulfill tonight?"

She was feeling sexually frustrated and needed to release that energy before taking on any further responsibilities.

He smiled, showing off his perfect smile. "No, seriously, this is a real business matter. You are too much!" he said looking at her.

"What!" Alex exclaimed, "I have not seen you in a minute, and, you know we never finished what we started."

"Yeah, I know," he replied with a hint of seduction in his voice. "We will wrap that matter up tonight, but right now this is a real deal."

Alex could tell that he was serious and she knew Sway well enough to know that when he was ready to talk 'business', he meant business. "Well, OK then shoot," she responded in a serious tone.

"I am thinking about opening up another shop," he said in a matter of fact tone.

"Sway, that is awesome! Where will this one be located?" Alex probed, ready to delve into his new venture.

"Well, hold up, I said I am thinking about it," he said, trying to calm Alex down. "This is where you come in. Before I approach Romeo with this, I would like to retain your services to go to Vegas, check out the location, and draw up a business plan listing the prospects of opening a business out there. Also, I will need a projection of the long- term overhead costs and revenue. I am going to need your straightforward input on this project because you will be overseeing it from conception to completion if we decide to proceed."

Alex was honored that Sway wanted her to take over the entire project, which showed her he trusted her fully with his business and his money. She was even more excited to be going to Las Vegas; she had never been to Nevada.

"Of course," Alex said as though she already accepted the job. "I should be wrapping up my paperwork for the Japan project within the next week or so. Let's schedule a flight and arrange a meeting with the investors. I am assuming for a project of this magnitude you have investors, right?"

"Yes, one. He is already a shop member and frequents the downtown location when he's in New York. I checked out his membership portfolio. He joined about a year ago and his business affiliations appear to be solid. And, his proposal sounds firm, but you know I don't trust any and everybody. I want you to do a thorough background check before you fly out there."

"Well, OK, I can check him out along with his proposal and then we can go from there. Schedule the meeting for sometime at the end of next week," Alex said pulling out her appointment book and jotting down some notes.

"Cool," Sway said as he veered off the Pelham, New York exit.

After selling *The Champagne Room* to Adam, Sway was content with his accomplishments and decided to focus on the four shops that were running smoothly and generating great income. He was also considering investing in more residential real estate. However, after the first of the New Year, he was approached with a proposition of a lifetime. Henry Mitken, a business entrepreneur, introduced himself to Sway one day at the shop, and informally mentioned his intention of opening a high end, upscale hotel in Las Vegas, and was wondering if Sway would like to open a spa in the mall on the courtyard level. Initially, Sway brushed the short, balding guy off, but the persistent little man came back for a shave and a massage a few days later, and handed Sway a detailed business plan that showed him great promise. The plan included a sixty-forty profit split from the hotel proceeds, and no split of the spa's revenue, making the deal entirely in Sway's favor. The added bonus was the total square footage of the shop would cover most of the ground floor, which would make it the largest spa Sway and Romeo would own thus far. It certainly sounded too good to be true. Over the past few months, Sway could not focus on anything other than the possibility of setting up shop in Las Vegas, and now that Alex was willing to come on board, Sway was feeling like this venture could not fail.

Sway pulled into the all too familiar driveway, and parked his Rover. Alex jumped out of the passenger side of the truck and opened the back door to grab Stevie, who was sound asleep. Sway grabbed the heavy luggage from the trunk and carried them effortlessly into the foyer of the house. He placed them on the marble tiled floor and inhaled the scent traveling through the house. The aroma of Mama Marie's homemade meatballs and spaghetti filled the house, and, for a split second, Sway thought he was downtown at *Tony Roma's.*

"Yo, Cain!" Sway called out. "Come get these bags and bring them upstairs to Alex's bedroom."

Sway did not hear a verbal response; instead, he could hear his son's footsteps coming from the lower level of the house. Cain was the spitting image of Sway except his skin complexion was that of ground cinnamon; a contribution from his mother's Puerto Rican heritage. His hair was pitch black, short and wavy, and his body was sculpted like a tri-athlete. His smooth skin and dark smoky eyes complimented his full lips and fine jaw line. He was a college pretty boy but his street knowledge, thug persona, and swagger clearly conveyed that he could hold his own and not to let his looks fool you.

"Hey Pops where's Alex?" Cain asked walking up to his father and giving him a firm handshake and a half hug.

"She's grabbing your sister out of the car. She's coming."

Cain lifted Alex's luggage just as easily as his father did a few minutes before and trotted up the steps as if he was carrying paperweights. As he reached the top of the steps, he could hear Alex entering the house.

"Hey Alex!" Cain called out. He sat the luggage on the floor in front of Alex's closed bedroom door and trotted back down the steps. He grew up knowing not to bust into closed doors. You never know what you will find behind them. As he reached the bottom of the stairs, his eyes met Alex's and together they exchanged a welcoming smile.

Cain respected Alex's ambition and independence, and he held her in high regard. He liked Alex from the first day he met her and he thought that she was great for his father. She treated Cain as if he was her son, despite the fact she was not much older the he. She took great care of his baby sister, and he could tell that she was not the gold digger type, trying to play his father for a "sugar daddy". He loved how she was making it successfully on her own, and accomplishing her goals with such style and grace. It was hard to dismiss the thoughts of how his mother was no competition for Alex when it came to class and all around appeal. Unlike Alex, Carmen never was independent and always felt the need to have a man in her life, even though she always tried to make Cain believe she was just trying to find him a good 'daddy'. Carmen loved men who made fast money and drove fast cars. And, it was an added pleasure if they hustled her drug of choice on the side. Carmen never kicked her life long drug addiction that she vehemently denied she had, and always minimized it as a 'social' habit. Back in the day it was helpful dating a major drug dealer like Sway because that meant Carmen would not have far to go to get her cocaine fix whenever she needed it. Carmen loved the high life. Her son's given name was proof of it. Although Sway named their son Cain, Carmen had no objections. At that time, Sway was becoming rich from selling it, and Carmen could not stop snorting it; they both loved it.

"Oh my!" Alex exclaimed. "Cain, you are so handsome. Look at you!"

Alex quickly passed a sleeping Stevie to Sway and walked over to admire Cain. The last time she seen Cain was over two years ago at her father's funeral when he was a nineteen-year-old kid, indecisive about his next move in life. She gave him a firm hug and realized that he was no longer a kid but a young man. She was overwhelmed with an unexpected feeling of pride for him, as any mother would feel towards her growing son.

"I am so happy you decided to stay so I could see you," Alex said pulling back, taking his hand and leading him into the kitchen.

The enticing smell of her favorite meal greeted Alex as soon as she and Cain entered the kitchen.

"Mmm ..., Mom you are making my favorite," Alex said, kissing her mother on the cheek, and sitting down on the stool at the island.

Cain sat beside her, and they both began to watch Marie finish preparing her divinely smelling meal. Marie reveled in the attention and began to move concisely and swiftly with her chopping knife. Alex and Cain snuck pieces of the piping hot garlic bread that was sitting in an arm's distance, and almost got caught when Marie spun around.

"Hey Baby Girl, grab the plates, and set the table in the dining room. We'll eat in there tonight," Marie said in one breath and spun back around to toss her salad.

Alex didn't respond; instead, she smiled brightly and slid off the stool to set the table. Cain remained seated, eyeing the garlic bread as he finished the piece he and Alex snuck from the breadbasket. Sway glided into the kitchen offering his assistance, but as always, Marie quickly declined and shooed them out of the kitchen. Sway tapped Cain on the shoulder and motioned his head in the direction towards the family room. The two men quickly slid out of the kitchen, and Sway turned on the television to *ESPN*. They sat down on the plush sofa and zoned in on the ten men racing up and down the basketball court. It was not long before they were interrupted by the women calling them to dinner.

****

"Mmm ..., Mama Marie that was delicious," Sway said, holding his stomach and leaning back in the chair.

"Glad you liked it but there is a pan of peach cobbler in there that still has to be eaten," Marie said, blushing from the compliment she had just received.

"I'm full," Alex said, stretching her arms and yawning, "and tired. I think I am going to call it a night. I will have some cobbler tomorrow Ma, OK?"

"Yup, don't worry about it. I know you are tired from flying around the world. Go on to bed, I will feed Stevie and put her down for the night, Marie said as she pulled herself up from her seat and began to gather the dishes.

"I'll do that," Cain interjected, popping up from his chair to help Marie clear off the table.

They drifted off into the kitchen, leaving Sway and Alex alone in the dining room. The two of them sat across from each other and spoke with their eyes, signaling one another to make the first move.

"I think I am going to take a long hot bath," Alex spoke in almost a whisper.

"I will be up in a minute. I have to eat some of your mother's cobbler, or she will think the worst," Sway replied with a sexy grin.

Alex took in his words, stood up from the table, and slowly walked out of the dining room. Sway watched her hips swing from side to side until she was out of his sight. He shook his head and was grateful that Marie had just placed his cobbler in front of him. He was ready to please Marie, by eating the entire meal she prepared, and Alex for being so sexy.

Before walking down the hall to her bedroom, Alex checked in on Stevie, who was still sleeping. As she approached her door she noticed it was closed and wondered why. Normally, upon returning from a business trip she would come home to a bedroom with a few items out of place and her walk-in closest in disarray. Stevie loved to play dress up while Alex is away, and, often left the remnants of her mess behind to let Alex know she did.

"Stevie must have really done a number on my room this time," Alex said aloud as she grabbed the doorknob with one hand and a piece of her luggage with the other.

She turned the knob slowly, fearful of what she would see on the other side of the door. She pushed the door opened without taking a step forward. She imagined shoes and clothes strewn everywhere and her make-up vanity totally destroyed. Instead, she was engulfed by the scent of the fresh roses that filled her room. The smile on her face could not be contained. Sway had done it again. Alex walked in slow motion looking at the bevy of roses sprawled out in every nook and cranny of her bedroom. She was so enthralled with the flowers, she did not even noticed the lacy black negligee sprawled out neatly on the bed. Alex walked over to a dozen of roses positioned neatly in a lovely glass vase on her window's ledge and breathed in deeply. The scent of a rose was her favorite fragrance and Sway knew that. He watched her from the doorway and was pleased with himself for once again making Alex smile.

"Welcome home, Baby," he said, startling her.

Alex jumped and turned around at the same time. The wide grin on her face said 'thank you'. Sway walked up to Alex's hourglass frame and hugged her body tightly. He was happy to have her back home where she belonged. He looked over at the bed and noticed the garment was untouched.

"You like the flowers but didn't like that?" he asked looking down at the bed.

"Didn't like what," Alex asked, following his gaze. "Oh, I didn't notice that." She leaned over, picked up the lacy garment and held it up to her fully clothed body.

Sway stepped back and tried to imagine her in it. "I have to see it on," he said, undressing her with his eyes. "Go put it on for me." The tone in his voice lowered to a sexy growl.

"Uh-uh, you have to wait. I am going to take a long hot bath like I planned, and after that I will put it on, sorry," Alex responded waving her index finger back and forth at Sway and walking into the adjoining master bathroom.

Sway followed her without persuasion, and they started to disrobe along side each other. Alex started to run her piping, hot bath water and poured in a few capfuls of soothing bath oil while Sway turned on the shower and hopped in. Alex slid into the oversized Jacuzzi tub, and grabbed her head pillow as her body adjusted to the water temperature. She sat down into the steaming water with a slight stiffness in her back and rested the pillow behind her neck. She closed her eyes. After a few minutes, she almost forgot Sway was there but his abrupt exit from the shower caused her to open her eyes and admire his muscular, dripping wet body. Although he would be forty in nine months, he managed to maintain a body of a man half his age. She watched his every move as he grabbed his towel and wrapped it around his waist. He did not look back at her but he could feel the heat from her stare, and sensed that he should prepare for another explosive night.

"Hurry up," he growled sexily as he walked out of the bathroom.

Alex smiled at his command. She admires a man who has the ability to take control. Her body heat began to rise and she could not decipher whether it was due to the water temperature or the man in her bedroom, but she decided to cut her *long* hot bath short, and fulfill the needs of the other yearning parts of her body.

It was not long before Sway heard her stirring around in the bathroom. Her movement interrupted his daydream as he blankly stared at the news anchorman on the television screen. He looked over at the bathroom entrance and waited for Alex to walk through it.

"You ready for me?" she rhetorically asked.

"Yup," Sway responded, not taking his eyes off of the doorway.

She sauntered up to the doorway, and stretched her arms above her head and held onto each side of the doorframe, causing the nicely fitted negligee to rise and reveal her nakedness. Sway had a devouring grin on his face and immediately pressed the off button on the television remote control. The soft, dim light illuminating from the small lamps on the nightstands and the multitude of roses filling the room created a romantic atmosphere. Alex walked over to the bed and climbed atop of it like a lioness on the prowl. Sway welcomed her by covering her with soft kisses on her collar bone and neck. She moaned in delight.

"I've missed you," she whispered in his ear.

He did not have to speak to respond, his growing erection told her that he was missing her just as much. They kissed passionately while Sway grabbed Alex by the waist and laid her on her back while she grabbed his thickness and massaged it to its peak. Their eyes met with both intensity and urgency to have one another. Sway grasped onto her hips to steady her motion. He wanted to take all the time he needed. He could tell that she had entered into her own heaven and he did not want to displease her by erupting too fast. He watched the angelic expressions her face made as she moved with grace back and forth beneath him. The two fell into a rhythmic pattern as beads of perspiration flowed freely from the pores of their skin. Sway could feel the blood rushing from the bottom of his feet to his groin and with both hands he firmly grasped her buttocks, and moved her body with his at a rapid pace. He continued to stroke her with force as she moaned in ecstasy. Within moments, they climaxed in unison like an orchestra reaching a great crescendo in a well-played symphony. Alex opened her eyes, delighted at the result of what just occurred and looked up at Sway.

"Thank you," she whispered.

"No … ," Sway replied. "Thank you."

Chapter 10

Journey
It's A Thin Line Between Love and Hate

After two weeks of hibernation from the outside world, the pigmentation around Journey's left eye had finally regained its natural honey hue color. All traces of Tiny's abusive explosion on the highway had diminished beneath her skin's surface. Journey initially woke up feeling like herself again, and slightly claustrophobic, so she decided to make today a day of pampering. She rolled out of bed around eight o'clock in the morning, and decided to at least finish payroll and the monthly employee work schedule before noon, so she could get out and treat herself to a few pairs of new shoes. But, her well planned day of a much needed spa treatment and shopping spree was overshadowed by the thought of Tiny being unfaithful. The unexpected phone call from the night manager at the gym, who was suppose to be home sick, caused Journey to be completely thrown off of her schedule, and now she was sitting at her desk, surrounded by unfinished business, wondering where her husband might be. Tiny left the house the night before around ten, stating that Sonny, the night manager, just called in sick. And, since it was too late to find coverage, Tiny quickly volunteered again to go in and pull a double shift. Although this was the fifth double shift Tiny worked since their reconciliation, Journey thought nothing of it. The past two weeks had been peaceful and almost stress free. Journey knew that his absence contributed to her serenity, but the few days that he did spend at home, he acted as if he appreciated her again. And, in an effort to regain her trust, he had his fertility testing completed, and he gave her sole responsibility of the work schedule, assuring that Tanya would never work on the same shift as Tiny again. Journey held onto these positives and considered them acts of good faith towards a new beginning.

When she saw the gym's phone number displayed on the telephone caller identification screen, she thought it was Tiny checking in to let her know what time he would be home for lunch: instead it was Sonny, asking if Tiny was planning on coming in because his shift was almost over.

"You mean, Tiny's not already there?" Journey remembered asking Sonny.

"Naw, I've been here since nine-thirty last night Jay, and I have not seen him. What time did he leave this morning?" Sonny asked nonchalantly.

"Before seven," Journey casually said, not revealing signs of anger to cause suspicion.

She wanted to interrogate Sonny and investigate if he had called in sick last night and reneged after the fact. Instead, Journey decided to internalize her insecurities.

"Well, maybe he had to run some errands," Sonny summed it up, "I will try him again on his cell. I will stick around until he comes, OK?"

"Thank you Sonny. Make sure you add the overtime to your time sheet," Journey replied with much gratitude.

Where did he stay last night? Why did he lie and say that Sonny called in sick? The questions regurgitated over and over again in her head. A part of her wanted to call Tanya at home to see if her husband was spending his time there, but Journey could not bring herself to stoop so low. *The truth is bound to come out, it always does*, she thought as she looked over at the clock. It read 11:30 a.m. She allowed Tiny to waste another one of her mornings with worry and frustration. She wanted to smack her own face for coming back to such misery when she was almost free two weeks ago. She hated the weak spirit she had birthed from this marriage because it allowed her to be governed by Tiny and his words; be it kind or harsh. She convinced herself to believe everything he told her that night on the phone when he begged her to come home. She entrusted him too fast upon her return home, letting her guard down to lift up the last ounce of hope in what was left of their marriage, only to be used like a fool. Journey could feel the insides of her stomach twist and turn at the thought of her husband sharing his love with someone else. It was bad enough that he felt justified when he smacked her around every now and then, but now he is spending the entire night out and totally disregarding the sanctity of their monogamous union.

"Only single men can lay their heads anywhere they please," she said aloud to herself as she stood up from her desk.

The heat from the anger forming in the pit of her being started to boil her blood. She was disappointed in herself for being so naïve, and angry at Tiny for making such a fool out of her. She paced back and forth from the kitchen to the living room trying to decide her next move. Common sense clearly told her the truth. She knew that Tiny was with Tanya, she could feel it in her bones. Yet, she struggled to make her heart believe it. She loved her husband and because she did, her heart would not accept that the promises Tiny made through the years, along with being told she was his one and only, the ying to his yang, and the air he breathed, were all empty.

Journey's mind continued to race as she became more infuriated thinking about the countless sacrifices she made to make her husband happy. She wiped the tears as they started to stream down her face. She shook her head as she replayed the memory of the day Tiny came home with the big idea of opening the gym. It was the same day she was offered a small part in an off-Broadway play. That was the day he started to take control. He convinced her that living out her dream of becoming a Broadway superstar could be accomplished at any time.

"That's what you went to school for. You got that in the bag. You can do way better than some small part in an unknown play," he convinced her.

Journey chuckled to herself as she reminisced about how the scene played out that day. He traipsed around the living room pointing out her many accolades in the form of trophies and framed certifications from theaters and schools, including her Bachelor's Degree from the *Tisch School of the Arts at New York University*. She became overwhelmed with her hidden desire to be awed and adored, and chose to believe every word that exited his mouth to be truth.

Tiny knew he could not open a gym without Journey's financial backing, so he convinced her to suppress her dreams and dismiss her years of hard work of being a stage actress to fulfill his own. He told her that she would have the same flexibility to audition just like she had when she worked at *The Candy Shop*, if not more, since she would own the business. She envisioned herself whisking away from one major audition to the next, while her husband managed their business. His well thought out plan delivered a promising future for them both. Journey quickly embraced his dream to be her own, and, soon after, convinced her father to relinquish a part of her trust fund prematurely to finance the start-up of *their* new business venture.

"I was such a fool!" she screamed, wishing she could suppress the memory back into her subconscious.

"I never wanted to open a damn gym! I did it all for you!" she said looking at their wedding picture encased in a crystal frame, strategically placed in the center of the fireplace mantle.

Without warning and completely filled with rage, she smacked the frame from its designated place, and watched it as it crashed against the hardwood floor. A thousand tiny pieces of shattered glass flew across the living room, just as she marched toward the kitchen.

"Bastard!" she screamed.

The sound of the phone ringing interrupted the tirade she was engrossed in. Journey stood still in the middle of the kitchen floor and breathed in deeply. She wiped her eyes with both hands and stared at the telephone with hatred in her eyes. She hoped it was Tiny on the other end of the line with a believable excuse to prove to her that the betrayal she was feeling inside was nothing more than a negative emotion born from her insecurities. She wanted him to calm her down and have reasonable explanation as to why he did not sleep in their bed the night before.

In a trance like state, she walked over to the white oblong telephone adhered to the wall and grabbed the cordless receiver from its cradle.

"Hello," Journey spoke into the phone, trying to sound calm and emotionless.

"Hey girl, what's up?" Alex happily sang into Journey's ear.

"Oh, hi Alex, when did you get back?"

"A couple days ago, sorry I did not call sooner. So, how is everything?" Alex asked, hoping to hear only good news.

As an awkward moment of silence penetrated the phone line, Alex started to become concerned. She quickly rephrased her question and inquired once again in a motherly tone. "Journey … I asked, how are things? Are you OK?"

"Yeah, I am OK, just tired of this shit," Journey said, walking back into her office and sitting down at her desk.

"What happened?" Alex asked, ready to erupt. "Did he put his damn hands on you again? I knew I should have made you come with me to Japan." Alex could not stop spewing words from her mouth long enough to get answers.

"No, no, he has not *touched* me since I been back," Journey said. "His ass has hardly been here. You want to hear something real foul Alex? He left last night telling me he was going to work a double shift because Sonny called in sick. Well, guess what?"

"What?" Alex echoed, bracing herself for the worst case scenario.

"Sonny called here this morning looking for Tiny! That big bastard never went in last night. Sonny never was sick. That was just Tiny's excuse to spend the night some place other than in our bed. This is the last straw for me Alex. I refuse to allow him to have his cake and eat it too!" Journey's voice jumped two octaves. "Alex he left here at ten o'clock last night. I know he is with her."

"Who?"

"That little whore, Tanya, that's who!"

"I thought he said he was just trying to make you mad with that Tanya story," Alex stated, slightly confused.

"That was the lie he told to pull me back into this hell he created for me."

Another awkward silence penetrated through the phone line, and was followed by the sound of Journey sniffling and trying to pull her self together.

Although she felt sorry for Journey, Alex did not want to be the friend who says the cliché "I told you so", so she opted to say nothing at all. She sat quietly on the phone and allowed her friend to release the pain and regret that filled her heart. Not knowing what to say or do,

Alex broke the silence, "I'm sorry Journey. Do you want me to come get you?"

"No," Journey stated defiantly. "I'm not running anymore. I want to be here when he calls or comes home, so we can get this over with. I have tolerated a lot of shit, but sharing my husband will not be one of them," Journey adamantly announced, wiping her eyes with the back of her hand and regaining her composure. "Plus, this is my damn house!" Journey added with a slight chuckle of certainty.

Alex snickered along with her and was relieved that Journey was not broken to the point that she would allow Tiny to have mistresses. Alex understood completely, since that has been a main staple for her not wanting to marry Sway. She could never trust Sway enough to think he did not have someone always waiting in the wings, willing to do whatever she would not do. "I know that is right," Alex chimed in. "But I have to be honest, I called you to talk to you about something else," Alex said making a smooth transition into a new conversation.

"Oh yeah," Journey's face brightened. "What do you have to tell me?" Journey leaned back in her reclining desk chair and waited for Alex to come forth with her worthy words of the day that hopefully would change her mood.

"Well, my dear, Sway has hired The A. Avery Agency to follow up on a business proposal to open a spa in …, Vegas!" she ended the sentence with a shrill that pierced Journey's eardrum.

They had always planned on going to Las Vegas but after changes in each of their circumstances; Alex having a baby and Journey getting married, that plan along with other adventures fell into the imaginary 'things to do' bucket.

"When do we leave?" Journey screamed.

"In two days, I know its short notice, but Sway and the investor are both anxious to get this under way. He booked flights and the hotel suite at the Bellagio."

"The Bellagio, huh," Journey happily responded with approval.

"Yes, the Bellagio. Sway wants his son to stay in the very best. Oh, yeah, Cain is here. You remember Cain, right?"

Alex knew that Journey remembered Cain. Who could forget him? He was the reincarnation of Sway; just younger and a tad bit shorter. Journey remembered seeing him at Mr. Avery's funeral. She paid little attention to him then; partially because of the circumstances but mostly because her marriage was at the tail end of the 'honeymoon' stage and her eyes were still only for her husband. "Of course I remember Sway's twin," Journey replied with a giggle.

"I know girl, they look just alike. Cain is even cuter than he was two years ago. He has a little swagger to him already," Alex said impressed. "He is going back home so I invited him to fly to Vegas for a couple of days to hang out and fly back home from there. That way when I am at my meeting you two can keep each other company."

"That was nice of you," Journey said admiring her friend's natural consideration and thoughtfulness. "This should be fun," Journey said with renewed vigor. She pressed the 'power on' button located in the center of the hard drive to her computer and watched the monitor light up with various fluorescent colors. "Two days is more than enough time for me to finish up here," Journey said looking at the stacks of paper on her desk, mentally prioritizing what task would be completed first.

"Are you going to let Tiny know that you are leaving?" Alex asked almost sorry for having to bring his name up.

"I doubt it," Journey flatly replied. "It's apparent that Tiny feels that he does not have to tell me where he is going, so I will cross that bridge when I come to it."

The two women discussed the final details of their trip and said their good-byes. Journey grabbed the pile of papers that were stacked near the left side of her monitor and sifted through the invoices, rearranging them in chronological order, making sure the bills received first would be the paid first. The sudden ringing sound of the telephone startled her and she grabbed the receiver without looking at the phone number displayed on the caller ID.

"Hello, this is Journey," her business voice sang into the phone.

She was no longer thinking about Tiny or his whereabouts. Leaving for Las Vegas had taken precedence, and she had suddenly become concerned with only completing tasks that would quicken her availability to leave for her much-needed getaway.

"Hey, what's up?" Tiny asked in a low guttural voice.

"You tell me. Where you been?"

"Man, you won't believe my night Baby," Tiny began his tall-tale. "When I got to work last night, Sonny was here and said that wasn't him who called in sick and that someone was playing games on my phone," he said trying to convince himself as well.

"So, of course I was pissed," he continued without pausing, "I got back on the highway to come home, blew a tire and bent the tire frame. My cell went dead right after I called the tow truck. The tow came a few hours later and I was so tired I copped a room at the motel next to the repair center. I would have called but I did not want to wake you. They fixed my shit this morning and I am just getting to the gym." Tiny finished his account of last night's events purely based on fiction with hope that his wife would believe at least a portion of his story.

Journey listened quietly to her husband, and was totally engaged in his storytelling. She identified all of the holes in his story, and could have tripped him up in his lie several times. Yet, the fact of the matter was she did not care anymore. He had rested his head some place other than home, and that was finally enough for her. Journey could endure almost anything Tiny placed upon her, both physically and mentally, but she knew she could never knowingly share her husband with another woman.

"Really Tiny, all of that happened?" she asked with sarcasm filtering the question.

"I swear Babe, it was crazy. I know it sounds unbelievable, but it really happened."

Coolly she asked, "well, are you OK?" not giving Tiny any indication as to whether she believed his nonsense or not.

"Yes Baby, I'm straight. I will be home later, OK," he replied.

Journey hung up the phone without responding and continued to work through the invoices as if the conversation never happened. Tiny, sleeping out every other night and lying to cover his infidelity had shown her the precise level on which he placed their marriage. It had become official. Journey had morphed into a woman scorned. With feelings of contempt and revenge, she thought it only fair that her husband finally get a taste of his own medicine.

Chapter 11

The Girls Fantasy

Journey stared out of the double-framed, living room window and wondered what was taking Alex so long. Their flight's departure was in less than three hours and she knew getting over the Whitestone Bridge would consume much of their time. Tiny was silently sleeping, and apparently had not heard Journey stirring about as she made sure she had everything for her weekend ahead. She told him the night before that she and Alex were having a "girls' weekend", but neglected to mention that it was taking place thousands of miles away in Las Vegas.

Journey swung her sweater wrap around her shoulders and folded her arms. She was dressed comfortably in a turtleneck and a pair of jeans tucked neatly in a pair of knee high, leather, three-inch, high heeled boots. Peering out of the window, she could hear the springs in their bed screech as Tiny tossed and turned. She closed her eyes and prayed that he was not getting up to send her off. She did not want to look in his face. She barely had since finally catching him sleeping around a couple of days ago. She hoped to be long gone before he woke up, but Alex being late had foiled that plan.

"Journey!" she heard his thunderous voice bellow her name from their bedroom. "You still here?"

Just was the word "yes" escaped from her lips, she was blinded by bright, white headlights pulling up to the curb outside of her brownstone. "But here is Alex now, so I will call you later, don't get up!" She grabbed her overnight and carry-on bags, and shuffled to the front door. She turned the doorknob quickly and pulled the door open. The sight of a hooded figure startled Journey and she jumped back a step. "What the hell ...?" Journey gasped, dropping the luggage on the spot.

"Sorry, I didn't mean to scare you. I came to help you with your things," a deep, masculine voice echoed from the hidden face. Cain pulled back the hood of his sweatshirt revealing his finely structured face that displayed a partial smile that resembled one that was all too familiar.

The fact that he was Sway's child was obvious, but it was his jet black, curly hair and thick eye brows, and neatly shaven mustache that caused Journey to look at Cain in a sexual way. He definitely carried the innate *Latin* sex appeal that only some Hispanic men were born with, and Journey could sense that Cain knew it. Journey returned the smile and breathed in a sigh of relief as she attempted to grab her bags. Cain responded to her cue, and grabbed for the bags as well. His large hand covered hers, and she quickly pulled back to allow him to take over. He sensed her nervousness, but did not respond.

"Oh, thank you Cain," Journey said, slightly embarrassed that her nerves had been rattled.

"No problem."

Cain lifted the luggage with ease, turned around and trotted down the steps back to the limousine.

Journey shook her head to come back to her senses, and closed the door behind her. *Wow, he has grown up over the past two years*, Journey thought as she followed Cain to the car and admired his swagger from behind.

Before getting into the backseat of the car, Cain gave the bags to the driver, who was patiently waiting with the trunk open. Journey and Alex greeted one another as Journey sat beside her. Cain eased into the seat across from the women.

"Hey girl, I thought you'd never get here," Journey said looking over at Alex.

"I know, I'm sorry we are late. My alarm clock didn't go off this morning," Alex confessed.

"Don't worry about it, I just wanted to be out of the house before asshole woke up," Journey said, causing Alex to laugh.

Alex was already busy with work, so after calming down from their comical outburst, she turned her attention back to the file folder sitting on her lap, as the limo swiftly navigated the streets toward the Interstate. She had to read over a few more details for the meeting that was scheduled to take place in less than six hours. Stillness filtered through the back of the limousine as Journey and Cain stared at one another. His striking good looks totally captured Journey, and she could not stop looking into his dark eyes. The fact that he was not intimidated by her gaze, excited her.

"So, Cain…, how have you been?" Journey broke the looming silence, not taking her eyes off of the incredibly gorgeous individual that shared her space.

"I'm doin' well," he replied in a cool, casual tone.

He had always been attracted to Journey, since their encounter at Stevie's first birthday party, but back then, he knew that she viewed him as a teenager. It did not help either that she was married to one of his father's closest friends. Cain reminded himself not to allow their flirtatious play to turn into anything more. Alex feverishly jotted notes down on her yellow paper pad, ignoring the sexual tension generating between Cain and Journey. Cain stared at Journey with intensity as she nervously licked her lips.

"You ever been to Vegas?" Cain asked.

"No, I haven't. Have you?" Journey asked shifting in her seat.

"A few times," Cain replied nonchalantly. "You will love it, I promise," he said with a smile that undeniably told Journey that this trip would be one to remember.

"I'm getting that feeling. You know what they say, what happens in Vegas, stays in Vegas," Journey responded leaning back into the cushioned seat and becoming restless as she anticipated their arrival to Sin City.

Interrupted by their shameless flirting, Alex looked up from her document and peered over her reading glasses. Without moving her head, she first shot her gaze over at Journey, then Cain, and shook her head back and forth. Under different circumstances, she would have reminded Journey that she was a married woman, but after finding out how Tiny has been treating her best friend, Alex thought it best to mind her business and let nature take its course.

****

The dry desert heat of Nevada greeted Alex, Journey and Cain as they exited the Las Vegas International Airport. In unison, they began to peel off the layers of clothing that was required for the winter weather still lagging around in New York, and had not yet allowed spring to take over. They quickly walked to the baggage claim area to grab their luggage, and connect with their driver. They followed the driver to their car and as they entered the back seat, Cain pulled off his long sleeved t-shirt and hopped in the air-conditioned back seat, after the ladies. With only a nicely fitted tank top covering his muscular torso, exposing his broad shoulders, Cain sat down next to Journey, and closed the car door. The moment his well-defined, muscular bicep touched her arm, Journey began to notice him as the man he had clearly become.

"Oh, my!" Journey exclaimed, impressed with his physique.

Cain, gloating in her admiration, flexed his chest as he sat back in the seat and smiled.

To avoid staring at his well defined arms and chest, Journey turned away from Cain and peered out of the window with Alex. It did not take long for them to become overwhelmed by their spectacular surroundings. As the car flowed down *Las Vegas Boulevard*, their appetite to experience Sin City grew. Their driver took the long route to their hotel, which allowed them to view several outrageous hotels on the strip. *The Monte Carlo, Caesar's Palace* and the *MGM* loomed high and wide as the car drove by. It was an unbelievable scene that could not be compared to anything they had ever seen before.

As their car pulled into the circular driveway of the hotel, the three visitors darted out of the back seat, and moved quickly to the lobby. By the time they checked in, the concierge was patiently waiting behind them with their luggage neatly stacked on a rolling luggage cart. As soon as the desk clerk handed Alex two gold card keys, she knew that Sway had outdone himself once again. When he told her that he upgraded their rooms, she expected that he would book nice suites for them, possibly adjoining but the card keys were designed to only go to one floor; the top, which meant they were staying in a penthouse suite.

As the threesome followed the concierge through the botanical gardens, they were awestruck with the splendor of nature displayed before them. The combination of scents from the array of rare plants, flowers and trees filled the air and captivated the guests. The women walked through the grandiose lobby, looking at the ceiling covered in a glass flower sculpture designed by *Chichuly*. They were speechless. As they walked toward the set of elevators, the concierge pointed out a long hallway lined with Italian marble columns and a wide path of custom designed carpeting that lead to the ringing sound of an active casino. A brochure or even the travel channel could have never prepared their eyes for such grandeur. The sight was immeasurable and clearly breathtaking. When they arrived at the bay of elevators, the concierge asked to see the key so that he'd know which elevator to take. As Alex handed him the gold key card, his demeanor changed, and he introduced himself, which he neglected to do at the onset of the guests checking in.

"Oh," he said looking at the gold plastic card, "my apologies Madam, my name is Sampson, and I will be available throughout your stay to accommodate all of your needs."

As they boarded the elevator, he continued to share information that could make their stay more enjoyable and comfortable. In the timely ride to the top of the hotel, Sampson had endless tips and ideas to share with the guests. He knew if he made a good impression, his guests would show their appreciation. His heightened desire to want to wait on them hand and foot did not go unnoticed.

Alex was used to this type behavior, which was common across the world. She use to think that is was because she was black, but soon discovered that the way one is treated in a hotel had nothing to do with the color of their skin. It took her some time to realize that those who work in the hotel industry respond to only one color: green. The more you have, the better you are treated.

After Sampson gave them a tour of the penthouse, drawing attention to endless amenities and lastly, demonstrated the remote operated drapes and blinds that covered the panoramic windows that revealed the Desert Mountains and the millions of lights below on the strip.

"Is there anything else I can do for you all before I leave you to your privacy?" Sampson offered.

Alex looked around the three-bedroom suite and noticed that he had placed everyone's luggage in their respective rooms, set-up the bar with a bucket of ice and placed her laptop case on the cherry-wood desk in the area of the suite designated for corporate guests to take care of their business matters.

Alex walked over to the oversized plush caramel sofa, grabbed her *Louis Vuitton* purse that effortlessly matched her luggage set, and pulled out a crisp one hundred dollar bill. She handed it to Sampson, who remained astute as he nodded his head in appreciation.

"That will be all, thank you. Can you please tell my driver I will be down in forty-five minutes?"

"Sure thing, ma'am," Sampson replied and hurried to the elevator to relay the message.

Alex shut the door and quickly entered the master bedroom to unpack her suitcase. She had to move fast. Sway scheduled her meeting with Mr. Mitken at four o'clock, and her wristwatch was reading two fifteen.

"Damn it, I don't have much time," Alex said aloud as she gathered her toiletries and ran into the adjoining bathroom.

The bathroom was stunning. Tiled with imported marble, with a jet-stream water bathtub, double sinks, etched in gold and a glass encased shower twice the size of Alex's bathroom at home. She wished she had more time to play with the gadgets and take a Jacuzzi bath but time was of the essence. She quickly disrobed and turned on the oversized showerhead and waited a few seconds before jumping in the soothing heated stream of water. She reminded herself to stay focused, represent her client to the best of her ability, and make sure the end result was beneficial to Sway. She lathered up her body, while silently reciting unwavering stipulations that she would demand. She always did this before an important meeting; it helped her remain grounded in the original pitch of the proposed business venture.

By the time Alex was fully dressed in her designer smoke gray, pin-striped suit, accented with an ivory cotton-silk blend, button down blouse, and putting on the final touches of make-up on her already flawless face, Journey was knocking on the bedroom door.

"Come in!" Alex called out, not taking her eyes off of her reflection in the mirror.

"Hey, what time will you be back?" Journey asked as she walked in and plopped down on the king-size bed.

"I am hoping to be back around seven. I believe the plan is to meet, discuss the proposal and check out the site today, so I can spend tomorrow with you guys."

"That sounds good," Journey said as she rolled over onto her back, "why didn't you tell me about Cain?" she asked, changing the subject.

"What do you mean?" Alex asked looking at Journey through the mirror.

"I mean …, that young boy has it going on."

"I *did* tell you, remember the other day," Alex said turning around to look Journey in the eye.

"Yeah, but you did not say he was sexy as all hell!" Journey laughed.

"Well, he's not sexy to me! His daddy is though," Alex concluded, unable to retain her laughter.

"OK, well I just want to make it clear that he just might get it this weekend, so don't judge me," Journey said, lowering her voice so low that it became barely audible.

"Listen, your secret is safe with me. Enjoy yourself," Alex said grabbing her matching briefcase and purse.

"How do I look?"

"Like Wall Street, Baby!" Journey replied, standing up and fixing Alex's collar.

Her suit jacket accentuated the curve in her waistline and the cotton-wool blend of the pant contoured her hips, lengthening her legs when paired with her four inch *Manolo Blahniks.* Journey and Alex walked to the door and looked over at Cain, who was sitting on the sofa, playing football on the built in *Playstation 2* displayed on the large plasma television on the wall. They shook their heads in unison and were sure that they were thinking the same thing … *he'll be OK for the next few hours.* The two women quickly collaborated on a plan to meet at *Picasso's Restaurant* down stairs in the hotel at seven thirty. Alex assured Journey that she would call if she was running late. They hugged and Alex was off to catch the elevator.

Chapter 12

Alex
Who's That Lady

Alex was thankful that the driver was a native of Las Vegas. Because of his knowledge of the city's back roads, she arrived at her scheduled appointment ten minutes early. Being prompt was paramount to Alex; it was a major indicator of professionalism. She entered the thirteen-story glass building with a professional strut, and waited patiently for someone to return to the security desk. After a few moments, she looked at her watch, and noticed her ten-minute lead was dwindling. Just as a loud sigh exited her mouth, a thin, clean-shaven man appeared behind the desk.

"Sorry for making you wait Ma'am. What floor are you going to?"

"Um, seventh, Mitken and Associates," Alex responded looking at the list of companies displayed on the wall behind the man.

"Please sign in," he replied and handed Alex the pen.

She pulled out her *Montblanc* from her purse and held it up as if to say 'thanks but I have one'. She considered this limited edition writing instrument to be her good luck charm. It was one of the gifts she received from her dad when she graduated college, and every time she pulled it out to sign her *"John Hancock,"* she would read the etched inscription along side of it, *To my Baby Girl. The world awaits your signature. Love Daddy,* before placing it delicately in its case.

The man pointed to the set of elevators to the left and Alex followed his silent indication by walking in that direction. She entered through the large steel doors and pressed the number seven button, and straightened her suit. The elevator sped smoothly upwards through the building, and chimed once it reached the desired floor. As the doors opened, Alex exited the elevator fully prepared to make a lasting first impression.

She opened the large, heavy glass double doors with white frosted etching that read in large letters *"Mitken & Associates, LLP."* Alex looked around, impressed with the company's unique contemporary design. Each office was encased in crystal-clear glass with hanging Venetian blinds to provide privacy when needed, and the sleek contemporary office furniture gave the space an up to date look just in time for the approaching new millennium. She sauntered over to the glass receptionist desk and leaned in slightly. The replacement of glass for actual walls, amplified almost every sound, making it somewhat hard to hear.

"Good afternoon. I'm Alex Avery and I have an appointment with Mr. Mitken," Alex said loudly trying not to scream.

"Oh yes Ms. Avery, both Mr. Mitken and his partner is expecting you," the perky blonde receptionist responded and stood up.

Without another word, the shapely woman walked around her desk and began to lead Alex down the corridor to the conference room. Alex began to feel her stomach tighten and her palms began to sweat. Although she had attended several important meetings with powerful prestigious men before, Alex always became slightly nervous before such an encounter. The woman pushed through the glass door and lead Alex into a large room decorated with an oversized boardroom table that easily accommodated twenty. Alex followed the woman to the end of the room where two men were seated at the head of the table. Alex clearly recognized Mr. Mitken as the balding, stout white man seated at the head, but she had no clue as to whom the brown-skinned attractive man was sitting next to him. *I didn't realize I was meeting someone else along with Mr. Mitken,* Alex thought as she extended her hand to introduce herself.

"Good afternoon gentlemen," she said in a professional voice as the men stood up to show her that chivalry was not dead. "I am Alex Avery from The A. Avery Agency."

Mr. Mitken quickly extended his hand and shook her hand with firmness. He was visibly flushed as Alex returned the firm handshake. It was clear that he had become more nervous than she was and the butterflies that were fluttering around in her stomach quickly disappeared.

"Oh, hello Ms. Avery, I am Henry Mitken and this is my silent partner in this venture, Mr. Derek Minor. You have to excuse me, but I am a little caught off guard. When Mr. McCoy told me that he was sending Alex Avery to represent him, I assumed you were a man, and obviously you aren't," he concluded while staring at her from head to toe.

"Well, thank you, I think," Alex said, showing off her pearly white teeth.

Slightly flattered, Alex quickly shook Mr. Minor's hand, and admired his handsome face while he pulled her chair out from the enormous table to allow her to sit down to join them. His tailor-made suit fit him like a glove, but Alex could tell that it was not his everyday attire.

"I'm sure Hank meant it as a compliment," Derek's deep voice flowed through her ears causing her to blush.

It was clear that an instant attraction had been ignited between the two of them and Alex quickly reminded herself that this was business. She did not know who this man was or where he came from, but he was totally throwing her off her game. His boardroom dialect was not typical nor professional, and the tattoo of a dollar sign on his neck that he tried to mask with a starched collar and neck tie, indicated that he certainly was not an alumni of any legitimate business university. Alex was intrigued.

"OK then," she said, clearing her throat, and pulling out the file from her briefcase. "Are you gentlemen ready to get started?" she asked rhetorically.

The three business cohorts began to review notes, raise pertinent questions and make necessary changes to profit percentages and stock ownership. Alex and Henry did most of the negotiating, while Derek reclined in his cushioned leather seat and listened to Alex spew her business terminology and divulge her finance knowledge. He was becoming aroused.

Derek was new to the logistics of legitimate business game and had never encountered a woman of her stature. He was impressed by her stern almost masculine business etiquette and admired that, at the same time, she was able to still present herself as a lady. Her business attire complimented her petite but shapely frame, and Derek found himself wondering how she would look in something more revealing.

His intense stare toward her caught Alex's attention, and she could tell he was looking right through her. The tiny hairs at the nape of her neck stood at attention and a chill raced up her spine. *He is sexy as hell*, she thought, breaking his trance with a smile. "Is everything OK Mr. Minor?"

"Perfect," he responded in a low growl. "And please, call me Derek."

Henry cleared his throat in an effort to remind Derek that he was in a business atmosphere and not a local bar lounge. It was apparent that Derek could not tame his overwhelming lure that Alex carried with her when she entered the conference room.

"OK," Alex awkwardly replied and turned her attention back to Henry. "Well, Mr. Mitken it seems that this partnership benefits my client the most. It's almost unheard of that someone coming in so late in the project would still obtain most of the stock options, thus giving him majority ownership in the project. I also find it odd that neither you, nor Mr. Minor, are interested in any profit from the shop that will house most of the ground floor of the hotel. That venture alone is sure to bring in large revenues, and, lastly, you are not asking that he contribute any monetary capital as good faith to a partnership and to set the whole deal in motion," she concluded with an inquisitive smirk on her face.

The deal they were offering Sway was too good to be true, and Alex was not going to allow someone to swindle her client, especially since he is making successful strides on his own. She folded her arms on top of the file, and clasped her hands together and awaited a justifiable explanation.

"Well, Ms. Avery … ," Henry shifted in his seat ready to respond.

"I got this Hank," Derek interjected and smiled at Alex. "Let's just say that we have been observing how your client handles his business over the past two years and we are impressed by his ability to generate so much dough from year to year."

That answer was not good enough. Alex needed more, especially since she was going to have to sell this fairy tale deal to Sway. She already could hear his questions laced with skepticism, pouring out at her like a flowing river. All of which would shoot holes in this mystical deal. Alex always heard Las Vegas was magical, but if she brought a Mickey Mouse deal back to Sway, he certainly would not be amused.

"What an admirable way for you to acknowledge my client for his continued success, however, this offer is ... , for lack of a better term, a little hard to swallow," Alex replied, stiffening in her chair and perched her lips.

"I know it sounds unbelievable but we have scouted various potential investors to partner with in this venture and because Mr. McCoy can bring in both revenue and prestigious clientele, he was our premier choice. We knew that we had to initially develop an enticing business plan to capture his attention at the onset of our proposal. Remember, Ms. Avery I am also a member of the Candy Shop and if I did not think this deal would not make all of us very wealthy, I would not be wasting your client's time," Henry said pulling Derek out of the hole he had dug for himself.

Relaxing a bit in her chair, Henry's answer somewhat satisfied Alex, and a sense of comfort started to ease the tension that was brewing inside her gut.

"I see," she responded looking directly into Henry's eyes. "I can understand that and Mr. McCoy did mention that you have been a member for quite sometime, so you know how his operation works first hand."

"Precisely," Henry added.

Alex smiled with affirmation that this was a done deal. The men followed her lead and graciously returned the grin. Alex looked at her wristwatch and noticed that six o'clock was slowly approaching, and she could not believe how time passed by so quickly. She began to gather her things, giving the men indication that the meeting was over. "Well, gentlemen, I think we are done here. If you make the final revisions on the acquisition agreement and email it to me by tomorrow, I will try to review it while I am in town, and send confirmation to initiate execution. However, there is one more thing," Alex said, grabbing the strap to her briefcase and standing up from the table. "Mr. Mitken when you approached my client you had given him the impression that this was a joint venture between you and him, where does Mr. Minor fit into this?" she asked for both business and personal reasons. She wanted to know more about him without being obvious.

Both men stood up with Alex and looked at one another for the answer. Henry quickly began to speak before Derek could say something to make Alex rethink her decision. "Mr. Minor's fairly new company is actually the financial backing for this project and he is taking all of the risk if it fails. Therefore, for those reasons he would like to maintain his anonymity. My company is the face of the operation because of its reputation, and experience in managing and operating multi-million dollar franchises."

The men could tell that answer was acceptable to Alex by the way she smiled and nodded as if it all made sense. Henry told Derek before the meeting to let him do all of the talking, and Derek promised to sit on the sideline, and allow Henry to work his magic, which he clearly did. Alex, being a beautiful woman instead of the stereotypical 'yuppie' businessman had thrown both men off, but Henry maintained his business savvy. Derek, on the other hand, had a hard time keeping his composure. This was Derek's first official business meeting. Normally, Henry handled all of their business affairs because they agreed from the onset of their partnership that Derek was not "white collar" material. He and Henry were total opposites, Derek, a former drug dealer and ex-con, and Henry, a Harvard Business School alumnus, divorced with two grown children. People often thought Derek was his bodyguard when they hung out, but they were actually just good friends.

"Also, Ms. Avery I know our meeting has run a little past schedule, but if you have time we would like to show you the location where the new shop will be," Henry added before Alex turned to leave.

She had totally forgotten about viewing the site because she was getting hungry and she had digested the airplane food a while ago.

"Oh yes, I am sorry, I was told that you wanted me to see the location. I do have dinner plans, but if it won't take long I would love to see it."

"It's not far from here. I can show you quickly and bring you back to your hotel," Derek interjected before Henry could open his mouth.

Alex was special; that was apparent to Derek, but he wanted to know what made her that way. This was his chance to find out who this woman was and why a man had not snatched her up. From the time she sat down for their meeting, he noticed her ring finger had not been claimed. Henry looked at Derek and wanted to stop what was transpiring but Derek was not only funding this project, it was his concept. He approached Henry a little over a year ago and asked him to check out a male 'spa' chain that he had heard of on the east coast. Derek even paid the hefty annual membership fee as an incentive for Henry to join. It was obvious that Derek wanted to use this time to get to know who this extraordinary woman was. Henry could not blame him, Alex was not only attractive, but smart too, and she carried an air of savvy that caused a man to pay attention to her. However, Henry did not want anything to go wrong at this point because everything was running smoothly.

"Um, maybe I should tag along to answer those questions Derek may not feel too comfortable answering," Henry said nervously as he adjusted his tie.

Alex looked at Henry, then at Derek, who was conveying a look that told her she would be OK. She could feel her cheeks become flush from the way he gazed at her, and she could not believe this was happening in a business meeting. There was something about Derek that made her want to lay down her inhibitions and disregard her number one rule in business: never mix it with pleasure.

"Ah, no Mr. Mitken, I think it will be alright if Mr. Min ..., I mean Derek, takes me to view the site," Alex said to Henry, but was unable to break the trance Derek's sexy eyes had put her in.

"Well, if you are sure it is OK, but please, feel free to call me with any questions my partner may not feel comfortable answering," Henry responded with a uneasy feeling building up in the pit of his stomach.

"Yo, chill Hank," Derek said calmly patting Henry on the shoulder, "I got this. Be easy. I will call you after I drop Ms. Avery off at her hotel."

The two men shook hands and lead Alex out of the conference room to the elevators. Henry said his good-byes and told Alex to expect the email by mid-morning. Derek followed her onto the elevator and pressed the lower level button.

The heavy doors closed causing Henry to disappear and leaving the two of them completely alone. Derek slowly backed up, leaned against the elevator wall next to Alex and stood silently. Alex started to feel flush again as she inhaled the captivating scent of his cologne. She breathed in deeply and did not realize her eyes had closed just as Derek turned to look at her. The look on her face was so soft and serene, for a split second, he had an urge to kiss her. She was definitely turning him on. As she opened her eyes she was welcomed by his stare.

"Oh, sorry, I guess the time difference is catching up to me," she lied, trying not to look guilty.

Derek smiled at her, showing off a sexy dimple deeply embedded in his right cheek. "This won't take long, but it can take as long as you want it to," he replied letting her know that he would make himself available to her if she needed him to be.

The elevator came to a sudden stop, causing a jolt in their step as they exited into the dimly lit parking garage. Alex followed Derek to a white on white Mercedes convertible. They got in and he sped out of the parking garage into the dusk. A nice breeze landed on Alex's face as Derek sped through the city. She was able to enjoy the well-lit attractions even better with the top down. She was falling in love with Vegas. This place was truly magical.

"So, Derek, are you from here?" Alex asked, trying to make light conversation.

"Naw, I'm originally from Mount Vernon, New York. I've only been out this way for about two years," he answered, not taking his eyes off the road. "I did not plan on staying here but on my way out to Cali, I met Henry gambling and we hit it off, and we ended up becoming partners."

Derek met Henry on the first night he arrived to Las Vegas at the height of Henry's gambling addiction. The two of them were seated at a high stakes black jack table where the betting started at five thousand dollars a hand to get in the game. They played against one another and the dealer until the wee hours of the morning, and became somewhat friendly throughout their wins and losses. Derek openly told Henry how he had been to prison, and that his probation had just ended. Derek flew out of New York the day after his probation officer wished him well and told him to change his life for the better. He was passing through Las Vegas for the weekend to party with a few showgirls, and then was heading out west to start his life over. Henry liked Derek's laid back style, and even though he looked like he would rob Henry before he would befriend him, his calm demeanor attracted Henry. It did not hurt that Derek was a master at black jack, and by following his instruction, Henry won over eighty thousand dollars that morning. And, although he lost it all later that day, before the two men departed, they exchanged information and promised to meet up before Derek left town. Derek went back to his hotel that morning with one hundred thousand dollars to add to the two million he had stashed away before going to prison. He was saving it to invest in something legit, so that he would not have to resort to hustling and thuggin' again. When Henry mentioned that there were ample investment opportunities right here in the city known as the City of Second Chances, Derek began to weigh his options. Derek felt that his meeting Henry was fate, and decided to stay around to see what transpired. Not long after, Derek purchased a couple of Laundromats that Henry invested in, and by the end of his first year in Vegas, Derek and Henry became partners and opened a motel. Derek's current net worth was more than a few million, and his life was finally changing for the better. He knew that he had to make reparations to those he had wronged when he was in New York dealing and stealing. This venture was his first step toward righting his wrongs.

"I was wondering how you two came together, its apparent that you two come from different worlds. You have an East Coast flare, definitely New York," she said, pulling him out of his walk down memory lane and back into the present.

"I hear that a lot out this way Alex. May I call you Alex?" he asked with a quiet laughter.

"Of course, you can," Alex said softly while inhaling the sound of his deep voice that somehow did not fit with the way he looked.

"Is your family still on the East Coast?" she asked trying to discover his roots.

"It's just me and my older sister. My moms passed away a while ago. That took a lot out of me." The tone of his voice lowered.

His memory honed in on that time-period when he was rotting in a prison cell while his mother was being laid to rest. It took him a considerable amount of time to forgive himself for not being able to say good-bye to the only woman he ever truly loved. He realized that was the price he had to pay for the life he chose to live.

"I'm sorry," Alex managed to say, clearly noticing that she struck his sensitive nerve.

"Thank you, but its all good. I know Moms is in heaven, so I am straight," Derek said quickly regaining his cool composure. "But like I was saying, my sister is still in Mount Vernon living in the same house we grew up in. I visited her last Christmas, but I am hoping to visit the East Coast more often."

He looked over at Alex and smiled, flashing his sexy dimple. Within what seemed like minutes, Derek was pulling into a graveled parking lot of an unfinished building site. The lot was massive and Alex immediately envisioned a forty-story glass encased building with neon lights flashing above. It seemed perfect. She stepped out of the car and forgot she had on a pair of her most expensive shoes as she began to walk carefully across gravel pavement.

Derek sat in the car and watched her hips sway effortlessly from side to side as if her heels were unaffected by the rocks she was pouncing on. She was the type of woman he needed in his life: someone to keep him on the straight and narrow. He could tell that she was not only intelligent, but also cultured. That is what Derek needed if he was going to stay legit: a woman to broaden his horizons. *He needed her.* After a few moments, he got out of the car and walked over to where she was standing. "So what do you think?"

"I think its going to be incredible," Alex replied, looking up at the sky imagining where the top of the hotel would end.

"Good, I am glad you approve. Now let me show you around," Derek said, using that as an excuse to grab her hand and carefully walked with her around the premises.

He pointed out where the main building would go as well as the smaller boutiques and eateries that were going to be built around it to give the hotel patrons places to go without going out on the busy strip. She loved the idea and mentally took notes so that she could relay every bit of information to Sway. As they walked back to his car, Derek stopped her from getting into the passenger seat by blocking the door.

"I told you that it would not take long, can I take you someplace to have a quick celebration drink before I take you back to your hotel?" his deep voice penetrated through her skin and traveled below her hips. She shivered.

"Um … ," Alex stumbled, totally caught off guard, "sure, I think I can sneak in one quick drink before I meet my friends for dinner, but we are no longer working, and this is not a date. Just two people going out for a quick drink," she cautioned him as she reminded herself of the thin boundary line between business and pleasure.

Content with that, Derek slid to the side and opened the door to allow her to sit down. He wasted very little time arriving at a quaint Mexican pub on a desert strip outside of the city limits. He pulled into the parking spot directly next to the only other car there.

"I know it does not look like much, but trust me they make the best enchiladas in Vegas and here is the only place you will get real homemade Mexican Tequila, not that *Jose Cuervo* bullshit in the bars!" he boasted.

"Sounds good," Alex said hungrily and looking at her watch that read 6:45. "I could use a little snack before dinner, and a shot of tequila should perk me right up." Alex jumped out of the car and walked into the dark, dingy bar behind Derek.

They immediately became the instant attraction since only the bartender, a waitress, and a half drunken Mexican man seated at the bar were in the place. Alex began to question if Derek was right about the food because the place looked like it had not been cleaned since it opened for business.

Derek could tell what Alex was thinking, by the involuntary grimace on her face. It made him laugh. "Seriously, trust me the food is off the hook," he said grabbing her hand and sitting down in a booth next to the window.

The waitress hardly gave them time to pull the menu from in between the salt and pepper shakers and the tin napkin holder before she was hovering over them asking if they were ready to order.

Derek gave the waitress an indignant look that if it had been back in the day, she would have regretted approaching him so quickly. He had to remind himself that he was no longer that person. "You know what ma, we'll have two chicken enchiladas and a couple rounds of your house tequila," he quipped, trying to keep his composure.

The waitress walked away without writing down the order. Alex stared at Derek and found it attractive that he took control and ordered for her. She missed that. She was so used to Sway letting her make all of her own decisions whenever the two of them did anything together, it felt nice to have someone make a decision for her again like Malcolm used to do. She leaned back onto the dingy red cushioned booth seat and smiled.

"What's on your mind?" His voice was putting her under a spell.

"It's nothing, really," Alex said coyly.

"I want to know anyway," he said leaning into her. "You fascinate me."

Alex could see that he was telling her the truth, and it scared her, but completely flattered her at the same time. She shifted in her seat and looked away just as the waitress sat down the small shot glasses filled with a clear liquid and a bowl of lemon wedges in front of her. Without waiting for Derek, Alex quickly licked the back of her hand, sprinkled some salt on it, licked again, grabbed her glass, swallowed the tequila in one gulp, grabbed a lemon wedge and sucked all of its juices from it. Derek sat in awe that she was a "pro" at drinking tequila, she didn't strike him as a woman who would know, yet she clearly was familiar with the method of the proper way of drinking it. Moment to moment, he grew more infatuated with her while observing everything she did.

"You really got a brotha' trippin'."

"Ahh," Alex said, shaking her head to get the tequila flowing through her body. "Why do you say that Derek, you didn't think a woman in a suit knew how to drink like a girl from the hood?"

"No, that is not why, just the opposite in fact. I'm feelin' everything about you, everything. The way you carry yourself, in and out of the boardroom, is turning a brotha on." He had to declare.

Alex did not know what was in the house tequila, but that one shot was making her hot. She slid out of her jacket and unbuttoned her ivory blouse, so that her cleavage could breathe. Derek took notice.

"Derek we have just spent less than three hours together, I can't have that kind of affect on you but thanks for the flattery, it *almost* can get you anywhere. Now, am I the only one drinking?" she asked, lifting her second shot glass.

He wanted to explain to her that he did not know where this was coming from either, but she was different from any woman he had ever encountered. He was used to women who loved and lived for that grimy lifestyle. He was always surrounded by women who were with him because something was in it for them. Derek was mostly familiar with the populace of lower class women with hidden agendas, and that is why he could not trust women.

Alex seemed different. He could tell that she was the real thing: no cover-ups. He was ready for a woman like Alex and after two years of searching, here she stood before him.

"Naw, you are definitely not drinking alone," he said and gulped his shot down without the salt buffer or the fresh lemon juice chaser. He waved at the waitress for another round, and began to pick Alex's brain. He was intrigued by Alex, and he wanted to get to know her better. "Does Alex stand for Alexandra?" he asked

Not wanting to go into the whole story as to why she and her sisters had boy names, she replied, "no, just Alex. Let's just say that my dad loved the names Alex, Reggie and Shawn, and so that's what he named my sisters and me. I know it gets confusing sometimes, but it works to my advantage in this business. It often catches people off guard like with you and Henry earlier today," she laughed.

They toasted their next shot to success and eagerly accepted the next round of shots the waitress set down in front of them. By the time the fourth round of shots landed on their table, the waitress was placing two large plates with steaming hot tortillas smothered in melted cheese before them. Alex looked at the meal and her empty stomach started to flip-flop. It looked too sloppy to eat.

"Trust me, try it," Derek said, noticing her apprehension.

She picked up the fork and dug into the gooey mess. As soon as she filled her mouth with the cheesy substance, it made her taste buds dance across her palette. "Mmm … , this is good!" she declared.

"Told you ma, you can trust me," his voice became steamy like the cheesy filled tortillas that they were eating.

They chomped on their food, while talking small talk. He impressed her with his reformation from being a convicted felon to a successful businessman. She admired his ability to overcome poor circumstances, and his will to break down stereotypical barriers and obstacles that many brothers like Derek face. Most of them find it too hard to live in society once they have been forced to live like a caged animal. She never held a man's past against him, especially a black man because she knew of their obstacles in society. In many ways, he reminded her of Sway, but a tad bit more thuggish. His vernacular and the hardness of his face told Alex that he was raised in and by the streets, so she appreciated his willingness to change. He also impressed her by not having children all over the world. Not many black men can say that they don't have at least one 'baby mama', and he did not have any, so he received extra credit for that accolade alone.

"So, do you have kids?" he asked between food bites.

"One, a daughter. She will be four in October," Alex said, beaming at the thought of her baby.

"Are you still with her father?"

"I was never "with" her father," Alex replied, making quotation marks with her fingers. "We were and still are friends. You know things happen, but I don't regret any of it."

"I can respect that. So are you seeing anyone?" he asked, cutting to the chase.

"Not really, you?"

"No, I am not seeing anyone at the moment. I played that game before, having a woman on every burner. I just want one woman for all of my burners, you feel me," he said in a serious tone.

His eyes captured hers and she understood exactly where he was coming from. *Why in the hell do you have to be way out here in Vegas*, she thought.

"Yeah, I feel you," she said in a soft low voice. She was feeling him, but she was not sure if the four shots of homegrown tequila was the reason why.

Alex was feeling mellow and losing track of the time, which was now past eight. "Damn it! Derek, will you excuse me, it looks like I am late for dinner," she said quickly sliding out of the booth without waiting to be excused, and walking outside.

Derek watched her from the window as she talked on her cell phone. He knew it was selfish, but he was glad that he had thwarted her dinner plans because he may never have a chance to spend time alone like this with her again.

"Hey, Journey what's up? Sorry, I missed dinner but I am still in a meeting, sort of," Alex spat into the phone.

"Hi Alex! Where are you?" Journey screamed into the phone.

"I am actually having a few drinks with … , well, I will tell you all about it later. Where are you guys? It's so noisy."

"Well, when you did not call at seven thirty, we said forget dinner and hit the casinos! Cain is teaching me how to shoot craps! I won five hundred dollars!" Journey screamed into the phone as if it were a million dollars.

"OK, you two have fun and I will meet you at the hotel later?"

"OK, oh and call Sway, he is looking for you. He said you were not picking up your cell!" Journey chimed and hung up before any good-byes were exchanged.

Alex checked her missed calls feature on her cell phone and saw that Sway called five times within minutes apart. She knew he wanted to know what happened at the meeting and she knew he would hunt her down like a thief in the night until he reached her. She looked back into the pub and saw Derek looking over at her. She held up her finger as if to say 'one more minute' and he nodded his head. She saw the waitress in the background placing more shot glasses on their table and she quickly dialed Sway's number. She was feeling a slight buzz and cleared her throat to gain what little sober poise she had left in her being. Sway could tell if she had been drinking and she did not want him to hear it.

"What up? Why in the hell haven't you been answering your phone?" Was all she heard when he answered the other end.

"Calm down, everything is fine. I did not call you, or answer the phone because I just came from the building site, which is very nice by the way," Alex said in a stern voice.

"Word!" Sway instantly became excited and no longer angry.

"Yes, word," Alex said with a smile, "I think if all goes well, as I expect it to, you are going to be a wealthy man."

"No, we are going to be wealthy. You know I am always going to take care of you," his sweetness oozed through the phone line.

Alex began to smile. He always knew what to say to her, but with him being miles away and her feeling high and uninhibited; she had to cut the phone call short, otherwise she would be torturing herself. She asked about Stevie and he confirmed that she was being well taken care of, and that he had a full day planned for the two of them starting early in the morning. The phone call lasted all of three minutes and

Alex rushed to get back inside to finish the fun night she had barely begun to have.

"Everything OK?" Derek asked as she sat back down across from him.

"Yup, it looks like my friends found something to do without me, so that makes me free for the night," Alex said licking her hand and pouring salt on the wet spot.

Derek looked at her with intensity as her tongue ran across the back of her hand. He imagined how it would feel on his skin.

"Then that means you can spend it with me," he said looking at her as she gulped down another shot.

Her glassy eyes showed him that the tequila was taking effect. His intention was not to get her plastered and could see it was time to leave, so he was hoping that she would say yes to them spending the rest of the night together.

Alex looked at his strong hands lying motionless on the table and then up at his finely shaven face. Everything she was feeling was going against all of her business rules. She stood firm on not having relationships with her clients, and Sway was the only exception because of the unique relationship they created way before ever doing business together. She could not handle another unique relationship, and she certainly did not want to do anything that would hinder the success of this new deal by starting something with Derek that in the end she would not be able to rectify. "I'm not sure that would be a good idea Derek."

"I think it's a very good idea," he said sliding out of the booth and pulling her arm so that she could get up to follow him.

No more words were spoken; none had to be. He smiled at her and the dimple in his right cheek softened his rugged look. She reciprocated with a wide grin as she held onto his hand and slid out of the booth. Derek dug in his pocket, and pulled out a hundred dollar bill and threw it on the table. He wrapped his arm around Alex's waist and they glided out of the pub as if they had known each other all of their lives.

Chapter 13

Journey
It's Our First Night Together

"Woooo!" Journey screamed at the top of her lungs. She and Cain had been glued to the craps table for over three hours and she was up by one thousand dollars. Gambling had never been her thing, but some how whenever Cain blew on her dice before she threw them; she felt a euphoric vibe, connecting her to the game *and* to him. It was as if the dice knew the number she needed to win, and they would fall in her favor. Cain loved every minute of her winning streak because he was benefiting from it as well. He had won over eighteen hundred dollars and if she rolled a seven on her next go, he would double his earnings.

"Come on Journey, Baby you got this," Cain quipped. It was hard to conceal his emotions that were running high.

She shook the pair of dice in her right hand so hard that her whole body shook. When she stopped shaking, she opened her hand to allow Cain to blow his luck over them.

"Ok Cain, blow some magic on these babies!" she said overwhelmed with excitement.

He quickly obliged and blew lightly over the white dice in her small hand, and she threw them hard against the backboard of the crap table. The dice tumbled many times before they slammed with force against the back of the table. Everyone around the table stood motionless as if the moment was being caught in time. The first die landed, displaying two black dots, just as the second die landed, revealing five black dots.

"Aayyyyy!" everyone cheered standing around the table.

"I won thirty eight hundred dollars!" Journey screamed in Cain's ear as she grabbed him and hugged him closely.

He took advantage of the moment and reciprocated by tightly holding onto her small frame. He was able to avoid physical interaction all night up until now. She felt good. He glided his hand up and down her back causing her to pull back just enough so that they faced each other. Journey and Cain stood with their arms wrapped around each other with just a few inches separating their lips. He had hoped he did not over step his bounds and noticed he hadn't when he saw the seductive smile on her face.

"Uh-uh, I have to keep my eye on you. You are a dangerous combination: a good luck charm and a naughty boy rolled up in one."

Cain licked his lips and gave her a look that told her their night was just beginning. They stood next to the crap table and stared at one another as if they were alone, ignoring the electrifying atmosphere that surrounded them.

"All bets in!" the dealer called out.

"Grab your chips and let's go have a drink," Cain demanded.

Journey did not protest. She grabbed her chips and threw them in her little bucket until it was full. Her total winnings for the night amounted to well over four thousand dollars, so she was compliant to Cain's idea to stop while she was ahead.

"I'm glad you stopped me. I would have stayed there all night," she laughed.

"I know, I could see the gambling gremlin in your eye," Cain joked as they walked into one of the hotel's bar lounge.

They found two empty stools at the bar and ordered their drinks.

"So, Cain, you think you gonna take Sway up on his offer to work in the family business?" Journey asked, drumming up conversation.

She could not stop herself from looking at his full lips as he licked them and thought about her question. The bartender walked over to them and placed an apple martini in front of Journey and a shot of Hennessy in front of Cain.

He took a sip. "Yeah, I think I am. I wasn't sure at first on how things were going to go down with me and my pops but he's straight."

"Your father is a good man, Cain. I think you will excel in the business simply by shadowing him and seeing how he runs his business," Journey said reassuringly.

"I got that feeling too; Pops ain't no joke when he handles his business. I got the chance to see him in action, and I see where I get my temper from," Cain said with a proud smile and looked over at Journey.

He caught her staring at his lips and she quickly looked the other way.

"What?" he asked, wiping his mouth with his hand, "Something on my mouth?"

She was embarrassed. She did not know what to say. She wanted to tell him that he got more than just a temper from his father, but chose not to. "No, it's nothing. It's just that I can't believe how much you've grown since I last saw you," Journey said, relieved she was able to think quickly on her feet.

"Well, you haven't changed," Cain said smiling at her. "You are still fine as hell."

His unexpectedly bold comment almost knocked Journey off her stool.

She blushed like a schoolgirl and modestly said, "thank you."

Worn out from gambling, and parched from screaming at the crap tables, they finished off their first round of drinks within minutes, and wasted little time ordering their second round. Journey discovered that as more liquor traveled through Cain's bloodstream, the more talkative he became. He told her about his relationship with his mother; and how he grew up fast, dealing with the type of men she chose to be with. It was a part of his life that he was not proud of, but he understood his mother always craved the fast life; had she not he would not have been here. Carmen never left the drug game, even after Sway got shot. Unsure if there was a hit out on his family, soon after Sway recovered from his wounds, he gave Carmen money to leave, and start a new life in San Diego with his only son. He made her promise to stay away from drug dealers and hustlers, even though they both knew that would be hard for her to do due to her cocaine habit. Because of her addiction, she befriended every known neighborhood drug dealer, no matter what city she would live in. And, as sure as the sky is blue, barely a month had gone by before Carmen had settled in sunny California and quickly found out where the "ballers and shot callers" were. She began to mark her territory. Every man she brought home acted like the gracious guest in front of Cain. However, that façade was always short lived because of his mother stealing their money or their product. Then a younger, defenseless Cain was forced to watch that same man beat his mother helpless. By the time Cain turned eighteen, he had physically filled out. He was towering over Carmen and staring her male friends in the eye. Once Cain realized that he could be just as intimidating to the punks who controlled his mother, his mere presence made it hard for a man to approach Carmen, let alone get close enough to put his hands on her. Cain continued to share his scandalous upbringing with Journey as they started on their fourth round of drinks. He explained his strategy to keep his mother away from the men she had become dependent on to feed her habit. He became a drug dealer himself. He was just a small-time weed dealer, but a drug dealer nonetheless. He sold weed to his college friends to make his ends meet because Carmen always used his child support money from Sway for herself. Cain told Journey that he would rather have his mother use his father's money than to have her depend on another man who would try to own her, and would beat her ass at his discretion.

Journey listened intently to Cain as he divulged his life story and he made her promise not to tell Alex or Sway. He did not want Sway to find out that his mother was supporting her habit with the money Sway sent to support Cain. Journey would normally steer clear of any man who sold drugs for a living, but she respected Cain for risking his life in order to save his mother from being abused. She empathized with his mother because no woman deserves to be beaten, regardless of the circumstances. Journey wished someone would save her too.

"I commend you Cain for doing that for your mother," she said, sipping on the last drop of her drink and picking up a mozzarella cheese stick from the appetizer platter she ordered while Cain was sharing his life story.

"Thanks, I love my mother. I mean she got mad issues, but she's still ma dukes," he said, downing the last swig of his shot of Hennessey. "So, how is the married life?" he asked, changing the subject and feeling slightly buzzed.

He wanted to know what was going on with Journey and Tiny because it could not be all good from the way she rushed out of the house earlier that morning. Cain also took notice that she was not wearing her wedding ring. Journey stopped chewing on her potato skin that she had just taken a bite out of, and suddenly became sick to her stomach. She was having a nice time up until now. She could not blame Cain for bringing up Tiny's name because he did not know that his father's best friend was beating her like those men used to beat his mother.

A somber look came across her face as she looked straight into Cain's sexy eyes.

"I don't want to talk about it," Journey said with firmness.

"Oh, OK, don't get mad yo, I was just changing the subject," Cain said, holding his hands up as if he was under arrest.

"I'm sorry Cain, it's just that I don't … ," Journey was interrupted by her cell phone. "Excuse me. Hello," Journey said into the little phone over the loud music blaring in the background.

"Where the fuck you at?" Tiny yelled into the phone.

"Excuse me?" Journey spat back.

"I said -- where in the fuck are you at? I just spoke to Sway and he said that you and Alex are in fuckin' Vegas! You did not tell me you were going to Vegas!"

"Just like you didn't tell me that you were gonna start spending your nights someplace else," Journey yelled, unable to contain her anger.

"What," Tiny stumbled.

Defiantly, Journey yelled back into the receiver. "You heard me, and yes, I am in Vegas, having a wonderful fucking time, so I will be home when I get home," Journey said with clenched teeth and much bravado.

"Journey! You get your ass back … ," Tiny's thunderous voice bolted through the phone just as she pressed the "end" button on her cell phone and threw it back in her purse.

Maybe it was the vodka but she suddenly felt a tremendous amount of courage, and proudly smiled at herself for finally having the last word. She wasn't sure if Tiny would try to kill her when she got home, and at the moment, by the way she was feeling, she really did not care. She was tired of being treated less than a woman of her worth. And, from Cain's recent compliment, she apparently still looked good. Right now she was thousands of miles away from the one person who was making her life miserable, and she was going to enjoy every minute of being free.

"You ai'ight," Cain asked unmoved by the event. He was used to this kind of drama. He calmly leaned back in his stool. Another sexy characteristic he inherited from his father: an ability to not let unforeseen circumstances rattle him.

Journey shook her head and breathed in deeply. "Yes, I'm sorry. Now you know why I didn't want to talk about it."

"And, we still don't have to," Cain replied giving Journey his undivided attention.

She was relieved that he did not care about the reason behind that turbulent phone call. They stared at each other wondering who would utter the next word. It was obvious that Journey needed to get her mind off Tiny and back on Vegas. After her luck at the crap table, there were only two other things left to do: party or have sex, she was ready for both.

"You want to get out of here," Journey finally broke the silence.

"I'm wit' you Ma, whatever you wanna do," Cain said seductively, looking just like his father.

Journey immediately could see what Alex saw in Sway. *Damn, this young boy is sexy*, Journey thought as she grabbed her purse and slid off the stool. "I want to party!" Journey exclaimed.

"Let's get out of here," Cain grabbed her by the hand and began leading her toward the bright red exit sign that hung above the lounge entrance.

They quickly walked over to the row of yellow taxis prepared to take the hotel guests to their destination. They climbed into a taxi and Cain instructed the driver to take them to another hot spot not far from their hotel. As they traveled down the strip, Journey sat in amazement at the bright neon lights reflecting off the tinted window of the taxi. No matter where she looked, her eyes were greeted by another illuminating structure standing high above her. When they pulled up to the curb of the club, Journey noticed that the party goers and Cain were in the same age range, so she knew he would blend right into the crowd of early twenty-something year-olds. She suddenly began to wonder if she could too. As the feeling of anxiety began to take over her nerves,

Journey realized that she had not been clubbing since getting married. She started to recognize the age difference between them, and stopped in her tracks.

Cain stopped walking and looked back at her. "What's wrong?"

"Cain, I think I am too old for this crowd," Journey said, looking at a young couple glued together leaning against a parked car in the club's parking lot. The two of them were French kissing like their lives depended on it.

"What! You buggin' … , you look better than most of the chicks up in this piece," he said with confidence and grabbed her hand to let everyone know they were there together.

They walked through the club and found two empty stools at the end of the bustling bar. The club was packed and the DJ had the floor jumping. Journey felt like dancing. Cain ordered their drinks and they bounced to the music on their stools until the drinks arrived. After downing her martini in a few gulps and with a sense of urgency, Journey jumped up from the stool.

"Let's dance!" she shouted.

Cain did not say anything; instead, he swallowed his shot, stood up and let Journey lead the way to the crowded dance floor. They danced non-stop through several songs until Journey's feet were hurting.

"Oh! Cain my feet! You are going to have to rub them for me when we get back to the hotel!" she screamed over the loud music, not knowing whether or not Cain actually heard what she was saying. She grabbed his hand and led him off the dance floor, toward the bar. Journey took a few napkins from the holder on the bar and began to wipe the sweat off Cain's face. They danced so long it felt like a good work out, which was something Journey had not done in awhile since working from home. Cain's muscles flexed through his drenched shirt. He ordered another round as Journey patted his face lightly with the small square paper napkins.

"So, after we down these drinks, you want to go back to the hotel so I can rub your feet?" he asked looking down at her with lust in his eyes.

"You did hear me." Journey stopped patting his face, leaned back and smiled. "Yes I would like that very much."

Their eyes connected and the stare became filled with sexual tension. Journey took a deep breath, and grabbed her drink that the bartender had just placed in her reach. She took a long sip and looked at Cain's glistening skin. He looked good enough to eat.

"Let's go," she almost demanded.

Cain looked down at her and saw that she was ready – *for him*. A devilish grin formed on his face; he gulped down his shot and slammed the glass down on the bar. Journey turned to walk out of the club and Cain followed closely behind. His good conscious reminded him that she was a married woman, but the little devil in him also reminded him that she was not happy. He could not believe that Tiny had been so stupid to mess up a good thing. Cain justified what he intended to do to Journey with the feeling that Tiny should be thanking Cain for making his wife smile tonight, which apparently, Tiny was neglectful in doing himself.

They approached an on duty parked taxi and climbed in. Cain told the driver where to take them. The air-conditioned taxi comforted the inebriated couple as they relaxed in the back seat ready to unwind in their lavish suite.

"Thank you Cain, I had fun tonight," Journey said with a slight slur, and grabbing his right thigh, "it's been awhile."

His thigh muscle involuntarily flexed as she squeezed his leg. Cain laid his head back against the seat and enjoyed her form of foreplay. The several shots of Hennessey had kicked in, and the promise he made to himself to not let things between he and Journey get out of hand was one that he knew he would not be able to keep.

"You're welcome," he replied with his eyes still closed. "Our night's not over yet," he coolly continued, opening his eyes and looking over into her pretty eyes, which were glazed over from the apple martinis.

"Mmm ..., I'm glad because I am not tired yet," she responded and moved her hand up his thigh a few inches.

Cain reached over and grabbed her left thigh to reciprocate the pleasurable massage she was giving him. Journey widened her legs to give his hand access to travel up her inner thigh to the crotch of her jeans. He could feel her sexual heat. She moved her hand up to his groin and rubbed gently, causing Cain to lean over and pull her in closer to kiss her. They moved in what seemed like slow motion until their lips touched, and Cain slid his soft tongue into Journey's mouth. Cain reached for her zipper and pulled it down without interrupting the passionate kiss. He slid his hand into her jeans underneath her panties and rubbed gently. Journey was warm and inviting, and he was hoping that the driver would get them to their destination sooner -- rather than later. She moaned as he slid two fingers into her moist flesh and slowly penetrated her. He continued to kiss her about the lips and neck with a tenderness that she missed from her own husband.

Journey was clearly in the pre-stages of ecstasy. She was feeling good and with his touch, Cain could tell just how good she was feeling. She was moistening to his touch and it made him anxious to be inside of her. The cab driver tried not to watch the "X" rated movie scene in the backseat of his car, but nevertheless, at every red light he indulged himself with another peek. Neither, Cain or Journey realized that they had an audience, and it was evident that they did not care. Cain hugged Journey and moved her body so that it was beneath his, and she was lying on the back seat. The cab driver's eyes widened just as the guy in the car behind him started to blow his horn. Unaffected by the sound, Cain continued to pleasure Journey with his kisses and his fingers as the cab driver pulled into the wide circular driveway lined with lights to the Bellagio Hotel entrance, the cab driver suddenly became overwhelmed with a feeling of awkwardness because he did not want to interrupt the lovers.

Making a loud noise as he cleared his throat, the driver broadcasted his announcement. "Um, excuse me … , but we're here," he said loudly, looking at the couple through his rearview mirror.

Cain suddenly stopped kissing Journey and looked up at the driver. As his eyes focused in on the reflection of the driver's eyes peering back at him through the rearview mirror, Cain shook his head and realized that they were still in the cab and not their suite. Cain looked down at Journey, who was covering her face with her hand. He imagined that she was realizing the same reality check. Cain quickly sat up straight in the seat, and allowed Journey to sit up as well and fasten her pants. A small part of her was embarrassed, but she was sure that the cab driver had seen worse in this lustful city. Journey felt a sense of relief knowing that the graying white man would never see her again. Cain zipped up his pants and pulled a fifty-dollar bill from his front pocket.

"Here you go my man," he said quickly as Journey opened the back door and slid out of the car unnoticed.

"Thank you," the cabbie chimed. "You all have a nice night."

Cain snickered at the man's comment, catching the subliminal message behind it, and slid out of the car and into the hotel lobby. Journey was already standing at the elevator, waiting for it to arrive, with the gold card key clearly visible in her hand. Cain walked up next to her and wondered if she was OK with what had just transpired in the taxicab.

"Yo, you ai'ight?" He looked over at her, hoping she'd say yes.

"Mmm, hmm," she moaned as the elevator doors opened. "But I will be better once we get upstairs."

"Then let's not waste anymore time," he replied and pulled her into the elevator.

As the doors closed, he pinned her against the back wall of the elevator, and started to devour her with warm wet kisses along her neck and chest. She wrapped her arms around his neck and lifted her body so that her legs wrapped firmly around his waist. Within seconds, the elevator came to a halt and the doors opened to a waiting couple. Stunned by what they were welcomed by, the tall man cleared his throat, while his petite significant other giggled under her breath.

"Oh, my bad," Cain replied turning around to face the couple. "We didn't realize the elevator had stopped."

Once again, Journey found herself in a slightly embarrassing situation. She quickly straightened out her clothes, and walked pass the couple without looking at them. Instead, she kept her eyes focused on the beautiful patterns in the hallway carpeting as she moved quickly down the long corridor.

"No problem. Hey, when in Rome you must do what the Romans do!" the man said patting Cain on his shoulder as they passed by each other.

"I hope you remember you said that when we get back to our room!" the petite woman sang to the tall man as the elevator doors closed.

Cain chuckled at himself for starting something he hoped homeboy could finish, and followed Journey to their suite. She quickly slid the card into the slot and opened the door to a dimly lit living room. Cain did not wait for her to turn around to face him. Instead, he scooped her up from behind and carried her into his bedroom. Journey felt like she was flying, partially from the affects of the liquor flowing through her body, but mostly because she never had someone literally sweep her off her feet before. Cain was full of surprises and she liked that.

"You sure about this?" he asked as he laid her down on the king size bed adorned with endless pillows. He hovered over her comfortably in a horizontal position.

"I couldn't be surer," she whispered and pulled his head closer to her face to kiss him.

They continued where they left off in the taxi, and Cain began to pull at his clothing with a sense of urgency. Journey followed suit and within moments, their bodies were bare and full of great expectations. Cain ran his hands all over her body causing goose bumps to form beneath her smooth skin. She shivered.

"Wait! Do you have a condom?" she asked, hoping he'd say yes.

Cain looked at her. He was fully erect and slightly caught off guard. He smiled at her pretty face and simply said, "No, I don't. I was not planning on sexing anybody this weekend."

He leaned in to kiss her again and wished she would just let nature take its course like girls his age did. Journey stopped him again.

"I think we should stop," she said as if it were an apology.

"I promise, I'll pull out," he replied in a whisper into her ear. "I want to feel you. I want you to feel me," he moaned, almost pleading.

She gave in. As a grown, responsible woman, she knew better. Yet, as a woman scorned, Journey knew he was about to make her *feel* better.

"You promise," she smirked with an expression of enticement.

"Hmm, hmm … ," he moaned as he widened her legs to gain access to her love.

In a matter of seconds, Cain could feel the softness of her flesh encasing his stiff being and he moved slowly to enjoy the massage from the friction of his penetration. They continued their lustful affair until Cain eventually collapsed on top of Journey, forgetting the pledge he had made an hour before.

"You liar," she said smiling, sliding her body from beneath his.

"I'm sorry," he gasped. "I didn't realize that you would feel so damn good." He returned the smile and hoped that she would forgive him because he clearly could feel the intensity between them, and he knew his body would crave her warmth again before the sun rose. He rolled onto his side to look at her face, which had an expression that told him she was fully satisfied. "Do you forgive me?" he asked with a boyish grin.

"Yes, I forgive you," she replied rolling over onto her side to face him and in a slightly more mature tone, filtered with the little dignity she had left said. "But next time you have to remember to keep your promise."

"So, there will be a next time?" he questioned, gliding his hand across her naked hip, landing at the curve of her waist, and pulling her closer to him. "I promise to keep my promise," he concluded before leaning in to kiss her again.

Journey responded with little hesitation. She surrendered to Cain's appeal once again and was enjoying the feeling he was infusing in her. She wished she could remain feeling this way. However, she was very mindful that in less than two days, she would return home to face Satan himself. She exhaled, closed her eyes and returned to the here and now, while Cain caressed her small breasts with soft kisses. She wondered where he acquired his lovemaking skills, but quickly dismissed it, and reconciled that he acquired it the same way he inherited the rest of his great qualities. *This apple clearly did not fall far from the tree.*

Chapter 14

Alex
I'm More Than a Woman

The desert night created a wind that gently caressed Alex's face as the wheels of Derek's Mercedes gripped the winding, deserted roads. Clueless to their next destination, Alex reclined back and felt no fear. Although, his masculine presence was slightly overbearing, he was also charming and sexy. She felt comfortable and safe, like she always felt when she was with Sway. The delightful interaction between her slight intoxication and the cool breeze, created a nice buzz. She closed her eyes and enjoyed how the car hugged the curves of the road. It felt like she was back at home in New York, riding on the *Dragon Coaster* at *Playland*. That amusement park was one of Stevie's favorite 'spur of the moment' fun activities.

Silently, Alex was grateful that Derek pulled her out of that little Mexican shack when he did because she had almost reached her drinking limit. She could feel her head slightly spinning, but miraculously the combination of the several shots of tequila and the greasy enchilada had no affect on her stomach. She was especially grateful for that. Slowly, Alex opened her eyes and they were greeted by the constellation in the moonlit Vegas sky illuminated by thousands of bright, tiny stars. She looked over at Derek and admired his deep dimple in his right cheek. Somehow, that one facial characteristic softened his overall persona.

"Hey, what's up, I thought you were sleeping," he turned to look at Alex.

"Mmm … no, actually I was just resting my eyes," Alex replied and looked at her watch. "I guess time is catching up with me." It was almost midnight and in another four hours she would have been up for twenty-four hours straight. "Maybe I should get back to the hotel," Alex said almost as if she was asking.

"Maybe you should stay with me tonight," Derek looked at her as he slowed down his car.

At that moment, the car turned onto a long driveway. In the near distance, Alex could see a lovely array of flickering porch lights. As they drove toward the lights, her vision began to focus on a newly built gated community of townhouses. Derek pulled up to the keypad next to the closed wrought iron gate and punched in a few numbers. The gates to the complex parted and without divulging where they were headed, Derek drove through the gate, and made a left onto the second driveway.

"Um, excuse me, where are we going?" Alex asked, sitting up straight in her seat.

"Oh, my bad, I thought you were sleeping and I didn't know which hotel you were staying at, so I was bringing you to my place for a little while to sleep it off," Derek thoughtfully replied.

His act of sincerity touched Alex. The kind gesture caused Alex to experience a déjà vu. An overwhelming feeling of safety engulfed her. For a quick moment she was reminded of the special times she shared with Malcolm. Her first and only truly love, who took care of her every need. Derek's arrogant decision to just bring Alex back to his place would have been something Malcolm would have done. So, instead of being insulted, she smiled at Derek to let him know that she approved of his attempt to perform a good deed.

He pressed the remote to the garage door, and smoothly pulled into the garage. He quickly turned off the engine to the car and hopped out to assist Alex. She welcomed his helpful attentiveness. She held onto his thick, firm arm to steady herself. She could not believe that of all places in the world, she would meet a man in Vegas, who possessed characteristics that were similar to both Malcolm and Sway. They walked hand in hand through the door adjoining the garage to a mid-sized mudroom. Alex was pleasantly surprised to see that he was organized and tidy. And, even more impressed by the several pairs of Timberland boots in all colors neatly displayed in wood cubbies stacked against the wall. One would have thought that he lived in North Dakota and not Nevada, but the boots confirmed that he would forever remain a New Yorker. Derek led Alex into a spacious kitchen that was sparkling clean. She wondered if he ever cooked on the spotless stainless steel chef's stove. The dining room table was decorated with a set of Waterford china. She was almost certain a woman helped him with selecting such an elegant pattern on the China to compliment the room's decor. She followed him into the large living room with a vaulted ceiling, and sat on the white oversized chaise lounge. Derek walked over to the mantle, pressed a button on the wall, and flames instantly appeared in the fireplace. Alex's eyes lit up and she suddenly started to feel awkward because she was feeling so comfortable. She had to quickly remind herself that Derek was someone who she was about to help generate millions of dollars. Her good conscious was trying to regain its ground, but her intoxicating, lackadaisical disposition was getting the best of her. She fixated her glazed over eyes on his bulging chest as he approached her.

"Derek this is really nice, but really, I can't stay long."

He did not respond, instead he sat down beside Alex and leaned in close. "I know what you are thinking," he stated, "you're saying to yourself that you should not be here because we just met *and* we are going to be working together, and you normally don't do this: right?"

She looked at him with an expression on her face that clearly told him she was freaked out. "That is exactly what I was thinking!" she exclaimed, amazed at his ability to read her mind. "How did you know that?" she wanted to know.

"Your face is telling it all," he said as a matter of fact followed by a slight chuckle.

Struggling to regain some sober composure, Alex sat up and put her hand up to stop Derek from going further. "*Well* … , is my face also telling you that a part of me *would* like to stay longer?" she asked.

"Yes, and that is the part of your face I am going to pay attention to for the rest of the night," he moaned in a low sexy voice, displaying his sexy dimple and covering her lips with his index finger. He leaned in and replaced his finger with his soft full lips, causing Alex to close her eyes. His mouth was partially open and the fact that he did not invade her with a full open mouth kiss, made the kiss more sensual.

The heat from the fireplace and his soft touch overwhelmed her and she pulled back. "I think I should go. I can't do this and you definitely know why," she firmly stated but at the same time hoped he was not upset.

He sat up and grabbed her hands, which seemed to fit perfectly inside his large hands. He had to respect her for her business etiquette. He admired that she did not mix business with pleasure. That was one of her characteristics that immediately drew him in.

"Listen Ma, would it make you feel better if I told you that we will not be working together on this project at all."

Alex pulled her hands back and folded them across her chest. "What are you talking about?" Alex began to feel like this situation was going to ruin Sway's deal.

"I am a silent partner in this deal," he confirmed. "You will be working directly with Hank on every level. That is my agreement with him. So, when you come to Vegas you can handle your business with him, and then chill with me afterwards."

"So, you mean, that you do not intend to meet the man you are going into business with, especially since he is going to own most of the stock in your project?" Alex asked, confused and starting to wonder if this deal really was too good to be true.

"Oh, trust me Sweetheart, I did my research on your client, Mr. McCoy," Derek said standing up and walking over to the bar in the corner of the room. "Would you like something to drink?"

"Do you have any ... , coffee, or tea, that would be great," she replied, still waiting for a justifiable answer, and at the same time needing something to help sober up.

Derek excused himself and walked into the kitchen. Alex sat back and tried to make sense out of what he just told her. *Why wouldn't he want to meet Sway?* She thought as she heard him tinkering around in the kitchen. She tried to figure out who this Derek Minor was by glancing around his living room. She did not see any collectible items from places abroad, which told her that he probably was telling the truth about once being incarcerated. Men his age should have at least traveled the Caribbean Islands a few times, and have some kind of picture, hand-carved wooden artifacts or some of those little woven baskets that can be found at any tourist stop to show for it. Hardly any books filled his bookshelf; mostly just magazines. He did possess a large screen television like almost all men Alex imagined, and it was hooked up neatly to a DVD player and a Playstation 2. *Men and their toys.* She smiled to herself as she heard Derek's footsteps come back into the room. She looked up at him, grabbed the steamy mug from his hand, and took a sip.

"Mmm … , thank you," Alex said allowing the warm liquid to flow through her body.

"Like I was saying," Derek sat back down next to her. "I am aware of how important this is to everyone, especially for me because I have the most invested in it. I just think that Hank is more experienced with this aspect of the business, and when I feel the time is right, trust me, I will meet all of the other parties involved. Your client also has a partner, doesn't he?" Derek asked, already knowing the answer.

"Well, you have done your homework Mr. Minor. Yes, he does have a partner, but he did not want to involve him until he knew this venture was actually going to occur," Alex responded, impressed and relieved.

"I can understand that," Derek responded. "Smart move, another smart move was hiring you," he concluded and looked Alex straight in the eye.

"How did he ever find you?" Derek asked wondering how the two of them met.

Alex stiffened as his question penetrated through her body. She was not prepared to answer that question this weekend. She never thought she would have to, especially under circumstances such as this one. She wanted to be honest and tell Derek that her client is also the father of her darling daughter. Yet, she felt that if she told Derek about the unusual personal relationship she and Sway had, he would see her as a hypocrite, especially after just being so adamant about not mixing business with pleasure. She decided that it would be best to leave the personal side of her and Sway's relationship out of this budding relationship with Derek. "My girlfriend and I worked at his first shop."

"Y'all were candy girls?" Derek interrupted her, partially impressed.

Alex laughed, but thought it was nice of him to think so, although Journey could have easily been one of the candy girls if she were a few inches taller.

"No, but thank you," Alex continued. "I was his business manager and she was his head bartender. He gave me my first opportunity to manage and he allowed my girlfriend the flexibility she needed to audition during the day."

Derek looked at Alex's face as it lit up while she talked about Sway. He could tell that she thought highly of him. Derek grabbed one of the remote controls that were lined up on the glass coffee table, and turned on the CD player. The sensual voice of *Jaheim* oozed out of the surround sound speakers embedded in the walls. Alex leaned back into the soft back cushion of the chaise, and cupped her mug as if she had as if she had been to this man's house a hundred times. It was so weird, but she felt like she knew him: like somehow they were connected. She watched him as he watched the flames glowing inside of the fireplace, and she wondered what he was thinking about. She took a sip of her tea. He made it perfectly as if he knew how she liked it. Derek could feel her eyes staring at his back and he turned to her.

"What's up, you OK?" he asked, looking back at her.

"Yeah, I'm good. Are you alright? You look like you are deep in thought," she questioned.

"I'm straight, just sittin' here thinking about how everything is falling into place for me. I feel like I have finally been forgiven for my past and God is making everything line up for me so I can right some wrongs," Derek said relieved as if a weight had been lifted off his shoulders.

Alex looked at him with a quizzical expression on her face. He had gotten a little deep, and she did not peg him for having a religious side but she appreciated the fact that he was spiritual, if nothing else. She also appreciated that he felt comfortable enough with her to tell her something that most men would keep so private.

"Well then, I am glad that I am here to help you see it through," Alex said with sincerity.

He nodded his head in appreciation, stood up, and walked over to the bar to sit his empty glass down. Derek felt good to finally be able to say that out loud. Once settled in Vegas, his life started to change for the better, and within a year, he was in a position to expand. Derek learned quickly that those who come to Las Vegas came with money. He wanted some of it the legitimate way. When he found the site where a hotel and shopping center would fit perfectly, he started looking on the Internet for upcoming boutique-type store franchises that would appeal to the upscale consumer. During his research, he found an up and coming male spa chain that catered to the upscale man. The idea was fresh and innovative and appealed to Derek immediately. He remembered logging on to the website and seeing Sway's face. Derek quickly Googled "Steven McCoy." He discovered that day that Sway was living quite well, and, in fact, he was named one of *Ebony's 100 Most Wanted Bachelors in 1997.* Sway's biography also indicated that he had two children. Derek assumed he and Carmen ended up together, and managed to produce another gorgeous kid. Seeing Sway's face plastered all over his computer monitor reminded Derek of how he used to be -- grimy and selfish. Yet, it also presented him with the opportunity to make amends with his former best friend.

Chapter 15

The Girls
You're All I Need

The rays from the sun on the horizon peeked through the drawn drapes and greeted Alex as she entered the dark penthouse suite. The living room was eerily silent and for a moment she wondered if Journey and Cain were even there. Alex threw her briefcase, suit jacket and shirt onto the sofa, slid out of her heels, and left them lying haphazardly by the door. She tiptoed across the room through the kitchenette over to the adjacent bedrooms. Both doors were closed and she wasn't sure which room was whose. Alex stood there looking back and forth at the doors and trying to decide whether to knock, or just peek in. She chose the latter. She approached the door on the left with caution, and placed her hand on the knob and slowly turned it. Her intentions were to crack the door just enough to see the foot of the bed. She was mindful of not wanting to invade Cain's privacy. She noticed that the bed seemed to be empty, so she opened the door a little wider. It was empty and still beautifully made with the mints on the pillows. *They still must be out,* Alex thought as she walked out of the room and looked over at the other door.

"Unless … ," she whispered, tiptoeing over to the other door and grabbing the doorknob.

Alex turned the knob slowly and cracked the door just as she did before. Only this time, she could see feet at the foot of the bed, and as she pushed the door open, she saw not only one pair of feet, but two.

Startled, Alex closed the door quickly, causing it to make a clicking sound.

Cain rolled over and opened one eye to look in the direction of the noise. When he did not see anything, he rolled back over and grabbed Journey's tiny waist to pull her closer to him. They had just fallen asleep after several hours of intermittent lovemaking. After the first round, he kept his promise and ran downstairs to the gift shop to purchase condoms. Even though Cain normally used them, he always frowned upon them because they made a woman feel artificial and the act itself seem somewhat unnatural. Yet, to his surprise, with Journey, the use of a condom had no effect on how good she felt during intercourse. Every time was explosive and he could feel her warmth penetrate through the paper-thin latex to his skin. Journey nestled her behind in the crease of his waist as Cain hugged her tighter, and tried to dose back off to sleep.

Alex quickly shuffled to the other side of the suite to her bedroom and closed the door behind her. She covered her mouth and shook her head.

"Clearly, Journey had made good on her promise," she whispered as she slid out of her slacks and slowly lifted Derek's t-shirt over her head.

She inhaled deeply as the shirt slid across her face. The refreshing fragrance of *Davidoff's Cool Water* overwhelmed her and she began to smile. She had a good night's rest and was wide-awake. Alex walked over to the bathroom and decided to take advantage of the jet-stream bathtub while the suite was still quiet and the sun was still making its way up the horizon. She disrobed slowly as the running water created a soothing sound that caused her body to relax. She slid into the hot water and shivered as her body temperature adjusted to its heat. She could not believe that she had just spent the night with a man she barely knew, and the true wonderment was that she slept like a baby. Derek had turned out to be a true gentleman. Alex turned off the water and pushed the jet stream button to create a whirlpool effect. She laid back and closed her eyes to recount the night before. She remembered how after drinking her tea, she began to dose off and Derek carried her to his bedroom. She was impressed that his knees did not buckle when he climbed the flight of stairs to the second level of his home. Alex was not overweight but she was an average sized woman, having a pant size that teetered between eight and ten depending on the time of year. Needless to say, she hated the holidays. When they entered his room, he impressed her more with the warm rust and gold colors that decorated his room and an oversized king-size bed that looked like it would swallow Alex up whole. The fireplace in his bedroom was already lit and burning brightly. He laid her down on the bed and offered her something to sleep in.

"I think maybe I should go back to my suite," she remembered saying to him as he grabbed a t-shirt from his dresser drawer.

"I don't want you to go," he stated as he handed her the shirt. "Chill with me tonight. Nothing is going to happen if you don't want it to. I can sleep in the guest room."

Derek sat on the bed next to her, grabbed her hand and began to touch her fingers lightly one by one.

She moistened to the stimulation of his touch, and the feeling he was creating inside of her body caused her to weaken. "I don't want to put you out," she said, trying to make up a valid excuse to leave.

They looked each other in the eye, and Derek flashed a mesmerizing smile. "Not at all. I am really feelin' you Alex, believe it or not. But a brother like me can show you better than I can tell you."

"Oh yeah, and how you gonna show me?" she asked, captivated by his charm.

He did not respond with words, instead, he leaned over and kissed her softly. His tongue was just as soft as his lips, and Alex slowly opened herself up to receive the passion he was pouring into her body. He pulled back just as she started giving in.

Alex looked at him as if she had done something wrong. "What's the matter?" she asked becoming slightly self-conscious.

"Nothing, trust me. I just don't want you to think that I brought you here for this because I didn't."

"I am not thinking that at all Derek. I know that nothing will happen unless I want it to," she said smiling at him, and standing up from the bed. "Can I use your bathroom?"

"Right over there," he replied, pointing to the partially opened door to a dimly lit room.

Alex walked over to the adjacent room and turned on the light. She looked back to see if he was watching her. He was, with a devilish grin on his face. By the time she returned from the bathroom, Derek had slipped into a comfortable pair of pajama pants and was putting another log on the fire. Alex was amazed that Las Vegas was so cool at night. She never imagined homes in Vegas would have fireplaces, and he had two. His shirtless chest was covered with an artful display of tattoos, and his chocolate skin glistened against the radiant glow that the flames were giving off. He was not as muscular as he appeared when fully clothed, but he was solid and his biceps bulged as they contracted while he shuffled the burning logs with the iron poker.

"Thanks for the shirt," Alex said as she climbed back onto his bed, unable to keep her eyes off of the sexy specimen standing before her.

"My pleasure, it actually looks better on you than it does me."

"I beg to differ," Alex smiled and leaned back against the cushioned headboard.

Derek walked over to the other side of the bed, and slid in behind her and positioned his legs beneath hers, so that they were in a spoon position. Alex melted in his arms and closed her eyes.

"I never did this before: spent the night with a man I literally just met," Alex whispered.

"I can tell," Derek said in a non-offensive way and pulling her closer to his body. "But it's OK because you will know me. I want you to know me."

They dosed off into the early morning hours, with Derek's arms securely wrapped around her waist.

Alex was awakened by the sound of someone's car alarm going off. She looked over her shoulder and found Derek sound asleep lying in the same position with his arm around her waist. She smiled. The moment reminded her of the only real relationship she once had with Malcolm. *That was so long ago*, she thought as she gently stroked Derek's arm with her manicured fingernails. She and Malcolm used to fall asleep in the same position without the need of having sex beforehand. It felt nice just to be close to someone. Alex continued daydreaming for a few moments more while she relished in the comfort of her newfound friend's arms, before waking Derek up to take her back to the hotel.

****

Alex was interrupted from her mental re-enactment of her extraordinary night by the sound of someone fumbling around in the kitchen. She opened her eyes and admired the bathroom décor, while the bevy of bubbles shot out of the jet stream holes embedded throughout the oversized oval bathtub. The massage she was receiving from the powerful force of water penetrating her skin felt almost as good as Helga's hands at her favorite spa back home. She wanted to know who was on the other side of the door, and hoped it was Journey because they had much to talk about, but the therapeutic recipe of hot water, soothing bath oil, and jet stream bubbles forbade her to move.

Cain tried to be as quiet as possible while he looked for the coffee filters. After Alex busted in his room he could not go back to sleep. He quickly made two cups of coffee and slipped back into his room before Alex came out of her room to catch him in his boxers. He closed the door behind him with his foot as he tried to hold the cups steadily in each hand without spilling a drop of the hot java. He walked softly over to the nightstand and gently placed the cups down. He sat at the foot of the bed and watched Journey as she slept. Several thoughts raced through his mind, but the one most prevalent was that she was his father's best friend's wife. Another thing that bothered him was that he did not care. Cain could feel the urgency in Journey to be desired when she surrendered to his advances fully and held nothing back. It was almost as if she was being released, freed from bondage. He always had a school-boy crush on Journey and Alex, but he knew Alex was totally off limits. It was no secret that his father loved Alex not to mention she was the mother of his baby sister. *That would be some Jerry Springer shit for real,* Cain silently laughed at the thought. Journey, on the other hand, was not totally off limits and she made it very clear to him. He lifted the sheet off her body and admired her curves. He slid his hand down the calf of her left leg until he reached the ball of her foot and started to rub it gently. She squirmed. He grabbed her foot with a delicate grasp so she would not move from his grip, and slowly began to massage the sole of her foot.

"Mmm … ," Journey moaned, but did not move.

Cain could see that his touch was receiving a positive response, so he grabbed the other foot and massaged it as he did the other.

Journey opened her eyes and looked down at Cain to watch him gently caress her feet. *Tiny never did this, even when he loved me,* she thought as she smiled at Cain. "That feels good, thank you," Journey said trying to adjust her body so that she could reach for the coffee cup, but not disrupt Cain at the same time.

"I keep my promises," Cain said jokingly.

Their eyes connected as Cain continued to rub her feet. She sipped on her coffee that was a bit too strong, but she appreciated that he even attempted; another gesture her husband never made during their four years together. She was happy Cain decided to join Alex and her in Vegas. She was also saddened by the fact that in less than twenty-four hours, she and Cain would be going their separate ways; him back to sunny California, and her back to misery and darkness in Harlem. Reality was slowly resurfacing in her psyche.

"So, what do you want to do today?" he asked.

"Um, I don't know," Journey answered, sipping on her coffee, "I think we should let Alex decide today since she did not have a chance to really enjoy herself last night."

"Yeah you're right." Cain agreed. "She was stuck with those stiffs all night."

****

Once Cain wrapped up his intimate foot massage on Journey and Alex finished relaxing in her bath, the ladies decided to plan their last day in Vegas by the pool, and Cain took that as an opportunity to play *Madden* football on the *Playstation 2*. The sun was shining brightly and their bodies glistened against its rays. The two women relaxed on their cushioned lounge chairs, and drank mimosas while they shared their surreal stories with one another.

"Then he took me to his house," Alex continued her story, not leaving out any details, "and we talked and talked, and then he carried me to his room," Alex concluded.

"That's so funny!" Journey interjected, looking over at Alex through her Gucci shades, "I think I remember Cain carrying me last night," she chuckled, replaying her romp with Cain in her head. "Girl, it must be the water out here! It brings out the sexy beast in a man!"

The women laughed like they were back in their college days.

"Well, I hate to bring up Sway right now, but if he is anything like his child, I can see why you keep him in your pocket for those times in need," Journey said in a completely satisfied tone.

"Please, stop! I don't want to hear the details of that part of your night with Cain," Alex laughed and held up her hand. "You know he is like a son to me!"

Journey shook her head. "No, you have to let me just tell you this, I woke up this morning to him massaging my feet," she chimed letting Alex know that Cain had won her over with that move. "It was so romantic Alex," Journey said leaning back.

"That does sound nice," Alex said impressed at Cain's bedroom skills. "Not even Sway has ever done anything like that!"

"Speaking of Sway, are you going to let him know about Derek?" Journey asked.

"He does not need to know about Derek, yet," Alex flatly replied. "It seems that everything is working out because Derek doesn't intend on introducing himself to the guys until later on during the process. That gives me time to see how far this thing between he and I go, and if it turns out to be nothing, well … , then nothing will have to be said," Alex spoke as if it were a well thought out plan.

"That makes sense," Journey agreed.

They soaked in the sun for a few hours more before running up to the suite to shower, change for brunch, and do a little shopping and sight seeing. Cain again, passed on the shopping excursion because he knew he would have more fun right where he was. They synchronized their watches, agreed to meet Cain later that evening for dinner and to take a final run through the infamous Vegas strip before they parted ways.

****

Alex made a mental note to thank Cain for asking the front desk to give them a wake up call as she rolled out of her bed, and tried to stop the floor from spinning beneath her feet. The enormous hangover was due to the threesome indulging in mouth-watering sushi and hot sake at *Nobu* in the *Hard Rock Café*. They took in a show, and sat through the entire *Cirque du soleil* performance in pure awe. They club hopped for a couple of hours before settling in at *The Bank Nightclub* in their hotel. The club provided a mature vibe, and allowed Journey and Alex to blend in with the over twenty-five crowd. The three of them partied hard into the wee hours of the morning, and Alex was reminded again that she was truly a lightweight when it came to drinking with Journey and Cain. She was also grateful that she booked afternoon flights. She shuffled to the bathroom and it felt like she was moving a lot faster than she actually was.

Journey stood in the doorway looking at her pitiful friend and could not hold back the laughter. "You know you can't hang with me," Journey chuckled and walked over to help her friend. "I thought you learned that in college."

"Shhh.., Journey you are talking way too loud," Alex grabbed her head with one hand and shooed her friend away with the other. "I am going to be fine, I just need to hop in the shower and regroup."

"You need to regroup alright!" Journey laughed. "While you regroup, I will take your bags out here, so Sampson can take them downstairs to the car. You have thirty minutes!" Journey sang as she grabbed one of Alex's overnight bags, and left the room.

Alex stepped into the shower and allowed the warm water to wash over her body. She stood there for a full five minutes before picking up the loofa sponge. When Journey told Alex she had thirty minutes, they both knew that actually meant a solid hour, so Alex took her time.

****

Alex waltzed out of the hotel renewed, rejuvenated, and ready to go home. She accomplished more than she expected to in Sin City, and now she was a witness as to why Las Vegas held that moniker. Although she thought about Derek all day while she and Journey hung out, she did not want to appear desperate, so she did not call him and she purposely turned off her cell phone. When she and Derek parted ways the morning before, she promised him she would call him before she left. Due to her hard partying, it was apparent that she would have to call him from the airport. Both Cain and Journey were inside of the car, sipping on orange juice and patiently waiting with the car door open, while the driver stuffed their luggage into the trunk. Just as Alex was about to slip into the back seat of the limousine, she could see flashing headlights out of her peripheral vision. She looked to the right of her, and noticed that is was Derek. The hard top was on his Benz but she could see his sexy grin from the distance between them, and suddenly she had thoughts of staying one more night.

"I'll be right back guys," Alex said, turning toward the shiny white Mercedes and walking towards it.

"Hurry up!" Journey yelled, stretching her neck to see who had captured her friend's attention.

"Who's that?" Cain asked as he looked out of the back window at Alex as she slid into the gleaming ride.

Journey made a quick decision to mind her own business, and said, "um, I'm not sure Sweety, let's shut the door to wait for her." She gently turned Cain's head so that he faced her.

Derek watched Alex quickly saunter toward his car in her nicely fitted jogging suit and her hair pulled back in a ponytail. She looked like a teenager. Once again, she impressed him with her ability to transform from an astute business woman to a girl from around the way. He was feeling something that he had never felt before. He watched her every move as she pulled the passenger door open and plopped down in the seat and looked over at Derek.

"Hey, what are you doing here? I was going to call you when I got to the airport," she questioned him, but he could see it in her smile that she was happy he was there.

"I had to see you before you jetted," he replied and leaned in to kiss her cheek. "I did not see or speak to you all day yesterday, so I had to check you before you left me," he smiled, showing his sexy dimple, causing her to melt into the white soft leather seat.

"How nice of you. I would have called, but we were out all night, actually we just woke up like an hour ago," she smiled and leaned in to give him a quick peck on the lips.

"I know you probably have to get to the airport. Let me take you. We can follow the limo," he said it as if it was a statement and not a question.

She looked into his deep brown eyes and could see that she would probably miss her plane if she sat and debated with him as to why he could not take her, so she agreed. She pulled her cell phone out from her bag, dialed Journey's number, and told her to pull off.

"Driver, you can go," Journey yelled to the driver. "That Mercedes behind you is going to follow us," she commanded as she pressed the button to roll up the divider that separated her from the driver.

"Who the fuck is that in the car with Alex?" Cain was behaving like the protective son.

"It's OK," Journey confirmed. His machismo was turning Journey on. "He's just one of the guys who will be working on your dad's deal. They probably have some last minute loose ends to tie up. But look at it as a great opportunity for us to say good-bye," she concluded by rolling over onto his lap so she could straddle him.

They both realized that this weekend was a one time only experience, and once they boarded their planes, their lives would return to normalcy. Cain would be back in school, taking finals and preparing for graduation, while Journey would mostly likely have to degrade herself in some form to make amends with her husband for hanging up on him, and flying out to Las Vegas in the first place. They stared at each other both knowing what was going to happen next.

Cain cupped her firm butt and placed his full lips over hers. He suddenly became determined to ensure that he sent her home with a smile on her face. He gently tugged at the string to her jogging pants to loosen them.

"We don't have anything," Journey whispered, but did not stop raiding Cain with soft kisses all over his face and neck.

"And, I can't promise to keep any promises," Cain added while sliding his hand underneath her panties.

"Then we have to be extra careful," Journey softly whispered in his ear while simultaneously unsnapping his jeans, so that his growing manhood could be released.

****

Derek gave himself quite a large distance between his car and the limousine. There were several cars between them, and it was becoming hard for Alex to keep an eye on the limousine.

"It's OK," he said, glancing over at her and touching her hand. "I know where the airport is," he laughed.

"I'm sorry," Alex chuckled at her behavior. "Of course you do," she stated and leaned back into the seat to relax.

"So, Miss Alex did you enjoy your first visit to Las Vegas?" he asked, hoping she more than enjoyed it.

"I had a wonderful time! Thank you for your hospitality. I look forward to coming back."

"I'm glad to hear that because I'm already missing you," he said in a sexy manner.

"I will be back soon," Alex responded, trying not to show how his words had flattered her.

"That reminds me!" Derek said hitting the steering wheel. "Hank told me to tell you that he emailed you the final documents."

"That sounds great. I will check my emails on the plane," Alex replied, making a mental note.

Derek looked over at Alex, and wanted to veer off the upcoming exit and take her back to his place. There was something about her that made him not only want to do right, but he wanted to do better. He remembered often planning his life while he spent those sixty-eight months in prison. When the lights shut down at eleven o'clock every night, and after his burly cellmate Big Will would dose off with a steady snore, Derek would sit up in his top bunk and stare out of the small caged window at the black sky. During the night hours he would vividly paint a different life. He would always revert to the age twenty-nine when he chose greed and power over loyalty and friendship. Derek's love for money quickly landed him in the company of men who loved money more than he did, and who had never heard of loyalty. Those bastards wasted little time snitching on him when they got hemmed up for drug trafficking thru New Jersey. On the very first day of being booked at Riker's Island, he realized that nothing is more important than a man's freedom. And, now, sitting in a brand new Mercedes with a gorgeous woman beside him, he was determined to do whatever it took to never have it taken away from him again.

"I wish you could stay with me for one more day," Derek said as he veered off the exit toward the airport.

"A part of me wishes I could stay one more day too, but I have to admit that I am missing my little girl," Alex said thinking about what Stevie was getting into back at home.

"I bet," Derek said, looking at her honey soaked skin radiate against the sunrays that poured through the open car windows.

Derek followed the airport departure signs and quickly caught up to the limousine. He pulled his car up to the curb behind the limousine, and shifted the gear to park.

"When will I see you again?" he asked, not wasting any of the precious time he had left with her.

"Soon. I am sure things will move quickly once the acquisition agreements are signed," Alex answered, slipping into business mode.

"What's going on here," he interjected, pointing his finger back and forth between them, "has nothing to do with business, remember?"

Their eyes locked in an intense gaze, and they leaned into one another until their lips touched. She could feel his sexual energy penetrate her through her body. She slowly pulled back and grabbed onto the door handle.

"Yes, I remember now," Alex smiled. "And, if you keep reminding me I am going to miss my plane."

"That would be cool, but I would not want to keep you from your daughter," he said politely.

Her smile widened at his sincerity and she leaned into to kiss his lips softly. "You are really sweet," Alex whispered.

Just before she could pull back again, he reached for her arm and held it tightly. They kissed each other with such passion that they did not notice they had captivated an audience. Journey, Cain and the limousine driver stood on the curb, watching the romantic couple trying to tear themselves apart from one another. As the driver placed their luggage onto the curbside check-in cart, Journey was witnessing Cain's growing anger.

"Yo Journey, go get her," Cain demanded.

Journey jumped at the command without any hesitation. She raced over to the sparkling white car, and knelt down beside the open passenger window.

"Um, excuse me!" Journey said clearing her throat, "Miss Alex, we have a plane to catch."

Derek and Alex continued kissing through Journey's attempt to interrupt, and stopped just as she completed her sentence. Alex looked over her shoulder at her friend.

"OK, give me a minute. You guys can go ahead inside. I am right behind you," Alex rambled as she motioned Journey away.

She and Derek watched Journey and Cain walk through the glass doors of the airport before turning their attention back to one another.

"I am going to call you later, OK," Derek whispered.

"You better," Alex whispered back and pushed the car door open this time. "But not too late, you know you are three hours behind me."

She slowly slid out of the plush car, and gently closed the door. Alex looked back at him as she walked away.

"Get home safely," he called out of the open window as he watched her disappear beyond the reflection of the glass doors.

Damn, she's all I need, he thought as he pulled off into the oncoming traffic and headed toward the expressway.

Chapter 16

The Girls ... back home
Me, Myself, and I

After going through the airport security checkpoint, Journey and Alex walked with Cain to his terminal. The women had a few minutes to spare since their flight was not due to leave for another hour. As the three of them approached Cain's destination, Alex tried to give Cain a hug good-bye but noticed his lackluster response. With a furrowed brow, she grabbed Cain by the arms and held them tightly.

"Cain, what's the matter?" Alex asked, not realizing that he just watched her kissing a stranger.

"Yo, Alex, I am not trying to get in your business, but who was homeboy in the Benz?"

Alex immediately realized that he must have been standing there when Journey interrupted her passionate moment with Derek. She was so wrapped up in the kiss she did not realize that there were other spectators besides Journey. "Oh," Alex stammered, "he's ... a friend." She did not want to get into detail, nor did she feel she really had to. She was almost positive that Cain had encountered at least one of his father's "friends" during his visits, so she felt that he surely should not judge her.

Cain looked at Alex with disappointing eyes. The scene he had just witnessed caught him completely off guard. He never expected any man to kiss her that way except for his father; despite the fact that he knew that Alex and his father were technically not a couple.

"Look Alex, I am sorry. I can't judge you," Cain said forcing a smile. "That shit just threw me for a loop, that's all." Cain tried to let it go. He hugged Alex again, this time with love and conviction. He knew that he was in no position to be upset with anyone. He had just spent the weekend with another man's wife, and was secretly looking forward to seeing her again soon.

Alex stepped up on her tiptoes and kissed him on his cheek. "We cool right?" she asked as she pulled back to look him in the eye.

"Always and forever," Cain smiled, and the look in his eyes told her that he was sincere.

They hugged again and Alex turned to walk away. She stopped in front of Journey, and told her to hurry up so they could catch their plane.

"I know girl," Journey responded, looking over Alex's shoulder at Cain. "This won't take long. We already said good-bye in the limo *if* you know what I mean."

Alex shook her head at her friend, happy that she too, enjoyed her first encounter with Sin City – Las Vegas. Alex continued walking toward the newsstand to buy a few magazines for the plane ride home, and to kill time while Journey parted ways with her weekend fantasy fulfiller.

Journey walked up to Cain and her eyes suddenly began to tear up. Her emotions overwhelmed her as she thought about their perfect weekend.

"Thank you Cain," she said as she reached up and wrapped her arms around his neck. "You were right, you showed me a wonderful time. It was just what I needed," she concluded, meaning that in more ways than one.

"I'm glad to be of service to you," he whispered in her ear and kissed her earlobe at the same time.

He felt her whole body tremble in his arms as he held onto her in the middle of the boarding section of the airport. They ignored the passersby as the two of them publicly displayed their affection for one another by kissing good-bye for the hundredth time. After a few moments, their lips parted and Cain wiped the tear from Journey's eye, just as it fell onto her smooth cheek.

"Don't do that," he said softly. "I'm going to be back in New York in a couple of months; for good," he reminded her.

"And, I feel good about that, but . . . ," Journey smiled weakly. "That still does not change things for me," she solemnly said, reminding him of her regretful state of matrimony.

They both knew that she was reluctant to return to her volatile marriage. She had no idea what to expect when she returned to Harlem in less than seven hours, and fear started to settle back into her psyche. Even in his absence, Cain could see in her eyes the influence of Tiny's intimidation.

"Who knows, things might change by the time I come back," Cain said, hinting that she should not stay with Tiny if she was not happy.

They hugged one last and final time, and slowly stepped back from one another as a voice echoed through the speakers announcing that Cain's flight was boarding. Journey watched him as he fell in line behind the other passengers, and disappeared through the tunnel connecting the plane to the building. They decided not to exchange phone numbers because Journey did not want to make matters worse at home. From the first night of their lustful tryst they solemnly made a pact that what happens between them in Vegas, shall remain in Vegas.

Journey wiped her eyes and breathed in deeply, as she watched the gate close to Cain's flight. She was crying because her fun was over, and because her misery was about to begin again. *I have to make some serious decisions when I get home*, she thought as she caught up to her friend at the bustling newsstand, and purchased some light reading material for the ride home.

****

The take off out of the Las Vegas airport was smooth, which Alex hoped was a clear indication of the rest of the flight home. She scheduled for a car to pick them up since she neglected to make arrangements with Sway to meet her at *LaGuardia Airport*. The women settled into their plush seats in the business class section of the airplane and simultaneously pulled out their magazines.

"Well, I guess you and Cain hit it off this weekend," Alex blurted out as she thumbed through the *Essence* magazine.

"I guess we did," Journey smiled, looking over at Alex, "we had a really good time, but that is all that it was. We both knew from the beginning that after the weekend, we would have to come back to reality.

"What are you going to do?" Alex asked, suddenly becoming concerned for her friend.

"I want a divorce," Journey said as though she had some time during her fun-filled weekend to give the matter some critical thought. "We could never go back to what we had in the beginning. Once third parties start filtering through the marriage, it might as well be over," Journey continued, "I mean it's not like the relationship you have with Sway. Your non-exclusivity is consensual, and I can respect that, but Alex, we are married. He made a vow to me, and he broke it first. Now all bets are off," Journey concluded, appreciating Cain a little more.

There was nothing Alex could say. She agreed with Journey one hundred percent because infidelity was her biggest fear. Deep in her heart, Alex always felt that if she ever conceded to Sway's pursuit, that one day she would find him in a compromising position with one of his many women, and regret sharing her love with him.

Nonetheless, now there is Derek, a man who swooped down into her life out of nowhere, and managed, within such a short time, to loosen a few of the bricks that encased her heart. From the onset, Derek spoke all of the words she wanted to hear from a man. He told her that he was ready to discover that one woman who would support him, and grow old with him. He was ready to have children and create a family of his own. He assured her that he had out-grown the days of rotating women, and maintaining notches on his imaginary sex belt. He wanted a monogamous relationship with a woman he could cherish. He was truly too good to be true.

"I just have to do it and get it over with," Journey stated, interrupting Alex in her sidebar thought.

"Huh," Alex was coming back into the conversation. "Oh yes, the sooner the better. You can stay with me if you want. You don't even have to go home tonight," Alex suggested, secretly hoping Journey would consider not ever going back to Tiny. She knew that Journey did not tell him that she was going to Vegas, and she vaguely remembered while they were partying, Journey mentioning to Alex that she hung up on Tiny the night before.

"Nope, I am not leaving my house Alex. You and I found that place together … , remember? And, when the landlord offered to sell it, he came directly to me and said he wanted to sell it to only me. You know he always liked us because we kept the place up. Not to mention, that he never warmed up to Tiny. And, for good reason! That is my brownstone," Journey demanded, raising her voice loud enough to cause a few glares.

"OK," Alex said patting her friend on the leg, "I hear you, but when you get home tonight, if he starts with any bullshit, leave right away and call me."

"I promise," Journey said trying to suppress the gloom that lurked in her near future.

"Now, it looks like you and mystery man made a little love connection this weekend too!" Journey exclaimed, turning in her seat to face Alex, so she could hear all of the details.

"He is something else," Alex began, "and he is the best kisser I ever had."

Alex proceeded to tell Journey how he was finally burned out from chasing women, and was ready to settle down and have a family. That alone, impressed Alex because that meant he was looking for one woman to be his only woman. A part of her still wanted to know the feeling of being in that position. She looked at Journey, and for a moment envied her, for even in Journey's awful situation, there once was a time when her husband held her in such high regard that she was his only one. Alex concluded her weekend experience with telling Journey that he promised to call her tonight, and she was already anxious to see him again.

"Girl, we haven't been in the air for a full hour, and you already missing that man!" Journey laughed at her own rhetoric.

"I know, I am not sure what he is doing to me," Alex laughed, fanning herself with the magazine, "I guess it's because he is not my usual type. He's done time and, has tattoos *everywhere* … ," she paused.

"But that is kind of sexy!" They both said in unison, looking at each other and both thinking about Tupac.

"Dang! You are right Alex, he does not sound like your type at all. And, he is a partner in this major deal?" Journey asked trying to figure out how this type of brother fit into the million-dollar equation.

"Girl, it's a long story and to be honest, I don't even know half of it, but both he and Mr. Mitken appear to be totally legit, and this venture seems solid, so I am prone to believe that this brother is just really trying to live right, and turn his life around. Who am I not to give him the benefit of the doubt?" Alex rhetorically asked.

"Well, I can say that he is a cutie," Journey said thinking back to when she interrupted the two of them.

"He kind of reminds me of that actor … Michael Jai White. You know the fine one from Connecticut."

"He does!" Alex agreed relieved that she was finally able to place his face. "All weekend, I was trying to picture who he reminded me of. Yes, that is who he looks like for sure.

"So … ," Journey continued to pry. "Did you or didn't you?"

"Come on Journey, you know me!" Alex blushed.

"Hell … , that means no then," Journey burst into laughter.

"Shut up!" Alex shouted, almost embarrassed for being such a square. "Actually if you must know, Miss Nosey, he was nothing short of a true gentleman. He did not want to seduce me because he wanted me to know how serious he was about getting to *know* me," she concluded and placed her hand over her heart.

"Oh how sweet! I bet poor Sway is going to have to work overtime tonight to relieve all of that frustration you managed to build up over this weekend," Journey managed to say in between her laughter.

"You really do know me!" Alex joined in, laughing uncontrollably.

****

The flight home was just as smooth as the take off in Vegas and Alex was grateful for that. She made a mental note not to leave the ground at least for another two months. Her mental stability was wavering, and she needed to literally become grounded again. She had flown almost around the world in a month, and her body was beginning to feel the affects of jet setting, as she and Journey got comfortable in the back of the limousine. She pulled her cell phone out of her bag, and dialed

Sway's number. It was only 8:00 p.m., so she knew he was not home yet. She was hoping he was at her place waiting for her. It rang a few times before she heard his sexy voice filter through her ears.

"What's up, you made it home?" Sway asked in one breath.

"Yeah, Journey and I are in the car now. He is about to drop her off. Where are you? I want to see you … ," Alex said lowering her voice.

"Um," Sway interjected, "right now is not a good time," he said into the phone while keeping an eye on his dinner date seated across from him.

"Excuse me?" Alex felt a wave of rejection jolt through her body.

"An old friend is passing through, and we are having dinner." Sway did not lie. "And afterwards, we will probably go have a drink," he said feeling bad that he could not accommodate his lover tonight but at the same time unable to break his gaze from Stephanie's lovely milk chocolate face. "I will come by in the morning, and we will have breakfast while we go over the new business proposal." Sway's speech was straight forward, almost as if he was talking to his business partner, Romeo instead of the mother of his daughter.

Alex pulled the phone away from her ear to look at it. She could not believe he was trying to play games with her. At first she did not realize the 'old friend' was a woman but the change in the tone of his voice when he mentioned meeting in the morning, clearly indicated to Alex that Sway was on a date. *He is so smooth*, Alex thought. She wondered if his date was also smart enough to know that a woman was on the other end of the phone. Slightly disappointed in her lover, Alex put the tiny gadget back up to her ear. "A breakfast meeting sounds good. Call me in the morning," Alex said flatly, giving Sway no indication of how she was feeling. She hung up without saying good-bye.

He hated that about her. He never knew when he tugged at her heartstrings. Her ability to behave so coldly both aggravated him and turned him on at the same time.

"Well, what did he say?" Journey asked.

"He's tied up tonight, some woman I am sure," Alex huffed.

A small part of her was extremely jealous of the woman who was spending the night with her lover. But a larger part of her was angry with herself for always settling on being number one, yet never demanding to be the *only one* . She was worth more than what she had become content with over the years. Although Sway was an awesome father, an incredible lover, and the most generous provider, the bottom line was that he also held an insatiable appetite for women, and Alex knew that from the day she met him. She could not expect him to change for her, especially when it was apparent that he was not yet ready to change for himself. Alex leaned back in the black soft leather seat and closed her eyes.

"Whatever," was all she could muster from her physically and now emotionally drained body.

****

When the limousine pulled up to the curb in front of Journey's brownstone, both she and Alex were relieved to see that there weren't any lights on. Journey let out a loud sigh of relief, and opened the door before the driver could, and jumped out of the car. She was tired, worn out and wanted to sleep in her own bed. She prayed that God would keep Tiny away from her tonight so she could rest. And, a large part of her sinfully wanted to fall asleep uninterrupted, so she could reminisce about her wild weekend with Cain. The driver helped Journey carry her luggage into the dark home, before shuffling back to the car to make his way to New York's suburbia. Journey thanked him and closed the heavy door behind him. She filled both her arms with bags and lugged all of them into her bedroom at once. Her house smelled of fresh cut roses, but she did not see any in a vase displayed on the kitchen or living room tables.

"He would not have been that thoughtful, especially after how I treated him this weekend," she chuckled out loud to herself as she turned on the light in her bedroom.

Her bed was freshly made with crisp clean linens, and her bedroom was oddly too clean. *Tiny would have never cleaned up after himself all weekend*, Journey's mind began to make accusations. She tried to shake her negative thoughts. She had not been home five minutes, and already her spirit was breaking. She could feel that something was not right, but could not place it. She peeled off her clothes, and hopped in the shower. Her good conscious kept repeating that Tanya was in her house while she washed over her body with the creamy shower gel. And, her good conscious was right. Had Journey taken a morning flight oppose to an evening flight, she would have found Tanya scrambling eggs on her stove, and having sex with her husband on her kitchen countertop. Journey wrestled with her thoughts and tried to outweigh the negative with the positive. She had finally accepted the fact that she and Tiny would have to part ways, and she was feeling strong enough to tell him. That in itself was the only positive she needed to focus on.

Journey quickly threw on some flannel pajamas once she showered and brushed her teeth. As she gargled mouth rinse staring at her reflection in the mirror, she noticed a lacy garment hanging out of the wicker hamper behind her. She spat the rinse into the sink, and quickly turned around as if the garment would disappear if she moved any slower. She walked over to the hamper and as her eyes focused in on the lavender laced piece of cloth, her heart began to race down into the pit of her stomach.

"No he didn't!" she said out loud as she reached for the pair of panties. "These are not my fucking underwear!" she screamed at the top of her lungs.

Anger quickly filtered through Journey's body as her breathing became heavy. Journey held the petite sized panties up into the bathroom light and examined them. She could not believe that she was standing in her own home holding Tanya's funky undergarment. Tiny had finally stepped over the line. She could never look in his eyes again without feeling betrayed and used. She wanted out. Journey balled the panties up in her hand and squeezed them as tight as she could, while imagining that they were Tanya's neck. She walked around her apartment, turning on all of the lights as she inspected every inch of her home.

"That bastard!" she huffed as she slid on her rubber gloves to shuffle through the trashcan in the kitchen.

She immediately found the empty box to a three-pack of Trojan condoms and her eyes began to water. She was not upset with Tiny for having sex with someone else. Her trip to Vegas made it easier for her to receive that blow, but she was enraged that he had so little respect for her that he would have sex with someone in her bed; most of all her nemesis Tanya. She wanted to cry. She wanted to fight. She wanted it to be over. Journey threw the empty box back into the trashcan, and scurried back into her bedroom.

"It's over!" she said it loudly as if Tiny was in the room. "I refuse to live like this when I know I don't have to."

She climbed into her cozy bed with the balled up panties in her tightly held fist and stared at the ceiling thinking about what was going to happen when she and Tiny confronted one another. A tear slowly formed and rolled down the side of her face as she tried to mentally prepare her body for the beating she may have to endure in order to be set free.

****

Alex opened the door to her home and could smell the sweet aroma of fresh baked apple pie. *That is why I am so thick;* she thought as her nose lead her straight to the kitchen.

"Hello! I'm home!" Alex chimed as she entered the kitchen where she found her darling daughter and lovely mother sitting at the kitchen table having apple pie alamode.

"Hi Mommy!" Stevie screamed at the top of her lungs with a mouth full of ice cream.

"Hey Baby Girl," Marie sang, scraping her bowl trying to gather the last remains of her delicious desert.

Alex quickly grabbed a bowl from the cabinet and the ice cream from the freezer. She warmed up her slice of pie in the microwave and prepared her treat. She sat next to her daughter where they ate their deserts, and talked about their weekend. A half an hour had passed and Stevie's ice cream had become a thick milky substance by the time Alex decided they had enough. Alex scooped Stevie up and carried her to the bathroom to bathe her and get her ready for bed. She missed her baby. Stevie picked out the book she wanted Alex to read, crawled into bed, and tucked herself in. Alex had only read to page four before she noticed that Stevie had dosed off. Just as Alex was folding the corner of the page down and placing the book on Stevie's nightstand, the phone rang. Alex dropped the book onto the plush carpeted floor, and rushed to her room to answer it before it rang again.

"Hello," she quickly said into the receiver.

"Hey you," the sound of Derek's voice caused her to smile.

"Hey you … yourself," Alex said softly into the phone and sat on her bed.

"Are you busy?" he asked.

"Not too busy to talk to you," she replied laying back on her bed feeling like she was back in high school again.

"I miss you," Derek said with a frown. "I am going to have to make arrangements to see you sooner than you think," he warned.

"I'm not going anywhere," Alex flirted.

"Those words are music to my ears," he chimed.

They continued to talk with hints of sexual innuendos laced throughout their two hour long conversation that eventually ended with Alex promising to call him after her morning meeting. Alex hung up the phone and stood in the middle of her room and looked into the self-standing full-length mirror to admire herself. Derek had managed to remove the disappointing feeling of rejection that Sway had instilled in her earlier that evening, by letting her know that if given the chance, he would take advantage of the opportunity to show her how it felt to be the only woman in a man's life. They both acknowledged that their happenstance meeting turned whirlwind romance was happening at an unbelievably rate of speed, but Derek told her that if she had spent over five years in prison, she would understand his natural sense of urgency. For him he had five years of his life to make up for, and therefore, precious time, he did not have to waste. She relished in their conversation as she replayed it in her head, while she prepared for bed. It turned out to not be a bad night after all. She climbed into bed and snuggled the soft pillow lying next to her.

****

Alex thought she heard the doorbell ring, but looked at the clock on her nightstand, which read 5:45 a.m. in red florescent lighting, and rolled back over to get a few more winks of sleep. The chime went off again.

"Who in the hell … ," Alex said, jumping up from her bed and trotting down the steps in hurry to answer the door.

She was moving so fast, she failed to ask who it was, and instead, she grabbed the *Louisville Slugger* bat she kept in the umbrella bin and opened the door.

"Yo hold up!" Sway said grabbing the bat while it was in full swing. "You ain't even gonna ask who is it? Just come out swinging!" Sway said, laughing and pushing both Alex and the bat back inside the house.

"Sway! It's not even six o'clock in the damn morning. We are all still sleeping! I thought you were on a date?" she said sarcastically as she tried to walk back upstairs to her room.

Sway closed the door behind him, and pulled her back off the second step and turned her around to face him.

"I never said I was on date," he said flatly.

"You did not have to," Alex smiled at him, "I know you Steven McCoy, better than you think," she said, trying to pry away from his tight grasp. "I thought when you said that we would see each other in the morning, you meant regular morning hours. Besides, you can't be done with your date already ..., it's not your style," she said trying to provoke him.

"Don't push me Alex," Sway's tone shifted.

It was clear that she was pushing his buttons. Their words were bouncing off the hollow walls in the large foyer as their voices rose in octaves as they spoke.

"Look Sway, I know how we do, I was not mad. I'm good ... , I mean we are good. So, you can go back to your friend, and come back at a decent hour to have our *business* meeting. You did not have to come here this early. Don't allow guilt to eat at you like that," Alex said unable to suppress her anger any longer.

She was a woman who was used to getting her way, and they both knew that. And, even though a small part of her felt special knowing that she was the only woman who he felt he had to keep happy, after her weekend in Vegas, Alex felt like she was finally ready to expect more from a man as well as in a relationship.

The callus attitude she conveyed, made it clear as to why Sway stood before her at this ridiculous time in the morning. He wanted to make everything right again, despite the fact that she still wasn't the only woman in his life.

"Look Alex," Sway began to ramble with his grasp becoming tighter. "You did not call me to tell me when you were coming home, shit you did not call me at all after we talked Friday night, so when Stephanie called and said she was in town, we hooked up for dinner." His honesty was something that Alex always appreciated in Sway. It separated him from the boys.

"Then why are you here?"

"Because you know here is where I would rather be," he said in a low sexy voice as he lifted Alex so that her legs wrapped around his waist.

She loved it when Sway took control in the heat of their love spats. He carried her into the living room, sat her down on the sofa, and hovered over her.

"Where's Mama Marie and my baby?" he asked in a whisper, leaning into her and grabbing her head with both hands and running his fingers through her soft hair.

"Sleeping," was all she could say in a low meek tone.

His large masculine fingers massaged her scalp and caused her body to collapse in total relaxation. The room was dark but had a natural soft glow from the sun rising, which created enough light so that they could see each other's faces. Silence hovered over them as they stared at each other while caressing each other in areas of their bodies that generated intense heat and anticipation.

Sway slid Alex's nightshirt over her head to view her perky breasts. He missed her. He watched her as she eagerly pulled at his belt to unzip his pants. She gently grabbed for his growing member and wanted to see it. Alex held it in her hand and caressed it gently as Sway pulled back and knelt down before her to part her legs. Alex leaned back into the soft sofa cushion and closed her eyes. Sway continued to provide oral pleasure to Alex as her mind kept rewinding to her night with Derek. She tried to shake the memory of someone else thousands of miles away. For the first time since meeting Sway, she found herself thinking of another man during their sexual exploration. Alex opened her eyes, and felt conflicted over stopping or letting Sway continue his attempt to please her.

She grabbed his head and slowly pulled it back. "We have to stop," she managed to say but still felt unsure.

"What's wrong," Sway looked at her, disappointed that she had stopped him from performing one of the moves he does best.

"I think I heard Mommy," Alex lied. She could not tell him that they had to stop because her mind was filled with the vivid image of another man.

Sway stood up quickly and tried to shake off his erection. "I don't hear anything," he said, listening to dead silence. "We can finish this upstairs," he suggested, feeling overly excited.

"Um, I think we shouldn't," Alex said, grabbing her nightshirt and pulling it over her head. "Stevie will be up soon and you know once she sees you, she's going to want you all to herself. Plus, we have plenty of ground to cover for this Vegas venture, so maybe it was a good thing you came early so we can get started," Alex concluded, turning on her professionalism, which always commanded Sway's attention.

Nothing stood in the way of Sway and his money; not even sex. He looked at her feeling slightly disappointed, but zipped up his pants and fastened his belt before walking toward the kitchen.

"You have a point," he said as he pulled out two coffee cups from the cabinet. "I will grab us some coffee and meet you in your office."

Alex released a sigh of relief and smiled at her self for being able to think of such good excuse so quickly.

****

Journey was in a deep sleep when she was awakened by the thunderous sound of heavy footsteps walking around in the kitchen. Before she could open her eyes to make sure it was Tiny, her body went into shock as the combination of ice cubes and ice cold water splashed against her body. She quickly sat up and screamed at the top of her lungs.

"Tiny! What are you doing?"

"What the fuck am I doing?" he roared as he dropped the bucket and walked closer to the bed.

"The question is what the fuck are you doing? You think you gonna lay around and sleep all day after partying all fuckin' weekend! You ain't leave no food here or nothing!" he ranted as he pulled her by the hair and dragged her out of the bed.

He pulled her body through the excess cold water that had fallen onto the hardwood floor. Journey tried to grab his hand and pry it away from her scalp. She could feel the handful of hair he tightly gripped in his hand, tearing from their follicles in her scalp. Tears began to stream down her face.

"Tiny, please stop!" she begged as he pulled her to her feet and wrapped his massive hand around her neck.

"Now you beggin'," he laughed. "The other night when you were wit' yo' girl, you thought you could talk shit, and hang up on a muthafucka!"

He slammed her up against the wall where the phone hung. Journey thought for sure when her back banged up against the phone console, her spine had shattered, but she could still feel her legs.

"Please, Tiny, stop before you kill me!" Journey grabbed his hand and made a weak attempt to pry it from around her neck. "I was drinking that night, I swear!"

"So, that is supposed to make it alright that you fuckin' hung up on me! You get around that fuckin' Alex and you forget that you have a husband at home!" he conveniently blamed Alex now for his abusive behavior.

Journey continued to pry at his hand. She was not going to allow Tiny to kill her without fighting back. However, the more she tried, the tighter his grip became.

"Tiny, stop! You are hurting me!" she screamed. "You promised that you would never hit me!"

"I ain't hit yo' ass … yet!" he screamed back. "Don't you ever leave me again like that," he demanded.

Journey looked at him as those words parted his mouth and a wave of courage overwhelmed her. She could not believe that he was making demands like that after having another woman in her home -- in her bed.

"Why? It's not like you missed me," she stated as a matter of fact.

"What? What the fuck did you just say?" He lifted her a few inches in the air by her neck. "What the fuck is that supposed to mean? You ain't ever leavin' me again. Are you crazy? You are my wife," he said it as if to remind her.

"You don't love me anymore," Journey gasped as tears flowed freely from her face, "or you would not be doing this."

Tiny looked at his pleading wife, and her helplessness fed his ego and the sense of empowerment came over him. "You got it wrong baby," his tone softened. "I do all of this because I love you. We have built a business together; I have too much invested in your sweet little ass."

"I know you don't love me, Tiny," she wept while staring in his evil eyes. "Because I know she was here."

Tiny's anger was transforming into rage right before Journey's eyes but she had decided the night before after finding Tanya's underwear that no matter what, she and Tiny had to end their unhealthy relationship at any cost.

Upset with himself for obviously leaving a clue for Journey to find, Tiny decided to take it out on her. He hurled her against the other wall and she landed on the floor. He stomped over to her and pulled her up by her hair.

"You know *who* was here?" Tiny questioned, trying to play it off. He slammed her up against the wall and punched a hole through it inches away from her face.

Journey was terrified but remained immovable in confronting Tiny with his indiscretion.

"What … , what makes you think I had someone here?" he asked, not loosening his grip. Journey pointed to the bedroom and Tiny dragged her back through the wet floor and over to the soaked bed. He quickly released the fist full of her hair as soon as his eyes made contact with the lavender lacy panties that he had just taken off Tanya's small body less than twenty-four hours ago.

Tiny grabbed the sopping wet panties, and held them in his hand as he looked down at the floor at his wife, who was sitting in a small puddle of water, sobbing uncontrollably. A sudden wave of guilt enveloped Tiny's oversized body, and he began to feel like he shrinking into the size of a man who literally befitted the name Tiny. He was upset with Tanya for being so careless, but more importantly, he had finally been hit with the reality that he should be upset with himself. He stood over his broken beautiful wife, who not only cherished him, but she loved him for who he was. He was not the same man who promised to love and protect her. Tiny couldn't speak because he was at a loss for words. He was caught, and suddenly the tables had turned. He knew it was not a good idea to play house with Tanya all weekend, but he was so angry at Journey for leaving him. At the time, it felt right. He held onto the wet panties and walked out of the bedroom. He stood in the center of their living room, and shook his head. He never intended on the little fling with Tanya to take on a life of its own, and now he regretted it. He needed to fix it, he just did not know how. He needed to be alone.

Journey lifted her body off of the cold wet floor and started to peel out of her wet pajamas. She was no longer crying, but relieved that she finally had Tiny in a corner. She rushed to grab some dry clothes and slipped into them before Tiny could come back into the room. By the time she was dressed in dry pajamas bottoms, she heard the front door close.

"Tiny!" she yelled. She heard nothing.

The apartment was still. It was as if a violent commotion had not just occurred less than five minutes ago. Journey walked into the living room and noticed that Tiny had left. *Coward*, she thought. She was happy that he was gone, but kind of upset that he did not allow her the opportunity to berate and belittle him for his adulterous activities. Journey walked over to the door and doubled locked it before picking up the phone to call the locksmith.

May - 1999

Chapter 17

Alex

I'm So Into You

Mother's Day was only a few days away and Alex was inundated with tying up the loose ends for her mother's surprise party. She and her sisters decided to do something extra special for their mother this year since Marie's seventieth birthday was the following Tuesday. They invited a few of Marie's former co-workers from the elementary school she retired from and all of her church friends, including Mr. Hopkins from the senior choir, who had been showing an interest in their mother lately.

A few weeks after her return from Las Vegas, Alex found it a little hard to swallow when the phone rang, and a man who was not her father, asked to speak with her mother. When Alex asked Marie about the gentleman caller, Marie made light of their connection and brushed him off. Her evasiveness caused Alex to pull her tired body out of bed that following Sunday morning to attend church to see this Mr. Hopkins for herself.

Once service had ended Marie introduced Mr. Hopkins to Alex, and it was clear that the two seniors were fond of each other. Alex witnessed a certain smile on her mother's face that Sunday morning. The same smile that Marie had suppressed since Alex's father died. It was the kind of smile that you cannot control when you are around someone who makes your body feel warm inside. On the way home, Alex told her mom that she was OK with Marie doing whatever she needed to do to continue to smile the way she did when Mr. Hopkins approached them after service. Finally, since her father's death, Alex was pleased to see her mother happy again.

This surprise event was another way of showing Marie that her daughters agreed with her enjoying herself, and they were all too honored to make sure celebrating her seventieth birthday happened in the most grandiose way. With college graduations occurring every week during this month, followed by graduation parties, they were lucky to find a place to have the surprise party on such short notice. They booked the smaller ballroom at the *Amarante's Seacliff Restaurant* in New Haven, Connecticut. The restaurant sat on a small cliff along the edge of the Long Island Sound, and overlooked the passing boats as well as the other side of the city. The picturesque view of the city, once the sun sets on the horizon, and its rays reflected off of the glistening water was perfect for a night of celebration. Alex was thankful that Sway was able to pull a few strings. Coincidently, one of the sons of the owner of the restaurant is also a member of *The Candy Shop*. At first, Sway was apprehensive because Alex's party was set to take place during the same weekend of Cain's graduation in California. He hoped that Alex could join him and Stevie in California. Yet, on the other hand, he also loved Marie, and would do anything to please her. So, to make sure his absence was not missed, as his gift to Marie, Sway not only booked the space, but paid for the event and told Alex to spare no expense to ensure that her mother fully enjoyed the festivity.

The spring breeze had finally settled in, replacing the New England winter that had gone into hibernation for the next eight months. Alex looked forward to the weekend she and her sisters planned because it was earmarked with expectations of an eventful summer season ahead. She had just returned home from the cleaners and her backless dress hung flowingly under the clear plastic, giving an appearance of newness. The house was quiet, which meant that Stevie was taking her afternoon nap. Alex walked into the kitchen and was surprised by her mother, quietly sitting at the counter, reading the paper and savoring a cup of coffee. Alex flung open the refrigerator door to grab a bottle of water before going up to Stevie's room to finish packing for her trip to California.

"Hey Ma," Alex said, leaning in and giving her mother a peck on the cheek, "did Sway call?"

"Yes. He said he will be here around four to pick up Stevie. Their flight leaves at six forty-five."

"Sounds good, I am going to finish packing her things now," Alex replied.

Alex held her dry cleaning, the bottle of water and her pocketbook with one hand, and trotted up the steps. Once in her room, she kicked off her sneakers and slid her small feet into a pair of soft awaiting slippers. As she stood up, the cordless phone lying on her bed began to ring. She grabbed it and looked at the caller id. The number was unrecognizable. She allowed it to ring again as she tried to figure out who it could be. After the third ring she answered it with caution.

"Hello."

"Hey you." Derek's deep voice oozed through her phone line.

"Oh, hi. I didn't recognize the number," Alex responded, slightly taken aback. "Where are you?" she asked shaking her head in wonderment.

"I'm not far," Derek chuckled at his ability to always stump her.

"Derek, stop playing! You can't be in Vegas, so where are you," the smile on her face brightened her unlit room, and she began to feel warm inside.

"I'm in Mount Vernon," he said as a matter of fact. "I want to see you."

Alex's palms began to sweat as her nerves started to bundle. During the past six weeks their extraordinary relationship was only two-dimensional being kept alive with a few steamy emails filtering through daily telephone conversations, ranging from politics to music. She loved talking to Derek because he was blessed with not only street knowledge but he was also a secret intellect. Alex discovered during one of their numerous conversations that among other things, he enjoyed classical music, poetry, and was learning how to play the stock market. He told her those were some of the attributes he took away from prison. He also told her that while wasting precious time being incarcerated like a caged animal, he realized that life is about choices, and he vowed not to make any more choices that would jeopardize his freedom, or waste his time.

And, now here he was, less than twenty minutes away, and physically available for her to see his face and touch his chocolate smooth skin. She felt a tinge of nervousness coupled with a slight sense of urgency surge through her body.

"I want to see you too," Alex found herself saying without thinking twice about it.

She missed Derek: his eyes, his smile, his sexy dimple. She held the phone tightly as she tiptoed into her sleeping daughter's room to grab her suitcase. "What are you doing in Mount Vernon?" she asked, curious to know the reason behind his sudden arrival to the East Coast. She had just spoken to him the evening before, and he did not mention that he would be so close to her so soon.

"My sister called me late last night, and needed me to fly out here to help her move. She finally sold my Mom's house, and she is moving to Yonkers. Her sorry ass boyfriend is missing in action, so she called her big brother," Derek explained, intentionally omitting the real reason of his impromptu flight to New York.

Despite the legitimate reason for needing her brother to come home to help her move, his sister, Dory specifically needed Derek to come and retrieve the gun she found hidden in a box in the basement. She told him that if he did not come to get rid of it within twenty-four hours, she would bring it to the police station and hand it over to them. Derek could not allow her to do such a thing. He had forgotten all about the .38 special that he hid behind the boiler in his mother's basement years ago, and he certainly had forgotten how many bodies were connected to it. He had no choice but to pay the airline an outrageous amount to book the next flight into New York.

"That is so nice of you to look out for your sister like that. It says a lot about you," Alex said impressed and pleased at the same.

Derek smiled through the phone at her approval, and was satisfied with not telling her about the gun. She did not need to know about it because he was already in the process of getting rid of it. As they spoke, he was waiting for his cousin to come over to take it off his hands. "Thank you but getting back to why I called you. I want to see you," he reiterated.

"OK, but how are we going to make that possible when you are here helping your sister move?" Alex replied, blushing from ear to ear.

"I am going to be done here by tomorrow, but I am staying until Sunday. Can I pick you up tomorrow for dinner?"

"That sounds lovely but your timing is slightly off this weekend," Alex said disappointed. "Remember, I told you that I was spending this weekend in Connecticut? My sisters and I are giving my mom a surprise party tomorrow night and I am going up there early tomorrow so I can help with the final touches," Alex said with a frown.

Derek was so excited to surprise Alex, he had forgotten all about her weekend. He was slightly disappointed as well, but he was determined to spend some time with the one woman who had managed to capture his heart with just her voice and emails in a matter of weeks.

"I miss you Ma," he moaned into the phone, "I am not leaving here without seeing your face."

Alex could not contain the butterflies he filled her stomach with every time he professed his desire to see her. Derek made her feel like she was the only woman who could fulfill his need for affection. "You are too much," she smiled.

"When will you be back from Connecticut?"

"Actually, not until Sunday but that is Mother's Day, and my daughter and her father may have plans for me, but," she paused, "you could come to Connecticut with me," Alex suggested, trying to make their meeting possible.

"Then consider yourself stuck with me until Sunday," he said pleased that they will soon be together, and not caring about her tentative plans with her daughter's father. Alex explained to Derek from the onset that she and Stevie's father had a unique and special relationship, but she also assured him that they would never be a couple. Derek believed her, and never allowed insecurity or jealousy to overshadow his intention to make her his woman.

Alex proceeded to inform Derek of the weekend activities as she packed Stevie's suitcase with clothes and her favorite toys. She wrapped up their conversation with giving Derek directions to her house, and telling him what time to pick her up the next day. Just as she was making Derek promise to call her again before the night ended, which he did without any hesitation, she could hear the excitement in Marie's voice.

Marie answered the door, only to find Sway, greeting her with a bouquet of flowers.

"Oh Steven, these are just beautiful!" Marie said in awe of the beautiful floral arrangement flowing out of the large crystal vase.

"Not as beautiful as you are," Sway said, giving her a peck on the cheek, "Happy Mother's Day and happy birthday. I am sorry I won't be here to help you celebrate both."

"Honey, I understand. Cain graduating is a once in a lifetime event. I will have plenty birthdays and mother's days for us to celebrate," she said patting his shoulder as he walked through the threshold of the door.

"Is my Baby Girl ready to hit the road?" he asked, changing the subject before he spoiled the surprise planned for her by talking too much.

Alex and Derek said their good-byes, and she tried to calm down the butterflies fluttering around in her stomach. She quickly ran into her daughter's bedroom to dress her while she slept.

"We'll be right down!" Alex yelled, causing Stevie to open her eyes.

"I'm sorry sweetie," Alex said propping her limp daughter up so that she could pull her arm through the sleeve of her jacket. "Daddy's down stairs waiting for you. He's ready to take you on the plane!"

Stevie's eyes grew wide when she heard the word 'plane'. She had quite the opposite reaction to planes than her mother. She loved to fly. It was astounding to the three year old that she could fly like the birds in the sky. Feeling rejuvenated from both her nap, and knowing she was about to get on an airplane, Stevie helped her mother by moving faster. Within moments, Stevie was fully dressed, trotting down the steps, and jumping into her father's arms.

"Hi Daddy!" she said moving her curly locks from her eyesight with her little hands. "Let's go!" she demanded.

"You must have told her we were going on an airplane," Sway said, securely holding his daughter, and looking over at Alex.

"I did, sorry," Alex said with a sheepish grin.

"You owe me now, you know that right," he said walking up to her so close, he invaded her private space.

Alex giggled like a schoolgirl because she knew that he was referring to his ride to the airport. Once Stevie learned how to talk, the two of them agreed to never tell her about flying until they were pulling into the airport parking lot. Otherwise, Stevie would talk endlessly about airplanes the entire way.

"I said sorry," Alex tried to suppress her laughter, "give Mommy a kiss." She looked up at Stevie and puckered up.

Stevie kissed her mother on the cheek, pulled back and hugged her daddy's neck. Sway looked at Alex seductively and kissed her lips lightly. As he pulled back, Alex began to feel awkward, almost like she was cheating on Derek. She quickly handed Sway the tightly packed Barbie suitcase, walked them over to the door, and kissed her daughter again. Sway leaned in to kiss Alex again, but this time she turned her cheek just in time to feel his soft lips gently land on her skin. She hoped he did not notice the change in her attitude. He did. Sway pulled back with a questionable look on his face, but knew he did not have enough time to find out the reason for her sudden apprehension to his affection. He stared at Alex from head to toe. She looked ripe in her nicely fitted jeans. Seeing her curvy hips and full lips, reminded him that they had not had any physical contact since the day after she came back from Vegas and he was missing the way she smelled, but mostly, the way she felt. He immediately began to think that maybe the reason for her hesitation was his lack of attention toward her lately.

However, little did Sway know that there was another man filling that void from long distance without any problems. Alex and Derek talked on the phone every night before she went to bed, and emailed one another throughout the day, everyday. Alex woke up looking forward to hearing Derek's voice, and found it hard to fall asleep at night without hearing it again. She was falling in love right before Sway's eyes: with someone else. Sway hadn't noticed because he was so distracted with the Vegas project that almost two whole months had gone by, and Alex had not called him for some tender loving care. Seeing her glowing face, and her hourglass figure fill out her clothing, made Sway aware that too much time had passed them by, and he was long over due.

"Call me when you land OK," Alex said with a weak smile, looking up at Sway.

"Of course, I promise," he responded, sensing her awkwardness as he walked away from her.

Alex watched them as he buckled Stevie up in her car seat, slide into the driver side of his SUV, and sped away.

****

Alex's nerves were on edge as she paced back and forth between the living room and the foyer of her home. Derek had gotten lost on his way to pick her up, and she was already thirty minutes off schedule. She could not blame him because she realized that her residence was neatly tucked away in the woods.. Yet, she was not in the mood to endure her sisters berating comments about not being on time. She mentally reviewed her list of 'things to do', and the quickest route to arrive at each destination. *I have to pick up the cake, Mommy's gift, and meet my cousins who are flying in from Cleveland.* Alex thought as she walked over to the dining room window to watch the long driveway, hoping that Derek would drive down it sooner rather than later.

The house was so quiet that it felt hollow and empty. Marie had driven up to Connecticut earlier under the impression that she was spending the weekend at Reggie and Mia's place to watch the kids. What Marie did not know was that later that night she would be surrounded by her family and friends to celebrate reaching another milestone. Alex smiled as she peered out of the window, imagining the excited expression that would soon be on her mother's face. The chime of her cell phone interrupted her daydream, and as she reached in her bag to grab it she noticed a shiny, black Maxima with tinted windows, cruising down her driveway. Her smile stretched from ear to ear as she sang into the phone. "Hello!"

"Where are you?" Her sister Shawn's irritated voice filled her ear.

"I'm walking out of the door right now," Alex said grabbing her overnight bag, and rushing out of the door.

"Hurry up; you know Ma is asking Reggie questions already. She is wondering why Reggie and Mia want to take *her* out to dinner when she is supposed to be watching the twins. Go get the cake and the gift in Westport, I will meet Jeffrey and them, and take them to the hotel. And, you meet me at my house, so we can get dressed," Shawn iterated her well thought out plan without taking a breath.

"Um … , "Alex stammered as she walked up to the trunk of Derek's car. "That sounds good. I will go to Westport, and meet you at the restaurant."

Alex quickly shuffled over to the passenger side of the car and opened the door to get in.

"What do you mean?" Shawn asked, sounding slightly frustrated that Alex was foiling her plan.

"I'm going to stay at the hotel," Alex stated as she sat onto the soft, creamy caramel, leather seat and leaned in to kiss Derek softly on the lips.

"Huh? Alex what are you talking about … ," Shawn was growing agitated.

"Listen, I will talk to you later at the party. I will be there on time, I promise," Alex said into the phone but did not take her eyes off of the driver of the vehicle.

She did not wait for Shawn to respond; instead she pressed the 'end' button on her cell phone and threw it into her pocketbook. Derek leaned in to kiss her again. He enticed her with the anticipation that he was going to French kiss her, but he didn't. Alex melted into the seat from the affects of his movie screen kisses, and she suddenly became elated that he surprised her with this visit.

"I missed you Ma," he whispered as he pulled back.

"I missed you too, but we have to be someplace in forty-five minutes, or my sisters are going to kill me," Alex said, overwhelmed with the feeling of being the one and only morsel to satisfy his hunger.

Derek chuckled at her nervousness and remembered what she told him about her older sisters. They were not only demanding, but also very protective, so his first impression should be a lasting good one, and getting Alex to her destination on time would be a step in the right direction.

****

The ride through the New Haven neighborhoods reminded Alex of her childhood growing up in Connecticut. She peered out of the window at the row of neatly kept Cape Cod style homes, and admired their curb appeal. It was apparent from the manicured lawns, and landscaped flowerbeds that everyone took pride in their home ownership. As Alex marveled at the scenery, Derek pulled into a parking lot embedded in a dead end street of the quiet residential neighborhood that sat on the edge of the water.

Alex peered around the partially empty lot, and was content that her sisters had not yet arrived. Derek backed his sister's car into the parking space, turned the ignition off, hopped out of the car, and quickly practiced his chivalry by opening the passenger door and extending his hand. Alex graciously accepted his invitation by placing her hand in his as he lifted her body up from the seat. Derek admired the way her backless dress hugged her body and accentuated her curves. He was never into thin women and appreciated those who did not mind carrying some meat on their bones. With each passing hour it was getting harder and harder for him to keep his composure in her presence. He had already commended himself for maintaining his gentlemanly side despite sneaking peeks at her while she dressed after checking into their posh room at *Premiere Hotel & Suites*. His eyes wandered up and down, gazing at the finished product, and felt like a lucky man.

Alex stood tall in her four-inch designer strappy heels as she shuffled to the back of the car to grab the cake and the gift out of the trunk.

"OK, remember what I told you about my sisters. Be yourself and you don't have to answer any of their nagging questions," Alex said, looking Derek in the eye.

"I'm cool," Derek said, lifting the full size sheet cake. "I have a baby sister too. I think I can handle your sisters," Derek concluded with a chuckle.

They quickly walked into the restaurant, and placed the gift and cake in their designated places. The inside of the main building of the restaurant looked like it was once a small comforting home of a sea merchant and his family. Alex and Derek walked around the premises to admire the architecture of the newer buildings that surrounded the main building. They were impressed with the flawless attachment thusly making the entire structure seem as if it was built that way originally. They breezed back into the great room to wait for guests, and found two cushioned chairs next to the bar across from the entryway. The two of them were so engulfed in a conversation about the progress of the Vegas project they did not notice that Shawn and her husband Ali had arrived. Alex could tell by the look on Ali's face as they approached her that Shawn was driving him crazy. Her sister had the tendency to over exaggerate even the smallest situations, and it would be unlike her not to worry everyone around her to death. Alex looked over at Derek and tried to prepare him for the wrath they were about to face. Before she could open her mouth, Shawn closed in on them.

"I can't believe you are not staying at the house! I had plans for us!" Shawn ranted, not noticing the handsome stranger sitting beside her baby sister.

"Well, hello and good to see you too," Alex replied and reached out to hug her sister. "Hey Ali, I am sure she drove you crazy these past few days."

The two of them laughed at Shawn's extreme behavior as they hugged, and Derek stood up to be introduced.

"You know your sister better than me," Ali joked and looked over at Derek. "What's up man?"

The two men immediately shared the universal brotherly handshake, half-hug, and pulled back from one another.

"Oh, Shawn and Ali, this is my friend Derek; Derek this is my sister Shawn and her husband Ali," Alex stated as she performed a proper introduction.

Shawn stared at Derek from head to toe, and silently commended her sister for always having such fine taste in men. Derek extended his hand out to Shawn and shook her hand firmly.

"Hello," Shawn said with a slight bashfulness. "Your hands are so soft. You obviously don't work with your hands, what do you do?" she asked, immediately starting her interrogation.

Derek chuckled at her blunt protectiveness over her baby sister, and looked over at Alex to let her know that her description of Shawn was exact and precise.

"Actually, I am an entrepreneur, and I invest in real estate," Derek said confidently, intentionally leaving his years of hustling and being incarcerated in his subconscious.

"Oh really," she replied impressed, "and, how did you meet my sister?" she inquired, holding nothing back.

"Um, excuse me," Alex interrupted and pulled her sister by the arm.

She practically dragged Shawn over to the entryway as they both smiled and waved at the arriving guests.

"Listen, Shawn, back off, OK?" Alex stated in a serious tone.

"Whatever do you mean?" Shawn asked as if she was clueless to her overbearing behavior.

Alex looked at Shawn and folded her arms. "I mean it Shawn. Derek is the guy I met in Vegas back in March, and he came here this weekend to surprise me, so stop acting like I planned to ruin the weekend you planned for me without my permission."

"Oh! So that is Mr. Vegas," Shawn said, forgetting that she was upset with Alex, and now becoming more inquisitive about Alex's new friend.

"Yes, that is him. So behave, and don't tell Ma or Reggie who he really is because I don't want Ma telling Sway that he was here at the gala Sway paid for," Alex demanded with pleading eyes.

"Yeah, that would be ugly," Shawn said, looking across the dining area, at the men they recently left standing behind.

"He is a cutie though," Shawn said, admiring the way Derek's suit hugged his broad shoulders and bulging biceps.

"Uh-huh, now you know why I am staying at the hotel." The two women chuckled as Mia ran into the ballroom to tell everyone that Reggie was outside helping Marie out of the car, and everyone should take their places.

****

Marie was not only surprised at the party, but she was touched that so many of her family and friends came out to celebrate her birthday. The crowd partied non-stop, and dined on delightful appetizers such as hand carved roasted pork with horseradish dressing, hand made crepes, and made to order pasta dishes. The more everyone danced, the more they ate. It was a wise choice to have appetizers served throughout the night opposed to a heavy four-course meal that would prevent people from wanting to dance the night away.

While the birthday cake and coffee was being served, Alex and Derek slipped out to the back of the restaurant to take in the view of the water reflecting off of the moonlight. They found a bench underneath a small tree, and sat down beside one another. Derek grabbed her hand as they looked out into the black night.

"Thank you for inviting me, I had a good time. It's nice to see such a close family," Derek said full of appreciation.

"You're welcome," Alex said squeezing his hand. "Thank you for surprising me this weekend."

"You're welcome. I think I did OK with your sisters," Derek said, seeking affirmation.

"Yeah, you did great. I knew you were doing fine when I saw you over at the bar downing shots with my sister Reggie," Alex laughed. "She doesn't drink with just anybody. You know those military people are paranoid, and never want to be around people when they are inebriated and vulnerable," Alex mocked at her sister's drunken paranoia.

"She is mad cool," Derek smiled, "like one of the guys."

"She would appreciate that comment," Alex laughed.

Derek leaned over and interrupted her laughter with his soft lips. He kissed her gently as he caressed her hand. "I can't wait to get you back to our room," he whispered between kisses.

"I think I am ready for you to take me there right now," Alex found her self saying in the heat of the moment.

Without wavering, Derek led Alex back into the party. Thankfully, people were leaving and that lessoned the guilt Alex was feeling as she said good-bye to her mother.

"I'm glad you had fun Ma," Alex said loudly over the music that blared throughout the ballroom, "I'm going back to the hotel now," Alex quickly concluded, hoping her mother would not ask any questions.

"When are you coming home?" was all Marie could say, with a wide grin on her face and Mr. Hopkins sitting close by her side.

If Alex did not know her mother any better, she would have thought her mother was trying to make sure Alex was not coming home for other reasons. Alex looked over at Mr. Hopkins while she kissed her mother on her cheek.

"I'll be home Sunday sometime. Tomorrow Reggie, Mia and Shawn are taking you and the folks from out of town to *Mohegan Sun Casino* for the day to do some gambling, shopping, and maybe get spa treatments. I probably won't make that," Alex said, smiling back at Derek, who was patiently waiting for her at the door.

Oblivious to Alex's hidden agenda, Marie smiled brightly at her daughter before thanking her, yet again, for a lovely evening, and confirmed that they would see each other Sunday.

****

Their hotel suite felt more like a sub-zero meat freezer thanks to the housekeeper leaving the air-conditioning on arctic blast. Derek quickly ran over to the radiator to turn the heat on. Alex jumped into the king-size bed and buried her fully clothed body beneath the blanket and floral print bedspread. By the time Derek looked back to see where she had darted off to, he only saw a lump in the center of the bed. He chuckled at her juvenile behavior, and loved the fact that she could tuck away her intellectual, serious side to let her guard down. Derek could hear it in her voice during their many conversations that her heart had been broken, and he wanted to prove to her that he did not intend to repeat that same fate. He quietly walked over to the large bed, making a conscious effort not to make a sound. Alex lay still beneath the blankets, breathing hard, and trying to hear where Derek could be. She felt like playing and so did he. He slowly leaned over the bed and began to tickle the lump with both hands.

"Ahhhh!" Alex screamed and laughed simultaneously. "OK, OK, I give! That is not fair, I told you I was ticklish and you used it against me." Alex flung the blankets away from her face to look at Derek. He was seductively smiling back at her. "You play dirty," she said, squinting her eyes at him.

"Is there any other way to play," he said, climbing on top of her and feeling the combination of heat from their bodies and the radiator. "You also told me some other things that I would like to use against you tonight," his voice became a whisper as he kissed her neck.

Alex reacted to his touch by arching her back, so their clothed bodies could touch. For the first time in a long time, Derek moved at a slower pace, in an attempt to try to savor every moment he was spending with this woman. He reached his ironclad arm beneath her body and unzipped her dress in slow motion. The anticipation grew inside of Alex as she waited for his next move, and allowed him to take full control over what was happening. The room was still except for the constant humming of the radiator, and the sound of them breathing heavily as they explored one another.

Derek helped Alex slide out of her dress with ease, and then undressed himself as Alex watched his performance in delight. A part of her was nervous because she knew with intimacy came more emotion, which for her, always proved to be fatal. Yet, her vulnerable side wanted to share a piece of her soul with Derek; something she has always kept so safeguarded, that up until this moment only one other man has had the privilege to receive just a smidgen of.

She wrapped her arms around his bareback, and gently glided her manicured nails up and down his skin, causing him to breathe deeper into her ear as he nibbled on her lobe. He remembered her mentioning that her earlobe was part of her erogenous zone. She squirmed in delight. Without interrupting his work at melting Alex into a state of surrender, Derek reached over and grabbed the condom that was conveniently placed on the nightstand. With one hand he opened it, took it out of the wrapper, and slid it onto his engorged penis. He looked deeply into her eyes and without speaking a word, asked her if this was what she wanted. And, without blinking an eye, she responded by slowly parting her legs to allow him full access to where she held her love. Derek entered her slowly and gently, trying not to cause any discomfort to her inner sanctum. He held her tightly as he penetrated her in a slow motion. Her flesh gently massaged him as he made long lasting strokes. They held onto each other as if their lives depended on it. There were so many things Derek wanted to say to her, but the only words that would form and exit his mouth were, "you feel so good." Alex would smile every time those words parted his lips, causing her hips to gyrate a little faster. The scenes played on into the morning until they both were depleted of every once of energy in their bodies, and tiredly fell asleep in each other's arms.

Chapter 18

Malibu, California
Journey
It Doesn't Hurt Anymore

The California sun mixed with the morning smog created a dull, somber mood, which was befitting for the way Journey felt. As she walked along the beach, which also doubled as the backyard to her parents' summer home, she watched the early risers jog past her with their loyal canine companions trotting along beside them. She had been in California visiting with her parents all week for Mother's Day, and now she was ready to return back to the hustle and bustle of New York City. The Big Apple had become her home, while her love for California had dwindled to nothing more than a family visit during the holidays. Journey had grown to love the daily rapidness of New Yorkers scurrying to catch the subway, or a taxicab. The heightened sense of urgency that everyone conveyed walking along the city streets always made Journey wonder where people were rushing off to. That distraction always kept her mind off of her failed marriage. Journey dug her toes into the warm sand as she walked along the shore, and peered up at the sky. She silently thanked God for removing her from the volatile relationship in one piece, and in tact.

It had been almost two months since Tiny dragged her out of bed to only have the truth about his infidelity finally rear its ugly head. After he left their home that day, Journey purchased a new mattress, had the locks changed, and had not seen Tiny since. At first, she thought he moved in with Tanya, but quickly discovered through staff gossip at the gym that Tiny fired Tanya, and literally moved into his office. Since walking out on her, Tiny called Journey several times to plead his case and beg for her forgiveness, but Journey stood firm on her decision to move on, despite the pain it caused in her heart.

"No, Tiny it's not going to work," she remembered telling him calmly over the phone. "I told you that if I ever caught you cheating I would leave, remember?"

"I remember, but I know we can make it work Baby, I promise. I will even go to counseling," Tiny pleaded.

Journey rolled her eyes up in her head. Since their separation, that statement had become so commonplace in his vocabulary that after the hundredth time of hearing it, Journey thought of it as his new way of saying 'hello'.

"Forget counseling," she remembered telling him. "You and I are beyond counseling Timothy." They both knew she was serious when she used his birth name. "You slept with that bitch in my bed," Journey tried to maintain her composure, "How would I ever be able to look you in the eye, and not think about you making love to her? I will never forgive you for that. I could never trust you again, ever."

Tiny heard the sternness in her voice, and knew that there would be no lie he could tell that would justify the lacy lavender panties Tanya conveniently left at his home. And, because of her carelessness, Tiny broke off their elicit affair. He tried to convince Journey that Tanya meant nothing to him. She was just a young girl, who knew how to stroke his ego, but he realized that was a huge mistake.

Journey listened intently every time Tiny called her with his plea, but she always remained unmoved. Her mind reminded her every time her heart would soften, that this man was not only abusive but unfaithful, which to Journey was the worst kind of abuse: betraying one's trust.

She reflected on their last conversation a few days before her departure to California. She explained to him that she wanted a divorce. She gave him forewarning that the rest of his personal property would be delivered to the gym, and that he would soon be served with divorce papers. She also put his mind at ease by letting him know that she did not want alimony, and that he could have the gym. "That gym was your dream, not mine. That place holds no good memories for me, you can have it," Journey remembered callously saying over the phone before hanging up on that man she once loved and adored.

Now, walking alone along the beach, Journey tried to decipher what was *her* dream. Ten years ago, she thought by now she would be a famous Broadway stage actress, commanding lead roles in plays like the *Lion King* and *Les Misérable.* Yet, by suppressing her desires and ambitions for the sake of her marriage, and to keep her man happy, Journey realized she had not accomplished any of her dreams. She felt like the years spent with Tiny, were years wasted. She had to admit, however, that she found some solace in knowing that her parents were not disappointed. They told her they were actually happy to have this happen now rather than later. Puzzled, Journey asked them why, and her father finally sat her down to read the terms of her trust fund. The provision that became seared in her memory was that upon her thirtieth birthday, which was in November, the trust would relinquish all monetary assets to Journey, making her a bon-a-fide 'Trust Fund Baby'. Her father told her that on her birthday she would have to meet with his financial advisors to discuss the best ways to invest the nine million dollars she was to receive. Journey was stunned at her parents' generosity as well as their wealth, and immediately smothered her father with kisses. It was always apparent that the Daniels family was wealthy, but Journey never knew her family's actual net worth, and now her father had given her some idea. Technically, she would never have to work again for financial support. She always knew that her father was money wise, and after making a hefty sum of money from his initial production deals, he immediately established trust funds for Journey and her younger siblings. Tiny was aware that Journey had a trust, but he never knew how much it was worth, or at what age she would acquire it. Knowing that she was about to receive this windfall made Journey even more anxious to sever her union with Tiny as quickly as possible. She did not want him receiving any of the money her father worked so hard for. He did not deserve the gym either, but Journey justified that one hundred thousand dollar advance her father relinquished from her trust a few years ago to get the gym started, as a mere drop in the bucket compared to what a Judge could order her to pay in alimony once her net worth would equal to millions. Journey was relieved that

Tiny revealed his true colors prior to her receiving her munificent inheritance.

"Everything really does happen for a reason," Journey whispered as her bare feet sunk into the sand.

Her dull mood was slowly brightening with sun as its rays burned off the morning smog. Journey waved at the neighbors as she dusted off her feet before walking up the wooden steps that lead to her parents back deck overlooking the Pacific Ocean. Her family was one of only four families of color who owned property on the beach, and Journey often wondered if her neighbors realized her father was actually white since he was never home during the day, and often slid in after the midnight hours. Their summer home was twice as old and half the size of their main home in Brentwood, but it was well decorated by an interior designer, and top of the line appliances filled the small, quaint kitchen. The imported furniture bore a cozy feel that immediately gave off a comfortable homey atmosphere. Unlike their Brentwood home that most would call a mini-mansion. With such spaciousness, that home provided an airy, less comfy feel. And, it was filled with antiques and priceless paintings collected during her parents' many vacations around the world.

Journey opened the French doors, walked through the kitchen, and found her mother in the family room watching the *Home Shopping Network*. Rap music was blaring from her brother, Dallas' room, and it could be heard throughout the whole neighborhood. He and his twin sister, Dahlila were teenagers. Their clothing, choice of music, and street vernacular revealed their age with ease.

"Ma, does Dallas have to have his music up that loud this early in the morning?" Journey questioned with annoyance in her voice as she made her way into the family room.

"Chile please, that is nothing. If your dad wasn't home it would be louder than that!" Journey's mother chuckled.

Not amused, Journey shook her head at her brother's inconsideration, and drifted toward her bedroom, which sometimes parlayed as a guest room. Journey sat on the firm bed that reminded her of her new bed at home, and reached for her cell phone. She made Alex give her Cain's number, and she had been contemplating calling Cain since she arrived on the West Coast, but did not want to appear to be desperate. She was fully aware that younger men usually made the immediate assumption that a female is "sweating" them if she reached out before he did. Yet, at the same time, Cain proved himself to be a mature man when they spent that brief time together. Journey had to admit; he not only impressed her, but sparked a curiosity inside of her. He intrigued her. She had not heard from him since their lustful rendezvous in Las Vegas, and she was anxious to bring him up to speed with the sudden turn of events in her life, and, more importantly, she wanted to hear his voice. She had no intention on leaving her husband only to fall into the arms of another man so soon, but there was something about Cain that made her crave him. And, since Cain understood her dilemma, and the emotional strain that came with an abusive relationship, he made it clear from the onset that he would be there for Journey to relieve her with the right kind of distraction whenever she needed. She needed him now. Journey held the little cellular phone in the palm of her hand, flipped it open and dialed Cain's number.

"Hello!" She heard his smooth, manly voice echo through the phone after the first ring.

"Um, hey, what's up," Journey spoke nervously into the compact phone.

"What's up, who's this?" Cain asked, not recognizing the voice.

"It's me … , Journey."

"Oh hey, what's up good lookin'," Cain replied with a smile. "How have you been?"

Journey could tell by the tone in his voice that he was asking that question generally as well as specifically.

"I'm fine! Really, I could not be better," Journey assured him.

"You sure about that?" his sexiness effortlessly oozed into her ear.

"I think I am sure, why?" Journey asked, playing into his game.

"Because I will be back in New York by the end of next week, and I could help you out. I mean if you needed to feel better."

Journey's heart began to race. "Well, actually since I'm single now … ," she spoke slowly so that he could hear every word.

"I know," Cain interjected, "that is why I am confirming that I will be back."

"Huh?" Journey was caught off guard. "How do you know?"

"Pops," Cain answered as if she should have known.

"Why would Sway tell you that? How does he know?" The questions fumbled out of her mouth.

"He was on the phone with Tiny when I picked him and Stevie up from the airport. I could hear my man crying and shit through the phone." Cain tried not to laugh, but at the same time held no sympathy for Tiny.

"Really," Journey replied, wanting to know what was said, but remained calm.

"Yeah, it looks like homeboy got it bad. He was telling my Pops how you changed the locks, how you want a divorce, and how he's sleepin' at the gym; all that shit! I think he wants my Pops to talk with Alex to find out where your head is really at. So, I just want to say that I am proud of you," Cain interceded with a friendly tone.

"You are?" Journey asked, softening to his encouraging words.

"Yes I am. You deserve better, especially if you always put it down like the way you put it down for me in Vegas," Cain said seductively, letting her know he had not forgotten their explosive weekend.

"You are right, I do deserve better," Journey confirmed. "But how about you, I think you deserve something nice for graduating from college," she said, turning the focus of the conversation on him.

"Oh yeah," Cain was growing excited, "you gonna give me that something when I get to New York?"

"Actually, I can give it to you before then." Journey lay back on the bed, and looked up at the ceiling as she imagined Cain hovering over her.

"And, how do you expect to make that happen because you know what I want, I can't get it unless you physically bring it to me."

"I can bring it to you," Journey continued to tease. "When do you want me to arrive with it?"

"Let's see, I graduate tomorrow, Pops and Stevie fly outta' here Sunday morning, so I am thinking Sunday afternoon would be just right," Cain planned, without knowing exactly how Journey was going to grant his wish.

"I think I can do Sunday late afternoon, no problem," Journey giggled into the phone like a schoolgirl. He made her feel young again.

"Do you need me to pick you up from the airport?" Cain asked, not believing she was coming to see him.

"Nope, I am already in California," Journey confessed. "I have a rental. I will drive down after having brunch with my mother on Sunday, and just catch my flight out of San Diego on Monday."

"Oh word! You are here and just now calling me?" Cain was a little disappointed.

"I know. I am sorry. I would have called sooner, but I needed some time to get my thoughts together. Now that I am no longer going to be co-owner of the gym, I had to determine where I should go from this point, career wise, that is. I needed some time to think."

"I can understand that," Cain replied, "I have been there. I was not sure about working with my father at first."

"That is exactly where I am right now," Journey sighed with relief. "I am not passionate about acting anymore, and I have been really considering going back to school to take a few counseling courses. I want to help other women who are in similar situations."

"I think that's mad cool. You would be really good at that. You should look into it," Cain said respectfully, thinking of how his abused mother would benefit from a few sessions with a counselor who could relate.

Journey smiled into the phone and could hear the sincerity in his voice.

"You are so sweet Cain," Journey answered him in a soft low voice.

"But getting back to me and you," Cain said. "Will you call me when you are on your way?"

"Of course I will but, before I let you go, can I ask you something?" Journey said with a slight hesitance in her voice.

"Anything."

"When Sway mentioned me and Tiny's situation, did you tell him about us in Vegas?" she was scared to hear his answer.

"Hell no!" Cain almost shouted. "Not at all, Sweetheart. This here ... ," Cain said pointing back and forth to his chest and the phone, "is between you and me. The only other person who knows about us is Alex, and we both know she is cool."

"You're right and thank you for not mentioning it to your father. I would hate for him to be in that awkward position."

"Naw, I don't want him in that predicament either. That would be whack," Cain agreed. "Listen, I gotta' go but I can't wait to see you."

"OK, have fun tomorrow. I will see you soon," Journey smiled into the phone, satisfied that she called him after all.

****

The ride down the West Coast in her rented *Lexus* coupe convertible was liberating, and in a sense inducted this chapter of Journey's life as another seed of growth and empowerment. With only the sound of the car's purring engine and wind breezing across her face, she sped down the coast. Journey found it amusing that only high end luxury car rental dealerships existed in Malibu. She had a choice between the coupe and the SUV, and decided on the convertible to enjoy the sunny, West Coast weather. She never drove back in New York, so zipping along the highways with the top down seemed even more tempting. She did not feel like listening to the radio. Instead, she opted to meditate on her afternoon brunch at the *Ivey* in Los Angeles with her mother, and the conversation they shared. Her mother choosing that location brought back fond memories for Journey, growing up in sunny California. Journey and her mother reminisced going there for lunch every Sunday, and seeing all of the Hollywood stars dining. Journey would talk through their whole meal, telling her mother how she was going to be on Broadway one day. She and her mother laughed at their memories while they munched on watercress salad, and pan seared salmon. As the waiter cleared their table and quickly mentioned that their latte's would be right out, Journey held onto her mother's hand and began to share how her life was during her marriage. Journey told her mother everything, from the onset of Tiny's abusive behavior to the lacy underwear she found in her hamper. She confided in her mother and told her of the beatings, and even the rape. Her mother tried to comfort Journey as best she could considering that they were in a public setting lacking the privacy needed for such a delicate conversation. She listened to Journey regurgitate the pain and anguish she suffered at the hands of Tiny over the past couple of years. She wished Journey had divulged this private matter at home, a place where they would have been able to cry hard, and shout as loud as they wanted. Mrs. Daniels was also angry at Tiny and she told Journey that although she never said anything, she never cared for him. She did not like the way he behaved around her. He always appeared to be hiding something. Now, she knew what that something was. Yet, she explained to Journey that she did not try to deter her daughter from being with the man she loved because she knew what it felt like to fall in love with someone so different from your self. Journey's mother reminded her of the hardships and blatant racial torture she and Journey's father faced when they met and fell in love, and most of the prejudice stemmed from their own families. Her parents were grateful that despite the obstacles they faced as an interracial couple, they were very successful. Her mother told Journey to be thankful that she got out when she did, and she advised Journey to never look back. After receiving affirmation from her mother, Journey felt justified and renewed. And, it also didn't hurt knowing that in six months, she would become a very wealthy woman.

****

The sun was setting along the horizon when Journey pulled into the Hilton Hotel. She quickly pulled into an empty parking space near the front entrance of the hotel, and grabbed her overnight bag from the back seat. She kept her luggage in the hatchback, and prayed that no one stole the car before daybreak. She tried to reach her destination before dusk, but the fender-bender on the opposite side of the highway caused Journey to be tied up in a long tailgating line. As she rushed to the front desk to check in, the elderly, but sweet desk clerk informed her that a handsome gentleman was already in the room awaiting her arrival. The frail woman handed Journey the room card key, and pointed in the direction of the elevators. Journey smiled at the thought of someone waiting for her. She pressed the elevator button more than once as if doing so would make the elevator come faster.

Journey stepped out of the elevator and looked both ways down the long corridor of the posh hotel. It was so quiet you could probably hear a pin drop on the plush paisley carpet beneath her flip-flops. Journey followed the sign that pointed in the direction of her room number. Once at the door, she stood still, suddenly becoming nervous. She tried to shake off the feeling and kept telling herself that this is *just Cain,* and that she's been with him before. Yet, this time would be different.

This time she was seeing him as a single woman; not a scorned, overly abused wife looking for a feel good moment.

She breathed in deeply, slid the card key into the slot, and turned the doorknob. As soon as she stepped in the room, she could smell Cain's cologne and once again, inhaled deeply. The television was on and the sportscaster on *ESPN* was going over the highlights of the baseball game that just ended. She could hear the shower running as she tip-toed into the bathroom.

As she stepped over his clothing that was strewn across the bathroom floor, she imagined how much fun the soapsuds were having as they cleansed his muscular body.

"Hey, Cain!" Journey sang just loud enough for him to hear her. Just as she was about to sneak a peek, he pulled back the heavy plastic, cream-colored shower curtain and smiled.

The pleasure of seeing her was written all over his face, and it was refreshing for Journey to see the delight dancing in his eyes. "Hi," she said, stepping back to get a full view of his nakedness.

"What's up?" he asked with a wide grin on his face.

Journey was not sure if he realized his innate sexuality, but he conveyed it with such ease, enticing her more. "Um … , nothing, what's up with you," Journey answered in a soft voice as she leaned against the sink.

"You want to come in?" he invited her into the shower.

"It looks like you are almost done, maybe next time."

Cain winked at her and pulled the shower curtain back to the wall. "I'll be right out! Then we can go someplace to eat," he yelled over the running water.

Journey did not respond, instead, with a smile on her face and feeling warm inside, she slid out of the bathroom, and walked over to the king-size bed and plopped her body onto it. The immediate comfort the soft bedspread provided, quickly gave Journey the idea of ordering up room service instead.

Chapter 19

New Haven, Connecticut
Alex
You're The Best Thing Yet

Alex was awakened by the sound of Derek having a conversation with someone at their room door.

"Yeah, don't worry about it, I already called the front desk," Derek spoke quickly in a low guttural voice. He was trying not to wake Alex up and brush the housekeeper off at the same time.

Alex rolled over just as Derek walked back into her sight. The daylight reflected off of the drawn drapes, providing just enough light in the room for her to focus in on his face as he approached the bed. Before she could ask who was at the door, he slid back into bed under the covers, and hugged her warm naked body tightly.

"That was the housekeeper, trying to tell me it was check out time," Derek whispered in Alex's ear.

With one eye open, Alex looked over at the alarm clock, and noticed it was already past noon. She looked over her shoulder at Derek to make sure he realized what time it was. "Derek, its way past check out time," Alex said, trying to lift her body against the weight of his forearm that had clamped her to the bed.

"Don't worry about it. I paid for an extra night, so we can spend a few more hours together," he said without moving. "Just lay with me," he whispered as his eyes closed, showing the initial signs of him dosing back off to sleep.

Alex looked at his peaceful sleeping face, and decided against reminding him that it was Mother's Day and that she had to get home. She stared at him for another moment and then gazed over at the clock. She mentally calculated her timing of getting home against Sway's flight arrival. It was their tradition to have dinner with Stevie on Mother's Day. His flight from California was not due to arrive until after five o'clock, and she figured that Derek would bring her home no later than four o'clock because he had a plane to catch. The possibility of the two men running into each other was close to nil. Comfortable with her plan, Alex nestled her body into Derek's grasp. Spending this time in person together opposed to envisioning each other's presence when they spoke on the phone, allowed the two of them to finally mentally and physically connect to solidify their newfound relationship. Alex dosed back off to sleep, feeling partially relieved that the night before, she finally told Derek the real reason she was so apprehensive in the beginning of their courtship. She explained that Stevie's father was also a client. Yet, despite that they were able to uniquely develop a co-parenting relationship that did not hinder their working relationship; she did not want co-mingling with clients to become habit forming. However, she held back telling him exactly *who* that client was because she did not want the Vegas venture to have any negative influences due to her personal connection with Sway. She did not want Derek becoming insecure because she and Sway still worked so closely together. Her better judgment told her to introduce that part of her unordinary life to Derek at their upcoming meeting with Sway and Romeo, which was only weeks away.

****

As Derek's car crossed over the New York State line on Interstate 95, Alex stared at the small digital clock on the dashboard of car, and silently prayed that Sway was running late.

"You OK?" Derek asked, glancing over at her, breaking her gaze.

"Oh, yeah, I'm fine," Alex said, looking over at him, and reaching for her cell phone. "I just have to call to see if my daughter is waiting for me."

A surge of guilt filled Derek. He was so enveloped in spending one-on-one time with Alex he had forgotten that she had plans with her daughter this evening. "I'm sorry Baby, I'll have you home in a minute," he said accelerating his speed.

Alex waved him off as if to say 'its OK' as she dialed her home number. "Hey Ma, is Stevie there yet?" she asked her mother as soon as she heard Marie's voice.

"No Honey, not yet. Steven called and said he was stopping by his place first to change clothes. They should be here shortly," Marie replied, looking at her wristwatch.

"OK, good. I am on my way. I should be there soon."

"I will let Steven know if he gets here first," Marie confirmed.

Alex hung up the phone and threw it back into her bag as she let out a loud sigh. She relaxed her shoulders and snuggled in the soft leather seat.

"Everything cool?" Derek asked, immediately noticing the change in her mood.

"Yes, they are not there yet," Alex looked over at him, with a glare in her eye that told him it was alright to slow down.

Now that she was satisfied knowing her baby girl was not waiting for her, she focused her attention toward Derek because it would be weeks before their next encounter.

"I'm really glad you came with me this weekend," Alex said, looking over at his dimple set deeply in his cheek.

The comment made him smile. "Me too," he said grabbing her hand. "You don't understand Alex, I have been waiting for a woman like you all of my life. You're smart, funny, intelligent, and at the same time not uptight, snobby and judgmental. There are not a lot of women out there like you. When I first saw you I thought you would never be interested in a man like me. At first, you kind of give of the impression that you go for the straight-laced, Wall Street kind of brotha'," Derek concluded with a chuckle.

"Really!" Alex exclaimed. "I might have gone out with one or two guys who fit that type, but I never had a preference really. If a guy has the right characteristics, he could come from almost any background, and work almost anywhere, as long as he is working. I have learned from my very first relationship that it's not about where you come from, but its more about where you are going, you know?"

"I feel you Ma, I'm glad you see it that way, and I want you to believe me when I tell you that I only have good intentions when it comes to you and me," he looked over at her with a wide smile on his face, causing his dimple to sink even deeper into his cheek.

She returned the smile and adored his confidence. It gave him an added boyish charm that made Alex want to support whatever plan he had in store. They talked as Derek maneuvered through the congestion caused by the holiday traffic. They reminisced about their weekend, and paid special attention to their private time together after the party. Once they arrived to their suite from her mother's bash, they never left until checking out a little over an hour ago. In between love sessions, they talked, ordered up room service, and stayed in bed to watch television while they regained their strength only to begin again. By the time they left the hotel, it was clear that they had taken their relationship to the next level. Alex stared at Derek as he chauffeured her home. She fixated her attention to the intricately designed tattoo of a dollar sign with the capital letter "D" etched in his neck. It was a work of art compared to the various tattoos he had all over his body. This one she favored the most. She was so caught up in his hypnotic spell that she was unaware that he had turned onto her street.

"We are here already!" Alex exclaimed, becoming filled with mixed emotions. She was anxious to see her daughter, but she hated that she and Derek were parting.

"Unfortunately, we are," Derek said as he pulled the car up to her front door and shifted the gear into park.

Alex immediately noticed Sway's car parked in front of the garage, and was thankful he was already inside. She did not want to deal with introducing the two men in her life to one another on this special day.

Derek looked at the shiny, parked BMW and assumed that it belonged to her baby's father since it was not parked there when he picked Alex up a few days earlier. He did not let it bother him; instead, he focused on the last few moments he had to spend with her until the next time. "I'm going to miss you," he said, pulling her attention back in his direction.

"Me too," Alex replied, turning her fixated stare from the parked car to Derek. "But we will see each other soon. These weeks will fly by, watch and see," she said trying to convince him as well as her self.

"I'm gonna call you later tonight when I get back home," Derek said softly but meant every word.

"I hope so," Alex smiled and leaned in to kiss his soft full lips.

The peck soon turned into a lasting passionate kiss, and Alex melted to his gentle touch as he ran his fingers across her cheek. They both hesitated as they pulled back to look at one another.

"I better go," Alex said, fixing her shirt and wiping her mouth with her index finger.

Just as she reached for the door handle, Derek grabbed her by the arm and pulled her in to kiss her again. The excitement of his spontaneous action raced through her body as she gave into his irresistible ardor for one moment more.

"Seriously, Derek, you have to let me go, or we will be out here forever, and you have a plane to catch," she reminded him, resisting his charm and opening the car door before he could reel her back in again.

"OK, OK, I'm sorry, I can't help myself. I will call you later, enjoy your dinner," he said sarcastically, finally allowing his jealously to rear its ugly head.

"Be nice, its just dinner. I'll be waiting for your call later," she said, looking back as she lifted herself out of the car.

The fact that she was going to wait for his call turned Derek on, and eliminated any fear that he harbored of Alex finishing off her night with another man. Derek hoped that once he and this guy met, any insecurity he was suppressing would dissipate once and for all. Alex promised him that day would come sooner rather than later, and Derek was totally prepared.

She gazed at him as she closed the car door. His smile told her that he was OK, making it a little easier for her to walk away from the car, and watch it drive away out of her sight. Alex turned around and walked up to the front door. Just as her hand grabbed the doorknob, she could feel herself being pulled inside of the house by whoever was opening the door from the other side.

"Oh, hey! I was just about to come out and meet your friend," Sway said casually as if he had already known that Alex was seeing someone.

"Excuse me?" Alex asked, as she tried to gather her bearings to prevent tripping over her feet and hitting the ground.

"Your friend. I was coming out to meet him," Sway said, looking Alex straight in the eye. "Your mother mentioned that you were still in Connecticut with your friend when I called earlier."

"Yes, she was right," Alex stood perfectly straight like a soldier. "That was my friend, but I don't want to talk about it right now. Aren't we going to be late for dinner?" she asked quickly changing the subject.

The two of them stood in the middle of the foyer as they could hear the pitter-patter of Stevie's tiny steps as she ran toward them.

"Mommy! Hi mommy, I missed you," Stevie screamed as she jumped into Alex's arms.

"Hey Baby, I missed you too. Are you ready to go to dinner?"

"Yup," Stevie answered, hugging Alex around the neck.

Alex kissed Stevie on the cheek, and yelled to her mother that they would be back soon before trotting back out of the door she had entered just moments before. Sway followed them and was becoming green with envy. His need to know this mystery man had suddenly catapulted to the top of his priority list.

****

The underground parking lot to the *Centro at the Mill Restaurant* in Greenwich, Connecticut was packed. Sway decided to let Alex and Stevie out at the entrance, and drove around the corner to the adjacent outdoor lot to park. Alex held Stevie in her arms and filtered through the line of patrons who did not made reservations, but hoped to get a table before the restaurant closed. She approached the hostess standing behind the podium, and told her what name her table was reserved under. The hostess immediately checked off the reservation, grabbed the menus, and a pack of crayons. Just as the hostess instructed Alex to follow her, Sway appeared and trailed closely behind. The hostess admired the attractive family as she sat them at a table in the corner of the restaurant. Stevie quickly adjusted her little body in the booster chair and began to color on the paper table cloth. Of all of the restaurants they have taken Stevie to, this by far was her favorite. Although, elegant and refined, the restaurant also functioned as a child friendly establishment. Adults could enjoy fine wine and conversation, while the children stayed occupied drawing mini masterpieces on the tablecloths made of large sheets of drawing paper.

While Stevie kept herself busy coloring, the idle chitchat between Alex and Sway mostly centered around his trip to California and Cain's graduation. It was apparent that Sway was very proud of his son because he could not stop talking about how it made him feel when he watched Cain walk up the steps of the outdoor stage to receive his degree.

"Man, I had tears in my eyes," Sway confessed.

"I can imagine," Alex said, enjoying the moment through his experience.

"Yeah, it was something to see, I wish you could have been there," Sway said slightly shifting the mood as the waiter placed their entrées in front of them.

"Me too," Alex said sincerely and meaning it.

"Do you?" Sway asked as he sliced into his perfectly cooked filet mignon.

"Yes, I do. What are you trying to say?" Alex asked. She was growing defensive, but tried to keep her composure.

"I'm just trying to say that it's hard to believe that it is a coincidence that this friend of yours pops up the same weekend I am out of town." Suddenly, Sway's jealousy began to overpower his ability to stay cool in such an awkward situation.

"What … , you are kidding right?" Alex asked, not believing that Sway was questioning her integrity. "Sway, you know I don't have to keep anything from you. We are better than that. How did you put it a few months ago? A friend of mine was passing through and we hooked up," Alex said repeating the same words that flowed from Sway's mouth not that long ago. She looked into Sway's piercing eyes, and for the first time could not read them. She expected him to confirm that their friendship was still in tack.

He stared back at Alex with intensity as he inwardly wrestled with his emotions. He hated that she was witnessing his struggle. Rejection and jealously were two feelings he hated having, which was why he made the choice long ago to not let his heart play into his relationships with women. And, although Alex is the only woman who has ever come so close to holding his entire heart in her hand, he somehow realized sitting before her that he had to safeguard it from her if he intended to keep it from breaking in two. He shifted in his seat and tried to get comfortable in the tense situation that he created. "Touché, you're right," he finally answered with a coolness in his voice that attempted to convey that he was unaffected by her new mystery man.

"Sway, I was going to tell you about him. I just was trying to wait until the time was right."

"Well, it appears that now might be the right time," Sway said looking down at his watch.

An involuntary smile lit up Alex's face at his invitation. "OK," Alex succumbed, grinning from ear to ear. "First let me say and I hope you won't be offended, but in some ways he reminds me of you. I just never thought I would find someone who really wants what I want in a relationship. He does everything to show me how serious he is, rather than simply tell me. That means a lot," Alex concluded as though she was talking to one of her girlfriends.

Sway witnessed the joy this mystery man was bringing to Alex by the way she was beaming, and for that he could not get mad. Anything that made her happy, made Sway happy. Ever since she gave birth to his daughter, Sway's only priority when it came to Alex was to ensure her happiness and well being. Of course, he would rather be the man making her glow the way she radiated in front of him, but he realized long ago that Alex would never let her guard down for him because of his history of having the inability to commit. He forced himself to listen to her as she went on about how attentive her "friend" was, and how she could not wait for them to meet because she was thinking that she was ready to introduce Stevie to him.

"So, it's that serious?" Sway asked, pushing the empty plate away from his reach, and leaning back in his chair. "You said you just met this guy a few months ago, you really ready for him to be around my daughter?" he asked, looking over at Stevie, who was stuffing a French fry in her little mouth.

Alex gave Sway a questionable look, disappointed that he was questioning her judgment. "Sway, do you honestly think that I would allow anyone around her if I thought that it would have a negative influence over her? Answer that carefully," Alex stated firmly as she crossed her arms and was becoming visibly upset.

Sway started to feel bad for ruining her special day, and quickly gathered up his emotions, and swallowed them whole. "Hey, my bad, I am sorry for even questioning you. I know you better than that, and you know I trust you more than anyone," Sway said, softening as he began to morph into his charismatic personality to lighten the mood.

Alex squinted her eyes at him and tried not to smile. He always had a way of putting an immediate end to any tense filled situation. That was one of his best qualities. It amplified his manliness and gave him a distinct swagger that not many men could emulate.

"So, when do I meet him?" Sway asked, trying to smile.

"When we go to Vegas to finalize the deal; he lives in Vegas," Alex said in a quick breath, trying not to put any emphasis on where Derek lived. She did not want Sway to put two and two together. "But enough about that, let's eat this delicious cake, right Stevie?" Alex converted all of her attention to the large piece of chocolate mousse cake perfectly placed on a miniature china plate sitting in the center of their table.

Stevie reached with her little spoon and sloppily dug it into the moist cake. Alex and Sway watched their daughter as she made a mess while they snuck looks at each other without saying another word. Both of them knew that no matter whom either of them would share their life with, the two of them would always remain connected.

****

The drive home from the restaurant was quiet and calm. Stevie had fallen asleep before they reached the state line. Sway popped in an old school R&B mixed CD, and cruised along the dark roads until he reached his destination. As he pulled into the driveway, Alex sat up in her seat and silently prayed that he was not planning on staying over. She hoped Sway realized from their earlier conversation, and from the lack of her reaching out for his affection during the past couple of months, that she had silently terminated the intimate part of their relationship. She was tired, and was looking forward to sleeping alone in her own bed. And, she was expecting her nightly call from Derek.

Sway stopped his car in front of the door, and looked back at his sleeping angel. Alex watched him as he examined Stevie from head to toe. The short moment seemed longer as his gaze revealed the obvious love that he had for his baby girl.

"Thank you Sway, as always I had a wonderful Mother's Day dinner," Alex said with a sincere tone, minimizing his minor outburst earlier in the evening.

"Anything for you, you know that. I left a little something for you inside. Enjoy the rest of your night, alright. I'm gonna get home, so I can sleep in my own bed," Sway said, letting Alex know that he knew how to play his position.

"I will see you next weekend," Alex said almost asking as she slid out of the car and opened the back door to retrieve Stevie's sleeping limp body.

"Yup, I will pick Stevie up around noon. I'm going to work out with Tiny in the morning. Your girl really did a number on him," Sway hinted as if it was Journey's fault that she and Tiny split.

Alex stopped unbuckling Stevie and peered over the headrest to look into Sway's eyes. Quietly she had thoughts of how his mouth was just full of surprises that evening. She was beginning to wonder if he had taken something.

"Wait a minute … ," her voice started out in roar, causing Stevie to turn her head. Alex softened her voice to almost a whisper. "I don't know what he told you, but I can bet you a million dollars, he ain't tell you everything. And, I am too tired to, so while you two are working out, ask him to tell you the whole story. Journey deserves someone who will treat her right."

Sway could see it in Alex's brown eyes that Tiny must not have disclosed all of the details of his break-up. "I definitely will," Sway confirmed, suddenly wanting to know what Alex knew. He could not wait to see Tiny face to face to ask him the real reason behind Journey filing for divorce.

Alex pulled Stevie out of the car and closed the door behind her before trotting up to the front door of her home. As she turned the doorknob to enter the house, she looked back and waved at Sway although because of the dark tint on the car windows she could not see if he waved back, but she assumed he did.

Once inside the house Alex slipped out of her shoes, and left them by the door. She carried Stevie to her room to prepare her for bed, which is never an easy feat when Stevie is sleeping. Alex tucked her in and made sure the *Barbie* comforter was wrapped securely around her body.

She tip-toed out of the room, and left the door slightly ajar, allowing the light from the hallway to peer through. Alex tiredly slipped into her room and was greeted by a large bouquet of flowers bursting out of a large crystal vase, and an elongated velvet jewelry box sitting neatly on her bed. Her eyes lit up and she released a loud sigh. "You've done it again Mr. McCoy," Alex said aloud as if Sway could hear her.

She walked over to the dresser and deeply inhaled the sweet botanical scent that the bouquet released. She grabbed the card and pulled it out of the small envelope. The inscription was simple and sweet. *For the world's best Mother, thinking of you always, Love Malcolm.* Alex smiled as she read the one-liner over and over again. With everything going on, she had forgotten that her annual flowers from Malcolm were due to arrive today. She looked forward to receiving her annual bouquet from Malcolm because it made her feel special knowing that she still held a place in his heart. She held onto the card tightly as she walked over to the bed, and reached for the jewelry box. As she opened it, the glow from the diamonds lit up the dimly lit room, and Alex's jaw dropped in awe.

"Oh my!" Alex gasped as she pulled the diamond necklace from the box and held it up in the air, "this is way more than a little something!"

Sway had impeccable taste when it came to jewelry, and the necklace was a spectacular addition to Alex's collection that he had created for her over the past four years. Alex was astounded as she shook and tried it on. She stood in front of the mirror to admire her gift. She looked at her happy reflection, and suddenly became overwhelmed with emotion. Her weekend had ended as perfectly as it had started thanks to the men in her life. She hoped that it was a clear indication of a blissful future with Derek, while maintaining lasting friendships with both Sway and Malcolm.

June - 1999

Chapter 20

The Girls
You Bring Me Joy

"So, are you ready for this weekend?" Journey asked Alex, as they lounged on the cushioned outdoor chaises in Alex's backyard, baked under the sun, and watched Stevie splash around in her kiddy pool.

Alex peered up at the blazing sun through her sunglasses on the hotter than usual early summer day, and took a long sip of her frozen cocktail. Her thoughts drifted off into the near future as she mentally played out the introduction of the two men in her life. She fantasized that Sway and Derek would immediately form a common respect for one another, and get along for the sake of her happiness. She realized the fantasy was a tad bit selfish, but she deserved to be happy, and finally she could see the possibility.

"Let's just say that I am ready, but we have to hope and pray both Sway and Derek are ready," Alex responded without looking over at her friend.

Journey shook her head and appreciated that it was Alex in this love triangle, and not her. "I think everything will go well," Journey said with a sense of assurance. "You know Sway is not the jealous type, so he won't trip on you in front of Derek. He is way too smooth for that," she confirmed.

"That is what I am banking on," Alex said in agreement, finding some comfort in knowing that even if Sway was jealous, he would never allow anyone see him succumb to that insecurity under any kind of pressure.

"This Derek guy is special, huh?" Journey asked.

"Yeah, I think so Journey," Alex replied as that certain smile formed across her face. "Its like he is Malcolm and Sway rolled up in one, but the added bonus is that he embodies the one characteristic they both lacked: the capability to commit and the willingness to do so."

"Commitment is key," Journey confirmed. "That is why, I will soon be single because of Tiny's lack of commitment," she concluded with a smile.

The two women chuckled at Tiny's expense and they both felt it was well deserved. Journey told Alex about her trust fund and brought Alex up to speed with the progress of the divorce proceedings. She also signed the deed giving Tiny full ownership of the gym. He begged her to reconsider their union as they sat across from each other in her lawyer's conference room a few weeks ago. Journey sat there staring at the groveling mess he had become. At the end of their meeting, her attorney reminded Tiny of the restraining order against him, which meant that he could no longer park in front of her home all night. She told Alex that under any other circumstance, Tiny's fanatic, stalker actions would have petrified her, but since Cain's return to New York, he was spending most nights with her to ensure her safety.

"So what's *really* up with you and my stepson?" Alex asked like a concerned parent.

"Huh! Cain and I are just friends, Alex. You know, almost like how you and Sway started out," Journey said downplaying the fact that lately she was, in fact, Cain's only interest and vice-versa. "Why do you ask?"

"Only because during the past few weekends when Sway dropped Stevie off, he mentioned that Cain had not been home, and he was wondering what little nymph had his son so sprung so quickly! You know how Sway is. He does not think a man should give all of his time to just one woman so soon, that's all," Alex said nonchalantly.

"We are just having a good time together, that's it. I have been acting as his personal guide around the City," Journey stated as a matter of fact.

"OK, you don't have to explain, I get it," Alex said, smiling at her friend to let her know that her business was safe and confidential.

Journey deliberately failed to mention that she sensed Cain was falling for her much harder than she was for him because she didn't want Alex lecturing her about messing with someone's feelings. Journey knew she was being selfish, but Cain provided that energetic spark she needed to get through such a crippling process. The emotional side of ending a marriage could have been much more severe if Cain was not there to soften the blows to her self-esteem, and to comfort her pain as her bruised heart healed. Despite the nine-year age difference between them, Cain harbored a mature spirit that often shone through his boyish charm. Journey recognized that he was at that age where young men try to gain ground with their sexual prowess, and she suggested that he date more. But his response would always be the same: that he has not met anyone yet like Journey who made him feel comfortable.

The two women took a moment to sip on their cocktails that were no longer frozen, but now just ice-cold, over-sweetened beverages. They watched Stevie play in the water while soaking up the sun as Marie made sandwiches for lunch. Alex appreciated her mother, not only because she did all of the cooking, but, because Marie never minded doing it. Marie brought out a tray of sandwiches and a pitcher of homemade, fresh-brewed ice tea and sat them down on the glass patio table. She did not have to call anyone to the table for lunch. In unison, Alex, Journey and Stevie gathered around the table, and munched silently on their meal. Everyone heard the telephone ring but neither, Alex nor Journey pulled themselves away from the table because they both assumed Marie would answer it. And, she did.

"Here Alex, I think it's your friend," Marie said, handing Alex the cordless phone and strolling back into the kitchen.

"His name is Derek, Ma. Hello," Alex sang into the phone with a smile on her face.

"Hey Baby, what's up?" Derek asked in one breath.

"Nothin' hangin' out in the back with Journey and Stevie," Alex replied in her schoolgirl voice.

"I can't wait to see you this weekend," Derek reiterated. He had been saying the same sentence over and over during the past several days.

"I know you told me," Alex replied, flattered by his need to see her face.

"I will have the driver bring me straight to your house as soon as I arrive," Alex said softly into the phone, forgetting her friend and daughter were in an ear's length of her conversation.

Journey looked over at Alex and began to chuckle. She had never seen her friend so vulnerable before. Usually, Alex kept her emotions encrusted in a guarded shell, which in turn empowered her with a witty, almost cold disposition when conversing with men who were interested in her. Journey always admired the edge Alex was able to maintain around men, and she decided that she would emulate her friend's attitude as her heart continued to heal from Tiny's abuse. This softer side of Alex not only surprised Journey, but showed her for the first time, a genuine happiness in her friend. "I have never seen this side of you," Journey whispered, trying to interrupt the unguarded display of affection Alex showed Derek.

Alex ignored her comment and listened intently to Derek's seduction. He had become a professional at swooning her over the phone. His voice caused her innards to tingle, and the sweet nothings he professed in her ear daily, always filled her with an overwhelming amount of anticipation of their next encounter. The excitement in Derek's voice was clearly conveyed, but Alex did not realize that it was not just because of her. Derek was especially overjoyed that the moment he had been planning for over two years was about to happen. He could not wait to make amends with his ex-best friend. And, although, he held no expectation of them ever forming that brotherly bond they once shared, Derek felt good knowing that he finally would have righted his main wrong, and prayed that Sway would finally forgive him. Derek was relieved that in less than forty-eight hours, he would no longer have to hide this secret from Alex. He hoped that she would approve of his way of apologizing to Sway, and not hold that horrendous part of his past against him.

"I know, this weekend is going to be extra special," Alex said into the phone, pulling him back into their conversation.

"I just wanted to hear your voice, Ma," Derek cooed. "I'll let you get back to your friend and daughter, but I will call you later," he said with a slight hesitance. A part of him wanted to keep her on the phone until she was in his presence again.

"Don't forget," Alex playfully demanded in a sensual voice before hanging up the phone. She was waiting with baited breath for the weekend ahead because it was the final step she had to take in order to bring her and Derek to the solid, committed, monogamous relationship she always dreamed of. After the introduction of her man to her "baby's daddy", there would not be anyone or anything standing in the way of her path to a real relationship. "I know they will get along," she said aloud to no one in particular.

"What?" Journey asked in an effort to get Alex to repeat herself.

"Sway and Derek, I know they are going to like each other. They act so much alike, it's kind of weird," Alex said, thinking of their similar mannerisms.

"That is probably why you've fallen for this Derek guy so fast," Journey added, "because he is Sway without being a womanizer."

Both women nodded in affirmation, and moved back over to their chaises as Marie grabbed Stevie to wash her up for her nap.

****

The smoke alarm chimed through Journey's apartment as a heavy, thick black fog billowed out of her oven. The slow moving mass filtered through the kitchen into the living room, and the charred, burning stench penetrated through everything it encountered.

"Oh shit!" Cain exclaimed, leaping from Journey's king-size bed, and running toward the kitchen.

Journey rolled over slowly, half asleep and inhaled a large amount of smoke, causing her to cough harshly and grab her chest. She quickly sat up in the bed and yelled for Cain.

"I'm in the kitchen!" he screamed. "We fell asleep and forgot about your chicken wings in the damn oven!"

"Oh, my God!" Journey jumped out of bed and ran into the kitchen.

"So much for trying to get a quickie in before dinner," Cain yelled over the beeping sound of the smoke alarm, trying to make light of the smoky situation while opening the front door and the living room windows.

"Lately with you, it's never been quick," Journey quipped, grabbing a dishcloth and waving it rapidly in front of the annoying smoke alarm, so it could stop blaring in her ears.

They moved rapidly through the house, flailing their arms around as they tried to push the smoke out of the brownstone. Once the spacious apartment finally cleared, Journey lit as many scented candles as she could find to combat the unappealing stench of charred chicken filtering through the house. They barricaded themselves in the bedroom with the door shut and stuffed a towel underneath it.

"I told you we should eat first," Journey looked over at Cain, who was stretched across the foot of the bed, channel surfing, trying to find any sport being captured on film.

"Don't put this all on me," Cain laughed. "It's not *my* fault you put me to sleep, but it is your fault that *you* fell asleep."

Despite that they almost burned to death, Journey could not hold back her laughter, and soon joined in with Cain. As the effect of the horrid turned humorous event subsided, it was soon realized that, although, they were both physically satisfied, they were also very hungry.

"What do you feel like eating?" Cain asked, as he grabbed his pants from the hardwood floor and slid into them. "You want to go out, or you want me to grab some take out?"

"Maybe we should go out to get some fresh air, but … ," Journey moaned as she cuddled up with one of the down pillows on her bed. "Take out sounds good, and the Chinese place I like is right around the corner. Remember where I took you the first night you came over? You won't have to move from your parking space either," Journey rationalized, as she nestled her body into the bed and pulled the cover up to her chin.

He looked at her and immediately realized that she had made the decision on take-out. He grabbed his sneakers and sat on the bed.

Journey stared at his back as it filled out the t-shirt he had just thrown on. She loved it when Cain catered to her. "The menu is in the kitchen drawer, I want some orange beef. If you order it before you go, it will be ready by the time you get there!" she called out as he headed for the kitchen.

Cain grabbed the menu and quickly scanned it to aide him in making the right decision. He liked almost everything on the menu. He had quickly grown to love East Coast Chinese food. It tasted far more authentic than the Thai food they pawned off as Chinese food on the West Coast, which he always found ironic because California was closer to China.

"Yo, Journey, I'll be right back, come lock the door!" Cain called out, conscious of the night sky hovering over the city. He was aware of the criminal activity that takes place as soon as the sun sets. What worried him more was that he did not know whether or not Tiny had finally stopped his obsession to stalk Journey. Although they had not seen his SUV parked near Journey's house ever since she signed the business over to Tiny, Journey was still not confident enough to believe that Tiny had finally moved on.

Journey rolled over as Cain's voice echoed through her ears and then quickly fainted away. She lay still for a few moments with the duvet cover pulled over her head to hide from the smell that still managed to seep into her bedroom. She took short breaths to avoid inhaling more of the burnt smell. Just as she removed the cover from her face and sat up in the bed, she heard the front door close again.

"What did you forget because you could not have picked up the food that quick," she said, jumping out of bed, and cheerfully walking into the living room.

Her cheerful smile suddenly changed to a worried look as Tiny's presence stopped her dead in her tracks.

"What are you doing here," she managed to say as she backed away from his reach. She did not want to appear to be afraid, but she was sure that he could hear the fear resonating in her voice. His silence scared her more.

"Tiny, what the fuck are you doing here?" Journey repeated her words slowly, this time with some authority.

"I was passing through the neighborhood," Tiny lied. He had pulled up to the curb across the street from her brownstone just as a man with a fitted baseball cap on, was leaving her house moments ago. Tiny was sure it was the same man that had been periodically coming and going to and from her house over the past several weeks, but he could never get a good view of his face.

Tiny slowly backed Journey into what used to be their bedroom. Journey stared at him and then looked over in the direction of his gaze to see what had captured his attention; the unmade bed. They both set their sights on the disheveled sheets and covers, and Journey could see Tiny's large chest expand and contract as his breathing grew heavy. She grabbed the phone and held it up in the air.

"Tiny if you don't leave, I am calling the cops!"

"I saw your friend leaving," he said, ignoring her threats, and taking a few steps toward her. "Is that the same man who has been spending so much time here?"

"Tiny, I'm dialing the fucking number. What I do is my business, this is my house, remember!" Journey screamed, pressing the buttons as hard as she could with shaky hands.

"You found somebody else already, Journey? You really ain't going to give me another chance?" Tiny asked, half-angry; half-pitiful.

"Yes, hello, I need the police!" Journey ranted into the phone, spewing her information at the dispatcher, trying to ignore Tiny's words, but watching his every move.

"Get Out! The cops are on their way!" she screamed as the dispatcher confirmed that a patrol car had been dispatched.

"Who is he Journey?" Tiny asked as he backed out of the bedroom. "Just tell me and I will leave you alone," Tiny pleaded. He wanted to know who this guy was, so he could tell him to stay away from his wife. The divorce was not final and until it was, Tiny felt that Journey still belonged to him.

"Tiny, you have to leave me alone, it's over. Get out, please!" she pleaded. She did not want him to get arrested. She feared that being detained would only anger him more.

"You are still my wife," Tiny reminded her.

"Not for much longer," she also reminded him.

Instead of grabbing Journey by the neck and trying to shake his love back into her, Tiny walked over to the door. He wanted her to believe him again. He needed her to believe in him again. Dealing with daily life over the past few months without her had been devastating to not only his emotional state, but it was affecting his health as well as work. After taking over the gym, he quickly discovered that Journey held all of its parts together so that the business ran like a well-oiled machine. Yet, under his management, it seemed to be fraying at the seams. He would do anything to get his life and wife back, but he knew if another man was taking up the majority of her time, Journey would have very little time to think about him. Tiny had to eliminate any chances for this man to have access to his vulnerable wife. He grabbed the doorknob, and looked back at the woman he let go, but was determined to get her back.

"I love you Journey, I really do, and I always will. I am sorry as hell that I treated you so bad. I hope that one day you will forgive me," Tiny stated with a touch of sincerity in his voice.

A tear welled up in Journey's left eye, and she breathed in deep to prevent it from falling. She appreciated his apology, despite it coming forth too late.

"I do forgive you Tiny. I have to in order to move on, but that is what you have to do also -- move on. This is what you wanted and now it's what I want too. Now, please leave before the cops come because I really don't want to see them take you away. And, please don't come back," Journey stated firmly, but kept her distance.

From her living room window, she watched him walk across the street to his SUV. She hoped this was the last time she would ever she Tiny again. As he pulled off, she could hear the police sirens approaching, and she could see Cain's athletic silhouette bouncing up the street with a white plastic bag in his hand.

The police car pulled up to the curb in front of Journey's house, and Cain's steps became shorter and faster. He was becoming more worried with each step. All of his worst fears congested his mind as he trotted up the cement steps of Journey's brownstone. The two officers stopped him at the door.

"It's OK, he's with me," Journey said with a trembling voice.

Cain pushed pass the police officers, dropped the plastic bag onto the coffee table, and pulled Journey into his arms.

"What's going on?" he asked, looking into her teary eyes.

"Tiny was just here," Journey said, holding back the tears.

"What the fuck you mean he was just here? Like outside, parked across the street?" Cain's questions were coming too fast for Journey to answer them one at a time.

The two police officers listened intently to the conversation to find out exactly why they were called to the scene.

"No, Cain, he was here, in the house," Journey confirmed.

"What! Did he touch you?" Cain asked stepping back to examine her face and body.

The police officers interrupted their conversation, and asked Journey if she wanted to have Tiny picked up for violating the protective order.

"Um, no officers, I don't. I don't think he will come back again," Journey tried to sound assured and confident.

"It doesn't matter officer," Cain interjected, "I'm taking her back to my place tonight. Right now as a matter of fact."

The officers agreed that was the best alternative to Tiny possibly coming back, and being arrested. The two uniformed men shook Cain's hand as they exited Journey's home, and made their way back to the patrol car.

"Grab some clothes," Cain demanded, as he closed the front door, and walked into the kitchen.

"Cain, I really appreciate this, but I don't think it would be a good idea for me to stay at your dad's place," Journey said, reminding Cain of the connection between her, Sway and Tiny.

"Journey, don't argue with me OK," Cain said calmly, approaching Journey and grabbing her by the waist.

"Everything is cool. Pops is leaving in the morning to go to Vegas with Alex for that meeting, and when he leaves Vegas he is flying straight to his spot in the Bahamas with one of his lady friends for a few days. Go get your stuff," he reiterated, squeezing her tightly.

Journey did not argue, instead, she pulled away from his grasp, and swiftly walked into her bedroom to gather a few articles of clothing and toiletries.

Cain sat on the sofa and tried to suppress his anger while he waited for Journey. Although, he did not know Tiny personally, he and Tiny have been in the same room a few times since Cain returned to New York, and on each occasion Tiny never showed a side of himself that made Cain see what Journey was attracted to. Tiny was loud, overbearing, and he often tried to impress Sway, but Cain knew Tiny's truth. A few times Cain wanted to pull Tiny to the side and tell him that his wife was finally being treated the way she should be, but Cain promised Journey that he would let her handle Tiny, in her own way.

"OK, let's go," Journey said, slightly out of breath, and overloaded with the weight of her baggage.

As Cain looked up at Journey, his initial thought when he saw the size of her bags, was that she was moving in, but quickly was relieved by the notion that over-packing was a natural trait in most women. He stood up from the sofa and shook his head as he unloaded Journey by taking the heavier pieces. They grabbed the Chinese food, turned off the lights and pounced out of the front door to Cain's parked *BMW M-3*. The shiny, silver speed machine was just one of the many gifts Sway bestowed upon Cain as soon as he arrived in New York. Cain sped through the city streets, and reached his apartment building in record time. As he pulled his car into a visitor parking space, he noticed that his father's SUV was missing. *Good, he's not here,* Cain thought as he turned the engine off and jumped out of the car to assist Journey. As they exited the elevator and approached the door to Cain's apartment, Journey stopped.

"What's wrong?" Cain asked, stopping in his tracks and looking back at her.

"Are you sure Sway is not going to flip out?" Journey asked, feeling a little apprehensive.

"He's not even here! Tell you what, come on, we will go to my room and you don't have to come out until he leaves; and I won't tell him you are here," Cain said walking over to her and tugging her by the arm.

They entered the dark apartment and like trained pets, they both removed their shoes. Cain neatly placed his sneakers alongside his father's pair by the door, and Journey held onto her pair and carried them into Cain's room. Cain turned on the light as they entered his spacious room. It was painted in a soft calming blue-gray and his queen-size bed was covered in a masculine striped comforter with a matching sham and pillowcases. The large mirror hanging on the wall across from his bed intimidated Journey because she had never been in a man's room with a mirror large enough to capture all of the naughty acts performed there. She tried to pry her eyes from the reflection staring back at her, and walked over to Cain's desk to view his impressive music CD collection. It was clear that his musical taste was centered on rap music, but Journey was surprised that he was drawn to authentic East Coast rappers, such as KRS-One, Rakim and EPMD. She perused around his room before finally sitting down on the edge of his bed, and waited for Cain to return with warm Chinese food. Just as she reached for the remote control, she could hear the front door open and close. Journey sat still on the bed and tried not to move. Sway had returned home, and the last thing she wanted was for him to find her in Cain's bedroom. Her breaths were short and even as she tried to listen to the conversation on the other side of the door.

"Hey, what's up Pops," Cain bellowed in a calm, cool and collected tone.

"What's up with you," Sway asked as he stepped into the kitchen and noticed that Cain purchased take out.

"Nothin' much, just chillin' tonight, ya know," Cain said patting his father on the shoulder. "I got company."

"Oh really," Sway replied, stepping back. "Cain, I told you about having women up here. You don't let every woman you meet into your home, you remember that right?"

"Sshh, keep your voice down Pops this one is straight. And, one day you will meet her, but tonight is not a good night, OK?" Cain assured his father.

Sway looked over at the closed door to Cain's bedroom. He wanted to bust through the door to see what kind of woman his son would think of as *special,* but decided to give his son the benefit of the doubt. "OK, but Cain I am serious. Don't be having a whole bunch of women up in my house. I have been living here for over three years and only two women have ever stepped foot in here, so take heed to what I am trying to say," Sway said seriously, looking into his son's eyes.

"I know, I know, you told me that when I first got here remember? Only Alex and Stephanie have been here. Trust me, this will be the only one for a minute," Cain assured his father and pulled him in to give him some dap.

The two men shook hands and gave each other a half hug before Sway walked into his bedroom, and closed the door. He smiled to himself, impressed that his son had inherited his swagger. Sway was kind of happy knowing that his son would have someone here to keep him company while Sway traveled this week, but at the same time, Sway did not want Cain making it a habit bringing home women who held no prospect of attaining an ongoing 'friendship' with Cain. Sway opened his closet door and grabbed his suitcase. He began to pack everything he needed for both his business trip with Alex, and his pleasure trip with Stephanie.

Since Alex's confession on Mother's Day, Sway began showing Stephanie a bit more interest hence he invited her to spend a few days with him in the Bahamas. Aside from Alex, Stephanie had been the only other woman able to hold Sway's attention. And, because Stephanie led her own life in Atlanta, the prospect of her trying to cling onto him on a daily basis was not possible. And, because of this, Sway found her even more attractive than he did in the prior years when she lived just a stone's throw away in Long Island. Sway folded his garments neatly and tucked them into the suitcase. He heard the phone ringing but ever since Cain moved in, Sway never answered it. Mostly, because its usually Carmen calling to cry about how much she misses her baby.

"Yo Pops, pick up the phone!" Cain yelled from the kitchen, while reheating his and Journey's meal.

Cain pulled the plates from the microwave oven and darted off into his room before Sway could come back to interrogate him some more about his company. Cain closed the door behind him with his foot, and handed Journey a plate. She took the steaming plate from his hand and placed it on the pillow that sat on top of her lap. Cain turned the volume up on the television and sat down beside Journey.

"I heard you and your dad out there," Journey said in between bites.

"Yeah, everything is cool. I told you it would be," Cain said leaning in and kissing Journey on the mouth, despite that both their mouths were full.

Journey reciprocated the closed mouth kiss while she continued to chew her food, and silently prayed that Sway would not come through the door.

Chapter 21

Las Vegas, Nevada
Alex
You, Me, and He

The plane ride was smooth and gentle, as flights always seem to be whenever Alex flown anywhere with Sway. On this particular trip, they were accompanied by Romeo and his wife, Jennifer. After identifying their luggage, the two couples were escorted by their driver through the exit doors. Quickly they climbed into the back of the awaiting limousine, and they were greeted by the cool breeze flowing from the A/C. As everyone got comfortable in their seats, the limousine moved smoothly through the congested traffic in the arrival section of the airport. Alex sat next to Sway and directly across from Romeo. She pulled out her agenda and began to review the itinerary with the gentlemen.

"The car will drop you, Romeo and Jen off at the hotel, and then the driver will return at three to pick you both up for the meeting, and remember that Henry's partner will be attending," Alex instructed as she peered over her reading glasses. She prayed that the meeting, as well as the introductions would go smoothly.

Sway and Romeo gave Alex their undivided attention, and learned through the years to not question her, especially while going over an itinerary.

"Jen honey, while Romeo is at the meeting, I scheduled a delectable spa treatment for you, so you wouldn't be bored," Alex said, smiling over at Jennifer, who returned the smile with much appreciation.

"You always take care of everything Alex," Jennifer praised.

"That she does," Sway added, looking at Alex and admiring her. He loved it when she wore her glasses. The spectacles made her look like a sexy schoolteacher.

"So, you are not staying at the hotel?" Romeo finally questioned Alex.

"Um … , no. My friend lives here, so I will be staying at his place while we are here, but I will be at the meeting on time, promise," Alex said looking into Sway's eyes, almost seeking approval.

As the muscle in his jaw tightened, Sway looked at her and with a sense of indifference that only he could convey, simply stated, "cool."

Alex rolled her eyes up in her head, and peered out of the tinted window. She refused to allow Sway to alter her mood. It had been awhile since she and Derek seen each other, and she was anxious and excited to start her weekend. As the limousine cruised down the main strip, Alex devoted her attention to landmarks that were becoming familiar from her previous visit, and were now embedded in her subconscious. She ignored the conversation that the other passengers were engrossed in, and tried to refrain from looking at her watch, again.

Sway noticed her uneasiness, and he tried to dismiss her behavior. It bothered him to watch Alex yearn for another man's affection. During the past several weeks Sway was able to maintain enough distance between he and Alex. And, although, he still craved to feel her, he had begun to get used to no longer making love to her. His long time friend, Stephanie had resurfaced at a time that provided a smooth transition for Sway. He continued to maintain several 'friendships', but Stephanie had become the closest to replacing Alex. Sway looked over at Alex as the car pulled up to the hotel entrance.

"So, I will see you later this afternoon at the meeting?" Sway asked Alex as he opened the door.

"Yup, I will be there, but count me out for dinner, I have plans," she said just as a smile formed on her face and her insides began to warm.

Sway could not contain his smile. A part of him was happy that she was happy.

"I hear you," he replied, "I am going to be pushing out early myself tomorrow. I am going to take a few days off to check on my place in the Bahamas," Sway said, letting Alex know his intentions without divulging his vacation plans with Stephanie.

"Oh," Alex responded and looked over at Sway, who was bending over and looking back at her through the open car door. "That sounds nice and peaceful, are you traveling alone?"

"Nah, not this trip," Sway said with a chuckle. "I will see you later. I am looking forward to meeting your friend, maybe he can swing by when the meeting is over." He closed the door with a slight force.

Alex rolled down the window to make sure she got the last word. "I will make a point of it," she said as a matter of fact before turning her head away from Sway's provoking gaze. Her emotions were starting to overwhelm her. She was anxious to have Sway and Derek finally meet, excited to see Derek, in more ways than one, and she was also feeling a little jealous that Sway was spending time with another woman in the Bahamas. She tried to not let that emotion take over. *Hey, he deserves to be happy too*, she thought as she watched him glide into the hotel and out of her sight. She rolled up the window before anymore of the refreshing breeze from the air conditioner could escape, and instructed the driver to the next destination.

Sway caught up to Romeo and Jennifer, who were both patiently waiting for the desk clerk to hand them the key card to their suite.

"Yo man, what's up with Alex having a "friend" out this way?" Romeo questioned Sway as if they were Alex's big brothers.

"Hey, I didn't ask any questions. She told me about him about a month ago, and I assumed she must have met this cat during her first visit out here. But you know me Ro, whatever is whatever. As long as she is happy, and this guy seems to be able to keep a smile on her face, so who am I to get in the way of that. You know the kind of relationship we have, so as long as she lets that brotha' know that I ain't going nowhere, it's all good," Sway concluded, suppressing his jealousy and trying to come to a justified resolution as to why Alex was preferring another man's affection over his.

"I hear you," Romeo confirmed, "it's just weird not having her here with us. So, you didn't meet this guy yet?"

"I am supposed to meet him while we are out here, but I guess that will depend on when our meeting is over," Sway said with a strand of indifference in his tone.

"This should be an interesting weekend," Romeo quipped as he grabbed Jennifer's hand, and proceeded to walk over to the awaiting elevators.

"That it should my brother, that it should," Sway commented as he followed Romeo.

****

Her anxiety began to take full control over her being as the driver drove Alex to Derek's house. Every time she saw him, seemed like the first time; and his overly excited reaction to seeing her face, always made her feel more than wanted, and much appreciated. He called her cell phone several times soon after her flight landed, but she did not answer it. She didn't want Sway or Romeo witnessing the magnetic power Derek had over her. Instead, she thought she'd surprise Derek with her arrival. As the driver turned onto Derek's street, Alex's palms began to sweat and an involuntary smile stretched across her face from ear to ear. Thanks to the car that was pulling out as her driver was pulling in, the gate to Derek's community was still open. The limousine pulled up in front of Derek's door, and the driver moved quickly to assist Alex with her luggage. Once she reached the door, she contemplated opening the door with the spare key underneath the welcome mat, or ringing the doorbell. She chose the latter.

She stood patiently, waiting for Derek to open the door as she waved good-bye to the exiting limousine. She could not help tapping her foot. She needed to see his face.

Derek trotted to the door wondering which neighbor needed to borrow something else from him. He opened the door without asking who it was, and found Alex standing before him with a pleasant smile on her face. "Hey baby, what's up? I have been calling you all morning!" he exclaimed reaching out to her, and pulling her body close to his.

He immediately began to smother her with soft kisses and a euphoric feeling raced through her body replacing her anxiety. Her body grew limp and submissive to his touch, and she found her self wanting more than just his soft kisses. Alex wrapped her arms around Derek's neck and held on tightly as he reciprocated the feeling. They pulled away from one another, just long enough for him to grab her luggage and close the front door.

Derek dropped the luggage where he stood and took Alex back into his arms. "What took you so long to get here," he whispered as he touched her lips softly with his.

"I was trying to make it here as fast as I could," Alex replied with a shy grin. "I had to drop my clients off at the hotel first, but I am here now."

"And, that you are," he replied and kissed her passionately.

Her legs had morphed into rubbery stilts and Alex was unable to stand on her own. She was grateful that he was holding her body tightly. They continued to kiss as Derek backed her up against the wall in his foyer. His hands slid down to her waist in search of her jeans' button and zipper. He needed to feel her to make sure she was really there. He quickly pulled her tucked in t-shirt out of her jeans and unfastened the button in one motion. She appreciated his ability to move swiftly without losing his momentum. He conveniently slipped the t-shirt over Alex's head, and pulled her jeans and lacy panties down to her ankles, making it easier for her to step out of them. She wasn't sure if it was part of a well thought plan or a coincidence, but by having on basketball shorts, allowed Derek to undress within seconds. The cool feeling the wall provided for her bare back counteracted the heat that was rising in between her thighs, and with a sense of urgency, she lifted her legs around his waist, without parting her lips from his. He graciously accepted the extra weight her legs applied to his being and held onto her tightly. They both knew that some form of protection should be involved at this point of their lustful tryst, but neither of them spoke a word and, instead, continued to kiss as Derek slowly penetrated her moist flesh. He released a sigh of relief. He often imagined how Alex felt without using a condom, and the actual feeling exceeded his expectation by far. He stroked her gently, trying to feel every part of her insides as his enlarged penis pulsated against the walls of her moist canal. Without letting her go, he pulled her body away from the wall and leaned her against the steps that lead to his second floor. Alex's moans turned him on more, causing him to move slightly faster as his thrusts provided a feel good pain that often comes with a man his size.

Alex relished in his ability to assist in maintaining her moisture. She showed her appreciation with the gyration of her hips in unison with the movement of his body. "Oh, Derek," she moaned as he cupped her buttocks with both hands and gently squeezed them.

"I really missed you Baby," he whispered in her ear while nibbling at her lobe.

"I missed you too," Alex replied and opened her eyes to get a full view of his masculine face. She felt lucky to have met a man who could make her feel this way. She appreciated Derek. And, she could feel that he was appreciating her.

Their bodies moved together in slow motion, as sweat beads formed on Derek's brow while he worked his magic on Alex. She gently glided her nails across his back, creating a tingling feeling that traveled from Derek's toes to his groin area.

"You're gonna make me come if you keep doing that," he moaned in delight.

"It's OK, you can. I'll be here all weekend," Alex purred.

And, within moments, he did, and collapsed on top of Alex. He made a conscious effort not to smother her, so he lifted himself onto his forearms. "You OK?" he asked with concern.

"Mmm … hmm," Alex sighed, exhausted from the trip and the tryst.

Derek stood up, slid back into his shorts, and extended his hand to Alex to help her stand up. Sheepishly, Alex slipped back into her clothing, and straightened out her hair, which was wildly out of place.

"Wow," she commented. "That was an exceptional welcome," she said, smiling at Derek as he lifted her bags and carried them up the steps.

"Sorry, I couldn't help it. You looked good enough to eat standing there on my doorstep!" he yelled from his bedroom. Within seconds, he was trotting back down the steps, and pulling Alex back into his arms.

"We have a few hours before the big meeting, so I planned a little something for you, but we have to hurry now that you've sidetracked me," he said, smiling brightly and showing off his sexy dimple.

"Oh yeah," Alex replied excitedly. "And, what would that be?"

"Come on, let's go," he said pulling her by hand, and rushing towards his garage.

"OK, but, shouldn't I freshen up, and maybe change," Alex suggested, hoping he would divulge where he was taking her.

"It will be just the two of us, and one other person," Derek hinted.

"Well is it someplace where I can eat? I am kind of hungry," Alex confessed.

"We'll grab something on the way," he promised, as he opened the car door for his lady.

****

"This is absolutely amazing!" Alex shouted into the small microphone that was attached to the oversized headphones covering her ears. Due to the noise of the helicopter propellers spinning above her head, she didn't realize she was yelling.

When Derek initially pulled into the small heliport, Alex's palms started to sweat profusely, and the gourmet sandwich she had just eaten was literally in her throat. But, as he parked the car, and pulled her out of it, Derek assured her that she would be safe, and that this was going to be fun. The forty-five minute helicopter ride was something Derek wanted to do since permanently settling in Las Vegas, but never found that right person to share the experience with because truth be told; he was afraid of helicopters.

"Yeah, it is, ain't it?" Derek asked rhetorically as he looked out of the window at the miniature city below.

The two newly formed lovers held each other's hands while they enjoyed their extraordinary tour of Nevada. The helicopter circled the city like a big eye in the sky before heading back to the heliport. Derek and Alex both wished they had more time to hover over Sin City, but their meeting time was nearing and they had to get back to his place to shower and change.

"That was incredible! Thank you," Alex said like a child experiencing her first time at an amusement park.

"You're welcome, and thank you for coming with me," Derek said with much appreciation. "I knew you could do it."

"Believe me, I had my reservations, but I feel safe with you," she smiled.

"I want you to feel that way because you are safe with me," his voice became romantic.

"Are you ready for the big meeting today?" Alex asked, ready to introduce Derek to Sway, so she could stop feeling like she is hiding something from the man she was prepared to become an open book for.

"I am so ready for this," Derek said, taking a deep breath. "I have something else planned today that I hope you will be OK with."

"Another surprise?" Alex questioned, completely drained from the one he just laid on her.

"Well, it's not really a surprise, although someone will be," Derek confessed. "It's more like redemption." Derek peered over at Alex with a serious face.

She immediately became curious, and wanted to know who needed to be redeemed and what did that have to do with her. Her glowing smile slowly disappeared. "Is everything OK Derek? Are you alright?"

"I'm cool," he assured her. "I am just glad you are here to witness something that I have to do. After I take care of this one last thing, I feel like we will be able to move forward without anything hanging over our heads, you feel me?"

"It just so happens that I feel you completely," Alex affirmed. "I actually have someone here for you to meet and once you do, I was hoping that you and I could go to the next level as well."

"OK, I'm wit' it," Derek confirmed and did not bother to ask who that person was. He assumed it was her daughter.

He remembered when Alex told him that she would know when she was ready for the next level in a relationship once she introduced that man to her daughter. *Who else could it be*, he thought as he drove along suddenly becoming anxious as he approached his house. He was hoping making amends with Sway would go smoothly and swiftly, so he could finally meet Alex's pride and joy.

****

Derek and Alex looked like the golden couple as they patrolled the Las Vegas strip in his shiny car. They were running a few minutes late for the meeting, but only had themselves and the quickie they performed in the shower to blame. They decided to take advantage of every minute they shared alone because they both knew that the weekend would be over in the blink of an eye, and Alex would soon be back on the East Coast.

Derek pulled into the parking garage, and found a spot next to the elevators. The two of them sprung out of the car and scurried to the elevators, knowing that tardiness was frowned upon in the professional world.

"Everything is going to be fine," Alex said with assurance as she straightened Derek's necktie. She noticed that he was visibly nervous. "My clients are really cool. Not your average millionaire stiffs," she chuckled, trying to make light of the importance of this deal.

"I hope he still is," Derek muffled as the elevator doors opened to Henry's office.

"Excuse me," Alex replied in an attempt to get Derek to repeat himself.

"It's nothing, never mind. Let's do this," he said, trying to muster up all of the confidence in his being. Derek did not know what to expect once he entered the boardroom to face the man he once tried to have killed. He hoped that during the past ten years, Sway's heart had softened with forgiveness. Yet, Derek sensed that it hadn't. He once knew Sway better than anyone, and forgiveness like commitment, was something Sway just did not do.

Alex and Derek approached the door to the conference room, and stood still before pulling the door open. Alex inhaled deeply. She was completely ready to introduce her new man to the only other man in her life. The two professionals burst through the double doors with an air of confidence, and Derek held a slight swagger. Sway and Romeo were deep in a private conversation when the sound of the doors opening caused them to divert their attention. It was unlike Alex to be late to anything, much less one of *his* meetings. Sway made a mental note to deal with her later, but right now he was ready to finalize this matter. At first, his eyes did not focus on the tall gentleman walking beside Alex because her business attire had captured his attention. But, once he finished admiring Alex from head to toe, he turned his attention to the rugged face attached to the form fitting Armani suit. Sway could not believe his eyes. He blinked -- twice, and without warning, he sprung from his chair and onto his feet, and his fist made contact with the right side of Derek's face.

"Oh my God! Sway what are you doing?" Alex screamed at the top of her lungs as Romeo jumped up from his seat and pulled Sway back.

"What the fuck are you doing here?" Sway growled at Derek, ignoring Alex. "You are so fuckin' lucky I don't have my gun, nigga!" Sway spewed his venom.

"Steven McCoy! Watch your mouth!" Alex found herself saying as she looked at Derek. She was totally confused. "What is going on!"

"I guess I deserve that," Derek said, rubbing his cheek. "I had that coming," he confirmed as he stared his former best friend in the eye.

"Muthafucka you deserve a lot more than that," Sway seethed, throwing his business etiquette out of the window.

Henry stayed seated at the head of the conference table, scared to move from the fear of getting hit, or allowing his cohorts to see that he had urinated all over himself. He had never been involved in such a violent setting, much less where he was the minority. For the first time ever in Derek's presence, he was petrified.

"Please, somebody tell me what is going on! You two know each other?" Alex questioned them both.

"Know each other, know each other," Sway repeated himself, trying to regain some kind of composure. "This is the muthafucka who tried to kill me!" He would not release Derek from his intense gaze. He wanted to kill him.

Romeo sensed it, and pulled Sway back near the window overlooking the city. "Yo, Sway calm down man, be easy. This ain't the place or the time for this shit. We gotta deal with him about that at a different time," Romeo said in a low voice in Sway's ear.

"Wait a minute, you mean to tell me you are the friend who betrayed Sway?" Alex looked at Derek with disappointment written all over her face.

Derek suddenly became utterly sorry for all of the past dirty deeds he took part in. He walked over to Alex and tried to grab her hands but she pulled back.

"I can't believe this," Alex said shaking her head. "He was the person I wanted you to meet," she said in a low voice.

"Excuse me," Sway interrupted, not sure of what he thought he just heard. "You wanted him to meet me? Meet me for what Alex?" Sway approached the couple with Romeo following closely behind. "*This* is your new friend?" Sway asked, hoping she'd say no.

Alex looked up at Sway with pleading eyes, and tried to hold back the tears, but was losing that battle. "Yes," she whimpered, "and, he is also Mr. Mitken's partner."

"What!" Sway screamed. "There is no fucking way I am going into business with this ... this," he stammered.

Derek stood still, observing Sway's every move. He allowed Sway to take a jab at him once because he owed it to him, but there would not be another one.

Sway leaned into Alex so close that their noses touched. "He will never meet my daughter, you hear me!" Sway said through clenched teeth with a tone of reverence and finality.

Derek shook his head, so that his ears could absorb what he had just heard. He was the one now befuddled. Alex had turned the tables, and everyone's secrets were being divulged haphazardly with no rhyme or reason.

"Wait a minute," Derek interjected, "Alex, this is your daughter's father?"

When she told him that one of her client's was also the father of her child, he never put the two of them together.

"Yes, Derek he is. I'm sorry, I should have told you the whole story, but I didn't know we were going to mesh so well so quickly," she immediately tried to explain.

Both Sway and Derek instantly fell victim to the sincerity and softness in the tone of her voice, and found themselves staring at her lovely pleading eyes. However, her gaze was only for Derek, and Sway noticed it.

"Yo, Ro I can't do this shit today man," Sway stated as he turned to face his business partner. "If I stay here any longer, I am going to kill this nigga." Sway walked over to the large oval conference table and grabbed his paperwork before heading for the door.

"Sway, wait!" Alex cried, breaking her stance with Derek, and turning to follow Sway. She quickly looked back at Derek and hoped he understood. She did not want Sway to walk away from the deal of his lifetime, and although everyone was overwhelmed with mixed emotions, she hoped that they all could sit down to at least try to deal with one situation at a time. More importantly, she could not have Sway upset with her for any reason. Her legs moved quickly, past the curious employees seated in the bullpen, to catch up to him before he could board the elevator.

"Please Sway, wait. Can I talk to you?" she begged as they walked into the elevator. She was grateful that they were alone because she felt that the conversation about to take place was not going to be pretty. "Sway what do you want me to say? How was I supposed to know?"

"You know what Alex, it doesn't even matter. The bottom line is, that is a friend you can't keep, period," Sway demanded with a stern look in his eye. They both knew he meant it. "And, to make matters worse, you're havin' sex with him," Sway felt his stomach turn.

Derek already tried to kill Sway once, and now that he was stealing Alex's heart from him, Derek was emotionally killing Sway again. It was a pain that Sway could not bear. He would rather have the bullets in his back again. Sway glared at Alex with great disapproval. "How could you sleep with someone so grimy?" Sway asked clearly disappointed at Alex's choice with whom she decided to depart from his love for.

His actions and words started to make Alex feel dirty and unclean. Suddenly a part of her regretted the explosive unprotected sex romps she had earlier with Derek. Yet, the other part had to defend her sense of character. "Look Sway, I asked you several times to tell me who did that to you, and you would always close up like a clamshell, so don't put all of this shit on me!" Alex said loudly.

Sway peered down at Alex, and for the first time since meeting her, felt nothing. He was angry and most of all, hurt. He could see that because of what just transpired, he and Alex's relationship would never be the same. Never again, would he be able to look at her with sexual hunger in his eyes because he would know that Derek had not only been there, but had the ability to make her fall *in* love, which was the one emotion Sway could never pull out of her. His resentment toward Derek grew fiercely at the mere thought. "You're right Alex, it's my fault for not telling you who shot me, but I'll tell you what. You have a very serious decision to make. Either you stop seeing him, or I fight for sole custody of my daughter," Sway said calmly as he exited the elevator that had finally landed on the ground level.

He walked quickly toward the exit while ignoring Alex's shrilling screams for him to stop. He realized that the ultimatum he had just given her, would destroy her happiness on one hand, or destroy their friendship on the other. Regardless, he would not allow her to fall any harder for the man who tried to snuff out his life on his thirtieth birthday. More importantly, he would never allow Derek to form a relationship with his daughter, ever.

Sway approached the waiting car, and slid into the back seat. His vision was blurred due to the tears that he tried to hold back. He was a man who did not believe in crying but losing the one woman he cherished was tormenting him. He was broken. He needed to go home to make sense out of what had just occurred, and he suddenly wanted to be alone. He pulled his cell phone from his suit jacket lapel and dialed Stephanie's number to cancel their island trip.

Alex's uncontrollable sobbing prevented her from leaving the elevator, so she rode it up and down until she could finally catch her breath and calm down. She could not believe that Sway was making her choose between her child, and Derek because they both knew that there was no choice to be made. She would have to end it with Derek. She wiped her face with her hands, and tried to gain as much composure as she could to face Romeo, Henry and Derek. As she walked back into Henry's office, she kept her head down, so his employees would not see how fast her eyes were able to swell from the millions of tears she managed to shed in such a short period of time. She walked back into the conference room with what little dignity she had left in her being. "I'm sorry about all of this," she said in a breathy voice, trying not to cry again.

Henry remained seated and nodded his head. He was more confused than she, and his only priority at the moment was removing these individuals from his office space, so he could change his soiled clothing. He was not sure what would become of his and Derek's business relationship, but the drama Derek brought into his workplace was unacceptable, to say the least.

"It will be fine," Henry tried to console her from a far. "I think we all need to adjourn this meeting for a later date. By then everyone's emotions should have settled, and we'll have our business caps back on straight."

"I think that is a good idea Hank. Ms. Avery and I have a lot to discuss right now though," Derek said to Henry but kept his eyes on Alex.

He was not sure what she and Sway talked about, but he could tell by her puffy eyes and bright red nose that she must had cried a river before returning to the conference room.

Romeo walked up to Alex and hugged her hard. "You want me to stick around," Romeo asked her like an overly protective brother.

"No, uh-uh, you go back to the hotel to your wife. I will see you at the hotel later, OK," Alex tried to convince him that she could handle herself.

"Alright, but if you need me, call me. I am going to get back to the hotel to make sure homeboy is cool. I will see you later," Romeo confirmed before saying a quick good-bye to the other two men and exiting the office.

Derek walked over to Alex and did not know if it was OK to touch her. "Hey," he whispered and reached out to her. "Can we go someplace to talk?" he asked.

Alex did not respond, instead, she walked over to Henry and leaned over so that their eyes met. "Mr. Mitken I am truly sorry for the outburst in here today. It was unwarranted and uncalled for. I hope that we all can come together on this because it is a great opportunity for all parties involved. Thank you for giving me some time to see if we can still work this out," Alex said, hoping to be able to save what was left of this venture.

"I think its only fair Ms. Avery, and please don't apologize. It's not your fault," Henry replied, staring at Derek with angry eyes. "Derek and I will need that time to regroup as well," Henry added.

"I agree Hank, and I apologize for not giving you all of the details of my intentions with this venture, and for having a hidden agenda. I will call you later," Derek said owning his part in the fiasco.

Henry did not stand up to see them out; instead he sat stoically at the head of his conference table and allowed his silence to dismiss them. Alex walked out of the office ahead of Derek unsure if she wanted to be seen with him or not.

"I know you are upset with me, but can you at least wait up," Derek ranted in a whisper, as he followed her into the elevators.

The few passengers in the elevator prevented Derek from speaking to Alex, and she was happy for that. They exited the building and walked over to Derek's car in silence, neither knowing where to start. He opened the car door for her, and stared at her every move as she brushed by him and sat down. This was the side of Alex, Derek had not yet seen: the quiet, angry side. He wasted very little time getting into the car, starting the engine and racing out of the garage.

"Alex, I am sorry." He thought by starting off with an apology would at least get her to look him in the face.

"Why didn't you tell me that you knew him?" Alex asked, trying to figure out why he kept that fact hidden.

"I didn't think you needed to know," Derek spoke truthfully. "I thought he was just a client of yours, but had I known of the deeper personal connection between the two of you, I would have never even approached you, to be honest. If you would have told me that Sway was your child's father, I would have stopped pursuing you on the spot. I would have concentrated primarily on why I initially set out to reconnect with him. Why didn't you tell me?" Derek asked, pointing to his chest, and a little upset that she never shared that important piece of this intricate puzzle.

Alex silently agreed with him that maybe she should have mentioned it once their relationship took a serious turn, but since she didn't know that Derek was the "friend" who tried to have Sway killed, she didn't think them meeting at this time made a difference. In less than one hour Alex had become part of three crumbling relationships because of intentional omissions and the harboring of secrets. Her heart sank as she thought about how she was going to fix the special unique relationship with Sway, continue the new loving budding relationship with Derek, and save the prosperous business relationship with Henry. Her mind raced and Sway's words rambled over and over in her head. She was the only woman who could tell when Sway was serious, and he spoke clearly with his eyes when he walked away from her, which told her he was. She looked over at Derek's somber face and wished she could turn back the hands of time, and handle the entire situation differently. But, because she couldn't, she realized that this was the last time they would see each other.

"I didn't tell you Derek because I wanted to wait until I was sure that what I was feeling was really love," Alex confessed with newly formed tears escaping her eyes.

His heart sank as soon as his ears heard the word "love", and he pulled the car over and stopped on the desolate road leading back to his house.

"What did you just say?" Derek needed to hear it again.

"You heard me, but now everything is out of control. He gave me an ultimatum and I have to take it," Alex cried, unable to hold it in.

"What do you mean?" Derek asked, utterly confused.

"I mean, when it comes to my child, there is never a choice. I choose her. I'm afraid that we are going to have to end this: right here, right now." Her words were barely audible due to the blubbering her cry had morphed into.

Derek could barely understand her, but he was able to recognize "end this". "Baby we don't have to end anything. I know Sway. He is mad at me and he should be, but he will get over it. Once he calms down, he will see that I have changed. I am not that person he knew ten years ago. You know the new me. We can't end it. I need you," Derek pleaded.

"I can't Derek. You don't … ," Alex whimpered, shaking her head back and forth. "You don't understand, Sway and I have a child together, and we take parenting very seriously. He already told me that it's either you or my daughter."

"He's making you choose?"

"Unfortunately, I'm so sorry but I can't do this anymore," she looked into his eyes seeking acceptance of the demise of their love affair.

"No, Alex don't say that. I will talk to him to make him understand how we feel about each other," Derek quipped, trying to think of anything to say that would salvage their relationship.

Alex looked into his pleading eyes, and could not help smiling at his sincerity and attempt to keep the flame they started, lit.

"That is the problem Derek, he already knows how we feel about one another, and he won't have it. Sway is in love with me, and had he and I met under different circumstances five years ago, I am sure I would not be sitting here with you now," she tried to explain.

It was starting to make sense to Derek. He had only researched Sway for the past two years, and apparently the relationship between Sway and Alex started years before that. Yet, that no longer mattered to Derek. It was too late because his heart was already into it, and he did not want to live out the rest of his days without Alex living them out with him. "Do you love him?" Derek needed to know.

"I do love him, but I am not *in* love with him," Alex honestly stated. "But, I also value his friendship, and I would never do anything to hinder that because it would affect the way we deal with each other and our child."

Derek wished he could understand the desire to have such a strong kinship with another person, but since he didn't have any children of his own, his mind could not yet conceptualize that kind of relationship between a man and a woman.

"I'm sorry Alex but I don't understand. I realize that you and he will always have to deal with each other, but it sounds like you are willing to sacrifice your relationship with me for a *friendship* with him," Derek said, trying not to sound insensitive.

Alex breathed in deeply and wiped her wet face with her bare hands. She could feel her emotions rebuilding the wall around her heart as she began to recoil back into her hardened self. Before the meeting, she wanted nothing more than to be able to further the blossoming relationship she and Derek were enveloped in; but the unveiling of his past, made it virtually impossible for them to continue to carry on an intimate relationship.

"And, that is what I was afraid of," she said regretfully. "You're not understanding what he and I have, and I am sorry that you don't. But, it doesn't even matter now because we have to stop seeing each other, or he will try to take my baby away from me. He would never allow his daughter around you! You tried to kill him Derek!" her voice grew louder, as the thought of that heinous act crept into the forefront of her psyche.

"I know and I am sorry for that. That's why I am trying to build this business out here; for him. Look, we have something Alex. I don't want that to end."

"Unfortunately, Derek it has too," Alex replied with coolness in her voice.

Alex turned away from his gaze and peered out of the window. It was killing her to have to end the one relationship she thought was on the road to forever, but she would never choose a man over her child.

"I wish you and Sway didn't know each other because things would be different," she said looking out of the window. "But the fact of the matter is, you two do know each other, too well," she chuckled. "And, because of the history you two share, you and I can never make our own. I am really sorry Derek, but I need you to take me back to the hotel," she said, refusing to look in his face, fearing that she would be recaptured by his magnetic charm.

"What about your things?" he asked, hoping that she would come back to his place, so he could seduce her back into his life.

"I will send for them. But I need to be alone right now," she began to cry again.

"Ok Baby, don't cry. I will take you to wherever you need to go," he solemnly said.

Derek made a u-turn in the middle of the road and started to head back toward the city. He drove at a slower speed, trying to savor what little time he had left to spend with the woman who would soon walk out of his life with his heart in her hand. He knew that he would have to reap all of the seeds he had sown, but he never expected karma to smack him down like this.

Chapter 22

New York, New York
Journey
Zoom

Journey had barely gotten a full hour's worth of sleep throughout the night knowing that Sway was snoring in the other bedroom across the apartment. She heard him when he got up and tried to quietly leave for his five a.m. flight. There was one moment, right before he walked out of the door, she could hear his footsteps walking towards Cain bedroom door, and then there was dead silence. She prayed he would not open the door to let Cain know he was leaving. She held her breath with the sheet over her head until she heard his footsteps fade away, and the heavy door to the apartment close.

The day passed by peacefully, and she tried not to think about why she was being held up at Sway's place for the weekend. She thanked Cain in more ways than one for being there for her, and for allowing her to sleep in all day. She lay in his firm bed, wearing just his t-shirt that he started out wearing the night before, and she waited for Cain to return with the pizza. She rolled out of the bed and stretched as her toes curled into the plush carpet. The city skyline was spectacular as the lights of the buildings flickered against the dark night. The view of New York from Cain's window was exceptional. Journey peered down at the city streets, and watched the pedestrians below shuffle up and down the sidewalk like little soldier ants. Walking around Cain's room and viewing the same artifacts she seen the night before, Journey decided to take advantage of being all alone in Sway's place. She eased out of Cain's room and looked around the dimly lit room to make sure she was alone. She perused the large studio style living room and dining area, and she admired the layout of the bachelor pad. She peeked in Sway's room, but was too afraid to walk into the room. She feared that he had cameras hidden somewhere. That thought did not seem too far fetched for someone as secretive as Sway. She had never been to Sway's place in all of the years she's known him. There was just never a reason to, until now. Cain had become her rock, and she was thankful that he was sent her way. She walked into the kitchen, and peered into the refrigerator to see what kind of foods the two bachelors consume on a daily basis. She was impressed to see vitamin waters, lots of leafy greens, and an abundance amount of fruit. There were a few sugary treats laced in between the organic goods, but for the most part they ate pretty healthy.

"No wonder he looks half his age," Journey said about Sway as if someone was listening.

The sound of the ringing phone startled Journey, and she jammed her finger in the refrigerator door.

"Ouch, shit!" she cursed as she shook her hand in an attempt to relieve the pain quickly.

The phone rang again. Journey stood next to the phone and looked at it while it rang several times more before hearing the answer machine come on. At the sound of the beep, her heart stopped when she heard Tiny's voice on the other end.

"Yo Sway, where you at man! I've been fuckin' callin' your cell an' shit, no answer! Yo, I need you to come bail me out of jail man! Fuckin' pussy ass cops picked me up for violating a damn protective order that bitch just put out on me. Yo, come get me man. I been here all fuckin' day. Two gees, that's all you need. I'm at the 33rd precinct downtown ... hurry up!"

Journey heard another click and then dead silence. "Bitch!" she said aloud at the machine as though Tiny could hear her. "I got your bitch, you bastard!" she said, looking at the delete button on the answering machine.

She was livid at Tiny for trying to imply that she just put a restraining order against him. It was apparent that he hadn't told Sway the whole truth as to why she left his abusive ass. And, she could only imagine the lies he told Sway to cover up his behavior and infidelity. *He is an ungrateful bastard*, Journey thought as the little devil inside of her told her to delete the message so Sway could not get it, and Tiny's big ass would have to sit in jail until Sway returned from the Bahamas. Yet, the angel inside of her asked her to let it go and move on, and not to waste any more energy on him. A devilish grin appeared on Journey's face, making it clear as to which part of her inner being she chose to listen to. She placed her manicured nail on the tiny button, and at the same time, she could hear Cain fidgeting with his keys at the door. She pressed the button quickly and looked at the message display to ensure that it indicated no calls. She quickly scurried over to the sofa and plopped down on it. Just as she reached for the remote Cain appeared with a large pizza box in his hand.

"Did I hear the phone ringing?" he asked as he walked over to the sofa and placed the large cardboard box on the table in front of Journey. "You can hear that shit way down the hall," he chuckled.

"Um, yeah," Journey stumbled, feeling a tinge of guilt surge through her body. "But they did not leave a message." She opened the box and was welcomed by the pleasant aroma of melted cheese and ripe tomato sauce.

Cain quickly ran into the kitchen to grab a couple of plates and two beers. He walked back over to Journey, handed her the chilled bottle, and sat down next to her. She pulled a slice of pizza out of the box and giggled under her breath.

"What's so funny?" Cain asked picking up the remote and turning the television on.

"I have a confession to make," Journey said sheepishly and looking deeply into his eyes.

"What'd you do?" Cain was afraid to ask.

"Well, someone did leave a message on your answering machine, but I erased it," Journey laughed.

"And, that's funny," Cain said, trying to find the humor in her juvenile act.

"Yeah," she gasped, "because it was Tiny!"

"Oh, word!" Cain chuckled. "What did he say?"

"The cops picked him up anyway and he wants your father to bail his big ass out! I wouldn't have erased it, but he called me a bitch! And, he made it seem like it was *my* fault that he is locked up in the 33rd precinct right now!" Journey exclaimed.

"Yeah, he is wild for that," Cain replied coolly.

"Oh well, Pops can't help his ass out right now anyway all the way from Vegas, so I guess he's stuck," Cain said, lifting a slice of pizza from the box and brushing off Tiny's current situation. He could care less. Cain thought Tiny was a coward, and he could not wait for the day when Sway would see that for himself.

Cain and Journey devoured the pizza in what seemed like one breath, and leaned back into the soft leather sofa in unison to digest the massive amount of carbohydrates filling their bodies.

"That was good," Cain managed to say as he lifted his t-shirt and rubbed his slightly protruding belly.

"Mmm … , yes it was," Journey agreed, standing up to clean up the mess they just made.

Cain slowly lifted his body, and followed suit by grabbing the empty beer bottles. Journey placed the food-stained plates in the sink and started to run the hot water. She was trying to make sure nothing was out of place in Sway's home.

"You don't have to do those," Cain said, walking up behind Journey and grabbing her by the waist.

"No, I want to do them now. You know, keep the place clean," Journey responded, looking over her shoulder at him.

Cain leaned in and kissed her on the mouth. Journey turned the running water off, and spun completely around to face him.

"You are so good at distracting me. I told you awhile ago that you were dangerous," she whispered while she allowed his hand to travel beneath the t-shirt and up and down her naked body.

"I like distracting you," Cain oozed as he lifted her body and sat her naked butt on the granite countertop.

Their kisses became more passionate as Cain entered Journey's warmth without hesitation and without protection. Journey wrapped her hands around Cain's waist to pull his thickness all the way in. Cain sucked on her small breasts as his leg muscles flexed while he slid in and out of Journey's juicy thighs. They were so wrapped up in their re-enactment of the infamous kitchen scene from the movie, *Fatal Attraction* that neither of them heard the front door opening.

"WHAT IS GOING ON HERE!" Sway nearly jumped out of his skin. He thought he had seen it all in Vegas, and he certainly was not expecting to walk into his own home, and find his twenty-one year old son sexing his best friend's wife on his kitchen countertop. The soft pornographic scene infuriated Sway, and his heavily pulsating temples made him feel like his head was going to explode.

"What the fuck Cain!" Was all Sway could say as he approached Cain, who was now standing in front of Journey, protecting her from Sway's forceful stare of unbelief that gripped his face like a muzzle on a vicious dog.

This was a side of his father Cain never had the opportunity to meet, and he wasn't so sure he was ready for the introduction under the current circumstances.

"Pops!" Cain gasped. "What are you doing home, you just left earlier this morning," Cain said trying to change the subject and pulling up his shorts.

"Boy, don't play with me!" Sway yelled. "Why in the hell are you fuckin' in my kitchen, and why are you doin' it with one of my best friend's wife?" Sway seethed through clenched teeth, and his eyes bulging. During the past twelve hours, Sway had managed to get sucked into all kinds of drama. He could not decipher which matter was worse.

Cain could see both the hurt and anger in Sway's eyes, but refused to back down.

"Boy? Yo, Pops I've stopped being a boy along fuckin' time ago," Cain stood up straight and faced his father like a man. "Listen, I am sorry that you had to see what you just saw. I am sorry as hell, but let it be known Pops calling me that boy shit ain't gonna fly," Cain apologized and tried to defend his manhood at the same time.

"Now you listen to me … , little man," Sway gritted as he stepped into Cain's personal space. "While you are living under my roof, eating my fuckin' food, and living the good life off my back, you will respect me!"

Fear started to creep up Cain's spine, but he tried to suppress it as he stared straight into his father's piercing eyes without blinking.

"And, I don't' know how you and her hooked up," Sway continued, pointing to Cain's closed bedroom door that Journey had managed to slide behind to gather up her belongings. "And, I don't want to know, but by you messing with her puts me in a very fucked up position, Cain. That's my boy's wife!"

"Soon to be ex-wife," Cain corrected Sway, with a hint of sarcasm in his voice.

"And, that's because of you," Sway said, disappointedly.

Cain backed away from his father to get a clear view of his face in order to make sure he was serious.

"Because of me?" Cain questioned. "Hell no, it ain't cause of me!"

"Tiny told me that Journey was leaving him for another man, and from the looks of it, you are the other man," Sway confirmed.

"Pops that bastard is lying!" Cain shouted, becoming slightly animated.

Journey could hear the men firing harsh words back and forth, and felt bad that is was because of her. She slipped on her sweats and flip-flops, and stuffed her clothes into her carry-on bag without folding one article. She stood at the door and held onto its knob, waiting for the perfect time to make her exit. She was mortified that Sway caught her having sex, much less with his son. She had no words to explain, and wished she didn't have to face him, but the front door was the only way out of the penthouse suite. *Damn, he would have to live on the top floor of a forty story building*, Journey thought as she tried to listen to the argument on the other side of the door.

"It don't seem like he's lying," Sway stated, protecting his friend and looking around his apartment at the proof of Cain and Journey's blatant infidelity.

Cain could see that Sway was having a hard time believing him. He had to make his father see Tiny for who he really was.

"You don't believe me? Go down to the 33rd precinct and bail your boy out for beatin' Journey's ass," Cain erupted, feeling slightly guilty for airing Journey's dirty laundry.

"What?" Sway asked, not understanding Cain's comeback.

"You heard me," Cain boasted. "Man please … , your boy is locked up because he has been hittin' on her, and he was at her place just last night threatening her. That's why she's here Pops. I'm protecting her from that crazy nigga!" Cain exclaimed, trying to justify his actions.

"Yeah, you protecting her alright!" Sway laughed. He could not help seeing the humor in the ridiculous scene he just walked in on.

Sway was more confused now than ever, and realized his night was just beginning because now he had to bond his boy out of jail. Sway had to find out why Tiny's wife was at his house laid up with his son. Sway stepped back away from Cain and rushed over to the door. "I am going to find out what is really going on Cain, and in the meantime you set up in Stevie's room for the night. Journey can stay here for as long as she needs to, but I can't have you two sleeping together until I find out the whole truth," Sway spoke in a fatherly tone.

He grabbed his car keys from the small table and opened the door. He looked back at Cain and shook his head. "You tell Journey to call her girl. I am certain Alex needs her."

Cain stared at his father, silently wishing that he would hurry up and leave, so he could stop puffing out his chest. As the door shut behind Sway, Cain collapsed onto the countertop in the same spot where Journey's naked butt had been adhered to. He breathed in deeply and was overwhelmed with embarrassment. He always figured that his father would catch him sexing a chick one day, but never like the way he just did. Cain stood up and attempted to retrieve his swagger as he approached his bedroom to let Journey know that Sway had calmed down, and to call Alex. By the time he entered his room, it was apparent that Journey was eavesdropping because she was already holding her cell phone and dialing Alex's phone number.

"I'm sorry Cain," Journey said, looking up at him, holding the small instrument up to her ear and waiting for Alex to answer. She didn't.

"Don't be sorry," Cain said calmly, and sat down on his bed beside her, "he was going to find out sooner or later, so it is what it is." His coolness effortlessly oozed out of his mouth as he spoke those words. He was definitely his father's child: calm, cool and collected.

Journey could hear it in Sway's voice as he left to rescue Tiny that he was almost over being upset about catching her and Cain christening his countertop. She just hoped that Sway would be able to see through Tiny's bullshit, and finally realize that Tiny is not the man who Sway thinks he is.

****

Sway sat impatiently in his car that was illegally double-parked across the street from the police station. His eyes were getting heavy from the exhaustion that was settling in his bones. He needed some sleep. He sat up straight in his car in an attempt to shake off the lethargic feeling that he could feel his body succumbing to. "Where is that damn bondsman?"

He stared at the dingy, tinted glass double doors leading into the dimly lit building. Sway hated police stations, second to hospitals, and refused to step foot in either of them unless it was absolutely necessary. As soon as he headed towards the station to bail Tiny out, he called Sammy, the bondsman to do the dirty work. Sway did not want his name attached to anything at any police station, so as soon as the two men arrived at the station, he handed Sammy the cash, and told him to make it quick. That was over an hour ago. Sway rubbed his eyes and checked his cell phone. Alex had tried over a dozen times to reach him since the blowup with Derek, and Sway was wondering if she had finally given up. She had.

He laughed under his breath as he slipped his phone back into his jacket lapel. He had no idea where their unique relationship was headed, but he sensed that it would be reduced to nothing more than a shared casualness in raising their daughter, and a mutual respect for one another with the omission of any intimacy. After discovering that his arch nemesis was Alex's new sexual conquest, Sway found himself feeling nothing sexually for Alex because he could never see himself coming second to Derek, ever, with anything. And, although, Sway realized that he and Alex were bound together for life, right now all he could foresee is a civil union shared with her for the sake of his child, not much unlike what his relationship had dwindled to between him and Carmen. He was thankful that he embodied calmness in his character that enabled him to deal with women on any level. He took the moment he had alone to digest the wad of confusion Alex and Derek had fed him earlier, and realized that he needed some space, so his heart could heal. Just as Sway looked down at his wristwatch, he noticed out of the corner of his eye, Tiny shaking the bondsman hand as they parted ways. Tiny trotted down the cement steps of the station and hobbled across the street.

"What up, man? What the fuck took you so long?" Tiny growled as he plopped his heaviness onto the passenger seat.

Sway looked over at Tiny, and involuntarily drew his head back when the smell of jail traveled through his nostrils and singed his nose hairs.

"I know, I know," Tiny agreed, embarrassed by his body odor, "get me the fuck outta here, so I can take a shower!"

Sway did not hesitate. He pulled off and headed toward Tiny's new apartment.

"So, tell me, why did I have to bail your ass out of jail in the middle of the night?" Sway asked, not looking at Tiny, and keeping his weary eyes on the road ahead.

"I told you why on the machine! You didn't get the message?" Tiny asked, somewhat confused as to how Sway could know to pick him up and not know the reason behind it.

"Nah, I wasn't home. I just got back from Vegas, which was a fucking disaster to put it lightly. I don't even want to start on that shit right now," Sway said, feeling his blood starting to boil at the thought of seeing Derek's face after all of these years.

"Cain gave me the message," he finally answered. "But, I need you to be straight with me and tell me why you and Journey ain't together no more. And … , no bullshit. Just give it to me straight, no chaser," Sway said, looking over at Tiny.

"What the fuck you mean *tell you why*?" Tiny questioned, becoming defensive. "I already told you why! She started seeing some nigga and cut yo' boy out of the picture," Tiny said, sticking to his story.

"Nah son, I don't think that is what happened at all," Sway responded with a slick grin. "Yo, you my boy and you know me. And, you know I know women, so with that said: when a woman, especially a married woman, leaves her man for another man, it means that her man started with the creepin'. So, who did Journey catch you with?" Sway questioned, giving Tiny just enough information to make him think he knew more than he actually did.

Tiny leaned back in his seat, trying to portray some sense of comfort with a serene expression on his face, but it was evident that his affair had become common knowledge. Sway was waiting for Tiny to hang himself, so he continued to supply the rope. He was becoming increasingly angry at Tiny's cavalier attitude, and outright lies on Journey; and Cain.

"Look Sway man, home girl from the gym had yo' boy open for a minute, but as soon as wifey caught on, I terminated that shit," Tiny lied, trying to save face in front of his best friend.

"Well you know once you open that door to infidelity, it's up to the woman to close it," Sway advised.

Tiny chuckled at Sway's advice and nodded his head in agreement.

"But that still doesn't explain why you got hemmed up," Sway said, searching for Tiny's abusive button, now that it was confirmed that Tiny started cheating on Journey first.

Sway hoped his boy was not putting his hands on Journey. That would not only be foul, but totally unacceptable. Sway was old school and understood the unwritten rule between men: Real men don't hit women -- under any circumstances, period. Sway kept asking questions hoping that Tiny would eventually explode. Sway needed to see that for himself.

"I said it on the fuckin' machine," Tiny's voice grew louder. "That bitch put a restraining order out on me!"

"A restraining order?" Sway asked shocked. "Yo, Tiny, they only grant those things if they have proof that a man is beating his woman. Man, you were hitting her?"

Tiny could see it in Sway's face, the transformation from a calm expression to an angered one as those words shot out of his mouth. He recognized that Sway and Journey were close, but she was *his* wife, and Tiny felt that he did not have to explain himself to Sway, or anyone else.

"Yo man chill out. I had to rough her up once or twice, but she did that restraining order shit to protect her little new friend," Tiny lied with casualness in his tone that angered Sway more. "She knows first hand what the wrath of Tiny feels like," Tiny spoke of himself in the third person with an air of admiration.

Once again the vein in Sway's forehead started to pulsate at the thought of Tiny laying a finger on his son in a confrontation because of Journey. Sway's breathing was becoming heavy as he turned onto Tiny's street and slowed the car down.

"She didn't need that restraining order shit for the man she is seeing right now," Sway confirmed, thinking about Journey sleeping at that moment in his son's bed.

"What?" Tiny asked, confused again.

"You heard me. You'll never confront the man she's with right now," Sway repeated with much bravado.

Tiny sat motionless in the passenger seat, trying to understand Sway's comment, as well as, his sudden alliance with Journey's new man. "What the fuck are you tryin' to say Sway?" Tiny questioned, seeking a straight answer, unlike the ones he's been giving since getting into Sway's car.

"Check it," Sway said, looking straight into Tiny's eyes. "Journey is at my house right now man. And, I don't appreciate you putting your fucking hands on her Tiny. That shit is whack!" Sway's voice was becoming forceful.

"At your house," Tiny repeated, stuck on those three words.

"Yeah, my house, with Cain!" Sway said unable to hold the admission back.

"You mean to tell me that she is lettin' little Cain hit her off?" Tiny asked, both flabbergasted and angry.

Tiny stared out of the window into the black night and surveyed the sleeping streets while trying to make sense of it all. He never imagined that Journey would be interested in someone so much younger than she, and he detested Cain for smiling in his face during the past several weeks, while sleeping with Journey the entire time.

Sway could see that he had finally struck Tiny's abusive nerve, and he wanted Tiny to fully understand where he stood in this newly formed love triangle. "I'm not exactly sure what is going on between them, or how long," Sway mentioned with a soothing stillness in his voice that irritated Tiny. "But, I do know that if you ever go near her, or my son again, I'll kill you," Sway affirmed with no reservation and with a seriousness conveyed on his face that told Tiny not to question, or doubt it.

"Yo, I need you to get out my car man," Sway said, disappointed at Tiny's behavior as he realized the type of the man Tiny had become.

Tiny wanted to make amends with his best friend, but he knew that Sway hated liars. He was given the opportunity to come clean with

Sway as soon as he got in the car, but instead, he decided to remain cowardly and irresponsible. And, because of it, he sacrificed one of his best friendships. Tiny looked at Sway, speechless, and while he tried to search for some final words that would resolve their issue, Sway returned a look that, instead, rushed Tiny along. "Ok, I'm out," Tiny complied, "but when shit calms down, I hope me and you can talk about this shit to straighten things out."

"I really don't have anything else to say, except that I don't get down with punks who hit on women. It ain't my style and you know that about me already," Sway stated, staring Tiny in the eyes. "And, you also know that I mean what I say, so don't fuck with me, or my family," Sway reiterated.

Feeling humiliated and ashamed, Tiny pried his heaviness out of the passenger seat, and closed the car door behind him. Of all people, he never wanted Sway to know of his abusive behavior, and now, not only did Sway know, but his son was able to slip in under the radar and sweep Journey off of her feet. And, there was nothing Tiny could do except, accept it. He watched Sway drive off into the black night that was giving way to the morning dusk that was invading its territory, and he imagined that this would be the last time he and Sway would cross paths. Their friendship had disintegrated into nothing during that short drive from the police station. Tiny realized as he watched Sway's car disappear down the street that the only way for him to hold onto what little dignity he had left would be to show both Sway and Journey that he could move on. Finally, he realized that he had to let Journey go. Their marriage was truly over.

Sway didn't look back as he made his tires burn the pavement, forming wide black track marks on the ashy gray pavement. It hurt him to end his friendship with Tiny because, aside from Romeo, Tiny was the only other man Sway trusted. He sped home in a race against the sun. He wanted to at least fall asleep while the night still loomed above. As he pulled up to the traffic light, he mentally assessed the drama that had taken place over the past eighteen hours. Here he sat, awaiting the light to change, so he can go home to an empty bed. Suddenly, he became saddened by the recent turn of events. It was almost ten years ago when he lost his best friend and almost his life. And now, in less than a full day, he had lost, yet, another best friend, and the life he had created with the only woman he was ever *in* love with.

The blowing horn pulled him back into the moment, and as he sped off, he had an epiphany. The revelation revealed to him that in order to not repeat the same fate again in another ten years, he would have to change, and maybe even settle down. With a slight reluctance, he pulled out his cell phone from his jacket lapel, and dialed Stephanie's number to let her know the trip to Bahamas was back on.

September - 1999

Chapter 23

White Plains, New York
Alex
I'm Catching Hell

After countless hours of therapy sessions with Dr. Clark during the bereavement period over the loss of her father, Alex thought for sure Dr. Clark had empowered her to cope with many circumstances, or situations she would have to face in the future. Alex never imagined that she would be sitting in the same old tacky brown leather chair again. Yet, after the Las Vegas debacle, and as the hot summer days melted into one another, Alex tried to recapture the unique circumstances she once shared with Sway. And, instead, Sway kept his distance from her. His rejection was more unbearable than she ever could imagine. For the most part their conversations only related to their daughter, or the Las Vegas project that Sway reluctantly decided to continue since Romeo agreed to solely oversee it. That relieved Sway of the added stress of dealing with Derek on any level. Sway knew the opportunity presented before him was too good to miss out on, despite that Derek was the originator of the venture. So, he rationalized that if he could not kill Derek, he would at least make Derek pay for all of the money he made Sway lose out on ten years ago. Alex was grateful that Romeo was able to save the deal. And, before the summer heat settled in for the season, all of the agreements were executed, and Alex's duty in the million-dollar venture was complete.

Derek made several attempts in the beginning of the summer to make contact with Alex, and even tried to visit her home on one occasion. Marie immediately turned him away, and she asked him not to call her daughter again. Eventually, he had finally respected Alex's decision and left her alone, except for the occasional middle of night phone call that was always answered by her drowsy voice. Alex could hear Derek's heavy breathing on the other end, and then the dial tone. She considered changing her number, but knew that on those rare occasions, he needed to hear her voice to get through the night. She understood.

And, as the summer days began to cool down, and the autumn season started to change the foliage from an array of greens to a beautiful display of browns, gold and oranges, the midnight phone calls became more infrequent, and then ceased altogether. Alex assumed that Derek had finally found someone else to fill the void she left in his heart, and she was happy for him. That assumption, coupled with Sway's blatant rejection made Alex decide that she had to find happiness for herself. She hoped that Dr. Clark would be able to assist her in finding a breakthrough, so she could at least smile again.

Dr. Clark's office was dreary and dark, yet, at the same time it created a comforting ambiance, which allowed her patients to relax while spilling their hearts out onto her dark beige carpet without hesitation. Two years had passed since the last time Alex was here, and she could not stop her heart from palpitating at an excessive rate. You would have thought that this was her first meeting with Dr. Clark. She waited patiently for Dr. Clark to come in and plant herself in the plush chair seated across from Alex's chair. There was also a decent chaise lounge tucked neatly in the corner for those who felt like they needed to lie down, but Alex always chose to sit up when divulging her most private thoughts to the therapist. Alex surveyed the room to see if any upgrades had been made since their last encounter. She found that Dr. Clark had actually attempted to brighten up the room by hanging crisp, cream-colored linen drapes over the oversized window that looked out onto the busy downtown streets of White Plains, New York. Alex's palms began to sweat as the clacking sound of Dr. Clark's pumps grew closer and closer to the closed door of her office. Alex stared at the doorknob as it turned clockwise and began to open.

"Well, hello stranger."

Alex heard a soft but strong voice enter the room before Dr. Clark physically appeared. Alex quickly repositioned her body in the chair, and tried to look as calm and collected as possible. "Hey, Dr. Clark, long time, no see." Alex heard her self responding.

They cordially shook hands and Dr. Clark quickly sat in her reserved seat facing her patient. Her creamy smooth brown skin radiated as the sunrays peeked through the drapes and touched her face. She was petite and, although she was not a beauty queen, Dr. Clark carried a beautiful, sophisticated attitude that made up for any physical attributes she lacked. She grabbed her pen from the bun in her hair and quickly jotted something down on her yellow legal pad. Alex always wondered what she wrote, but never asked. For all Alex knew she could be doodling. The room was still for a moment and then Dr. Clark lifted her head to speak.

"So Alex, tell me, what have you been doing over the past two years?"

Alex breathed in deep and closed her eyes to prevent the tears from flowing too soon. So much had happened, she really did not know where to begin, and she knew if she said that Dr. Clark's response would be, "start from the beginning." Alex stiffened as she thought about her dad's funeral, and a tear managed to form and escape from her left eye. Alex wiped it away quickly and smiled. She missed her daddy, but that was not why she returned to Dr. Clark for guidance. Alex cleared her throat. "For starters, I have been working like a mule since leaving the Candy Shop and starting my own business consulting firm which, by the way, is flourishing so much so that I was able to take the summer off to spend it with my daughter," she managed to say with an accomplished grin.

Dr. Clark smiled and jotted something else down on her pad. Alex stared at her hand as it moved quickly across the pad as Alex continued, "Stevie is doing great, and my mother has finally adjusted to living with us. I think it helps keep her mind off of daddy not being here any longer."

Dr. Clark continued to write as Alex spoke. A moment of silence took over the room as Alex began to reminisce about her first session with Dr. Clark. The thought was vividly clear in her head as Alex could hear herself telling Dr. Clark how her life was going to change forever because of her father's sudden death.

"I see you still have some strong emotional feelings over the loss of your dad," Dr. Clark stated as a matter of fact.

Alex cut her eyes at the doctor, taking the comment a little too personal. She breathed in deep and thought carefully before speaking. Alex needed a confidant right now, not someone to struggle with.

"I just miss him," Alex said softly with a weak smile.

"I know and I am sorry Alex, truly, I am. I know when I lost my mother it took years before I was able to think of her without shedding a few tears. Just know with time, comes comfort."

"Thank you doctor, but I'm fine," Alex said, getting comfortable again.

She was ready to get to the reason why she had returned to Dr. Clark for guidance. She needed to hear the Doctor's voice of reason once again. Dr. Clark once helped Alex relieve herself from the blanket of guilt she felt for not marrying Sway before her father had a chance to see his baby become a bride. It had been only the doctor, who agreed with Alex that she should not marry Sway if she was not truly capable of loving *and* trusting him fully. She made Alex realize that having a baby with someone doesn't mean you marry that person. Times had changed and Dr. Clark made Alex realize that people who judge her for being a single parent would have to learn how to adapt to the new age of how families are made up. Of course, Sway thought Dr. Clark was the devil in disguise and wanted Alex to stop her sessions until Alex sat him down one day, and explained to him that all the love in the world could not make someone trust another person. Those were two separate emotions, and it was unfortunate that she did not hold both with the same weight for Sway.

"And Sway ... , how are things in that department?" Dr. Clark said, interrupting Alex's thoughts.

Alex looked at Dr. Clark with questioning eyes, wondering if the doctor already knew that Sway's latest actions are what drove Alex back into her office.

"It's funny you should mention him," Alex said shifting again in her chair and becoming uneasy.

"Oh yeah, why is that?"

"Because he is part of the reason why I am back in this seat," Alex said, almost angry at Sway for not letting their lives revert back to the way it used to be.

Combining Sway's dismissive attitude toward her with spending the summer nights tucked away in her bedroom mourning the death of her whirlwind romance with Derek, Marie encouraged Alex to seek some therapeutic help to enable her to regain her zest for life. Alex stared at the doctor as a flood of tears formed in the bottom lids of her eyes.

"It all just fell apart!" Alex cried, slightly startling the doctor.

"What fell apart Honey?" Dr. Clark asked as she jumped up from her seated position, grabbed the Kleenex box, and handed it to Alex. "Just take a deep breath and calm down," she said rubbing Alex's shoulder in an attempt to relax her client. "Tell me what happened."

Alex took a few deep breaths and wiped her face, partially ashamed for coming apart at the seams so quickly into their session.

Dr. Clark sat back down in her plush chair, and refitted her reading glasses to a comfortable position on the bridge of her nose.

Alex smiled meekly and began her tale of woes. She started at the beginning just as the doctor would have suggested. Alex told Dr. Clark about her very first encounter with Derek. She took her time to reiterate the fairytale love story she was able to bring to reality in a matter of only a few short months. As Alex reminisced about her whirlwind love affair, she omitted nothing; and during the hour-long session found herself laughing at some of the things Derek use to say, and crying because she would not hear those sweet nothings being whispered into her ear ever again. She often surprised the doctor with juicy sexual innuendos. And, Alex found that she had totally captivated all of the doctor's attention toward the end of the story when she looked up and found the doctor seated at the edge of her chair with her mouth gaped open, unable to jot anymore words down on her yellow pad.

"Derek dropped me off at the hotel that day. I ended up catching a taxi to the airport, and flew back home with just the clothes on my back and my briefcase. We haven't seen each other since," Alex concluded her story. "So, you see Dr. Clark because of Sway's past history with Derek, I could never create a future with Derek," Alex said, suddenly saddened by the cause of events once again.

"Wow!" Dr. Clark exasperated and leaned back in her chair. "Alex, you can't make that stuff up. Actually, we can turn that story into a book, or even a movie," she jokingly suggested to lighten up the mood.

"Yeah, I know, maybe I should," Alex chuckled, feeling slightly better now that she released all of the pain she had been harboring. "Who would have thought that the world is actually that small?" Alex questioned in wonderment.

"Oh, but it is my dear," Dr. Clark confirmed, "you know what they say, that there are only six degrees of separation between you and a stranger you see passing on the street. And, in your case it took less than that."

"Well, I guess my dilemma has proven that theory to be somewhat true. But the problem now doc is, now that my relationship with Derek is over Sway no longer is interested in me intimately, and it hurts like hell to feel unloved and unwanted," Alex said with a sigh.

"Yes it does hurt, but you know first hand that with time comes healing," Dr. Clark reminded Alex.

"I know, but I am tired of healing," Alex argued. "I want to feel loved and appreciated again, like how Derek made me feel," Alex sulked.

"And, you will find that man who will make your heart skip beats again, but you have to get out and see what's available. You told me earlier that you spent the entire summer held up in your bedroom, or out on your patio. When did you go out to socialize?" Dr. Clark asked, ready to delve into finding some possible resolutions to help her client find happiness within again.

"I did go out a few times with Journey and Cain. He's Sway's son, and that is a whole other story to be told at another time," Alex giggled, thinking about Cain and Journey's fiery relationship.

Dr. Clark quickly looked up from her pad and peered over her eyeglass frame at Alex. She wanted to hear about that escapade too, but quickly realized it had little, if nothing, to do with why Alex was seated across from her. "And, how did that go, hanging out with Journey and Cain?" she asked.

"Not so good," Alex frowned. "The club scene is just not me. Not to mention, Cain is a lot younger than both Journey and I, so the places we frequented consisted of men his age, and I don't have time to raise another child," Alex quipped. "Journey, however, blends in without any problems. I guess it's because she still looks like a teenager. Not to mention her divorce finally going through has had a positive affect on her attitude. She told me she finally felt free," Alex said, relieved that her best friend had ended her debilitating marriage.

"But, you know what the ironic thing is, doc?" Alex rhetorically asked. "I'm free too, but I don't like the way it feels. I just thought that once I ended it with Derek, Sway would be OK, and we would at least be able to maintain the unique relationship we built over the years. Instead, he told me that he could never play second fiddle to Derek, and that every time he thinks about me in a sexual way, all he can see is Derek making love to me, and me enjoying it," Alex stated disappointedly.

"Men and their double standards," Dr. Clark retorted. "The nerve of Sway to feel that way, and you and I both know Alex, had this been a reversed situation, he would not only expect you to forgive him, but to get over it quickly," Dr. Clark said, slightly perturbed at Sway's behavior.

"Yes I know, but on some levels I understand where he is coming from because before I knew that they knew each other, he could see it on my face how Derek was making me feel, and Sway never made me feel that way," Alex confessed.

"Alex, I understand why are you so conflicted, and believe me, I know it is hard maintaining a relationship with Sway for the sake of your daughter, but I strongly encourage you to start letting go of the "special" part of your relationship with him, so you can heal," Dr. Clark prescribed her medicine to mend the broken hearted.

"I agree," Alex said wiping her face again with a worn Kleenex. "It's just that I don't want to meet the same type of man anymore. I don't want the Wall Street business type, nor do I want the ex-thug turned legit. I just want a professional man, maybe the doctor or lawyer type who knows how to handle business and his woman," Alex said growing anxious as the thought of Malcolm raced through her head.

He had become the professional man she now sought after, but Alex did not want to re-enter his life at this time just because hers was falling a part. She hadn't spoken to Malcolm since her daughter was born, and aside from receiving his annual Mother's Day flowers, Alex had no idea about how Malcolm was living out his life. With him running his own pediatric practice in New Jersey, she could only imagine that by now some cute, petite nurse had scooped his tall, dark fineness up, and was catering to his every need. *It wouldn't be fair*, Alex thought as she silently considered giving him a phone call, but decided against it.

"They too, can be a handful sometimes," Dr. Clark chuckled, pulling Alex back into their conversation, and away from her mental dilemma.

"Excuse me," Alex said, shaking her head to push the thought of Malcolm back into her subconscious.

"Doctors and lawyers can come with just as much drama," Dr. Clark assured Alex.

"Yeah I know, men are men," Alex affirmed. "But I kind of have one specific doctor in mind, but it's been years since I last saw him. He's probably re-married now with more children, and I am sure his practice is flourishing in New Jersey. I definitely could not see Malcolm being single. He's a true catch."

As Malcolm's name exited Alex's mouth, Dr. Clark stopped writing and looked up at Alex with a quizzical expression plastered on her face. She wondered if the Malcolm Alex just mentioned is the same Malcolm who Dr. Clark befriended a couple of years ago at a Physicians Conference in Phoenix, Arizona. *It has to be the same person*, Dr. Clark thought as she and Alex locked eyes in an intense stare off.

"What's the matter Dr. Clark, did I say something?" Alex asked, trying to recant the words she had just spoken to ensure she did not offend the good doctor.

"No, no Alex, it's nothing, I just thought of something," Dr. Clark replied, trying not to look too suspicious. She had suddenly begun her mission to play cupid, or at least attempt to, despite it going against all of her professional ethics. Dr. Clark had immediately made it her business to find out if her good friend Dr. Malcolm Irving is the same man who apparently could potentially make her patient truly happy again.

"Listen Alex, what I am about to do is totally unethical because physicians normally do not fraternize with our patients, but a few collogues of mine and I are hosting a Halloween party next month, and I would like for you to come," Dr. Clark said.

"Really," Alex replied, a little taken aback that the doctor would want to risk her license or her professional reputation. "Dr. Clark, I know I am a bit of a mess right now, but in all sincerity, I don't want any charity right now. And, I couldn't handle it if you lost your license to practice."

"Alex, this is not charity, I just think you will have a good time, or at least a different kind of time," Dr. Clark laughed, not divulging her true reasoning for the abrupt invitation. "And, if my colleagues ask, I will just tell them that you are my new receptionist." She stated as a matter of fact.

"What the hell," Alex said as an acceptance to the doctor's invitation, "but can I bring my girlfriend?"

"Of course, but you both have to come in costume, the more outrageous the better. My date and I are coming as Scarlet O'Hara and Rhett Butler," Dr. Clark chuckled.

"That does sound like fun," Alex said, thinking of a costume to wear.

"Yes, I believe this year will be quite different from previous gatherings. At least, I hope so," Dr. Clark added. "It took months to get my date to finally go out, so I really hope we have a good time."

"I am sure everything will be fine," Alex assured the doctor. "He is going to see what a great person you are and fall to his knees."

"Oh, it's nothing romantic between us, strictly platonic to say the least, but he's a hard nut to crack. He is very much to himself, and also very selective when it comes to dating. He's dated a few women in our profession since I've known him, but he never opened up enough with any of them to create anything more than a few more dates before showing signs of disinterest," Dr. Clark concluded.

"Well, maybe he will meet someone nice at your party," Alex said, trying to sound convincing.

Dr. Clark smiled graciously at her client, and with a slightly devious twinkle in her eye, simply stated, "that is my plan."

Alex peered into the doctor's eyes, not knowing how to take that statement, but chose not to delve into the doctor's mind. She hoped that the doctor was not trying to set her up. Alex never enjoyed blind dating or matchmaking because neither ever amounted to anything more than a good dinner and boring conversation.

"OK, enough about the party. This session is supposed to be about you," Dr. Clark said, clearing her throat. "I will send you the formal invitation, and I will remind you at our next session in a few weeks. Now, are you going to be OK until then?"

Alex looked at her wristwatch and noticed that they had conversed way past her one-hour session. She appreciated Dr. Clark for not kicking her out before consoling her until the next time. Alex had to admit that she felt better.

"I am going to be OK, and thank you Dr. Clark for seeing me on such short notice. I know that my mother would have called you excessively had you not taken her first call. She was concerned for me, so she looked you up in the yellow pages. I am glad she did." Alex smiled at the doctor as she stood up and stretched her arms up in the air.

"I am glad she did also, and I am looking forward to our next session. But, until then concentrate on going that extra mile to pamper yourself, and don't brush any prospects off. It is always good to get out into the world to see what it still has to offer," Dr. Clark said with a positive grin on her face.

"I'll try," Alex huffed, "but no promises."

Alex and Dr. Clark shook hands as the doctor led her to the closed door to her office. They hugged and Alex exited the office feeling rejuvenated and somewhat alive.

Alex was suddenly looking forward to attending Dr. Clark's Halloween party. She pulled out her cell phone as she entered the elevator to call Journey to make sure she would attend the event with her.

October - 1999

Chapter 24

New York, New York
The Girls
Do You Still Love Me

The chill in the air caused Journey's bones to shiver, and she wanted to smack her own face for not putting a turtleneck on beneath her fleece. It was barely five o'clock in the evening and the sky was already dark like it is in the late night hours. Journey stared at the little digital clock embedded in the dash board of her new *Mercedes CL600 Coupe*, and hoped Cain would exit out of the glass doors that led to the airport baggage claim area sooner rather than later. He and Romeo had been in Las Vegas for the past several weeks, overseeing the final touches on the hotel and the new *Candy Shop*. Journey thought it was nice of him to call her the night before and ask her to pick him up from the airport, but now he was running late, and cutting into her time. She had several errands to run in order to prepare for the Halloween Party the following day. Journey lightly tapped her manicured nails on the shiny new dashboard, and fixated her eyes on the glass doors, willing Cain to rush through them. Just as flashing red and blue lights appeared in her rearview mirror and a policeman exited the patrol car, Journey could see Cain's handsome face and his strong arms pushing the door open.

"I'm leaving right now officer," Journey said with a pleasant, girly smile.

"Hurry it up Miss," the officer replied in an unfriendly tone.

She hated the police sometimes. Cain noticed the policeman approaching Journey in a car that he had never seen before, and put a little pep in his step.

"Evenin' officer," Cain spoke as politely as possible as he opened the passenger door to Journey's car and threw his bags in the backseat.

The cop acknowledged Cain with a head nod, and a look that told them to move it. Cain slid in the passenger seat, leaned over and kissed Journey on the cheek.

"What's up? I see your trust fund kicked in," Cain said peering around the spanking brand new vehicle.

"Yup, and this is just a gift to myself. You like it?" Journey asked, smiling hard and pulling into the ongoing traffic.

"Love it," Cain said in admiration. "And, it fits you perfectly. So, what have you been getting into since I left?"

"Nothing really," Journey replied, keeping her eyes on the road. Driving in New York City proved to not be as easy as she thought. Defensive driving is the only way to get around in the Big Apple. It made Journey nervous.

"Alex and I are going to some uppity doctors Halloween party tomorrow night. I might meet a doctor," Journey teased.

"You need a doctor to handle your crazy ass," Cain joked.

Since saving Journey from Tiny's unexpected visit back in June, Cain and Journey's sexually overcharged relationship had dwindled down to a very tight knit friendship, with sex only being involved sporadically. Journey felt so bad after being caught in the act with Cain by Sway that she sat Cain down and told him that they would have to create some space between them, and that he would have to begin seeing other women because in no way was she ready for another committed relationship. Cain reluctantly agreed, but realized that Journey was right and soon after, they both found themselves dating other people during the summer months, and respected one another enough to always be truthful and not lead each other on. They began to mimic the kind of relationship Alex and Sway once shared.

"Naw but seriously, that sounds cool," Cain concluded. "Maybe Alex will meet someone too."

"I hope so," Journey sighed. "My girl has been miserable since the big blow up happened."

No one hardly ever spoke of the melee at Mr. Mitken's office on that disastrous summer day, and when they had to, it was always referred to as "the big blow up." Journey hated seeing her best friend so lonely, and she prayed that the Halloween party would at least provide enough masculinity to intrigue Alex enough to distract her from her constant feeling of despair.

"Yeah, I know," Cain affirmed. "And, I am sure it doesn't help that Pops and Stephanie are really trying to make it happen."

Journey quickly glanced over at Cain, not expecting to hear that Sway had really decided to make anything "happen" without Alex being involved. Yet, Cain's comment confirmed what Alex had been telling Journey all summer long; that Sway no longer feels for Alex the way he used to. Journey suddenly felt a wave of empathy rush through her body, and she felt sad for her friend. For she knew what it felt like to lose that special kind of love that someone once cherished you for.

Journey shook her head in disbelief. "So, you are saying that Sway and Stephanie are like a couple, couple?"

"Yo, I think so," Cain stated as a matter of fact. "Stephanie has been staying at the crib off and on since I've been in Vegas, and I think she is staying over this weekend."

"Staying for the weekend?" Journey repeated, wondering if Cain knew what he was saying. "You know this weekend is your little sister's fourth birthday, right?" Journey reminded Cain.

"Oh shit, it is huh?" Cain said, suddenly remembering what date it was. "Well, this will be interesting."

"I just don't want Alex going through anymore drama, especially on such a special occasion," Journey said, hoping that Sway would consider Alex's feelings during the weekend ahead.

Journey cruised through the city streets as though they were floating on a magic carpet, and glided into a parking space in front of Cain's building with ease. Cain looked over at Journey and was happy to see her face. Although, he had hooked up with a few nice looking ladies in Vegas during his business trip, there was nothing like looking at someone you truly cared about.

"You want to come up, it's been a minute," Cain teased, displaying a sexy grin.

"Yes it has," Journey confirmed. "But, I have several things to do before the party tomorrow night and Stevie's party this weekend. Can I have a rain check?" she asked with a smile.

"For you, of course. You know I can always accommodate you when you're ready." Cain's voice turned into a sexy growl. He was the true incarnation of his father.

"Mmm … , remember you said that," Journey said, melting at the thought of his arms wrapped around her body. "Bring an overnight bag to Stevie's party Sunday, so you can spend the night with me afterwards," Journey found herself speaking without thinking first. It was clear which part of her body was talking.

"You got it," Cain agreed as he climbed out of the car and pulled his bags from the backseat.

Journey watched him trot through the front door as the doorman held it open for him, and then he disappeared. *That young man is too much*, Journey thought as she pulled out of the parking space.

****

Alex was so immersed in her work that she did not notice Sway standing in the doorway to her home office. He gazed at her while she typed what sounded like a thousand words per minute on her laptop, with her reading glasses hanging on the tip of her perfectly shaped nose. He would always love her. However, he finally accepted that he was in fact getting older, and the kind of relationship he needed, was one that he could never create with Alex. Sway had painfully moved on, and to some extent was content and surprisingly happy. He accomplished maintaining a long distance, monogamous relationship with Stephanie for the past few months. Finally, Sway had succumbed to an inner peace that came with no longer juggling women, and running himself weary for a variety of sexual excursions. Even though he could never love any other woman in the same way loved Alex, he knew that Stephanie loved him in that same way. He decided to appreciate her for it because he understood how special it was to have someone express that kind of love toward you. It was time to share that with Alex.

"Hey," he said almost in a whisper, trying not to startle Alex. He did.

"Oh, hi," Alex said, jumping in her chair. "You just scared the mess out of me."

"Sorry," Sway chuckled. "You got a minute?"

"Yup," Alex answered. "Come in and sit down."

Sway slowly entered the office and sat down in the chair across from Alex's large desk. He looked into her framed eyes, and admired her beauty. He loved it when she wore her glasses.

"What's on your mind, Steven?" Alex questioned, wondering the sudden urge to speak to her privately.

For the past few months, he barely spoke to her at all. Gratefully, she was finally at a good place thanks to Dr. Clark and her therapy sessions, and could now accept how she and Sway's relationship would remain: platonic.

"I need to tell you something," he said in a serious tone.

"OK," Alex said, folding her arms on her desk and giving him her undivided attention.

"Stephanie is flying in this weekend. You know she is a stewardess. And, I wanted to talk to you about her coming to Stevie's party Sunday."

Alex's eyes widened, clearly showing Sway that she was unprepared for that question, but at the same time he could see that she was trying to portray an unaffected expression on her face. "Wow, Sway, that is some kind of question at the last minute, don't you think?" Alex asked, slightly taken aback.

"I know, I know, but she ended up covering for a co-worker who fell ill overseas, and she always stops by when passing through New York. Plus, I think it's time she met Stevie," he said lowering his voice, hoping Alex would not flip out.

"You do, do you?" Alex asked, leaning back in her chair and becoming visibly uneasy. "It's that serious between you and her, Sway?" Alex wanted to know. She needed to know.

"I know you're not going to believe me, but yeah it is," he stated. "Look Alex, you and I both know that there will never be another you in my life, and if we would have started out differently, you and I would be together. I finally accepted the fact that we will never have the kind of relationship we both want, especially now. But, I will always take care of you and my daughter. You know how I feel about you, and you will always be at the center of my heart, but I am finally ready for that one on one type of thing, and Stephanie loves me the same way I loved you."

"So, are you in love with her?" Alex asked, feeling rejection creeping into her gut.

"You are the only woman I was ever in love with," Sway told her without any reservation. "But I do love her enough to show her I appreciate that she is *in* love with me, and I know her love is real. We go back further than you and I."

Alex looked into Sway's beautiful but aging eyes, and could plainly see that he cared for Stephanie, and that he was sincerely seeking Alex's blessing. Alex found herself empathizing momentarily with Sway because she completely understood what it felt like to receive the kind of affection that only comes from someone totally in awe of you. She missed Derek. Alex smiled at Sway to let him know that she approved of his effort to seek out and maintain happiness and a sense of stability. He would be turning forty in a couple of months and she did not want him to be alone. And, he was right, Stephanie held onto her second place position for so long that Alex felt it only right to pass the torch onto her. At least Alex could let Sway go, knowing that the woman she was releasing him to, would love and adore him in the way Alex always wanted to, but never could.

"Thank you Sway for saying that and you know that I will always love you too," Alex said looking at him straight in the eyes. "And, if you think that Stephanie is the one, and you are that serious about her, then yes she can come to the party. I think Stevie will like her," Alex said positively, letting Sway know that it was truly all good.

Sway smiled at Alex as he stood up to leave, and appreciated her maturity. Stephanie had been nagging him for weeks about meeting Stevie because she knew that would mean Sway was taking their relationship to the next level. Plus, it would be confirmation that the *intimate* relationship he shared with Alex, was in fact finally over. He felt relieved that he would not have to hear Stephanie hassle him about it anymore.

Alex watched Sway swagger out of her office and out of her sight before releasing a loud sigh. A large part of her was sincerely happy for Sway, but there still was a small part of her heart that immediately recognized its emptiness, and she suddenly became sad. Alex sat back into her plush chair and pulled out the drawer where she kept her mail. She picked up the black and white envelope and pulled out the engraved invitation to read it again:

The Physicians of Westchester County
Cordially Invite You To Their 3rd Annual
Halloween Extravaganza
@ The Hyatt Regency Hotel Grand Ballroom
Boston Post Road, Greenwich, CT
Friday, October 29, 1999 @ 7:00 p.m.
Wear your best costume!

Alex smiled at the piece of paper as she read and re-read it again. She silently prayed that she would at least be in good company where she would be able to have a decent conversation, and a little fun with the male species. She needed a spark in her life again to light the path to a future that promised peace and happiness. She yearned for it. She needed it. *I hope there is at least one man there tomorrow night worth talking to,* Alex thought as she slipped the invitation back into its envelope and threw it back into the drawer before shutting it closed.

Chapter 25

The Girls
Always and Forever

"These costumes are a bit much," Alex said, looking at her reflection in the floor length mirror in her bedroom as she and Journey slipped into their identical Catholic schoolgirl uniforms.

Journey stood next to Alex to admire their transformation. She had driven up to Alex's house earlier with the costumes to get dressed. "What are you talking about?" Journey asked, looking at Alex up and down. "You look adorable!"

"You're just saying that," Alex disagreed. "You just don't want me to find something else to wear."

"Well, that is partly true, but it's also true that you look great Alex," Journey said, complimenting her friend.

Alex had lost at least ten pounds during those dreadful summer months, and, instead of packing the pounds back on, she changed her eating habits, and started power walking in the mornings after taking Stevie to preschool. Smiling at the reflection of a toned body, Alex had to admit that she almost looked like a college kid again. *Extra weight really does age you,* she thought as she twirled around to get a view of her round behind in the almost too short plaid pleated skirt. Journey even went so far as to rent the Mary Jane shoes, and she purchased the bright white knee high socks to perfect the look.

Alex had to give Journey credit after all. They really did look adorable. "Thank you Journey, but flattery will get you nowhere," Alex chuckled.

"OK then, I guess we are ready to meet some doctors!" Journey nearly screamed as she pulled Alex away from the mirror and out of the bedroom.

****

Journey whipped her coupe up to the entrance of Hyatt Regency Hotel and by a nose hair, she missed hitting a lanky, spiked haired valet who was standing on the curb.

"Sorry Honey," Journey snapped as she climbed out of the car, and handed him the keys.

Alex hopped out of the passenger seat and adjusted her skirt. It was apparent by the expression on the valet's face that their costumes would definitely turn a few heads at the party.

"No … no, problem at all Miss," the valet said with a wide grin as he slid into the plush driver seat Journey just abandoned.

"And, be careful with my baby!" Journey yelled as the valet sped off into the parking garage.

The two women shook their heads in unison and sauntered into the hotel. The Grand Ballroom was superbly decorated in Halloween décor, and, at the same time, the massive room held onto its elegance and charm with its high ceiling, spectacular chandeliers, and imported dining furniture. Alex was impressed that the deejay was playing a nice medley of music as she and Journey approached the ballroom entrance. And, she was equally impressed by the crowd of outrageous costumes filling the dance floor and most of the seats around the tables.

"Looks like you can just sit anywhere," Journey howled over the music and bopped her head to the beat at the same time. She was ready to party.

"I guess so, but let's find Dr. Clark first, so she knows that we are here. She said that she will be dressed as Scarlet O'Hara, let's just hope that no one else decided to dress the same way," Alex laughed and pulled Journey into the crowd.

The two of them shuffled through the crowd of witches, goblins and ghouls, catching glares from the men and snares from the women.

Journey was glad that they were the only ones dressed as schoolgirls. It caused some much-needed attention for her friend. Journey knew when she picked them up from the costume rental shop that the uniforms would.

As they approached the bar in the back corner, Alex noticed Dr. Clark standing next to the men's bathroom door. Alex told Journey to order their drinks, and she waltzed over to where Dr. Clark was standing. "Dr. Clark!" Alex spoke loudly without trying to yell.

"Alex! You made it," Dr. Clark greeted Alex with open arms.

The two of them hugged quickly and pulled back to admire each other's costumes.

"Yes we made it," Alex said. "And, she picked out the get ups," Alex said bashfully as she pointed at Journey, who was flirting with the bartender. "And, don't be surprised, if she's back there tending the bar before the night is over!" Alex laughed as she and Dr. Clark watched Journey make her moves on the handsome olive skinned, dark haired Italian man.

"She's not shy is she?" Dr. Clark rhetorically asked, admiring Journey's gumption.

"No, she's not shy at all," Alex laughed.

"So, where's your Rhett Butler?" Alex asked, making conversation.

"He's in the men's room," Dr. Clark answered, suddenly feeling awkward. It dawned on her as she looked back and forth at Alex and the bathroom door. *What if this is not her Malcolm,* Dr. Clark thought, hoping Malcolm would not come out of the men's room until Alex was out of sight. She thought it best for them to find one another on their own just in case their reunion did not turn out to be a blissful one.

Alex looked over at Journey to make sure she did not sneak off with the bartender, and Journey signaled for Alex to come get her drink. "I believe she's beckoning me," Alex said. "Dr. Clark I am sorry, but I better get over there before she gets into trouble. I will have to meet your date later, but thanks for inviting me. This is just what I needed."

"You are very welcome Alex, and please call me Monica. We will definitely catch up with you two later. I have to say that this year the group has proven me wrong. They are really letting go. So please, go enjoy yourself," Dr. Clark said, politely nudging Alex in the direction of her friend, and feeling relieved that Malcolm did not exit the men's room.

Alex took the doctor's advice and joined Journey at the bar before mingling on the dance floor with a man hidden behind a very believable Spiderman costume. Journey latched onto a very nice looking brown skinned brother wearing a toga sheet that conveniently showed off all of his muscular attributes. The two women danced into the late night hours and shared an equally fun time, with the only difference being Journey accepting a few phone numbers, and Alex, declining every advance. Alex could not let her guard down enough to let anyone in. She could not deny that Spidey ended up being a very handsome bi-racial man from Phoenix who was in town specifically for the event. The fact that he was long distance was just enough for Alex to make that her excuse to not exchange numbers and politely dismissed him.

As Journey continued to wear out the dance floor, Alex dipped out into the hotel lobby for some fresh air. She found a small bench tucked in the corner and sat down to rest her weary body. Alex slipped off the thick-heeled shoes and rubbed her feet. She hoped no one was paying attention to her, but someone was. Alex could feel a set of eyes staring at her, and she raised her head to find out where the penetrating gaze was coming from. And, there he was; Dr. Clark's Rhett Butler, and *her* Malcolm. Alex thought for a second that her heart stopped beating altogether, but then she realized that she was breathing so heavy, her chest was visibly contracting and expanding. His sexy smile was making it hard for her to calm down. Alex sat upright and leaned her back against the bench, staring at the tall dark handsome figure approaching her, and not believing her eyes. Anxiety had taken total control over her body, and Alex did not know whether to stand, sit, or run, so she remained still. As her eyes focused in on his chocolate brown skin, it became clear that the man now standing before her was in fact the very same man who owned her soul. *He still looks like Big Daddy Kane,* Alex thought and a smile slowly appeared on her face as she peered up at his fineness, and she began to feel warm inside.

"Hey stranger," Malcolm's deep voice traveled through her ears down to the pit of her warmth.

"Hey, yourself," Alex smiled.

"Mind if I sit here?" Malcolm asked while sitting down beside her, not waiting for an answer.

"I thought that was you on the dance floor with Spiderman all night. What are you doing here?" Malcolm asked, curious to know if the masked arachnid was Alex's new man.

"Yeah, that was me, acting like a damn fool. Spidey was kind enough to put up with me all night," Alex chuckled at her own jovial behavior. "My therapist invited me. You know her, Monica Clark."

Alex looked into Malcolm's eyes to witness his reaction. She wanted to know if he was more interested in Dr. Clark than he was leading Dr. Clark to believe.

"You have got to be kidding me!" Malcolm exclaimed, shocked at the rare coincidence. "What a small world."

"I'm afraid it is," Alex said, not believing that silly six degrees myth was actually playing out again in her life, so soon.

Malcolm immediately noticed the change of the tone in her voice as she made that comment and looked over at Alex.

"She and I are just friends Alex," Malcolm said reassuringly.

"Excuse me?" Alex questioned.

"I said she and I are nothing more than friends. She has been trying to get me to hang out with her for awhile, and I only accepted her invitation this time because Malachi is spending the weekend with his mother," Malcolm explained.

"So, this is not a real date?" Alex questioned, trying to make sure Malcolm did not harbor any feelings for her doctor.

"Not at all; Monica and I are just friends. I met her here and I'm not even sure if she knows I have a room here for the night. I figured I was not going to be in shape for trekking back to Jersey tonight."

Alex focused on his eyes to make sure they were speaking the truth because over the years, she learned that you can't trust every word that exits a person's mouth, but their eyes somehow always tell the truth. And, Malcolm's did. Alex thought about her first meeting with Dr. Clark, and suddenly realized why she was here. It was all coming together.

"I think she invited me here tonight because of you," Alex confessed. "I mentioned your name during one of our sessions, and coincidently, she invites me to this party against all of her principles, and it's totally unethical."

"I am glad she did," Malcolm whispered into Alex's ear.

Her insides melted as the heat from the soft sound of his voice travelled through her body. She remembered that feeling, and she missed it. "I just wished she would have mentioned it to me that she knew you," Alex said as a weakening feeling started to overwhelm her knees. She was grateful that she was already seated.

"But she didn't," Malcolm rebutted, looking into Alex's eyes. "So, what are we going to do now?"

"Nothing," Alex said without thinking. She was filled with so many emotions it felt like the first day of high school her freshman year when she and Malcolm first met.

He always had the ability to simplify her thinking, and lead the way. She missed that.

"What do you mean nothing?" Malcolm said grabbing Alex's hand. "Don't you see it?" he asked her, hoping she did.

"See what?"

"Alex don't you see that this is fate. Do you remember that letter I wrote you four years ago? Do remember what it said?" Malcolm asked, trying to remind her.

He didn't have to. She memorized the letter word for word, and thought the exact same thing the moment she looked into his eyes from across the room. It scared her. She quickly slid her tiny feet back into the wedged heeled shoes.

"Malcolm, I can't do this right now," Alex said, standing up and taking a few steps forward.

Malcolm shadowed her and was closely on her heels. "Look, Alex, wait up," he said, tugging at her arm to slow her down. "Take a walk with me."

Malcolm did not wait for a reply; instead, he guided her to the exit that opened up to the outdoor botanical courtyard. As they walked through the maze of dimly lit but finely trimmed brushes, Malcolm slipped out of his jacket and placed it over Alex's shoulders.

"I wasn't going to come tonight," Malcolm's declaration came out of the sky. "But Monica told me that I had to come because there might be someone here I would be interested in. And, she was right because here you are," he said, stopping in their tracks and turning to face her. "I just need to know one thing."

"Oh yeah, and what do you need to know?" Alex sarcastically asked, having no intentions in playing a game with her high school sweetheart.

"Are you and that Sway cat together?" Malcolm asked with a serious expression on his face, letting her know he was expecting the truth.

"No, we're not. We weren't able to create that typical family unit that you thought we would," Alex said, no longer dwelling on the past. "But we are still friends, and he is an awesome father," Alex beamed, commending Sway.

"I always knew he would be," Malcolm concurred. "But, I have to be honest. I'm relieved that you're not with him because now there is nothing standing in my way," he concluded, stepping into her personal space.

Alex wanted to back up, but her shoes were rooted into the ground as if she was planted there. Malcolm hovered over her, just like he used to do when they were love struck teenagers, and kissed her softly on the lips. The familiar feeling caused her to melt into his arms, and she allowed him to take full control over their passionate moment. Malcolm wrapped his firm arms around Alex's body and wanted to hold onto her forever. He never thought that he would have the opportunity to hold Alex again, and this time by any means necessary, he was not letting her go.

Alex pulled back from his strong embrace and gazed up at Malcolm. "Malcolm, I have been through a lot lately, and although I want to believe that this may be fate, I'm scared. I just can't afford to let my heart suffer again, ever," Alex explained.

"Alex, you know me. It's me, Malcolm; you know I would do anything to show you how you should be loved. You still hold my heart in your pocket girl," he snared with a devilish grin as he pulled her body close to his. "I love you Alex. I've never stopped loving you, and now that you are in my arms again, I am going to create the life for you that I promised over ten years ago. This time I am going to see it through," Malcolm spoke with both love and determination.

Alex was at a loss for words. She believed every word Malcolm spoke: not because those were the exact words she needed to hear from a man, but because those words were coming from the one man whom she felt was truly her soul mate. The kind of love that the two of them shared transgressed beyond the skies, and through the universe. It was a feeling deeper than love, for it was directly linked to their souls. They have always known that, and now she could not deny it. Her eyes welled up with water, and as the tears fell, Malcolm graciously wiped them away.

"I want to spend the rest of my life with you, Alex. I want to be a stepfather to Stevie, and the father of the babies you plan to have. I want to take care of you like I always told you I would. I never gave myself a chance to ever want that with anyone else," Malcolm confessed as though Alex was dressed as a Catholic priest rather than a schoolgirl. He wanted her to believe him. He needed her to believe him. A part of him regretted walking out of her life a second time after Stevie was born. He often kicked himself for not fighting for Alex, and, instead, giving Sway the opportunity to break her heart again, which apparently he had. Malcolm was determined to fight for Alex now. They continued walking as he professed his love for her over and over again. As they re-entered the lobby of the hotel to return to the party, Malcolm noticed that he had worn Alex down. They were holding hands, and catching up on the past four years.

"Can you believe that she will be four already? Her party is Sunday," Alex beamed.

"Time does fly," Malcolm agreed. "I have not seen Stevie since your dad's funeral, but I would love to see her again," Malcolm said, stopping Alex in her tracks again. "I don't want to sound pushy, and I promise not to rush anything, but I just always felt a connection to your daughter since the day she was born, and I want you to see Malachi again because he certainly had a connection with you," Malcolm said calmly.

"If I let you back in my life Malcolm you won't disappear again, will you?"

Malcolm shook his head, and pulled her in again to hug her precious body. She reciprocated the hug by wrapping her arms around his waist, and as they stood in the middle of the lobby, neither of them noticed Dr. Clark and Journey witnessing their affection from across the room.

"I think that's your Rhett hugging my twin over there," Journey snickered, pointing her finger at Alex and Malcolm.

Dr. Clark's face became flushed as she grinned excitedly at the sight of her date fondling her client. "Yes, it is" Dr. Clark beamed. "Somehow I knew that he was the Malcolm Alex spoke of."

"Malcolm?" Journey repeated, looking at the doctor. "Your date is Malcolm Irving?"

"Yes it is, and I am so happy that the two of them found each other before the night ended. I was beginning to worry when Spidey would not let Alex off of the dance floor," Dr. Clark chuckled, completely satisfied with her act of matchmaking.

"Hold up doc," Journey said pulling the doctor by the arm. "I'm confused. How did you know that they know each other?"

"During one of our sessions, Alex mentioned his name and that he was a doctor with a practice in New Jersey. I said to myself how many successful black doctors are in New Jersey with the name Malcolm?" Dr. Clark questioned and the two women laughed at the irony.

"He's her first love," Journey replied in a sudden dreamy tone of voice, as they watched Alex and Malcolm embrace and caress one another as though they were not in a public place.

The two women stood still across the lobby and became enamored with their view as they watched the two soul mates reconnect in a way that only soul mates could. It was apparent that Malcolm and Alex were in a world of their own standing in the middle of the lobby, and affectionately gazing into each other's eyes. Dr. Clark was witnessing a side of Malcolm that she was sure none of their other medical collogues have ever seen. She could see that he embodied a strong mass of emotion and could give affection freely. It finally became clear that he was holding it all inside for Alex.

"That is why he is so standoffish," Dr. Clark stated as though she was observing a medical experiment. "He loves *her*," Dr. Clark stated her diagnosis.

"And she loves *him*," Journey replied and pulled the doctor back into the party. "Come on doc, there are enough single physicians in here for us to pick and choose from," Journey laughed.

Malcolm's embrace felt so good, Alex wished he would hold onto her for the rest of the night. As they pulled back from one another, Malcolm walked with Alex over to the ballroom.

"So, like I asked earlier, what are we going to do about us?" Malcolm asked again, sitting down on the same bench that he and Alex occupied a couple of hours earlier.

"I guess we have to start all over, and take it day by day," Alex smiled as she allowed him to pull her body down onto his lap.

"OK, so what's up for tomorrow?" Malcolm asked.

"Don't you think you should at least end your night with your date?" Alex nervously laughed, flattered by his pursuit.

"I got that under control, don't worry about her. Although, she might not want to counsel you anymore after I tell her that you are going to be my wife," Malcolm joked but was very serious about his intentions for the future.

"You are still crazy!" Alex giggled like the schoolgirl she was dressed up as.

"But, I am serious. Now, what's the plan for tomorrow?" Malcolm questioned again.

"Nothing, I will be preparing for Stevie's birthday party," Alex answered.

"Am I invited?"

Alex looked into Malcolm's eyes, and somehow could clearly see forever. She pondered the idea of him attending Stevie's party, without first consulting with Sway. But then she realized that Malcolm has been in Stevie's life since birth, literally, and since it was clear that Sway has moved on with Stephanie, Alex was sure that he would not mind if Malcolm attended the party as well. At least, Sway did not harbor any ill feelings toward Malcolm, and from the looks of it already, Malcolm was not intending on going anywhere this time around.

"Of course you are," Alex smiled and leaned in to kiss him softly on the lips.

December 31, 1999

Epilogue

Las Vegas, Nevada
Everyone
Love and Happiness

"I can't believe how nice this place turned out!" Romeo shouted over the blaring music at Sway, while Jennifer and Stephanie sat across from them, engrossed in their own conversation. "And, who would have thought that it would have been finished just in time for your fortieth birthday!"

Despite that interior work was still being done to the upper levels of the hotel, Romeo was excited for several different reasons. The grand opening of the new Candy Shop was a huge success, he and his wife Jennifer were finally moved into their newly built home that sat on eight acres outside of the city of Las Vegas, and he was happy for his friend, Sway, who finally decided to settle down. When Sway asked Stephanie to quit her job and move back to New York to live with him, everyone, including Alex, thought Sway had lost his mind. But he hadn't. After Stephanie met Stevie, and Sway saw the genuine likeness between them, he knew that she was the closest thing to Alex he would ever have, so he made sure to secure it by keeping Stephanie close. She was moving in immediately after the New Year.

"Yeah, I have to admit Ro this place is bangin' hard. I love everything about it, and you and Cain deserve all of the credit. He did an exceptional job. I think he will do well taking over the Atlantic City spot," Sway said proudly.

Everything was coming together, and his night was going smoothly. He made it clear that Derek was not to attend the grand opening because it also parlayed as his fortieth birthday party. The last time Sway celebrated his birthday with Derek, it turned tragic. Sway was adamant about Derek being no where on the premises on this special night. He still did not trust him. Derek respected his wishes despite that he would miss his opportunity to see Alex once again, but Derek was also aware that she had rekindled an old flame with her high school sweetheart, and that she was very happy. At least, that was what Henry told him. Derek decided to back off, and allow Alex to receive the kind of love a woman like her deserved. And, in a small spiteful way, he was content that she was not receiving it from Sway. Selfishly, he found solace in knowing that neither he, nor Sway won her affection in the end. Unbeknownst to Derek, Sway felt exactly the same way. Sway was actually happy that fate had brought Malcolm back into Alex's life. Sway knew Alex very well, and he was always aware that Malcolm was the only man she ever truly loved. He appreciated Malcolm for reconnecting with her soul, and finally making her heart whole. And, although Sway once wished it was him completing the only woman he was ever truly in love with, he had finally arrived at a place in his life where he was complacent with his position in Alex's life, and satisfied that he would always be in it.

"This is a hell of a turnout too," Romeo stated as he peered around the large nightclub that was housed on the first floor next to the shop. "Is Alex coming?" Romeo asked.

"Yeah, she and homeboy should be here any minute. I think they are coming with Journey and some new doctor Journey is dating," Sway answered with an air of casualness. "But, they better hurry up," Sway growled, looking at his wristwatch. "It will be midnight soon, and I want to ring in the New Millennium with all of the people I care about!" he howled over the blaring music as he grabbed Stephanie's hand and held it tightly.

Despite that his friendship with Tiny never mended, Sway was still overjoyed that Journey and Cain decided to tone down their May/December romance. It excited Sway to see his son date an unlimited amount of women his own age because Sway wanted Cain to be able to decipher the good ones from the bad ones. He was truly a proud father. Sway was also very excited for Journey, who he found out had recently become very wealthy through a trust fund established for her by her parents. She was also finally dating someone around her age who is intelligent, humorous, mild-mannered, and comes from a similar background. Sway commended her new man for showering Journey with all he had to offer.

****

As the limousine pulled up to the *Triple M Resort,* Journey and Alex were both impressed by the long red carpet and flashing lights donning the walkway. They felt like movie stars as the driver opened the door to assist them out of the car. The finely suited gentlemen slid out behind their dates, and quickly caught up to the gorgeous women to lend their arms.

As they walked through the hotel lobby that was filled with astounding waterfalls, they admired the manmade streams, overflowing with tropical fish. The two couples sauntered through the large airy area and peered through the windows of the boutiques and shops embedded in the lining of the hotel walls. They entered the nightclub that was nestled in the rear of the building, conveniently named, *Club Sway,* and spotted the man of the hour with his party seated in the VIP section of the club.

"Hi everyone!" Alex shouted over the music, as she kissed cheeks and gave hugs. "Sway and Stephanie, you both know Malcolm, but Romeo and Jennifer, this is Malcolm; Malcolm this is Sway's partner and his wife."

Malcolm graciously shook their hands, kissed Stephanie on the cheek and gave Sway some dap. Journey followed suit and introduced her date to everyone. They all sat down, and mingled into the ongoing conversations. As the night wore on, a very tipsy Cain finally arrived with two voluptuous beauties dangling from each arm, and fully enjoying the New Year festivities. The group danced, ate and drank into the night, and as the eleventh hour was coming to an end to ring in the New Year, Malcolm pulled Alex into a corner.

"You are fresh!" Alex laughed as their bodies squeezed into the dark corner.

"I didn't bring you over here for that, although I can't wait for that to happen," Malcolm said, reminding her that they had yet to consummate the renewing of their relationship.

"I think tonight will be your lucky night," Alex teased, but the alcohol traveling through her veins told her that statement may very well be true.

The two of them agreed at the onset of them getting back together, that they would wait until she was ready for intimacy, She did not want to start off with sex because it would make matters worse if what she and Malcolm are trying build falls a apart too soon.

"I'm hoping that luck will run in my favor since I am in what some call the luckiest place in the world," Malcolm said, wrapping his arms around her body. "But, I wanted you all to myself right now because I have a very serious question to ask you," Malcolm became stone-faced.

"*Ten, Nine, Eight*". The crowd behind them screamed as they all watched the countdown on the plasma screen televisions hanging on the freshly painted walls.

Malcolm quickly tucked his hand in his front pocket of his designer slacks, and pulled out a small velvet ring box.

Alex looked down at his hand as he lifted the open box up to her face. The three-carat heart shaped diamond frightened her. Tears began to fill her eyes, and the clear vision of Malcolm's face had suddenly become a watery blur.

"Alex, I know I should have been asking you this question a long time ago, and I am sorry it took me so long. And, I am sorry that my childish actions back in day, caused us both great pain, but despite all of that, I hope you are still willing to be my wife. Will you marry me?" Malcolm bellowed over the crowds' screams as he knelt down on one knee, and grabbed her left hand. He carefully took the ring out of its box and slid it onto Alex's finger.

She was in shock, but in the most extraordinary way. She was not only being asked to marry someone, but the man asking her was the only man she ever wanted to ask her that question. She wiped her eyes to get a clear view of the solid but clear rock on her ring finger, and then looked lovingly at a kneeling Malcolm.

"Yes, yes of course I will!" Alex shouted for the world to hear as the partygoers rang in the New Millennium for the new life Alex and Malcolm were destined to share.

The End...for now